KT-407-547

ACC. No: 05147804

'Phillips is back with a most intriguing and compelling story of grief, loss, memory and the quest for the truth. With rich characterisation and a lively setting, this story will enthral you to the end.'
LIZ NUGENT

'*The Hiding Game* is filled with characters who will grab you by the throat from beginning to end. Absolutely gripping storyline, expertly crafted, an addictive page turner. I loved it.'
PATRICIA GIBNEY

'*The Hiding Game* has everything you would expect from a Phillips novel – a pacy crime procedural full of twists and turns, with poignant insights into the emotional bond between mother and child. A cracking good read.'
KAREN PERRY

'A riveting, ripped-from-the-headlines legal thriller set in A Small Town in the USA with dark secrets and murky lies which Phillips has pulled off not only with authenticity, but aplomb.'
CATHERINE RYAN HOWARD

'Phillips is at the top of her game. *The Hiding Game* is riveting, thought-provoking and compulsive. A five-star read.'
ARLENE HUNT

'A gripping courtroom drama with a courageous new heroine in Heather Baxter. Pacy, tightly plotted and full of suspense. *The Hiding Game* was worth the wait!'
ANDREA CARTER

'Phillips sends us down into a rabbit hole of buried trauma, disjointed memories, fractured relationships and ruptured lives in the search for justice and redemption. An undoubted master of the psychological thriller.'
CORMAC O'KEEFFE

'Best known for her Dublin-based crime fiction, Phillips makes a very successful trip Stateside with *The Hiding Game*. As always, research is her strong point, and the oppressive na                    llips draws together                    er.'

Louise Phillips is the author of four bestselling psychological crime thrillers, each nominated for Crime Fiction Book of the Year at the Irish Book Awards. She won the award in 2013.

A recipient of several awards, art bursaries, and residencies, Louise's work has appeared in many literary anthologies. In 2015, she was a judge on the Irish panel for the EU Literary Award, and in 2016, she was longlisted for the CWA Dagger in the Library Award. Recently, her first two novels were published in the US.

*The Hiding Game* received an Arts Bursary for Literature from the Arts Council of Ireland.

@LouiseMPhillips
www.facebook.com/LouisePhillipsAuthor
www.louise-phillips.com

Also by Louise Phillips

*Red Ribbons*
*The Doll's House*
*Last Kiss*
*The Game Changer*

# THE HIDING GAME

## LOUISE PHILLIPS

**Llyfrgelloedd Caerdydd**
www.caerdydd.gov.uk/llyfrgelloedd
**Cardiff Libraries**
www.cardiff.gov.uk/libraries

HACHETTE
BOOKS
IRELAND

Copyright © 2019 Louise Phillips

The right of Louise Phillips to be identified as the Author of
the Work has been asserted by her in accordance with the
Copyright, Designs and Patents Act 1988.

First published in Ireland in 2019 by
HACHETTE BOOKS IRELAND

1

All rights reserved. No part of this publication may be reproduced, stored in
a retrieval system, or transmitted, in any form or by any means without the
prior written permission of the publisher, nor be otherwise circulated in any
form of binding or cover other than that in which it is published and without
a similar condition being imposed on the subsequent purchaser.

Cataloguing in Publication Data is available from the British Library

Trade paperback ISBN 9781529304107

Typeset in Garamond by redrattledesign.com

Printed and bound in Great Britain by
Clays Ltd, Elcograf, S.p.A

Hachette Books Ireland policy is to use papers that are natural, renewable and
recyclable products and made from wood grown in sustainable forests. The logging and
manufacturing processes are expected to conform to the environmental regulations of
the country of origin.

Hachette Books Ireland
8 Castlecourt Centre
Castleknock
Dublin 15, Ireland

A division of Hachette UK Ltd
Carmelite House, 50 Victoria Embankment, EC4Y 0DZ
www.hachettebooksireland.ie

*For Monica*

All the characters and events in this publication are fictitious.
Any resemblance to real persons, living or dead,
or real events is purely coincidental.

# Patriot Eagle

## Brutal Murder of Young Mother
## REMAINS UNSOLVED

Gerry Gillespie

Thursday, June 9, 1994.

A month on from the vicious murder of Elizabeth Baxter, a young mother whose dead body was tragically discovered by her ten-year-old daughter, Heather Baxter, police in Corham arc still struggling to find her killer. The date, 9 May 1994, remains circled in red on a calendar in the hall, acting as a grim reminder of how the lives of the Baxter family, mother Elizabeth, father Charlie, and daughter Heather have changed for ever.

On the afternoon of the killing, a storm had formed north of Lake Ontario and slid off the coast, bringing the first snow in early summer in a hundred years. According to recent reports, young Heather was drawn from her bedroom on hearing a noise outside. She told Sheriff Hodgson she paused at the door of her late sister's room, highlighting the earlier tragedy, three years before, of Elizabeth's other daughter, Mia, who died at only five days old from septicaemia.

Heather said the door to the baby's room was ajar. It was dark inside with the heavy curtains pulled over to keep out the light. A crib, empty, except for a quilt with different-coloured elephants, stood in testament to Mia's short life as the mobile above it hung in silence. The only photograph in the room depicts the infant, with her port-wine birthmark in the shape of a half-moon on her right cheek, being held by her mother. Who could have known they would both die far too young?

A shocked Heather gave the police a scant description of the intruder, having caught a glimpse of him as he entered the house. She described him as medium build with wide shoulders, wearing dark overalls and a black ski-mask to cover his face. Sheriff Hodgson told reporters that when the child saw him she wanted to call out to warn her mother, but the words wouldn't come. 'They were stuck inside my head,' she said, 'trapped.' Instead, she hid in a blanket box upstairs, terrified. Soon after that, she heard the first scream, followed by a crashing noise, as if metal pots were hitting the ground at speed.

According to police, at some point the intruder left the kitchen, and moved throughout the house, ransacking each of the rooms. Did the young girl peek through the small slits in the blanket box? Did she see the man kick in her parents' bedroom door, swiping the contents off the top of the dressing-table? Did she follow his movements as he entered the baby's room, ripping the quilt from the empty crib? The answers to these questions may never be known as the child insists she cannot remember anything from shortly after she hid in the blanket box.

Hours later, with the house in darkness, and freezing cold, she climbed out and walked downstairs. Outside, inches of snow piled on the window-sills. She told police she was in a kind of trance until she reached the kitchen and in the darkness, saw her mother's dead body on the kitchen floor, the blood pooled around her chest, as her honey-blonde hair lay like tangled seaweed on the bloodied white tiles.

The crime-scene photographs act as a stark reminder of the evil inflicted on this young mother, with multiple knife wounds to her upper chest, her legs discoloured from the start of bruising, and the skin on her wrists scorched from the rope used to tie her hands. We can only imagine the horror she felt. Perhaps her knees went weak as the intruder dragged her to the floor. Was his voice loud, shrilling, or did he act in silence? Did the knife attack happen before or after the sexual assault?

Hours later, the little girl knelt beside her mother's dead body and pulled her skirt down over her exposed legs, offering a final act of respect in death.

To date, several people have been questioned about the killing, including Elizabeth's husband, Charlie Baxter, but only one remains in custody, Lucas García, or the Medicine Man, as he has become known. It was Heather's scant description of the intruder, including the colour of his eyes, that linked García to the crime. Now, a month afterwards, it is still impossible to know if Elizabeth Baxter died straight away. Many believe that even if her daughter had come down earlier and raised the alarm she might not have saved her. The child, emotionally strained, still has no recollection of what happened from the time she hid in the blanket box to hours later when she found her mother on the kitchen floor. Undoubtedly, the murder has cast a dark shadow over the small coastal town of Corham, with so many unanswered questions. Perhaps none of us will ever know the truth. On that dark day in May, did Elizabeth Baxter know her killer? Did she know she was going to die? And if the dead could speak, what would she say?

# 1
# HEATHER

The traffic on Route 3A to Corham is travelling at a snail's pace. The early August sun has pushed the temperature past ninety degrees and the glare on the windscreen is blinding. I try to ignore my cell phone, but the caller is persistent.

'Heather,' Jim Handcock's voice bellows down the line, pronouncing my name *Heathah* with his heavy South Shore accent, 'are you having a tough time getting here? We expected you a quarter of an hour ago.' His voice already feels like an unwanted pull back to the past.

'It's been bumper to bumper,' I reply, realising I'm less than ten miles outside Central Boston and my city voice has already slipped. 'Traffic is moving faster now. I won't be long.'

'We'll be here waiting for yah.'

I turn the air-conditioner up another notch and switch on the radio. The local station, Country Way, has the latest on Abby Jones, the young girl awaiting trial for the murder of the baby, Jacob Rotterdam. 'With many people screaming for justice for Jacob,' states the radio presenter, 'Abby Jones will soon face a jury, and this community, like the grieving parents, will at long last get the answers it deserves.'

As the presenter switches to another news segment, I think long and hard about the teenager, Abby Jones, the reason I'm heading out of the city to the town of my birth.

I take my exit from the Interstate, passing the lumber company on the right, and Raintree woods on the left. It feels like I'm entering an old life, one I thought was dead to me, one I didn't plan on returning to so fast.

The closer I get to Corham, the more residential the landscape becomes, with wealthy upper-middle-class homes, nestled behind tree-lined driveways, dotted on either side. Further south will bring me to Pike, and its picturesque harbour, but instead I keep my mind focused, as I drive to the Handcocks' house, on whether or not, considering our shared history, I will defend their niece.

On Main Street, I pass the old pharmacy, now a day spa, the window display in shades of aqua and gold. What used to be Ryan's hardware store has changed too, now specialising in high-tech machinery. Jeremiah Ryan died ten years ago, but I imagine him now, like a ghost from an old life, turning up at his store every day, rain or shine, in sickness and in health, much like his marriage vows.

There are tourists on the sidewalk taking photographs. I hear Grandma Lorrie's voice in my head, talking about them creeping all over town in summer, and soon I'm passing St Anthony's Church. Although the bell isn't tolling in the white wooden tower, I hear it loud and clear.

I take a sharp right turn with memories of the church and my mother's funeral, despite the intervening years, clawing after me: the closed casket, the stained-glass windows, with all the saints looking down in judgement, the smell of incense, strong, potent, and the people from the town, whispering, watching me with their accusing eyes, telling me what I already knew – I'd failed her.

Nearing the coast, I pass homes with private beaches. I think about how our old house in Corham, not even thirty miles south-east of Boston but still a universe apart, was always at odds with this wealth. As the road rises, and the coastal town of my birth, with its New England-style colonial homes, comes further into view, it immediately engulfs me, letting me know it still exists, as does the code of silence around my mother's death.

I turn into Hobart Lane, the most affluent address in Corham, and one, like the rest of the town, embedded in my childhood. In spite of the heat, I open the car window to hear the sea, its rhythmic pulse beating against the cliffs. I breathe in deeply, the air a mix of dry heat, salt and seaweed, visualising in the distance the hypnotic astral blue of the ocean, remembering how many times, growing up, I went to the water's edge, wanting to get away from a life I didn't choose, one without a mother, and how that life was sometimes filled with a loneliness I didn't know existed until she died. I have learned over time how loss can make you fragile or strong, or both.

Ten minutes later, I drive up the curved pathway of the Handcocks' home.

Parking, I switch off the engine, and instantly, without the air-conditioner, the heat is oppressive, bearing down, August heat, like a firecracker ready to explode, sapping the last of any surplus air. I jerk the rear-view mirror around and check my make-up. For a split second, I see the younger me, ten years old, full of questions, and afraid.

Outside, a line of sweat builds up on the back of my neck. I buzz open the trunk and take out my leather briefcase.

As I hear my footsteps crunch on the gravelled drive, I have the distinct sense of being watched. I catch a glimpse of someone looking down from upstairs. At first, I think it's the sun playing tricks on the windows, but then with my hands shielding my eyes, for a second I see the darkened shape, before the light changes again and it's gone.

The doorbell echoes in what I know is a marbled hallway. The house is the largest in Corham. Everything about it is big and bold, a loud, clear statement about money, lots of it. Moments later, footsteps approach. They sound light and delicate, but swift, getting ever closer to the door. I wipe the perspiration off the back of my neck. A young girl with dazzling blue eyes greets me. She is dressed in a maid's uniform, her auburn hair tied up tightly in a bun. I visualise her in hipster jeans and a T-shirt, socialising with friends, rather than being another possession of the Handcocks. She doesn't get a chance to ask my name, because from behind the double staircase Alice Handcock calls out. 'Heather, how kind of you to come at such short notice.'

I watch her glide towards me, as if she is the ruler of all she sees. I step into the grand hallway, filled with over-the-top marble sculptures of naked men, probably paid for with the easy money the Handcocks made before the real estate bubble burst, when they, unlike others, had the good fortune to pull out early. Like me, the sculptures belong someplace else. Not here.

When I got the phone call from Jim Handcock a few days ago, wanting me to defend his niece, Abby, my immediate instinct was to say, 'No,' even if my brain told me this might be the trial of the decade. With my small private practice and limited resources – compared to the bigger corporate firms – I would have been crazy to outright turn it down, even if it meant a complete reshuffling of case files and playing catch-up fast. None of that matters now. I know that the real reason I'm here is the same reason I want to be somewhere else: all the unanswered questions from my past.

The house is cool, each room and zone perfectly balanced to fight off the oppressive heat. Alice is exactly as I remember her, her skin barely covering her bones. She has attractive features, and honey-blonde hair the same shade as my mother's. Twelve years younger than her husband, she looks the epitome of a life lived in the gym and at the golf club. She is wearing three-quarter-length white linen trousers, light gym shoes and a sleeveless red cotton top. Up close, I spot the signs of early Botox intervention: immovable forehead skin, a slightly rigid jawline. Now in her mid-forties, she has been married to Jim since she turned eighteen, but she could easily be taken for far younger than her years.

'Hello, Alice,' I say.

'Oh, Heather, it's been far too long. It was your grandmother's funeral, wasn't it, the last time we met?'

I nod.

'Jim is so keen to chat with you.' She indicates that I should follow her. We walk towards the garden out back, but we come to an abrupt stop in the conservatory, filled with tall leafy exotic plants. Within the green foliage, I see him, the man who, as a child, I feared because everyone feared him. Power in a small town is everything.

He looks slightly out of breath, as if he rushed to get here. Was he the person upstairs? He has gained weight, his hair is thinning, and his eyes, although hidden behind sunglasses, are obviously staring at me. There is a can of beer on the wrought-iron table in front of him. He sits down and removes his glasses. I sense Alice's disapproval of the can. She reaches into the drinks cabinet and takes out a glass, pouring the beer into it.

'Heather.' He beams, looking up at me, reaching out to shake my sweaty hand. I think about the shape in the upstairs window again. I tell myself to get it together. If my mother had lived, she and Jim would be the same age and, like most folks from Corham, they would have known each other their entire lives. That's the thing about small towns: people in them spend a lifetime tripping over each other whether they want to or not. No one openly talks about her killing, but it's always there, in the fabric of the place and trapped inside me. It never goes away.

Jim and Alice settle down beside each other – presenting as a team. I sit opposite, on a chaise longue patterned with giant sunflowers. Jim tells me about a new family in town. Alice shares a short anecdote from the golf club. I ask about business, knowing he has recently switched to renewable energy while still running a car dealership in Winthrop, and a transport company monopolising operations along the South Shore. They ask about Boston and my practice. I hate small talk. I swiftly shift gear, needing them to get to the point, still hearing the words of the radio presenter in my head, talking about people screaming for justice, as I wonder, yet again, why they called me.

Their demeanour promptly changes. Jim puts down his beer. Alice rests her hands on her knees. This is their cue to talk about Abby. Both sit up straight. Their body language tells me they find this conversation uncomfortable. Alice takes the initiative. 'It was Jim's idea to contact you.' She smiles at her husband. He nods back in affirmation.

'I understand your previous attorney quit?'

'I wouldn't call it that, Heather.' Jim sits further forward. 'He had personal issues. Besides, he couldn't even manage to get Abby out on bail. What kind of attorney is that?'

I want to tell them the reason Abby has been behind bars since her arraignment months before is the evidence stacked against her, but instead, staring at him, I say, 'Your niece's statements to the police were damning.'

'We've all seen enough TV shows,' says Jim, 'to know things said to the police under pressure are not always the truth.'

'Our old attorney,' Alice adds, 'said his wife left him.' Her voice is deadpan. 'Apparently she took the children and drove out west to Arizona. It seems he had abuse problems. You know, Heather, drink, drugs, but still functioning at the top of his game. An adrenalin junkie, you might say, who happened to crash out at the most inappropriate time.'

'He came highly recommended,' Jim says, 'the best money can buy.' He reaches over and touches my knee. 'But you, Heather, you're one of our own.' I catch Alice staring at his hand, maintaining her composure. When he takes it away, I pull my knees further back. Is that why they contacted me? Because I'm from this town, because I have history here, and they think, like everyone else from this place, that I'll do their bidding?

'I won't lie to you, Heather,' he continues, 'we need your help. Abby needs your help.'

I think about the images in the newspapers. Even before the Handcocks' phone call, I already had a more than keen interest in the case. The girl, at nineteen, had been repeatedly scorned in the media, with references to the mark of the devil on her face, a similar port-wine birthmark to my late sister Mia's. A lot was already stacked against the teenager, who seemed ill-equipped to deal with any of it. Is that why I'm considering this case, because I see myself in her, a girl far too young to recognise the high stakes involved?

'How is your father doing?' Jim asks distractedly.

'I haven't seen him in a while.' My voice sounds sharper than I intend. I've barely spoken to my father in months.

A silence hangs.

'Well,' he replies, 'Charlie has always been a law unto himself.'

'Indeed,' I say, already hating them knowing so much about me. They're both staring. I plaster a false smile of reassurance on my face.

'Heather, are you going to take this case?' Jim looks anxiously

11

at Alice. 'We realise Corham doesn't have the best of memories for you.' He turns back to me.

I hear the tension in his voice. I know Abby is his niece, but *why* does he care so much? This trial is going to cost him plenty. Is it guilt for all the time she was in foster care? I understand guilt better than most, but Jim Handcock never struck me as the guilty type. I take the legal pad out of my briefcase. 'That depends, Jim. I need to ask you a few questions first, and as for my memories, let's all agree that the past is in the past.' I sound more assured than I feel.

He nods.

'I believe you both knew the Rotterdams prior to Abby's engagement as a live-in nanny.' My voice sounds professional, efficient, but still it feels strange asking them questions. Our roles have changed. I'm no longer the child from the poor background seeing them as adults, people considered to be pillars of the community. Here, in this room, we're on an equal footing. And they need my help.

'That's right,' says Alice. 'They were a lovely couple.'

'Were?'

'I mean, before all this messy business. We became quite friendly shortly after Morgan began advising us on investments, but now … Well, all those things they're saying about Abby, they're shocking. Isn't that right, Jim?'

'They sure are.'

'He was such a beautiful baby, though,' Alice adds, her voice full of regret. 'I can't say I ever saw such a gorgeous child before.'

Jim sits forward again. 'Look, Heather, I don't know who or what harmed that baby, but it sure as hell wasn't my niece, and I want the rest of the world to know it. My reputation is on the line here too.'

'Your late grandpa,' Alice cuts in, 'is said to have been the greatest attorney born in these parts.'

'So I hear.' I make a note in the legal pad about their previous relationship with the Rotterdams.

'A great guy,' Jim adds.

I wonder how much about my grandpa either of them really knows.

'Tell me everything you can about Abby,' I say, looking from Jim to Alice. 'Starting at the beginning, including why you took her out of foster care to live with you.'

'Does that mean, Heather,' he asks, 'that you're gonna take the case?'

'I'll let you know as soon as I hear what you have to say, and once I've talked to Abby.'

'We don't have a lot of time.' Alice eyeballs me in a way I remember from childhood: a don't-dare-mess-with-me stare.

'I realise that,' I say, 'which is why I've set up an appointment to meet her at Framingham Correctional this afternoon.' I look from Alice to Jim. 'It's important I believe her.'

'I warn you, Heather, she can be a bit odd,' he adds.

'Odd isn't guilty,' I retort.

'No,' he agrees, 'that's true, it ain't, and Abby hasn't had the easiest of lives.'

'You were going to tell me why you took her out of foster care.'

'We didn't exactly take her out of care. It was more that she came to us.'

'We never had children of our own,' Alice adds, with an inflection of regret.

'Go on,' I say, looking at Jim.

'Abby was released from DCF when she turned eighteen.'

'The Department of Children and Families?'

'Yeah,' he says, his body stiffening. 'She had the option to enter an independent-living programme, with kids of her own age, but by then she was sick of sharing a room and people constantly being around her.'

'Oh?'

'So, as I said, she turned up here. Rang on the doorbell the same way you did just now.'

'It was like seeing a ghost, wasn't it, Jim?' Alice looks at her husband.

'What Alice means,' he swallows hard, sharpness in his tone, 'is that Abby looks a lot like my sister.'

I already know about Jim's late sister, Olivia. How as a teenager she ended up pregnant and unmarried, having linked up with a guy called Jones. They slept rough in Boston and, hooked on heroin, overdosed a few years later, within weeks of each other, when Abby was barely three. In a place like Corham, though, no matter how far you travel from it, your story still belongs right here.

I promptly move things on. 'How did Abby end up going to the Rotterdams?'

Jim hesitates. Alice instantly takes over. 'The girl needed space, and besides, Boston wasn't a million miles away. All those difficult years meant she found it hard to settle. Jim thought working, keeping busy, would ground her more, didn't you, Jim?'

'She was bored doing nothing,' he agrees, swallowing the rest of his beer a little too fast. I sense they may be holding something back, but I let it slide for now.

Four completed pages of a legal pad later, I hear more about Abby's difficult life in and out of foster homes. How she was still unsettled when she came to live with them. It was Alice who saw how much she loved children, and Abby agreed that earning her own money would help her feel more independent. When the opportunity came to work for the Rotterdams, it seemed like a good idea, but tension soon developed between herself and Vivienne Rotterdam. Abby thought Vivienne was too controlling. Jim put it down to the girl's restlessness, nothing more.

'You're so like your mother,' he says, as I stand to leave. I don't answer him. I don't want him talking about her. His words feel like an intrusion into something private, something other people think they own, even if they don't. I hear my mother's words in my head – *Be fragile, be strong.*

Alice leads me out through a side corridor. I've never been in this part of the house before. Animal heads hang on the walls, but my eyes are drawn to a mahogany and glass cabinet. Inside, there is an assortment of miniature elephants, at least fifty of them, sitting on mirrored glass shelves. Many are made of crystal, others of clay, while some are coated in metallic paint. I stop.

'They're Jim's,' Alice says dismissively, as if she wants to rid herself of any responsibility for them. 'He had them imported from all over the world.'

'Really?'

'He's been fascinated with elephants ever since his daddy promised to take him on safari as a boy. It never materialised, of course, but the fascination stuck.'

I stare into the cabinet, seeing my adult self reflected in the glass. I know exactly what I'm looking for: a miniature silver elephant with an ivory trunk held upwards towards the sky.

'Are you all right, Heather? You've gone quite pale.'

I don't answer her. I'm thinking about my mother's red box of mementoes. I see the miniature elephant she had in it as clearly as I see its counterparts on the mirrored shelves. Was it a present from Jim Handcock?

Alice moves in closer. 'Jim was always very fond of your mother,' she says quietly, as if reading my thoughts. 'It's partly why he's so fond of you. I hope you're not going to let him down.'

I turn to face her, matching her stare. 'As I said earlier, Alice, I'll let you both know how I get on with Abby.'

'We'd appreciate that, although there is something you should know.' Her words are almost teasing, as if we're about to share a secret.

'What?' I ask, mildly irritated by her intimate tone.

'Jim may not have been completely honest with you about Abby.'

'Meaning?'

'It is possible,' she pauses, hesitant, 'that he has an unhealthy fascination with the girl.'

'Unhealthy?'

'I don't have to spell it out for you, Heather, do I?' She stares at me as if she knows something I don't. 'I could be wrong,' she continues, 'but it wouldn't be the first time a man becomes besotted with a young girl, especially one who is related to them.'

Her words feel cloying, but I note them all the same, my mind drifting back to a few months earlier, when I was back in Corham for Grandma Lorrie's funeral, and how afterwards practically everyone in town went up to my grandparents' house. Samuel, my uncle, was there too. Meeting him again, after nearly a decade of living somewhere else, and avoiding being around him, had unsettled me more than I wanted to admit, as if he could still find minute cracks in my skin to crawl into. He told me he had started the twelve-step programme, looking to make amends for past sins, all the terrible things he had done, but that the voice of the devil was still urging him on. He touched my arm. I balked.

That was when the first shred of memory came back, and I saw the shadow standing over me. Initially I thought I'd imagined it, but then I was back there, in my old bedroom, and the dark shadow was moving around the room. I heard the chorus of birdsong, too, as a light summer's breeze came in through the opened window. Since that first recall, other fragments of memory have come back too, each so tiny that, no matter how many times I replay them, they refuse to become whole.

As Alice directs me outside, my eyes dart back to the cabinet with the miniature elephants. Again, I visualise the silver elephant belonging to my mother. At the door, Alice waits until I'm outside before she says, 'Lucas García is back in town.'

The name explodes in my head. I glare at her.

'He's been here for a while. He's opened an alternative healing shop. Who would have thought?'

I don't answer her.

Outside, the sun is even hotter than it was earlier. My throat feels dry. I swallow hard, walking away from the house. Again, I hear my feet crunch on the gravelled drive, and with every step I take, I know Alice is watching me. Opening the car door, I stare back at her. She doesn't wave or acknowledge me. Her face is too far away for me to read her thoughts.

As I drive off, another idea takes hold, one that isn't based on rational thinking but, rather, a sense of inner warning, and a feeling that somehow, being here this afternoon, with the Handcocks, I have already put certain things in motion, things I may soon regret.

# 2
# HEATHER

The first thing that hits you about Framingham Correctional is its large and oppressive size. Framed within reddish-brown stone walls and rows of rectangular sash windows, as the oldest correctional institution in the US it exudes dominance. Even the most optimistic of inmates on first viewing must doubt they will ever leave. I stare at the steel poles surrounding the building, meshed from the ground up with barbed wire and cameras watching a person's every move, daring anyone to get in or out without permission. I think about Abby, wondering if she is still in that early stage of hope, believing she might soon leave.

At the entrance, the solid and forbidding structure casts an elongated darkness on the ground below, and in the clawing temperatures of the afternoon, it is as if the barbed wire is somehow curling in on itself. Before walking through the red double doors with 'MCI FRAMINGHAM' in bold white letters above, I glance across at the female prisoners out for their daily exercise. There isn't a piece of greenery anywhere. Some of the women move in groups, but most are walking alone, dragging their feet along the concrete. If Abby Jones is found guilty, this place will become her life.

Inside, I go through the normal security checks, reaching the visitors' area in less than ten minutes. I had noted 'Special Circumstances' on my prisoner-visit request, meaning there were two possible outcomes: either I'd find myself sitting in a room with others, and a glass panel between myself and Abby, or we'd get an empty visitor's room. I am relieved to hear it's the latter.

As I wait for her to arrive, the sense of being trapped in the small grey room, with its high walls, is formidable. Water gurgles through the pipework overhead. There is a tiny north-facing window high up, allowing in only a little light. A double-tubed fluorescent fitting hangs from the ceiling by four linked chains. The prisoners' canteen is nearby. I smell supper being cooked and I imagine the women thronging in, eating their meals from the metal plates and bowls. It isn't hard to understand how a person could lose themselves in a place like this. Especially when they know they're going to be locked up for a very long time.

A female security guard opens the door. Abby walks in. Her face is blank, her shoulders bent forward, her hands locked together in handcuffs. Female inmates entering the visitors' area can wear normal clothes, but there are strict rules about attire. Everything must be neat and presentable – a top with long sleeves, pants, socks, flat shoes, foundation garments, and no wired bras. Abby wears an oversized grey sweatshirt and navy leggings. Her jet-black hair is tied back in a short, tight ponytail. She looks younger than her nineteen years. I stare at the birthmark in the shape of a half-moon on her face. I can't help but think of Mia, and how, like Jacob, the baby Abby is accused of harming, each had their lives cut tragically short.

When she sits down, I mentally review the case notes again, thinking about that damning interview between her and the two police officers, when she admitted shaking the baby. The officers gave a very different account of what Abby said from the one she put forward later. There are always differences, contradictions between what people believed they had said to the police and what was recorded. Still, first statements are important, and things blurted out directly after something horrific has happened can often be closest to the truth.

I study her, noting the marked resilience in her expression. She looks like someone who is used to relying only on herself.

'Hello, Abby,' I say.

'Hello.' She keeps her head down.

'I'm Heather Baxter.'

'I know who you are.' Her tone is flat.

'I'm guessing then that you also know I'm here to listen to your side of the story.'

'I've explained it all before.'

'Yes, but today I'll need you to explain it again, to me.'

She looks up for the first time. 'Uncle Jim says I should trust you.'

'And he's right.'

'I didn't kill the baby. Do you believe that?'

'I don't know, Abby, not yet, but I'm here to *help* if I can.' I pull a file from my briefcase. The top documents are the statements from the interviewing officers. 'Let's start with your police statement.' I take her lack of response as agreement. 'According to the police, you admitted shaking Jacob. You even demonstrated on that day how you did it.'

'They had me all mixed up.'

'The reports go on to say that you dropped him into his crib from a height.'

She doesn't respond, and her face is giving nothing away.

'And when you were asked if you had shaken Jacob before, you said you might have done.'

'I was trying to be helpful. I didn't understand what was happening.'

'Both officers recorded identical statements in their notebooks.'

'You don't believe me, do you?'

'I didn't say that, Abby.' I keep my voice calm. 'Why don't you take me back to the day Jacob died, and tell me, in your own words, exactly what happened.'

Her recall isn't poles apart from the original statements, but it communicates a very different premise. She panicked when Jacob didn't wake up. Her shaking of the baby was to revive him. When the officers questioned her, she wasn't sure what they were asking. She was in shock. She didn't want to believe what was happening. He had been poorly earlier that morning, coughing and a little out of sorts, but nothing serious. How could she possibly have known he would die? At first, when she went upstairs to check on him, she got scared because of his lack of response. She started to rock him back and forth, and feeling even more frightened, her rocking became frenzied. She put him down in the crib, unsure of what to do next.

'I freaked out when he wouldn't open his eyes.' Her voice is high-pitched. 'I kept calling his name. Like I said, he'd been unwell earlier. I thought it would pass, but it didn't. It was awful …'

'Did you shake Jacob violently?'

'I didn't. I swear. All I wanted was for them to stop pushing me. I couldn't think straight.'

'Abby, I'm going to ask you a few questions,' I lock eyes with her, 'and I want you to be absolutely sure about your answers. Remember,' I say, 'your trial is only weeks away.'

If I believe her, I know the time pressures won't matter because I won't be able to walk away.

'Okay,' she says, repositioning herself on the chair.

'I'll know if you're lying,' I insist, glaring at her, drilling my words home.

She nods.

'Did you kill Jacob Rotterdam?'

'No.'

'Did you lose your temper with him?'

'No.'

'Did you panic when you realised you'd gone too far? Was that what happened, Abby?'

'No, no, no, I couldn't have.'

Mentally, I'm already putting her on the witness stand, because that is exactly where she will soon be. She looks at me as if I'm crazy, as if the questions are so ridiculous she doesn't even know where to begin. I study my prospective client, the intermingling of her fingers, her slightly hunched shoulders, her exhausted, strained eyes. She looks as if she's physically fading away. Do I believe her? I don't know yet, not for sure. I change tack.

'Your uncle said you didn't want to enter the independent-living programme.'

'No, I didn't.'

'Why not?'

'I was sick of people being around me. I'd have had to live with roommates. I'd had enough sharing in foster care.' She looks around the room, her revulsion at her new reality immediately showing on her face.

'But, eventually, you would have been independent.'

'I don't trust *eventually*. I don't trust *them*.'

'Who?'

'Those in charge.'

'I see.'

'Do you?'

She's testing me, too, sizing me up. 'Perhaps not,' I say, 'not fully.'

'People lucky enough to have loving families never do.'

'I know you lost your mother,' I say, 'when you were three years old,' aware of how loaded my words are.

'I lost her before that, but yeah.'

'That must have been difficult.'

I see tears forming in her eyes and, despite her hardened resolve, I already know I want to believe her.

'I've always felt different from other people. I used to think it was not having parents, a mother and a father.' She pauses, staring at me. 'But it wasn't that. It was being unwanted.'

Was I unwanted? Abandoned so many times by my father, Grandma Lorrie only taking me in out of a sense of responsibility, but never, ever, out of love. 'I understand that, Abby,' I say.

'I thought I wasn't deserving of love, you know, and maybe I wasn't.' She shrugs her shoulders.

'Abby, what happened back then wasn't your fault,' I say, aware of how many times I've repeated the same thing to myself, and how often the words rang hollow.

'Did you ever see darkness, Heather?'

Her question feels unexpected. 'What do you mean?'

'When the world goes black, so dark you can't think?'

I see myself as ten years old again, how I heard the clock ticking before seeing the intruder. Then I heard my mother scream, and things began to crash to the floor, and after that, her muffled cries, before I hid, unwilling or unable to protect her. 'Yes, Abby, I have.'

'That's what it was like, when Jacob wouldn't wake up. Everything went dark. I couldn't think straight. I didn't know what to do.'

Her words could be the same as mine, from the day my mother

was killed, when everything went black, and afterwards there were all those hours of nothingness, until eventually I found her and knew nothing would ever be the same again.

'Heather, I couldn't have harmed Jacob. I couldn't have done any of those things they're saying.'

I visualise the photographs of Jacob from the news reports, the beautiful, happy baby boy with a head of dark hair, and those deep whirlpools of brown eyes. It is hard, even now, not to think about what might have been, imagining him as an older child, a teenager, and then a man. Everything changes with the death of a child. The sense of injustice is unfathomable. It is something beyond acceptance. Again, my mind shifts to Mia, and how, after she died, my mother changed too. I see myself holding my mother's hand as she stares into the empty crib, and my father is nowhere to be found. How, later that day, I was the one who put my mother to bed, I was the one who went to town to get whatever groceries we could afford, who tried, in my childlike way, to make her better. None of it mattered, because once she lost the baby, there was no going back to our life before.

'Heather,' Abby pleads, 'tell me you'll help. If you won't, I don't know what I'll do. I can't take much more of this. I—'

I don't let her finish her sentence. 'It's okay,' I say, 'you're stronger than you think.' *Be fragile, be strong.*

Neither of us says anything for a moment, but a million thoughts fly through my head, because, I already realise, I see myself in this young girl, motherless, feeling unwanted by the world, unloved, and, far too young to understand what any of it means, still partly reeling from shock. If I walk away from Abby, from this trial, I will become like all the other people who, in one way or another, have abandoned both of us.

The more we talk, the more I believe her. Considering her age and obvious vulnerability, she would have been an easy target for blame, feeling trapped, like me, when something unimaginable happened, and she was isolated and alone. Abby may have the Handcocks on her side, but they can't defend her in a court of law, and by the time we part ways, I have accepted the case, along with the belief that the world is stacked against Abby Jones.

It is only when I'm halfway home to West Roxbury that I see the black sedan. It maintains a five-car distance behind me. I had noticed it earlier, too, after leaving the Handcocks' house, but I put my unease down to an overactive imagination playing havoc. In the rear-view mirror, I see a male frame, his face shadowed by a wide-brimmed hat.

Is it Lucas?

I immediately push away the question, but when the car fades out of view, the relief is instant.

# 3
# ELIZABETH

*In my mind, I am still running through the woods, and my direction is uncertain. My feet are bare and muddied. There are scratches on my upper arms, but I have no memory of how I got them. The desire to run, and to keep on running, is strong. I can't look back. I have to find her. 'Mia,' I scream, over and over, but she doesn't hear me. She can't hear me, because she is no longer here. Mia is dead.*

*At times like this, when everything is quiet other than the sleeping night, the faintest sound can give me hope, fool me into believing she's still here, until I grasp again that she's gone. She isn't real. Not any more.*

*Some people think that after you die, you see a bright light at the end of a tunnel, or an open door willing you to the other side. I wonder if my baby girl saw either of these things.*

*The doubts will keep me awake for hours.*

*I have changed, I know. Deep in my core, I am different. It is as if there is a 'before' and 'after' me, and neither of them gives me solace.*

*Lately, in the early mornings, when Heather is at school, I have started going swimming. I take the route along Atlantic Road to Sandy Beach. The place is usually deserted at that hour. It's how I like it.*

*It's over a year since Mia's death. The beach and the water are like a sanctuary to me now, vast and mysterious, and, by extension, at times I feel hardly human, with the seemingly endless ocean beating against the shore. I tell myself not to worry, that things will soon change, and looking out at the vastness, I can become a creature of that world, instead of the person I really am, with all the complications of a life I'm locked within.*

*A couple of months ago, on a warm morning in April, Lucas García came to the beach. When I saw him, I thought at first he was a drifter, a nobody passing through. I was annoyed at being disturbed, and I was soaked from head to toe, having just come out of the water. As my toes intertwined with the pink seaweed, I tried to dry off fast, feeling self-conscious. He was standing by a large boulder a few metres away, wearing what looked like a Panama hat. He swigged from a small bottle. I noted the strangeness of this, drinking so early in the morning, but in that moment I was more concerned with the interruption than wondering who he was or why he was there. Later, he told me, it was one of his potions, the kind to clear your mind of negative thoughts, but what spiked my curiosity most was the way he looked at me. There was a familiarity about him and his piercing green eyes. It was as if they knew all the thoughts swirling around in my head. He didn't say anything for a very long time, and soon my instincts were tinged with something else. That something else scared me. It told me this man could be a mixture of temptation and danger.*

*I became more conscious of my appearance, pulling the towel tightly around my body. My swimsuit, still wet, was stuck to me like a skin I needed to rid myself of. As I stood there, my feet sinking further into the sand, my awkwardness and fear fought one another. I thought I might topple over. He took another swig, and raised his other hand in recognition, as if it was the most natural thing in the world.*

*'I won't harm you,' he said, sensing my unease.*

*I turned my head away, gazing downwards instead of at him. I don't know how long I stood like that, but when I finally looked up, he was gone.*

*It was as if I had imagined him. I searched the beach, thinking I would find him, but he'd disappeared, although a part of me already knew he would be back. It was only a matter of time.*

# 4
# HEATHER

As I head towards our offices in Central Boston, for my first pre-trial session with Mark Hickman and Robin Finch, my side-chairs for the trial, I catch a glimpse of Long Island in the distance, no longer linked to Moon Island since the demolition of the bridge. After meeting the Handcocks, it's as if my old and new life feel the same way, disconnected, only now, taking on this case, I'm speeding back into a past I'd fooled myself into believing I'd left behind.

I continue along Franklin Park, and soon I turn into Beacon Street, passing Dunkin Donuts on my right. When I reach our offices on the first floor, Robin and Mark are already in the conference room, sipping takeaway coffee. Mine still has the lid on it, waiting.

Robin, like me, is in her mid-thirties, but married. She is tough, old school, and she tells you things straight. Mark is younger, less experienced, with reddish-blond hair and pale skin, thanks to his Irish grandparents. At times, he appears like an over-eager puppy, but as a top graduate from Harvard, he, like Robin, will be invaluable.

We take our seats at the table.

'Okay,' I say. 'I know we all love a challenge.'

They both return a grin.

'I also know,' I add, taking the lid off my coffee, 'that we're racing against the clock.'

'Making it all the more challenging,' says Robin.

'And interesting,' pipes Mark.

'Okay,' I say, 'let's start. Robin, what's the first thing that hits you about this case?'

'Abby was in the wrong place at the wrong time.'

'You mean she was the last person with Jacob.'

'Yes. As with many of these cases of alleged abuse, without witnesses, the last person with the infant is the first in the firing line.'

'Let's quickly go through the events of that day.' I flip open my notepad. 'When the Rotterdams left the house that morning, apart from a light cough, Jacob seemed fine, and neither Vivienne nor Morgan felt the need to check in later that day.'

They nod in agreement.

'Towards lunchtime, Abby put Jacob down for a sleep. She says he seemed a little more poorly, his cough was slightly worse, but he settled quickly. While he slept, she phoned her friend, Ashley. She admits to not keeping a key eye on the baby monitor, but directly after the phone call, she went back upstairs to check on the baby. In her statement to the police, she said she wasn't sure how long she was on the phone.

'But we now have the subpoenaed phone records from the prosecution,' says Robin. 'It was over an hour.'

'Which is damning,' I say, 'giving us a time gap when nobody is watching the infant. There is simply no way of knowing what happened while he was upstairs alone.' I look back at my notes. 'It was only when Abby went upstairs that she realised something was terribly wrong. She also says she can't remember what she spent that hour talking to Ashley about.'

'Sounds like she's being deliberately evasive,' says Mark.

'Maybe, but with Abby,' I say, 'a lot goes down to trust. I'll be pushing her on it again.'

'The important factor here,' says Robin, 'is that once retinal haemorrhaging was found, it was taken as an inflicted injury, and the logical assumption became child abuse.'

I look down at my notes again. 'When Jacob was admitted to hospital, initial X-rays revealed haemorrhages in his brain and eyes. According to the chief medical examiner, Boris Wesley, the triad of symptoms associated with Shaken Baby Syndrome, or SBS, as it's commonly known, were all present.'

'Which would have been an immediate flag for child-protection services, even if Jacob had survived,' adds Mark.

'But we also know,' I say, 'there have been several cases where alternative reasons for this kind of haemorrhaging have been identified.'

'The point is,' says Mark, 'as yet we don't have an alternative reason.'

'It's not up to us to supply one,' says Robin. 'It's the job of the prosecution to prove guilt beyond reasonable doubt. Our job is to establish sufficient doubt, and if the police are correct about the harm done to Jacob, then common sense tells us it should have been the start of a very long investigation. When you consider the time line here, this feels like a rush to justice.'

'You mean, Abby was an easy target?'

'Precisely.'

'So far,' I say, 'the line I've taken with the media is that there are many other potential reasons for the injuries, and that our experts over the course of the trial will prove this and, most importantly, that the injuries had nothing to do with Abby. This case will rest on one set of medical experts against another. We need the jury to understand that, in the absence of any other identifiable cause for the triad of symptoms Jacob presented with, it doesn't mean one didn't exist.'

'Still, we can't get away from the fact that Abby was the last person with Jacob,' adds Robin, 'and we have a missing hour, no matter how sorry she is about not checking the monitor.'

'A missing hour, no witnesses as yet, no other plausible reasons for the injuries, and very little time,' says Mark. 'Looking at the autopsy photographs, seeing a child so young, people will find it hard to believe there isn't a solid reason for the death. Without a solid alternative, they will look for someone to blame.'

'And Abby is sitting right in front of them,' I add.

'The death of a child,' Robin interjects, 'especially an infant, will have emotions running high.'

I briefly look away, remembering how, after my mother lost Mia, I knew nothing on earth could console her because when there were no good feelings left inside her, all she could feel was sadness.

'It will be an open courtroom too,' Mark adds. 'It could easily turn into a media circus.'

'We'll have to be careful,' I agree, turning back to them. 'One wrong move, one misguided statement, and we'll be knee-deep in damage control.'

'From a media point of view,' says Robin, 'it could split female opinion. On the one hand we have a young girl who, we will argue, has been wrongly accused of a crime. On the other, we have a mother who has lost her child.'

'Woman against woman,' I reply, 'and both potential victims.'

'The challenge of putting up other reasons for Jacob's death, outside Shaken Baby Syndrome,' says Mark, 'is that you introduce a grey area into the jury's mind.'

'Go on,' I say.

'There will be debate over forensics and medical opinion, but as soon as we introduce other potential causes, like a previously unidentified fall causing earlier trauma, genetics or even metabolic disorders, we're also putting ourselves in the position of having to prove them. With medical opinion divided on SBS, that may be a problem, and a big one.'

He flicks through the autopsy photographs. 'You can't look at these, Heather, and still think rationally. Without a full explanation to hand, it will be hard for people to imagine how a young life can simply end. The prosecution has marked these items one to ten in order of importance to the state. They're going to hit home hard with them.'

'You mean, they'll look for a visceral reaction.'

'Exactly.'

'The jury selection will be critical too,' adds Robin. 'Boston is no different from the rest of the country when it comes to Shaken Baby Syndrome. One half of the experts believe it's the only cause for the triad of symptoms presented, the other half that there are many other reasons, including unknown causes.'

'There was a case I found in Wyoming,' Mark says, sitting forward, 'which could be useful. An ex-drug addict was accused of killing his baby son after his wife died of an overdose. The case looked simple on paper. The child arrived at the hospital with the same triad of symptoms as Jacob. It turned out, after his wife died, that the father went to rehab and got himself cleaned up. He was doing a good job as a father.'

'What happened?' I ask.

'This guy wasn't well educated, nor did he have much money. Everyone wanted to take the simple route. Ultimately, he was convicted, with thirty years' jail time. Currently he's still locked up, but what's important is that a retrial now looks likely.'

'On what grounds?' Robin asks.

'The mother had an unusual blood-clotting problem. The Innocence Project took the case on and pushed for the mother's medical records. It took a while, but eventually the blood tests gave them another reason for the infant's death, namely genetic blood abnormalities.'

'It's not beyond possibility,' I add, 'that something similar happened here.'

'Also,' adds Robin, energised, 'I think the DA's office took a few shortcuts, which we can expose.'

'Why am I not surprised, with Assistant District Attorney Finlay Clarke running the show?' asks Mark, sarcastically.

'With Finlay,' I emphasise, 'be prepared for the unexpected. But I agree with you, Robin, about the shortcuts.' I stare at them, remembering how the rush to justice in my mother's case, or lack of it, is partly why her death remains unsolved. 'The greatest threat to the truth can come from those who respond to a crime jumping to a false conclusion. The DA's office may have tried too eagerly to fill a vacuum.'

'Any other areas we should look at outside of the medical data?' asks Mark.

I think about my mother, and how depressed she became after Mia's death. 'Yeah,' I say. 'I want you to look closely at Vivienne Rotterdam. We all have our weaknesses, find hers. Was she ever aggressive? What kind of birth did she have with Jacob? Did she suffer post-natal depression? Anything that will help us. And I agree with your earlier point too, Robin. It's the women in this trial who may be put most under the microscope.'

'We'll need to cast doubt on the time line too,' adds Robin, 'because, right now, it puts Abby in the frame.'

'Even if the X-rays revealed haemorrhages in Jacob's brain and eyes,' I say, 'which, according to the prosecution's medical experts, can only happen if the baby is shaken, there is no getting away from two other factors, apart from finding an alternative cause for the haemorrhaging. First, the infant was ill on the day he died. Second, minor historical fractures were found in his upper arms. These are arguably common in an infant of this age, but even if they're of little consequence, they'll help us extend the time line, and if we can get our medical experts to establish a potential time-lag, it will be harder to point the finger at Abby. Perhaps the root cause of the haemorrhaging, considering the ill health of the baby, didn't happen the day he died. Maybe, as Mark mentioned, he had an earlier fall, weeks or even months beforehand. If we think it's possible, we need the jury to think it's possible too.'

'Further examination of the bones,' says Robin, 'will take time.'

'Then,' I say, 'we may have to hope for a long trial, but either way, we need to find something Finlay has missed.' I turn to Mark. 'I want you to look into all potential medical causes that could result in the same or similar symptoms. Look at the usual suspects: viruses, genetics, blood clotting, you name it. We also need to cast doubt on the medical witnesses for the prosecution by having our own experts who believe the opposite. Remember, the Handcocks' pockets are deep, so let's use them, but our strategy is clear. We need to identify other solid reasons for the symptoms presented, extend the time line, put forward medical experts whose opinions will cast doubt on those of the prosecution's, focusing on the historical bone fractures too, while looking at the people closest to Jacob, including Vivienne Rotterdam. If we are to convince the jury, we must also bear in mind, the loss of a child's life is an emotional landmine. It will affect everyone, especially the jury.'

# 5
# HEATHER

The weeks since my first meeting with Abby have disappeared far too quickly, with endless journeys back and forth from Boston to Framingham, clearing the decks of everything other than this case file, and trying to achieve in weeks what should take months. In as much as anyone can get to know a relative stranger fast, I have attempted to do so with Abby, including discovering certain uncomplimentary aspects of her past, and how at times her difficult behaviour meant she had more than her fair share of foster homes.

I have also become increasingly aware of similarities between the two of us, other than that we both lost a mother at a young age. Abby, like me, has learned to depend mostly on herself rather than relying on others and, also like me, she has lived through moments, particularly in her early life, when she has felt extremely vulnerable.

I check the time on my cell phone – 7 a.m. In a few hours, I'm due to see Assistant District Attorney Finlay Clarke, the lead prosecutor in Abby's trial and my old boss. The meeting will be at his offices in Central Boston. An *informal get-together* – his words, not mine – and fitting, he said, considering our shared time in the prosecutor's office. What I'm really expecting is our opening battle, something aside from our first day in court. I could have refused, but that would have been perceived as weakness, which I have no intention of gifting him.

My cell phone rings. It's Mark, and at this hour of the morning, it can only mean bad news.

'You're not going to like this, Heather. I've got more information about Abby's time at DCF.'

'Spit it out.'

'She had a bad spell in 2011, after spending time with a family called French. She was given counselling. It seems the authorities had issues with the foster family. Rumours of possible child abuse, but nothing proven. Either way, the counselling didn't go well. There is a record of Abby having a violent outburst.'

'But she would have been a child.' I pause. 'How violent?'

'She completely lost it with staff. She had to be sedated.'

I repeat, 'She was only a child.'

'Yeah, but.'

'What was the name of the psychologist she attended?'

'Dr Perrotta.'

'Okay, see what you can get on the French family. I'll ask Robin to look into the doctor.'

'Will do.'

Seconds later, I hear Robin's voice. 'Sorry to call so early,' I say, 'but when you get to the office, talk to Mark about the latest from DCF. I want you to look at Dr Perrotta, the consultant psychologist assigned to Abby. It seems there was a violent outburst after she left a family called French. I know we're playing catch-up, but we can't risk missing something.'

Hanging up, I catch a glimpse of myself in the bedroom mirror. I look as tired as I feel. The last few weeks have meant a series of long days and nights, with very little sleep. I know I'll need a clear head for my meeting with Finlay, which is why when I reach our offices, less than an hour later, I decide to go for a short run.

As I make my way around Boston Common, the air has a fresh tinge to it, and the sun, although bright, doesn't yet possess the suffocating heat that will soon settle on the day. There are plenty of early-morning joggers, women and men in running gear, who, like me, will soon put on a new skin, suits, formal attire for their professional day.

Since setting up my law practice, after years of double and triple jobbing, doing everything from waitressing to research work for private law firms, and only partly using the trust fund set up by Lorrie to finance it, I have learned to love this city. I feel content within its lush greenery and high-rise buildings, the scent of cherry blossom in late spring, the smell of fresh pastry and coffee in the mornings, the various bijou shops and cafés down side-streets, the mix of young and old, all within the steady heart of the city, a place with a constant pulse, moving forward and never looking back, and so different to Corham.

As I run, I allow a light breeze to consume me, almost instinctively moving with increased agility, feeling the rising sweat on my body as it gets into a more uplifting rhythm. I hear my feet hit the pavement, the repetitive sound resonating upwards within a place where, if I try hard enough, I can push all other thoughts out of my mind and become invisible.

Turning into Arlington Street, I concentrate on the mundane – a well-dressed woman, with manicured nails and a smart hairstyle, sipping takeaway coffee, a couple of grey squirrels escaping up a tree. I keep running, past various stone-stepped houses, typical of Central Boston, with their small, neat front gardens, all the time clearing my head for whatever Finlay has in store. By the time my run is over, I feel like a different me, capable of taking on anyone, including my old boss.

I know Finlay won't comment on me switching from prosecution to defence. That path is well trodden: many others like me, without political ambition, have also left for a more lucrative private practice. The extra money wasn't my main reason, but he won't care about that. Telling Finlay I wanted to help others by defending them would be wasted on him.

Three hours later, I get off the Green Line and walk towards Cambridge Street, taking a right at the next intersection into Bullfinch Place. Soon I'm in the elevator climbing to the top floor and Finlay's offices, with their panoramic view of the city below. I imagine him sitting at his desk, remembering how he touched me once, placing a hand low on my back, applying gentle pressure but with too much intimacy for it to be purely sociable. When I pulled away, he had seemed amused – desire, or a test? With Finlay nothing is ever certain, except what he wants you to know. At the time, I was a rookie in the prosecutor's office, raw and naïve, filled with all the things youth allows, before I'd been knocked around enough times to realise that working within the law, you need to be smarter and faster than the rest if you want to achieve anything. When I set up my private defence practice, he sent me flowers, the message on the card 'Watch that beautiful back of yours.' A cheesy threat, but a muted warning all the same, telling me he still considered himself professionally superior.

As the elevator rises, another thought slips in, a clawing reminder that Finlay knew me before I perfected the necessary façade to ensure other people couldn't work out what I was thinking. Sometimes, even now, when he looks at me, it's as if he's saying, *You don't fool me, Heather Baxter, no matter how hard you try.* Equally, I know I need to prove him wrong.

I stare at my reflection in the glass, aware of the dark rings under my eyes from the lack of sleep. I applied concealer to the worst parts, but it doesn't hide everything. I chide myself, for the umpteenth time, that only a mad person would take on such a big case with just weeks to trial, but I already know the answer goes deeper than that. It goes beyond the similarities between me and Abby too, losing a mother as a child, or having to face adversity far too young. It even goes past any crusade on my part, worrying about what would happen to Abby if, like her previous attorney, I let her down. It's partly connected to the birthmark, the same as my sister's, the baby girl who never got a chance to fulfil her potential. And, somewhere deep inside me, I recognise another truth: for so long I have avoided Corham, and my past, or any connection to it, but I have always known that, one day, something would bring me back.

I haven't seen that black sedan since the first day I went to the Handcocks' house, or the man whose face was in shadow under his hat, but he is never far from my thoughts. I step out of the elevator and walk towards the reception desk. Finlay's PA gestures me towards his office. I tap on the door.

'Come in, Heather,' he calls.

I open the door, then close it behind me. 'Finlay,' I say, holding out my hand as I walk towards him.

'Well, don't God and the law work in mysterious ways?' he replies, standing up. His suit is impeccable, his shirt a textured white cotton with a blood-red tie. He is slightly tanned. It suits him.

'How's that?' I ask.

'Bringing us together again, like old times.' He smiles.

'Like old times,' I reply, not rising to the bait.

'Take a seat, Heather. There's no need to stand on ceremony.'

We both sit down. There are four floor-to-ceiling windows behind him, framing the city streetscape.

'Did you hear, Heather, that Wilburn Kendell has granted media access?' He smiles again.

'I knew it was to be decided upon, but I'm not surprised.' Is he staring at the dark shadows under my eyes? I keep my gaze fixed on him.

'He's agreed to the cameras in court too, filming every nuance of the trial.'

'I guess that's his prerogative.' I place my leather satchel on the floor beside my feet.

'It surely is, Heather, it surely is.' He pauses, moving his glasses further up his nose. 'You look well.'

'As do you. The tan suits you,' I say. 'But let's get to the point, Finlay. You called this meeting, not me.'

'Still in a hurry?' he muses.

'Point,' I say again, smiling insincerely.

'Heather, we go back a long way,' he pauses once more, looking concerned, 'and I have to ask, are you confident you're best positioned to grasp the enormous emotional trauma of this case?'

'Meaning?'

'Well,' he says, dragging out his words, 'to have an infant taken from you is truly a cruel and awful thing.'

I think about my mother and Mia. I think about what a shithead Finlay is. 'Are you questioning my credentials?'

'Not at all, but you're at such a tentative juncture in your career.'

'I suggest you concentrate on your side of things and stop troubling yourself on my account.'

'You're not a parent either.'

'Neither are you.'

If I'm not careful, he'll have me defending myself faster than a speeding bullet.

'It may be difficult for you, Heather, at this point, to comprehend the intense suffering involved.'

Asshole.

'I comprehend it far better than you give me credit for, but if you're trying to offer guidance, Finlay, remember, I don't work for you, not any more. So, it's probably best if we don't waste our time.'

He puts his hands up in defence. 'Okay,' he says, 'but this is a complicated one.' His southern drawl becomes more evident with each word.

'I hear you have high plans for Congress,' I say, putting the boot in, telling him I know how important this case is for him.

'You flatter me.' He laughs. 'Did you know, Heather, that fifteen years ago I had a difficult case in North Carolina? That's where I learned the ropes, in my own backyard.'

I nod, already aware of his Southern roots.

'Well, there was this black kid up for rape and attempted murder.' He stands up and walks over to the water dispenser, filling a paper cup. He makes a gesture, asking me if I want some.

'No, thanks,' I say. 'I'm fine.'

'I thought the trial was going to be about what that boy did to the young girl. You see, he went and whipped her up from a country road, the one she walked to her part-time job at the local ice-cream parlour. She was a good kid, came from a nice family, and although they had plenty of money, they were honourable folks, wanting her to help pay her way through college. That's what the part-time job was for.'

'I'm listening.'

'The boy held her for two days. In that time, he raped her day and night, like she was a free ride at a rodeo. He bit her, poked her, put his cigarette butts out on that pure white body of hers. Hell, he even laughed when he told her that in the end she would plead for him to kill her.'

'Any chance you could get to the bottom line?' I ask, wondering what he's up to, looking far too damn smug.

He squashes the empty cup in his hand, before firing it into the trash can. 'He also told her, Heather, he would put her body in the water, and that she would sink to the bottom with the stones he would add in for good measure. Her family would never see their little darling again. The fear that young girl felt was unimaginable but, lucky for her, the police caught up with him before he could take her life.'

'Point?' I repeat again, my body already repositioning itself to cut this meeting short. I have no intention of letting him play me.

'The point, sweet girl, is that there is a very important lesson here.'

'Which is?'

'You see, Heather, it turned out that the trial wasn't only about what that boy did to that nice white girl.'

'No?'

He shakes his head. 'No. What it was about was one black boy too many being beaten to a pulp while in custody, and how the white police officers threatening him said he would never get out of there alive. How he would die for what he did to that girl, if not legally then by whatever means was necessary. What I'm saying, Heather, is this. Don't fool yourself into thinking that this one is going to spin out about simple justice.'

'No?'

'This trial, Heather, as far as the media are concerned, may well break down to a rich-man-poor-man affair. The young nanny who spent most of her life in foster care, her lack of education, and the Ivy League Rotterdams who had everything: money, position, power. A respected professional couple, in the right circles, lucky to have the God-given gift of a child, their own flesh and blood, their light and joy, only for him to be taken away from them.'

'Finlay, I don't see—' I stand up.

He keeps on talking. 'I already see the upcoming media headlines.' He spreads his arms out wide and high. 'Right now, they're out to get Abby, the girl with the mark of the devil on her face, but they could soon shift and look at the Rotterdams, seeing the pillars of a society they hold dear, and they will ask, Why? They may even ask, why did they leave their child with an unstable young girl? And when that happens, the truth, like my boy from North Carolina, may not matter so much. The only thing that will matter, Heather, is that those rich folks gave their baby to an ill-educated, ill-equipped young girl, and everyone will hate them for it. And shall I tell you why?'

'Do I have a choice?' Prick.

'Because the good folk of our nation like to see themselves in the likes of the Rotterdams. The professional couple who have it all. A status they either have or aspire to. Which is why they will care a whole lot more about Jacob Rotterdam than about another child who is, in their eyes, less worthy. Their grief for the loss will be stretched to a point they can't imagine possible. How could they bear something like that happening to them? And it's precisely at that moment, Heather, that the doubled-edged sword comes into play, and they will look for people to blame.'

'Abby?'

'Or even the Rotterdams.'

'I don't see anyone pointing the finger at them, but it sounds like you're telling me I've already won the trial in the media.'

He smiles again. 'Nothing of the sort, Heather,' he says, dropping the soft tone in his voice, replacing it with a hard edge. 'All I'm doing, for old times' sake, is offering you a friendly warning that, whatever tactics you may envisage using, I'll always be one step ahead of you.'

With the exit of the soft tone, some of the veneer goes, his mask slipping, until all there is, is his ruthless ambition, and the message sent loud and clear: You are not capable of stopping me.

'For what it's worth,' I say, with practised calm, 'I don't need you to tell me that, when it comes to this trial, we're not simply dealing with a court of law, or that in the media things can, and will, get tricky, but I appreciate you laying your cards on the table, for old times' sake.'

He raises his eyebrows.

'And it would be a foolish opponent, Finlay,' I add, moving towards the door, 'who believes that threatening their years of experience is going to achieve anything other than raising the stakes.'

'I can't tell you,' he says, 'how much I'm looking forward to working with you again.'

'Whatever happened to that boy?' I ask, curious despite myself.

'Oh, in the end he was found guilty. DNA, thankfully, doesn't lie.'

Finlay is so close to me now I can smell his cologne, the one he told me was inspired by a historic emperor, celebrating strength, power and success. 'However,' he says, 'because of the marchers with their banners outside the courthouse every day of the trial, claiming police injustice and so forth, the thing went national, and the boy got fifteen years instead of life.'

'I see,' I say, already regretting my curiosity.

'In the end, Heather, nobody was happy, not the young girl, who won't leave her house any more, or her parents who can't look her straight in the eye, or the protesters, who still feel the white man won out and the black man suffered.'

'Times have changed,' I say.

'Have they?' He allows several beats to pass. 'I don't reckon things change that fast.'

I take a step back.

'Don't you want to know where he's serving his sentence?'

'No.' I've already had enough of this circus.

'In some soft, low-security prison where he gets nice meals every day. I understand he's made some friends. Sure, I even hear tell,' his voice close to laughter, 'that he took up college studies.'

'I'm guessing the young girl never went back to college?'

'Her name is Celine, by the way, and, no, she never did go back. Although I'm glad, Heather, the irony isn't lost on you.'

I open the door to leave.

'Before you go, Heather, there is one other thing.'

'What?'

'Daniel Petersen, from Corham.'

'What about him?'

'He's working for us now.'

'When you say "us", you mean the DA's office?'

'Yes. It's good to have a local guy on the ground in Corham, what with Abby being the Handcocks' niece. Keeping an eye on things locally often delivers benefits.'

'I see.'

'Always a pleasure,' he whispers in my ear.

I barely resist the temptation to say, *Fuck you*, knowing he would use any emotive response as a tiny victory. Instead I smile and pull away, telling myself he can have as many small victories as he wants, once I win the one that matters.

Outside, instead of heading to the Green Line, I hail a cab, asking the driver to let me out near the Charles River, wanting to reflect on everything Finlay has said. Walking in the shade, I turn the corner onto Beacon Hill, and it is only then, in the distance, I see him, the man sitting on the stone steps, looking downwards, wearing a battered Panama hat.

Stuck to the spot, I wonder if I'm imagining him. I walk on, but the closer I get to the man, the more uncertain I feel. Part of me wants him to look up, another part doesn't. It can't be him. Can it? Since my first visit to the Handcocks' house, I've been recalling more memories, including seeing that miniature silver elephant buried in the soil, its trunk turned upwards towards the sky. I stop only inches from the man. He looks up, curious. The sun blinds him. I concentrate hard, looking for something familiar in his lined blotchy red face, as his eyes stare at me.

It isn't him. It's a stranger. I walk on, slightly spooked.

'Hey,' he shouts after me, 'do I know you?'

I look back, feeling somewhat like a fool. 'Sorry,' I say. 'I thought you were someone else.'

*

Later that evening, at home, to take my mind off things, I order Italian takeout and get ready to watch some mindless television. I flick through various channels, avoiding all news reports, before finally settling on an episode of *The Wall*. I enjoy answering all the trivia questions, but during the ad break, while I wait for the food delivery, I find myself absentmindedly searching my phone for anything interesting on the Handcocks. I may be defending Abby, but they're still part of it. I flip from one article to another, until I see a newspaper report about a girl called Lexie Gilmore. She used to work for the Handcocks as a maid and, according to the article, she was nineteen when she went missing. I examine the date, too: a few months before my mother was killed. Everyone believed the girl skipped town. For a time, it was all people talked about, until they had the juicier story of my mother's death.

The persistent buzz of the apartment intercom pulls me from my thoughts, telling me my takeout has arrived, but as I tip the delivery boy, I decide to make my own discreet enquiries into what else the Handcocks might have been up to in the intervening years. For that, I will need someone unconnected to the practice. It's been a long time since I spoke to Alex, but if anyone is going to find out something that others have missed on the Handcocks, she will.

# 6
# ELIZABETH

*Earlier tonight I crept into Heather's bedroom. She'd left her bedside lamp on. There was a book lying open on her pillow. I sat on the bed thinking how much like me she was, always appearing troubled, always questioning.*

*I felt her forehead. She had gotten sunburned this afternoon. I'd covered her body in calamine. She looked like an Egyptian mummy, all white and stiff. I smiled at her, so earnest in sleep.*

*The bedroom was quiet and filled with the kind of silence that engulfs everything. I knew Charlie wouldn't be home tonight, not after the argument we'd had, and I found myself, almost unwittingly, thinking about Mia's father again.*

*Sometimes we used to meet near the wildlife sanctuary. Being there, in the woods, I felt the same comfort I often get near the ocean, as if it's a place I can escape to and become lost within. I see us as we walk close together, the ground underfoot damp and mossy, with small twigs constantly snapping underneath our feet. Deep in the woods, dense with tall pines, holly trees and squirrelly oaks, I would listen hard for the sound of animals, a coyote, fox or deer. LEAVE ONLY FOOTPRINTS – TAKE ONLY MEMORIES, the words engraved on the wooden sign at the entrance. What memories have I taken?*

*I know we never arrived together. It was far too risky. I also know meeting in secret added another layer of excitement. But that was then. Now all I can think about are the reasons why being with him was wrong.*

*I have realised something else lately. More than anything, back then, our desire for each other was driven by a kind of desperation, one we shared, and when the sound of our lovemaking was swallowed by the swaying trees, each of them spiralling tall, I pretended things would be okay, only they never could be, not with him.*

*Since I saw Lucas at the beach a few weeks ago, he has come back several times. With him, I sense a form of desperation too. I warn myself not to make the same mistakes again, but equally I know I can't be sure of anything, not any more.*

# 7
# HEATHER

Driving to Alex's house the following day, I get the phone call from Robin telling me Dr Perrotta has been added to the prosecution witness list.

'What else have you found out about him?'

'The day of Abby's violent outburst, the one when she had to be sedated as a child, it seems Dr Perrotta pulled back from being her therapist, handing her case file over to another psychologist at DCF.'

'Do we know why?'

'He claimed potential *transference*.'

'Which is what exactly?'

'It's a theoretical phenomenon, principally characterised by manipulative behaviour in which the patient consciously or unconsciously transfers certain feelings and emotions towards the therapist to gain favour.'

'Then we already know what Finlay's inference will be. Despite Abby being only eleven at the time, he will paint her as someone capable of manipulation to get whatever she wants.'

Hanging up on Robin, I pass myriad wooden New England homes on the way to Alex's place in Dorchester. Some look the worse for wear, and not for the first time, despite believing Abby didn't harm Jacob, I wonder if she's telling us everything.

On reaching the town centre, at the traffic lights, I think again about that black sedan, and how I mistakenly thought the man sitting on the stone steps yesterday was Lucas.

The lights change from red to green, and suddenly I see my mother, pregnant with Mia, as she lifts her hair, asking me to close the clasp of her necklace. This fresh memory feels like all the others, disconnected and important in equal measure.

When, finally, I park the car outside Alex's house, instead of going inside I wait, belatedly wondering if this is such a good idea. Born in the Bronx, New York, Alex is mainly suspicious of others, except those closest to her. Once, I might have been considered the latter, but it has been a long time since I've been in touch. I look across at Alex's house, which, like many in Dorchester, is a two-storey wooden building with a steep pitched roof and a narrow porch. It's in need of a bit of TLC, although painting and decorating would be low on her priorities. This is partly why we used to click so well. She never sweats the small stuff, even if I do. We met in the DA's office when she worked as an in-house investigator. Now she operates as a PI, a lone wolf. She always preferred working on her own. She is someone who is prepared to take risks and do whatever it takes, and right now I need her to dig into the Handcocks and find out if there is another reason, outside family ties, why Jim is prepared to invest so much money in this trial. That requires filling in all the gaps from the time I left Corham to now.

I get out of the car and walk towards the front door. For a brief moment, I pause again. What if she's with someone? Maybe I should have phoned ahead. Last I heard, her latest lover was an out-of-work actress who was going to make it *big* some day. I'd lay money on 'some day' being the attraction, fitting nicely into Alex's desire to pick up strays, both animal and human.

She told me once, after far too many tequilas, that I intrigued her, and that people with dark histories were like magnets, inextricably attracted to one another. She also told me that she could be anyone people wanted her to be.

I ring the doorbell. I smell fresh coffee.

As I wait, I'm picturing her small but fierce frame, dressed in black from head to toe. She was always far too pretty to be punk, but far too street to be typical. I like her sassiness and intensity, not to mention she's damn good at her job: she saved my neck when I was a young prosecutor more than once after I'd messed up.

The door swings back on its hinges, and there she is, in the flesh. She's wearing a Marilyn Monroe-style wig, blonde and big. She gives me one of her you're-kidding-me looks.

'Well, heavens to Betsy,' she says, looking me up and down, 'to what do I owe this pleasure?'

'In the neighbourhood, you know,' I joke.

'Yeah, and I'm Snow White waiting for Prince Charming.'

'You alone?'

'I'm alone.' She smiles, opening the door wider.

I take a step into the hallway. She stands back to let me pass.

'It's been a while,' she says, 'not that I'm the sensitive type.'

'Does that matter?' I ask.

'No, it doesn't, not now that you're here.'

'I smell coffee.'

'And I smell trouble.' She gives me a wink. I already know she's forgiven me for not being in touch.

In the kitchen, filling our cups, she says, 'I see you've been putting in long hours,' noting the dark shadows under my eyes.

'Are they that obvious?'

'Pretty much.' She touches my cheek with the back of her hand. It feels soft.

I stare at the tattoo of the phoenix rising from the ashes on her arm, as she pulls her hand away. It reshapes itself as she sits down. There is a side table filled with half a dozen coloured wigs on mannequin heads, and jewellery hanging around their necks. One has a pair of dark sunglasses. I imagine her wearing a raincoat with the collar up, looking like something out of a Dick Tracy novel, enjoying the pretence of being someone else.

'Aren't you hot in that wig?' I ask.

'What? You don't like it?' she scoffs, teasing.

'I prefer the real you,' I say. The words hang in the air.

'Sometimes,' she says, 'so do I.' She takes a sip from her coffee, eyeing me over the cup rim. 'Okay, what's really up?' She applies a facial expression she's perfected for discovering the truth. Before the DA's office, she spent a couple of years working as a nurse's aide in a psychiatric hospital, the Ding Wing, as she called it. Seeing other people locked up, she said, with their weakness out on show, taught her more about humanity, or the lack of it, than most people could learn in a lifetime.

Layla, her black pitbull, another stray, pushes open the kitchen door and flops at her ankles.

'Do you ever miss it?' I ask, ignoring her earlier question.

'What?'

'The DA's office.'

'Nope. Do you?'

'Sometimes,' I say. 'Putting away the bad guys has a certain appeal.'

'It's all a game of cat and mouse, whichever side you're on.'

'I've taken on a new case.' I blow the hot steam off the coffee.

'I heard – Rotterdams and Abby Jones.'

'You don't miss much.'

'I make a point of knowing things.' She keeps her gaze steady.

'I met Abby for the first time a few weeks ago.'

'And?'

'I believe her. I don't think she harmed the baby.'

'You sure she isn't fooling you? Folks are capable of almost anything, given the right set of circumstances, and some are capable of getting there a whole lot faster than others.'

'She reminds me of someone too.'

'Who?'

'My sister. She had a similar birthmark.'

Alex stands up, walking towards the wigs, fingering through a long brunette one with curls. 'Being sentimental isn't going to help either of you. You need to stay focused.'

'I know that.'

'And letting that girl get under your skin because of some family resemblance …' She lets the unfinished sentence hover.

'I understand what's at stake.'

'If this gets personal, it'll make you weaker.'

'I know that too.'

Suddenly I want to tell her about all the stuff I've been remembering, and before I change my mind, I blurt out, 'I've been remembering things.'

'What things?' she asks, sitting down again.

'About before.'

'Your momma?'

'Yeah.'

'Since when?'

'Since a few months back, after my grandmother's funeral, and then later, when I agreed to take on this case.'

She gives me a sympathetic look. I don't want her feeling sorry for me. Maybe this is a mistake. 'Look,' I say, 'that's not the main reason I'm here.'

'No?' she retorts, her tone gaining an edge, sensing I'm holding back. The cell phone in the back pocket of her jeans rings.

'Let me take this,' she says.

I watch as her muscles tense, as if they could snap at any moment. She pulls the wig off, firing it down on the table like a skinned animal, revealing shaven black bristles underneath as she walks towards the array of wigs again, all the time keeping her back to me. I had heard rumours about her and Finlay at one point. It's a topic we have never discussed. Alex's relationships with women and her odd indiscretions with men are her own business, but it didn't surprise me. Finlay would find her attractive. She would find him interesting. He would fall within her inclination towards risks, for the sake of finding out where they would take her.

She hangs up, turning to face me, her back now to the wigs. 'Before you tell me why you're actually here, let me warn you, you're up against a helluva gunslinger with Finlay.'

'I can handle him.'

She raises her eyebrows. 'Don't underestimate him, Heather. Beneath that smooth talk of his, he's as hungry for control and power as a cornered rat is for escape. Anyhow,' she says, 'you made a good call, switching sides. For starters, there's more dollars on the private defence side of things.'

I'm tempted to ask what she saw in him, but I don't. 'I'm not in it for the money.' I sound sharp.

'Okay, Florence Nightingale. I'm on your side, remember.'

'I know.'

Layla licks her ankles.

'You picked up any more strays recently?' I ask, fishing to know if there's someone new on the scene.

'Maybe. It gives me a reason for getting up in the morning.' She shrugs and smiles.

I smile back. 'By the way,' I add, 'the case is being televised.' This new piece of information puts us back on safer ground.

'Which is why Finlay will love it.'

'The big guys always get the big cases – you know that as well as I do.'

'Especially the televised ones,' she says. 'There's no buying that kind of publicity, and Finlay isn't going to fuck around with it.'

'He has McKenna as one of his sidekicks.'

'McKenna is tough.'

'Because he's an ex-cop?'

'Because he's mean and smart.' The Marilyn wig still sits between us on the table. 'How come you've been brought in so late?'

'The previous lead defender had personal issues.'

'I see.' She folds her arms, leaning back. 'What were the numbers from the indictment?'

'Nineteen to four in favour of a true bill.'

'Jesus Christ, Heather.'

'It's always heavily loaded for the prosecution.'

'Yeah, but even if folk think you can indict a ham sandwich, it isn't always true.'

I shrug my shoulders.

'All I'm saying, Heather, is sometimes the cards can be stacked against you. What's your biggest weakness?'

'The medical examiner's report is toxic.'

'Boris Wesley?'

'Yes, and according to him, the triad of symptoms presented –

bleeding behind the eyes, the subdural haematoma, and the brain swelling – means there's only one possible cause and that's physical abuse. He's so damn respected it might as well be God Almighty on the stand.'

'What is Finlay's main argument?'

'Basically, when Jacob got irritable, Abby got angry. She didn't, or couldn't, deal with him, so she shook him out of rage, causing fatal damage.'

'And your theory?'

'Medical opinion is split down the middle on Shaken Baby Syndrome. Boris Wesley is on one side of it. Other specialists disagree.'

'And you're depending on the burden of proof being on the prosecution to prove guilt before a reasonable doubt?' she asks, almost mockingly.

'Anything else is against Abby's constitutional rights.'

'We both know when it comes to cases like this, where a child, particularly an infant, someone defenceless, is harmed, it doesn't matter if it's against the Constitution of the United States or not. The burden of proof is often reversed, and don't kid yourself otherwise. Finlay isn't going to mess around. He'll be ready to sell his own blood or that of anyone else who happens to come within a hundred-mile radius.' She eyeballs me. 'Why are you really taking this on? And don't give me any bullshit.'

I sip my coffee. It tastes cold, and suddenly sickening. I think about Jacob Rotterdam. I think about how his parents will never see him again. I think about the younger me, and the days after my mother lost the baby, that empty crib, and how my mother refused to let it be taken from the house, no matter how much my father wanted it gone. I think about all the nights afterwards, when I felt so alone, making my own supper, waiting for the night to turn to daylight and back again, when I didn't have a mother because she was lost within herself, and there was no father either. He had done another temporary disappearing act after a couple of guys called at the house looking for money, and suddenly he needed desperately to be somewhere else. I think again about how Abby faced life far too young without a mother, and how I understand what it's like to no longer feel loved. I think about her birthmark, too, and how from that very first day I've thought of Mia, and how life can be so unfair, and sometimes, when things go against you, you just need one person in your life to believe in you, the way my mother once believed in me.

'Because,' I say, 'I don't have a choice. Abby Jones is innocent.'

'You always have a choice,' she snaps, annoyed at my obvious vagueness, getting up from the table again. This time Layla follows her. 'Okay,' she says, her voice suddenly accusing. 'Why are you actually here?'

'Because I need your investigative skills.'

She tilts her head to the side. 'Don't you have your own in-house investigators to do your dirty work?'

'Are you looking for a compliment?'

'Are you offering one?'

'Look, I need you to do some digging for me into the Handcocks.'

'Why?'

'I don't trust them, I never have, and I'm suspicious about their belated so-called support. Besides, I don't want anything surprising coming out of the woodwork. It's been a long time since I've had any real connection to them or Corham, and I need you to fill in the blanks, find out what's lurking behind all that gloss and money, especially if it affects Abby.'

'You're hilarious.'

'What do you mean?'

'I assume it's the deep pockets of the Handcocks paying for all this.'

'You assume right.'

'Won't they mind you using their money to spy on them?'

'They hired me to defend their niece. I'll do whatever it takes.'

'All right,' she says, slightly changing tack. 'I'll consider it, but there is one other thing.'

'What?'

'If you're so sure Abby Jones didn't harm Jacob Rotterdam, then who did?'

'I don't know, perhaps nobody. My gut tells me Abby is telling the truth.'

'Gut doesn't usually do too well in court.'

'Perhaps not, but I am sticking with it for now. As you said yourself, I need to stay focused.'

She looks away, pensive. I push her for an answer. 'Will you help?'

'It will take time digging into the Handcocks,' she replies, still looking away, 'but, yeah, as soon as I have something concrete, I'll let you know.'

'Great.'

'Heather?'

'Yeah?'

'If you ever need to talk to anyone about that memory stuff, or anything else, you know I'm here, right?'

'Yeah,' I say, 'I do.'

# 8
# MARCIA

Marcia Langan's fingers hit the keyboard of her laptop faster than she can talk. It's a wrap on the front page of the *Patriot Eagle*, mainly local news – a car crash the previous night, preparation for the town fair, and a photograph of some teenagers from the local dance troupe, enjoying the sun at Sandy Beach. Gerry Gillespie, the editor of Corham's local newspaper since he was out of diapers, calls her from his office.

She doesn't rush. Rushing makes you appear eager. She clicks 'save', before closing the other open tabs. The screen goes black. She admires her reflection.

'Glad you can honour me with your presence,' he says, as she hovers in the doorway.

'Happy to oblige, Gerry, as always.'

'I'm thinking we should do a piece on Heather Baxter.'

'The lead on Jones's trial?'

'That's right. There's a lot of history there.'

'I grew up here, Gerry, remember. Everyone in town knows about

Heather's mother. The story is practically a tourist attraction,' she adds, believing sarcasm to be one of her strong points. 'You wrote a piece on it, didn't you, Gerry, back in the day?'

He flinches. 'Yeah, I did.'

'I'll get in touch with Heather. She shouldn't be too hard to track down.'

'No, leave the direct contact to me. Just find out all you can on the upcoming trial, and we'll move things from there.'

She gives him one of her brightest smiles. She'd wondered if he'd avoided covering the trial because of the Handcock connection, not wanting to get on the wrong side of one of the newspaper's main benefactors, but obviously Heather's involvement has shifted things.

'And don't you go flying off on any tangents, Marcia. Run everything by me first, do yah hear me?'

'You're the boss.'

'See that you remember it.'

Back at her desk she picks up her purse and turns off the lamp, ready to leave. At the front door she hesitates, hearing Gerry dial an outside line. He has it on speaker phone. This could be interesting, she decides, so she hangs back, moving close enough to his office door to hear a female voice say, 'Hello.'

'Heather? Is that you?'

'Who is this?'

'It's Gerry Gillespie from the *Patriot Eagle*.'

There is silence at the other end of the line, before the female voice asks, 'How did you get my private cell number?'

'Daniel Petersen.'

Another silence. Gerry fills it. 'Look, I know we haven't spoken in some time, but I'd be interested in talking to you now that you're the lead on the Abby Jones trial.'

'The trial is not up for discussion.'

'I understand. I was thinking more of a life piece. You know, local girl made good …' He lets his words trail off.

'I've made good now, have I?'

Marcia detects an edge to Heather's voice.

'I didn't mean to offend.'

'Do you remember what you said about me, Gerry, in that newspaper article all those years ago? The one you wrote a month after my mother died?'

'I remember every word.'

'So do I.'

There is another long silence.

Marcia waits.

'Look,' Gerry says, filling the void, 'I didn't mean to …'

'I will *always* remember your words, how you said I gave my mother respect, a final act, you called it. Nobody else ever mentioned that. All they talked about was the other stuff, how I hid in the blanket box. How I might have saved her.'

'I know. I wrote those things too.'

'Yes, you did … but even if I didn't protect her, I didn't want anyone seeing her that way.'

'You were only a child.'

'I don't remember that mattering a whole lot.'

'Heather, if you consider doing the piece, it will be your chance to put the record straight.'

The line goes dead. Marcia hears Gerry pace the room. She needs to get away before he realises she's been listening in. It's clear to her he intends to approach this in a sensitive manner, but most successful people in the media aren't much into sensitivity. He asked her to find out information, and she will. Potential scoops like this don't cross your path too often, and she has every intention of finding out as much as possible about Heather Baxter. She doesn't plan on staying at the *Patriot Eagle* for ever.

Outside, she puts a call through to Sheriff Blanco. He's always had a shine for her. They agree to meet the next day down at Popfinn Beach. He also gives her the other contact number she needs, for Lucas García. She waits until she's in her car before she keys it into her phone. 'Hi there, Lucas,' she says, in her cheeriest voice. 'It's Marcia Langan of the *Patriot Eagle*.' The words roll into one another, as if she and the newspaper are one and the same. 'I sure would like to chat with you.'

*

The next day, driving towards Popfinn Beach, Marcia has the music turned up full blast. She is still annoyed that Lucas García didn't want to play ball, but Sheriff Blanco will come up with the goods, she's sure of it. It still irks some of the locals that Lucas never did time for Elizabeth Baxter's murder. Despite old Sheriff Hodgson's best efforts, the case never got past the grand-jury stage. Still, when she gets talking to Blanco, she isn't going to mention any of this because, with Blanco, it's always best to let him think he's the one in control.

As she reaches their rendezvous, plenty of people are already on the beach. She slows down, passing a few rundown bars at the seafront, Daddy Dog, Barefoot Bob's, the Yellow Parrot. Unlike Corham, Popfinn Beach screams trailer trash, with its closed-down arcade and various signs of disrepair, no matter how pretty the beach is.

At the Beach Front Bar, she parks opposite, turning her car to face the road instead of the sea.

When she spots the police car turning onto the beach road, she drops her reflective sunglasses over her eyes. They'll offer her protection of sorts, distance. Blanco likes pretty women. Being in the police force is a power trip for him. When it comes to mixing with the snakes, they don't come much sneakier than him. But if anyone knows about the secret underbelly of Corham, he does.

He parks the police car, taking his time getting out and walking over to her.

'So, Marcia, I'm guessing this isn't a date?' He leans against her car, lighting a cigarette. The seagulls flap around his feet. He doesn't pay them any heed.

She laughs, encouraging his attention for now. 'I sure would love you to tell me everything you know about Heather Baxter. You know, Blanco, the real stuff.'

He raises his eyebrows. 'That might take a while.'

He's already loving this, she thinks, and he'll probably string it out to massage his ego. 'I have the time,' she says, pressing the record app on her phone.

'You can put that thing away, Marcia. There isn't going to be any recording.'

'Fine, have it your way, but I promise you, Blanco, I would have wiped it.'

'I didn't get this far in life depending on others so I've no intention of starting now.'

'Let's start with the old killing,' Marcia says, putting her phone into her pocket.

'It was an awful tragedy,' he says. 'The town's never gotten over it.'

Yep, she thinks again, he is going to string it out. 'I wasn't born back then,' she says, 'but I'm assuming Heather had a tough time of it.'

'She sure did. After the murder, she moved into Lorrie's place.'

'Her grandma?'

'That's right. She was ten years old when her mother was killed.

The girl left Elizabeth Baxter lying on the kitchen floor for hours, and in a pool of her own blood too.'

'Maybe she was frightened.' Marcia takes a step closer, adding some false empathy. 'After all, she was very young.'

'She was old enough to do something. Folk don't like things like that. Around Corham, you need to be squeaky clean, and folk here are not that quick to forgive or forget.' He stubs out his cigarette. 'Her grandma never forgave her either. She blamed Heather for not saving her little girl. If it had been Samuel, Lorrie's son, who ended up dead, the girl would have done the world a favour.'

'And the father, Charlie Baxter? How exactly did he fit into all this?'

'That man has drifter in his blood. Not good with money either.'

'It must have been hard for Heather's mother, if he wasn't around too much.'

'I guess so.'

'She came from money, didn't she?'

'That's right. Grey and Lorrie Lawson idolised Elizabeth until she got mixed up with Charlie.'

'When they eloped?'

'Yep, and neither Grey nor Lorrie wanted any more to do with her then.'

'A bit harsh, don't you think?'

'As I said, folks around here aren't too good at forgiving. It was Charlie or them. There was no middle ground.'

'What was she like, Elizabeth, as a young bride?'

'She was full of fancy ideas. She probably thought Charlie was her hero, but he wasn't going to be anyone's hero. He was always running away from something, or someone.'

'What about after the killing?'

'He kept his distance then too.'

'Really?'

'Every now and then he'd come back to Lorrie's place to see Heather, but he most likely wasn't wanted there either.'

'Her grandma raised her?'

'She did. Grey was dead by then, which gave Lorrie's Bible-thumping even more zeal.'

'I hear yah,' she says, 'and then Lorrie died a few months back, didn't she? We covered it in the newspaper.'

'You did.'

'From what I recall, Heather didn't hang around after the funeral.'

'She was here for a time, long enough to look respectable, but she didn't want to be. Everyone could see that.'

'I heard the reading of the will has been delayed.'

'It got held up because Lorrie wrote on it. Nothing important, just a few scrawled words insisting she wouldn't be cremated. It will resolve itself soon enough, and when it does, most of the money will probably go to Samuel.'

'Her uncle still lives at the big house, doesn't he?'

'Sometimes, but he likes to roam too.'

'Like Charlie?'

'The way I see it, Marcia, certain people are good at spreading themselves around, but not so good at the day-to-day living.'

'What about the sister, Mia? The baby who died.'

'The child had one of those things on her face, you know, a birthmark, like Abby Jones.' He looks away as if repulsed.

'What kind of birthmark?'

'A port-wine stain. I think that's what they call it.'

Interesting, she thinks. 'Why don't you tell me a little more about Elizabeth?'

'Not much more to tell. Grey kicked her out of the house when she married Charlie. The girl was only seventeen at the time and, as I said, no doubt full of romantic nonsense. Real life turned out to be a whole lot different, though, what with no money, and Charlie not being around too much.'

'I heard rumours of an affair,' she says.

'The one with Lucas García?'

'That's right. He was accused of the murder, wasn't he, but got off?'

'Yep. He was pulled in shortly after Elizabeth was buried. Some said Sheriff Hodgson, my predecessor, had a personal vendetta against him, mainly because he wasn't from these parts, but either way, the sheriff didn't like him one bit.'

'Outside of bias, what did the sheriff have?'

'The description the girl gave. Hodgson helped her to put the sketch together of the guy's build. She had the colour of his eyes too. Green, they were. Folk think Hodgson coaxed the information out of her, but the overall description bore a strong resemblance to García, and it was the oldest reason for murder in the book.'

'Rejected love,' she pipes. 'The affair was over by then, wasn't it?'

'That's right,' he says. 'As old as Adam and Eve.' He lights another cigarette.

'Was there anything else?'

'His fingerprints were all over the house.'

'Pretty damning,' she agrees, already knowing about Lucas and the fingerprints, like everyone else in town.

'I guess it might have been, if they'd got a match on the sperm test too.'

She hadn't known about that. She could probably have gotten it from the public record, but it's always good to get information first-hand.

'It didn't match?' she asks, encouraging him.

'No, but Hodgson argued there might have been more than one man in the house. The only witness was Heather, and she was hiding in a blanket box upstairs.'

'Where's Hodgson now?'

'Retired. He reached the magic number, thirty-two years' service at the age of fifty-five, and went out on a full pension.'

'He doesn't still live in Corham, does he?'

'Got himself a nice place further up the coast, near Salem. I can get that address for you, if you want.'

'Sheriff, what would I do without you?'

'You know me, Marcia, always willing to oblige.'

'Can I ask you something else?'

'Sure.'

'I hear Heather went into her shell a bit after the mother died, became withdrawn.'

'She was sickly for a time. Refused to eat and everything.'

'But she recovered?'

'She sure did. Picked up her life, became top of her class, all the way through high school, and then later.'

'When she went to Harvard?'

'Correct.'

'Paid for by Lorrie?'

'Correct. Heather got to do all the things her mother didn't get a chance to.'

'Big responsibility on someone's shoulders?'

'Maybe, but she's the one still alive.' He smirks.

'And the Baxter place? It was torn apart at the time of the killing, as if the killer was looking for something.'

'That's right.'

'Odd that the place was ransacked.'

'I guess.'

'Does anyone have any ideas as to why?'

'No – or none that ever made sense to anyone, except the killer.'

She waits for him to take another pull of the cigarette before asking, 'What can you tell me about Lucas?'

'Did you call him last night?'

'I did, but he hung up on me.'

'What do you want to know?'

'He was called the Medicine Man, yeah?'

'More like Witch Doctor, if you ask me.'

'Why?'

'Because the guy is strange and probably dangerous with it.'

'I heard he made up potions.'

'That's right.'

'Anything else?'

'Have you heard about voodoo, Marcia?'

'Yeah, a bit.'

'Best you keep it that way. You don't want to be meddling with that kind of thing.'

'Why do you think he came back to town?'

'Most likely to make trouble.'

'And the voodoo?' she says, trying to get him back on track.

'What about it?'

'How is it connected to Lucas?'

'Marcia, don't go poking your nose into things you don't understand.'

'I'm not easily scared.'

He looks at her long and hard, as if considering whether or not he should tell her any more. 'All right, then,' he says, 'if you're sure.'

She waits.

'He made those doll things. You know, like little people.'

'Voodoo dolls?'

'Exactly. As I said, Marcia, that man is strange, and deadly dangerous with it.'

# 9
# HEATHER

After another long day, I head towards West Roxbury, or Westie, as it's known, and home. Situated barely south-west of Boston, I have always liked its proximity to the city. Three years earlier, I opted for a slick two-floor unit off Baker Street, one with a sunny aspect, hardwood floors, modern interiors, and neighbours who for the most part are transient, and keep themselves to themselves. Some tenants are long-term, like Joe, the gay Tom Hanks lookalike, who has a keen interest in bees, Mr and Mrs Patel, the elderly Asian couple, or Mira, the yoga trainer. I only know these scant details because of Abel, who helped me carry in boxes on the first day and likes to hear himself talk. A successful marketing executive, he goes through women faster than takeout, and his lack of depth appeals to me, in the same way as living here does, surrounded by people. Unlike in Corham, you can be as invisible as you want to be.

At the next block, a florist takes in a late delivery of bougainvillaea, purples and pinks, the scent so intense it spills out onto the street, but before I turn onto Baker Street for home, I spot a woman holding her child's hand tight, like a fist. My mind immediately skips to Jacob Rotterdam, and how much is at stake. The death of a baby brings out the best and the worst in people, and so far, our strategy of playing off one medical expert against another, or digging for more answers, doesn't feel like nearly enough. Parking the car, I spot Abel, dressed to impress, wearing a white shirt that probably cost him the earth, a pair of casual black slacks, and a light jacket flicked over his shoulder.

'Seeing anyone special?' I ask, not particularly interested, but glad of the light relief.

'They're all special, Heather, you know that,' he laughs, 'but none like you.'

'Save the chat-up line,' I fire back at him, 'for whoever the lucky woman is.'

He gives me a wink before sliding into his bright blue Porsche.

Turning the key in the front door, I'm already thinking about kicking off my shoes and drinking something cold straight from the fridge. Once the shoes are off, I flick on the television. An old episode of *Desperate Housewives* appears on the screen. I don't care. All I want is noise. I lower a large glass of ice-water from the cooler and head to the shower.

The water feels good on my skin, but soon my mind flicks back to Lucas García, and the part of my past I have run away from for far too long.

It's probably why, directly after the shower, I abandon all thoughts of chilling out, and make the last-minute decision to drive to Corham instead. Suddenly it's as if I need to be there, and within an hour I arrive at the familiar cluster of low buildings and the fuel station on the outskirts of town. On Main Street, I pass the shops, with their different-coloured fronts, and the old blue water pump that hasn't worked for years. It's surrounded, in the fading sunlight, by bright orange and yellow marigolds.

There are several roads leading out of town. I would have taken one to school, another to home, and later to Grandma Lorrie's house. Turning a corner, I see the single-storey police station on my left, next to the fire depot. Out front, there are a couple of patrol cars and two shiny fire engines parked underneath the low roof, all ready to take flight. A group of young girls gather together. It is late, but still warm, and their thin summer clothes flap in the evening breeze. They look happy, and immediately I have a sense of not belonging, not to this town, or to my past. So, why am I here? But I already know the answer. Lucas García.

I visualise him with his Panama hat, his sallow skin and tight dark hair, wearing creased linen trousers and a shirt to match. The two top buttons of his shirt were often left open, revealing strands of hair on his darkened chest, his New Orleans accent setting him up as an outsider from the beginning.

And then I see him, walking back towards the town centre.

I slow the car. He has a tight white beard now. Unlike my father, who changes his appearance every time he reinvents himself, Lucas still wears his Panama hat, tilted forward at the front, keeping his face in shadow.

This is stupid, I tell myself, putting my foot down hard on the accelerator, and pulling further away. I aim for the next right turn. Around it, I will find the stone façade of the library standing proud, but as I'm about to take the bend, I catch a glimpse of Lucas in the side-mirror. He has turned in the opposite direction and is looking straight at me.

\*

By the time I reach home for the second time, my head is in overdrive, and I'm unable to get Lucas out of my mind. I pace the bedroom floor, agitated. I hear a car stop directly outside. I walk towards the window, but by the time I look out, all I can see is the red flicker of brake lights disappearing into the darkness, leaving the empty street with an eerie feel.

I place my warm palms against the window. The coolness of the windowpane fuses with my skin. Damp spots drip beneath. I draw a stick person on the glass with my index finger, a girl, me, and then a smaller version, Mia. Maybe it's the trial, but I keep thinking about her too, remembering the mobile hanging above her crib, and the quilt with the different-coloured elephants on it. It feels as if something is hidden in the memory, urging me to look deeper.

I know now I'm not going to be able to sleep. I switch on my laptop, searching the newspaper archives for that old article by Gerry Gillespie. Over the years, I've read it many times, but still I keep going back to it, and every time I do, the words feel new, and the old horror returns.

Seeing Lucas again has unsettled me. I think about the afternoon he took me to the Handcocks' house. Back then, he'd become something of a surrogate father to me, my own hardly around at all. At the time I trusted him, like you would a kind relative, and my mother trusted him too. Alice Handcock had been very sick, and he was bringing herbs to make a potion. I had begged my mother to let me go with him, thinking it was some kind of great adventure, but when I reached the Handcocks' house, it all felt very different, as if things were happening that I didn't understand, and, being a child, I became scared.

I push the thought away and walk back to the window. I see a fleeting movement outside. It happens so fast that I wonder if I'm mistaken, but then I see it again, the shadow moving in and out of focus. I know someone is out there, looking up at the apartment block.

A part of me doesn't want to go downstairs, but another pushes forward. When I open the front door, the street outside is empty. I walk along the pathway, looking up and down. Whoever it was seems to have gone, although I still have the sense that they could be close by. My breath under the streetlight looks like tiny puffs of smoke. I turn to walk back inside, tripping on the lobby step, and instantly my body breaks into a cold sweat. I feel something around my neck, like a thread from a spider's web, thin and clinging. My hand pulls away a strand of hair. I slam the door, acutely aware now of every noise or movement. My breathing is rapid, but I breathe even faster on entering the apartment, when I see my bedroom door is closed. I'm sure I left it open.

I turn the handle. I hear the creak of the door opening, and then I see it, resting in the centre of the bed, drawing me in like a magnet.

I listen hard again, as a fresh layer of sweat builds up on my palms. My heart skips every second beat. I think about how easy it would be for someone to kill me, to do the same to me as they did to my mother, the way a life can be over in seconds, without warning or care.

As I walk towards the bed, my eyes concentrate on the thing staring back at me, the top of it resting on my pillow. At first, the small doll feels fragile, but then I look at the face. There is something grotesque about it. I touch the strands of hair, the same shade as my mother's. I want to throw it away, to rid myself of it, but then I look at the fabric sewn with the different-coloured threads. It takes me just seconds to realise it came from a blouse my mother used to wear. Who would have her old clothes? Did Lorrie keep them?

I think about Lucas again. Could he have left it? I put a hand to my neck, remembering pulling away the strand of hair a few moments earlier. What if he's still here? What if he didn't leave?

I run through the apartment, the same way the intruder must have done on the day my mother was killed. I switch on the lights in every room, but they're all empty. I'm out of breath by the time I come back into the bedroom. I look at the doll again and, no matter which way I turn it, I see the same thing, my mother lying on the kitchen floor, as my past crawls over me. Right now, the only thing I can be sure of is that whoever left the doll wants to send me some kind of message. It is their way of telling me they can get close.

I stare at the fabric, green polka-dots, visualising my mother wearing the blouse. The first time she wore it was at a carnival in town, and the reason I remember it so clearly is because of Daniel. He came with us after he was given a camera for his birthday. He took photographs of anything and anyone, including my mother. I remember thinking how beautiful she was, having the kind of good looks that attract men, but mixed with a certain aloofness. As I imagine her now, though, what I see most is her sadness, as if the bright polka-dots were nothing more than a camouflage, directing others not to look too deeply.

My cell phone bleeps on the bedside locker. The noise startles me all over again. When I pick it up, there's a message from Daniel. It feels weird, because I was just thinking about him.

*Heather,* it says, *I need to see you.*

Ever since Finlay told me that Daniel was working for him, I've avoided making contact, but the truth is, I've avoided him for some time, the same way I've avoided so much of my past.

I tell myself that if we have to meet before the trial it might as well be sooner rather than later.

I message back. *What about tomorrow morning? Saturday, 11 a.m.?*

Ten seconds later, he replies. *I'll see you at the diner*, as if we're kids again, arranging to grab a soda together.

I stare at the makeshift doll, before firing it into the trash basket. I walk towards the window again, as the two stick-people fade on the glass. I think about Mia's crib. I see myself staring down at the baby's quilt, while the mobile above the cot plays 'Rock-a-bye Baby'. All of a sudden, thinking about the baby's room, another thought strikes me, like a new slice of memory, warning me that there is someone or something in the room I need to protect.

# 10
# ELIZABETH

*Few people understand why I married Charlie, choosing a life that was a million miles from the one I had known. It seems silly now, how much like my father I thought Charlie was. How it was those perceived similarities and his differences that first drew me to him. I thought my father was carefree. The man who took us on vacation, who mapped out our adventures as if anything was possible, who turned ordinary things into leaps of imagination. I thought he was the man who saw his daughter as the apple of his eye, and every other cliché that comes to mind. But it all changed when I married Charlie.*

*To marry below your social status turned out to be the biggest sin of all. I met a different father then, the one I didn't know, the same man who argued in court, who did everything in his power never to lose, the one capable of being ruthless, uncaring, the man who could turn his back on his only daughter as if she had never existed. I used to think my mother had the bigger share of cruelty. I was wrong there, too.*

*At seventeen, I made the mistake of believing Charlie was the personification of my father, the fun-loving man I adored. Only Charlie's* sense of fun and freedom wasn't framed in a steady life, where laughter and games happened when the day job ended. It was something unguarded. And with that came another side of him, the side that put certain things in motion, things capable of changing everything, including me.

Now, I am no longer a naïve teenager, but because of Mia's death, there are times I know I am still completely lost within myself, and whatever I've been yearning for over these last few months, in a way it had to come to me.

Summer is fast approaching, and Lucas and I have gotten closer. At first, I thought the last thing I wanted was to begin an affair with him, especially after losing Mia, but I have made another discovery recently. The thing I have most wanted over the last few months, other than having my baby girl back, was to be loved again. The second time Lucas came to the beach, he stood so close to me I felt his breath on my face. I was attracted to him in a way I hadn't felt for anyone in a long time, which was why we began to meet regularly at the shoreline. He is different from other people, and I feel different from others, too.

One morning, I couldn't turn up at the beach and the following day I arrived earlier than normal. When I didn't see him, I thought he was paying me back for not turning up the day before. I went for a swim, wondering if I'd ever see him again, although getting into the water, I had the sense that someone was watching me.

In parts of the beach, the houses above have a clear view of below, but inside the smaller coves, you are completely hidden. When I came out of the water, he was waiting for me. He didn't say anything. Instead, he took my hand, and I followed him.

There is a disused cabin further up. I knew he was going to take me there. I was shivering, and at first when he touched me it was as if it was happening to someone else. Then his hands were on my body. He said my name, over and over, as if it was a chant. The air tightened between us. I felt separated from the world, off kilter, like a broken spinning top that kept spinning, long after it should stop.

# 11
# BLANCO

Blanco is still thinking about his meeting with Marcia Langan when he gets the call about a family dispute in a house off Popfinn Beach Avenue, and all thoughts of Marcia vanish. He heads straight there. The caller said they heard a female screaming, and shortly after that the sound of breaking glass. He is familiar with the address. He is familiar with Billy Townsend, too, and his vicious temper. Had it not been for Billy's family connections to the ex-sheriff, Hodgson, he might have ended up in prison long ago.

Parking down the street, Blanco walks with a quiet, confident stride to the front door. His right hand is close to his firearm should he need it. The house on the sea front is down a dirt track. A tattered Stars and Stripes flag curls in the breeze as Blanco waits and listens.

It isn't long before he hears the woman screaming for mercy, then Billy Townsend yelling obscenities at her, high on another rampage. When Blanco knocks on the door, the screaming and swearing stop, but no one answers. He knocks again, announcing himself loudly, before Billy finally opens the door.

'What's going on, Billy?' he asks.

'Yah're not needed here.'

Blanco smells something. 'Billy, are you on a substance?'

'Fuck off – I'm not taking no lectures from you.'

'Keeping it official, that's all.'

'Whatcha want?'

He stares past Billy to the two small children, a boy and a girl, hanging back towards the kitchen. 'Can I talk to your wife?'

'She's fine,' he spits, 'and she doesn't want to talk to you.'

'If she doesn't come to the door, I'll be coming in.' Blanco's hand moves closer to his firearm.

Billy looks down, then hollers, 'Get out here, Linda, and tell this cop you're okay.'

His wife seems to drag herself out to the hall. Her white cotton blouse covers a black bra. The blouse is torn at the front. She folds her arms tightly together, hiding what she can. Blanco takes in the bruising on her arms. 'Linda, what are those marks you have there?' he asks.

'They're nothing,' Billy answers for her. 'She fell down the stairs.'

'Billy, I'm warning you. Don't go hurting her any more. Are you listening to me? I don't want to be called out again.' He looks from Billy to his wife. 'Linda, do you want to press charges?'

Again, Billy answers for her. 'No, she doesn't.'

'You stay quiet now, Billy.'

When she finally speaks, her voice is barely above a whisper, her eyes look downwards: 'I don't want him arrested.'

'You sure about that?'

'I'm sure.'

'Billy,' Blanco says, 'you need to listen to me.' He puts his boot into the hall, ensuring Billy can't close the door.

'I'm listening.'

'You're mighty testing my patience. Do you know what I could do if I had the mind?'

'What?'

He takes out his Sig Sauer .40 calibre. 'I could step inside and have a nice look around, make sure Linda over there,' pointing with his weapon, 'goes and puts the children somewhere safe. She could make herself safe, too, as far away from any more accidents as she can get. Then the two of us could have a proper chat. One in which I might have to defend myself against a wife beater.' He presses the barrel of the Sig into Billy's cheek. 'Do you think anyone around here would care, Billy, if I killed you?'

He doesn't answer.

'Another call like this and I won't waste a prison cell on you. Do you hear me?'

'I hear you.'

Walking away, Blanco knows it's only a matter of time before he'll be making the next social call. But right now, after talking to Marcia, he has other, more pressing matters on his mind, including Lucas García, and the cold case of Elizabeth Baxter. Obviously, he hadn't told Marcia everything. She is a journalist, after all.

Back at the station, Blanco sits in his chair, pulling out a set of keys from his pocket. He flicks through them looking for the one to the bottom drawer of his desk. In it, he has an old photograph of Elizabeth Baxter, looking all young and innocent. It's the same photograph the police used for the media after her dead body was found. Her face stares at him as if caught in time. He isn't comfortable with Billy Townsend causing trouble. When Billy is under pressure, he gets messy and indiscreet. As he slams the desk drawer shut, the one thing Blanco is sure of is that he needs to be on his toes unless he wants a whole load of shit to start unravelling all around him.

# 12
# ELIZABETH

*When Mia died, I entered an abyss I didn't think I would be able to pull myself back from. Which is partly why I started writing in this journal shortly after she died, wanting to force my mind to make sense of all the things that happened, and have happened ever since. Losing a child goes against everything. A beginning shouldn't be an ending, but when it is, other silly things, worries, desires, things that may have consumed you for hours on end, fade into oblivion, taking second place.*

*Tonight I have been thinking about my father, too, and how, when I went to the funeral, I knew the eyes of the town were on me. Of course my mother blamed me, the same way she blamed the world for any wrong that ever happened to her. She didn't have to tell me again how I had thrown their love in their faces, marrying Charlie, ruining everything. How I was no longer the trophy daughter, the one they spoke about with pride, the girl filled with promise. I was soiled goods, like my brother, and another disappointment.*

*After the funeral, when we went back to the house I grew up in, it was strange thinking about my father no longer being there. I was so* obsessed with my own thoughts that I didn't notice Heather wandering off. When I couldn't find her, I became frantic, until I saw her playing in the grounds outside, a place she barely knew, a place where I had spent most of my life. She had climbed up into an oak tree, and I had nearly missed her as I passed by, but then she called out. Climbing down, she had a ten-dollar bill in her hand, gripped tight, like a prized possession. I asked her where she'd got it. When she said Uncle Samuel gave it to her, I froze. He'd told her to buy candy with it.

'Did he touch you?' I asked. 'Think hard,' I said, my words angry, knowing my own fears were fuelling a sudden desperate rage.

'No,' she said, over and over, shaking her head.

I grabbed the ten-dollar bill. I told her never to take money from him again. She started to cry. I knew I had frightened her. Then I said everything would be all right, that she wasn't to worry, that I would make everything okay, that I was there for her, that I would keep her safe.

Only I didn't do any of those things because a few days later Charlie came home from his disappearing act, and when he did, he didn't mention Mia, not once. It was as if she'd never existed, and then the darkness of my depression gripped tighter still, until whatever demon was locked inside me didn't care about anything else, no matter how hard I wanted it to.

The loss of Mia changed everything, and once again, I pushed everything else away, except for the one thing that screams at me now. When Heather climbed down from that tree and, more than anything, I wanted to believe her, I knew I couldn't trust my brother.

# 13
# HEATHER

I park the car beneath the shade of a sycamore tree, looking across at the diner where I'm due to meet Daniel. It feels strange being here again. Corham may be less than an hour outside Boston, but it might as well be another world.

I would prefer not to see Daniel, but failing to turn up isn't an option, especially for an old friend. I step out of the car and walk across to the diner.

The bell over the door chimes as I open it. Inside, I adjust my gaze from the sharp sunlight outside to the darker interior. A waitress pours coffee at the counter. She smiles, wearing a fake pink flower in her shoulder-length curled blonde hair. Her tight uniform is blue and white, matching the café's design. I hear her say, 'You're welcome,' to the men drinking coffee at the counter. I look for a table out of the way, but somewhere I can keep an eye on the door. I'm early.

The waitress carries a tray of cupcakes from the kitchen, arranging them on a two-tiered display stand, the kind that swirls around so you can make your choice. Immediately, I feel a quarter-century younger, ready to get my fingers sticky with the sweet icing. The waitress stands back to examine her creation. 'Why, isn't that perfect?' she says aloud. I have a knot in my stomach, thinking about Daniel. 'I'll be right over to you, honey,' she calls, her voice chirpy.

There is an elderly couple in a booth near the door. The man nods. The woman keeps staring. I recognise them. I know they recognise me too. I pick up a menu. It hasn't changed much. I almost laugh. It's as if this town and I are somehow stuck in a kind of a time warp.

'How are you doing today?' asks the chirpy waitress, blocking my view of the door.

I look up and, now that we're closer, I recognise her as well. 'I'm doing fine, Lola.'

'Oh, my, is that you, Heathah?'

'One and the same.'

'Darling, you look amazing.'

'And you haven't changed a bit,' I lie.

'I wish,' she says dreamily, talking fast, 'but another thirty pounds can do that to a girl. I guess working in a place like this with all its temptations isn't ideal. The pancakes,' she laughs, 'are far too yummy.'

'In that case, Lola, I'll have a large black coffee and the tastiest blueberry pancakes you can find.'

'Coming right up. Oh, my,' she says, 'it's so good to see you again.'

Her sweetness is catching. Maybe this won't be so bad. It's not as if Daniel and I ever had an argument. It's more that I haven't been in touch and, knowing him, he'll want to talk about that too.

I'm digesting Lola's pancakes when the door chimes ring, and I see him. I push the plate aside.

He waves, walking towards me.

I stand up to give him a hug, intentionally keeping a slight, but discernible distance between us. 'Hi, Daniel,' I say. 'It's good to see you.'

'You too,' he says. We sit down. His right knee touches mine under the table, sending an old, but familiar spark of attraction through me, as if the younger me is sitting opposite him.

'You already know I'm working for Finlay?' he asks, repositioning his knee.

'He took pleasure in telling me.'

I notice Daniel isn't wearing his glasses.

'Can I bring you a coffee, Dan?' Lola roars.

'Thanks, white, no sugar.' He turns to face me again. 'You look very well. Kind of different.'

'It's the long days and late nights,' I joke. 'They're giving me an elusive, desperate appeal.' My voice is too loud, nervous, as if I'm some idiot teenager.

'Maybe I just forgot how good you look,' he says.

'You too,' I reply, pointing to the lack of glasses.

'Operation a few years back.' His cheeks go a bright pink.

I smile, remembering how he was picked on in school, teased about his glasses and his slight squint. Even back then he saw more than most, observing the smallest details, things other people would miss, and how much I liked that about him. I notice a few random grey hairs mingled in his beard, too, and without thinking, I look down at his fingers – no wedding band.

'No,' he says, realising what I'm looking at. 'I'm still not married.'

'That makes two of us.'

'Maybe we were meant for one another,' he says, adjusting the cutlery.

'Stop it, Daniel,' I say, attempting a laugh. 'We tried romance once, remember? We make much better friends.'

'Is that why you haven't been in touch?'

I think about all the phone calls I didn't return, all the messages left unanswered. How deep down, I know the real reason I haven't been in touch is because of what he knows about me. 'I'm sorry, Daniel,' I say, and I mean it.

He moves the salt and pepper canisters together into the centre of the table. He straightens the napkins, too, beneath the knives and forks. That was the other thing they teased him about – his obsession with things always being neat and tidy, nothing ever out of place.

It feels odd sitting here with him, as if very little has changed when everything has. Once we were close childhood friends. Later, as teenagers, our relationship went deeper. He talked about getting married some day. I didn't, and then I left Corham for good. Initially, it was to study in Boston, but somehow I knew I would never come back to live here, and I think he knew that too.

Lola brings the coffee and tops up my cup. When she is far enough away, I say, 'You know Lucas is back in town?'

'Yes,' he says, stirring his coffee. 'Are you worried?'

'I don't know why he's come back, that's all. It's strange, don't you think, that he should return, after all this time?'

He stops stirring his coffee.

'A couple of things have happened lately too,' I say, my voice low.

'What things?'

'I thought someone was following me a while back, but I might have been wrong, and then, the other night …' My voice trails off.

'What?' Frown lines appear on his brow.

'Someone was in my apartment. I don't know who,' I add, my voice racing, 'but they left something.'

'What?' He looks at me perplexed.

'A doll,' I say. 'They left a voodoo doll.'

A certain clarity appears on his face. 'You think it was Lucas?'

'I don't know, but someone wanted to let me know they were there.'

'Who was the doll supposed to be?'

'My mother, I think.'

'You think, or you're sure?'

'It had something belonging to her on it.'

'What?'

'Fabric, from a blouse she used to wear.'

'Jesus, Heather, you've got to go to the police.'

'And tell them what? That I thought I was being followed?'

'About the doll, and someone breaking in.'

'No.'

'Why not?'

'Because,' I say, stalling, 'what if the doll came from someone who knows what happened to her? What if they wanted to send me some kind of message?'

'Even more reason to go to the police.'

'I don't want to, not yet, not until I have a better handle on things.'

He looks at me, baffled.

'I've been remembering stuff too.'

His facial expression becomes more pensive. Extra frown lines appear on his brow. 'What stuff?'

'Different things. It's been happening ever since Lorrie's funeral, as if a box is opening up in my mind. Sometimes I hear things, like birdsong, or the mobile playing above my sister's old crib. Other times it might be a door opening, a shadow in a corner or …' I pause, not sure how much I want to tell him.

He repositions his spoon at the side of his cup. 'You said the doll wore fabric that belonged to your mother?'

'Yes. You took a photograph of her wearing the same blouse at that carnival we went to years ago. It was shortly after your birthday. Do you remember?'

He nods, looking concerned, as if placing the last piece of

information in the section of his brain most likely classified as 'Further Thought'.

I don't feel any better having told him. In fact, now that I have, I'm not sure I've done the right thing.

'I assume,' I say, 'you wanted to meet me because of Finlay,' switching the conversation.

'Partly,' he says, holding my gaze.

'Look, Daniel, I know I went off the rails for a while a long time ago.'

'You don't have to explain yourself to me.'

'I know, but still, I'd prefer it if you didn't mention anything about it to Finlay.'

'We've all done things we regret.'

'I know that, too,' I say.

His hands cup mine. They feel familiar, intimate, the hands of friendship, of something we both once felt, something pure. 'Heather, I promised you a long time ago I would never tell anyone about that, and I never will. It will always be our secret.'

I believe him, but there's something about how he emphasises 'our secret' that curls around inside me, leaving me less sure.

# 14
# HEATHER

It's three weeks since I met Daniel, as the trial begins in earnest at Suffolk Superior Court, in Central Boston. We always knew we would be against the clock, having been brought in so late, but after weeks of effort, pulling together as many medical specialists as we can, including bone marrow experts, we are still no closer to finding a concrete reason for Jacob's death. Alex was right: in normal circumstances, the onus is on the prosecution to prove guilt beyond reasonable doubt, but in this case, where a child's death is concerned, the lack of a viable alternative puts us in a weak position, no matter how much doubt we cast on the medical evidence.

Jim and Alice Handcock sit directly behind me, as Finlay begins his opening statement. The absence of contact from Alex is worrying too, although it's not unusual for her to keep her silence until she has something worth sharing, but still.

Abby is sitting to my left. She looks aloof, distant. I can be that way too, so it's easy to recognise in others, but as I study members of the jury, looking in her direction, I know they're not warming to her.

Robin and Mark are beside me also, and, like me, they are now staring at Finlay, who is gliding around the courtroom with his usual ease. I take in the smallest movements of his hands, the familiar lightness of foot, how he slows down or increases speed in the same uninterrupted flow. He has been on his feet for over half an hour. He is in his stride. I've seen it all before, and I know that behind every movement of his body, every change of tone, and every word, he has a plan.

At times, his facial expression changes from gloomy to intense. On other occasions, he looks angry, the muscles on his forehead strained, especially when he mentions Jacob. All of it, in other circumstances, might gain him an Oscar, but it doesn't matter what I think. What matters is that many people in the room already believe him.

He is retracing the hours before Jacob's death, locking in the jury, six women and six men, as well as every single journalist at the back of the courtroom. It impossible not to dwell on the gravity of it all, as the air fills with the horrible sense of what might have been.

As an adult, I understand how, after Mia died, her short life became extra precious, more treasured, partly because my mother had to love her even more fiercely, especially in death. And right now, if things were different, instead of Jacob being the victim, if he was still alive, he would be at home with his parents, safe and happy, attempting his first steps, or some other milestone. Only I can't dwell on that now. My focus needs to be on Abby. I think about the first time I met her, how lost she looked, just as I was all those years before, and how, when all the facts were added up, Abby became the easy target for blame, in much the same way as I blamed Lucas, even though, many times, I've wondered if I was wrong.

Everyone is hanging on Finlay's every word. He moves his emphasis to the phone call Abby made to her friend Ashley on the day Jacob died. The conversation lasted for over an hour, he says, according to the subpoenaed phone records, yet neither of them can remember what they had discussed.

'Don't you think this is mighty strange,' he asks the jury, 'that an entire one-hour conversation could be forgotten?' He pauses, allowing them to consider the implication of his remark, before putting his own spin on the truth. 'Unless,' he continues, 'the content of that phone call, and the issues discussed, were something neither party wanted others to know about.'

I click the button on the top of my pen up and down, my feet ready to take flight, contemplating whether to object to his slight against my client. But with Finlay it's all about balance, and jumping in too soon isn't a wise move.

Glancing to my left, I see Robin and Mark giving me a questioning look, both, most likely, thinking the same as me, that there is still something about that conversation with her friend that Abby doesn't want us to know. So far, no matter how much we've pushed her, she's remained evasive. Perhaps she thinks she's protecting Ashley in some way. Perhaps whatever they spoke about has nothing to do with Jacob, but the not knowing is harming us, so one way or another, I plan on getting it out of her. On autopilot, I do a quick double-check on Abby. She's wearing the navy suit we decided upon, with a skirt that covers her knees. She looks like she's going for a job interview instead of defending her life. The blouse, also carefully chosen, has a hint of pink, buttoned up to the neck. She will wear the same, or similar, throughout the trial. Appearances shouldn't matter, but they do. I look at the jury again. Even at this early stage, their body language can give you clues. One jury member, in the front row, a well-dressed woman in her early sixties with short grey hair, cranes her neck. The woman to her side, attractive and half her age, raises her tinted eyebrows, while the man behind her coughs, as if it may help his obvious discomfort.

Many are from Boston. Some are from further afield in Massachusetts. They range in age from late twenties to early sixties, all white. The woman with the grey hair is the oldest. The jury chairman, a man in his fifties, has a pointed nose and a poker face that, in Finlay's opening statement, is giving little away. He doesn't look like a man who is easily swayed, but juries can surprise you, and their decisions are always a gamble.

Finlay had made the jury selection an arduous affair, drawing up a pre-selection questionnaire of more than three hundred items. His team objected to anyone similar in age to Abby or who had a hint of liberalism about them. Our focus was primarily made up of avoiding parents with young children or babies, even though you don't have to have either to understand the magnitude involved. After five days of decision-making, both sides accepted the jury.

Below the defence table, I reach over and pat Abby's hand. It is ice-cold. Finlay has his back to us. He pauses and, for a moment, the only sound I hear is the low drone of the air-conditioner before he picks up where he left off.

If I didn't know better, his hand gestures would amuse me: waving his long arms, energised, walking in a semi-circle with his hands positioned tightly on his hips, illustrating his intensity. Everyone in the room is watching him. The cameras at the back are focused on him too. Regularly, he makes eye contact with the public at large, while the journalists, to a man and woman, sit upright in their seats, ever eager, alert.

I glance at Abby again. She is also staring at Finlay, as if she, too, is being taken in by his storytelling appeal, as if his words are new to her. Her detachment worries me.

'Six hours after being admitted to hospital,' Finlay continues, 'Jacob fell into a coma.' He pauses. 'Sadly, because of the various injuries and subdural haematoma, he died later that day.' He catches my glance before turning solemnly to the jury. 'The ophthalmologist observed retinal haemorrhaging, and later confirmed his findings were characteristic of what is commonly known as Shaken Baby Syndrome. We will be referring to this in greater detail over the course of the trial but, for now, the truth we firmly believe is this: Jacob's death was not an accident, but rather one of sustained abuse.'

He opens his jacket, placing his hands on his hips once more. 'We have a huge responsibility, folks, especially you, the members of the jury.'

I watch as some of them make notes on their writing pads. He waits until they have finished, allowing them time to recapture his gaze before continuing, 'We will prove to each one of you that Abby Jones is guilty, that she is capable of cold-blooded murder, and that while Jacob Rotterdam was in her care, the baby was shaken with such force, and for a sufficient period, to ensure maximum and ultimately lethal damage.' He thumps the rail in front of the jury. 'Abby Jones is an angry and resentful young woman, and this anger and resentment manifested itself in her actions towards a wholly innocent child.'

I leap to my feet. 'Objection, Your Honour. The prosecution is introducing derogatory opinion as fact.'

'Sustained.' Wilburn Kendell looks across at Finlay. 'Mr Clarke, play by the rules.'

'I'll rephrase.'

He gives me a glance, aware this is his turn to impress the jury. My turn will soon follow and, hopefully, it will show Finlay's words up for the fabrication and exaggeration they are.

'We believe,' he continues, 'Abby Jones was aware she was harming the baby, and that the trauma administered to him had serious and deadly consequences—' He stops mid-sentence, before striding over to the prosecution table and looking at his watch. He picks up a brown manila file, shaking it back and forth.

'We contend that the rage which roared in Abby's mind that day, as baby Jacob was shaken repeatedly, was immense.' He continues to shake the file, only placing it down on the table when his watch bleeps.

'Ladies and gentlemen, I have recorded one minute on my watch. Medical evidence in this case will confirm that Jacob Rotterdam was shaken for a minimum of ten minutes. That is how long it took to sustain the deadly injuries to this child.' He puts a hand to his brow. 'Look at the clock on the wall. Think about how long a period that is, and while you're considering that, there is something else, too.'

Every member of the jury looks from the wall clock to Finlay, synchronised perfectly.

'This trial, I hope, will give Jacob Rotterdam a voice, a child who lost his life because of a wicked, evil act.' He eyeballs each jury member. 'Medical evidence will establish that the irreversible injuries he sustained came from violent abuse, which we believe was done by Abby Jones in a frustrated, resentful rage, both on the day he died, and earlier. We know he had small fractures in his arm, historical ones. He also presented with the triad of symptoms medical evidence will prove are indicative of abuse but, apart from the injuries sustained, what is undeniable is this. Abby Jones's prolonged delay in alerting others to the baby's deteriorating condition – when, in her own words, he showed signs of being unwell, coughing and being out of sorts – prior to his afternoon nap, and her failure to notify his parents until it was too late, allowed precious hours to be lost.' He pauses again. 'In our opinion, this delay contributed to his death. Was she aware of the enormity of what was at stake? We will argue that she was. We will also argue that not only did Abby Jones grievously injure Jacob,' he walks closer to the jury, 'but her actions immediately afterwards made his death inevitable.'

He takes another two slow steps towards them. 'Jacob cannot speak to us today. He has been deprived of the opportunity of life, and we are charged with the responsibility of making sure the truth is heard. And, make no mistake, we intend for his voice, even in death, to be given justice, and for the horrendous pain inflicted on him, despite the harrowing facts surrounding this case, to be examined with absolute vigour.'

Although outwardly Finlay gives no sign of obvious pleasure, it is there all the same. He places his hands on his hips again, raising his voice for dramatic effect.

'During this trial, we will look at scores of medical data, facts, ladies and gentlemen of the jury, that cannot lie, unlike the accused in this case.'

'Objection, Your Honour,' I say, leaping out of the chair, and taking a few steps forward. 'Council is deliberately slandering my client—'

Wilburn Kendell raises his hand, stopping me in mid-sentence. 'I've already warned you, Mr Clarke. You're treading dangerously. The jury will ignore that last remark.'

As I return to my seat, my eyes are drawn to the back of the room. I'm suddenly aware of the man standing there, his green eyes holding my gaze. I swallow hard, remembering the doll I fired into the trash basket weeks before. Lucas is still staring at me as I look away, returning to my position at the defence table, knowing from the moment Alice Handcock told me he had come back to Corham that he would seek me out, and now he has.

Kendell's warning against Finlay is soon forgotten. I take a deep breath, sitting up straight, as if the physical movement will realign my thoughts.

I hear Finlay's voice. 'During this trial, ladies and gentlemen, we will painstakingly take you second by second through what happened to Jacob in the closing hours of his life. Until finally,' he says, facing the jury, 'you will be in no doubt that Abby Jones viciously took the life of this innocent and defenceless baby, the only child of his loving parents, Vivienne and Morgan Rotterdam.'

The eyes of the jury turn to the Rotterdams. Both are the essence of composure, except for a tear escaping down the side of Vivienne Rotterdam's face. She brushes it aside, but not before every member of the jury sees it, imagining what it must be like to lose your only child, as I do too.

# 15
# HEATHER

Kendell dismisses the jury shortly after Finlay's opening statement. It's going to be a long trial, and he knows from experience how heightened the first day can be. If nothing else, the jury will be fresh in the morning for my opening statement, but before Abby is led away, I pull her to the side.

'I need you to think long and hard about that conversation you had with Ashley.'

Her blank stare doesn't help my mood.

'It's not important,' she retorts, far too quickly.

'Think on it overnight, and we can talk again early in the morning.'

Before the courtroom is fully emptied, with Robin and Mark to my side, I scan the room for Lucas, but he has already gone. This is probably his way of letting me know he can watch and follow me any time he wants. The same way I once watched and followed him, all those years after my mother's death, when, in my early twenties, I was still unable to come to terms with him walking free.

I used to be besotted by that man of magic. I used to look up to him as a replacement father, someone capable of kindness, of being there when my real father wasn't. I would watch him for hours, studying his every move, including the way he kept adjusting that hat of his, like it was a part of him. Sometimes he would let me run my fingers along the rim, as he talked about the intricate weave and how its creator had spent weeks preparing every strand, separating them into pairs, and how, over time, the hat had grown and grown. During that summer, when he and my mother were together, I used to pretend life was made up of the three of us, and that perhaps my father would never return.

The day Lucas took me to the Handcocks' house, as the maple leaves changed from yellow to orange-red, he told me the hat was special because it held the weaver's soul, and I had wondered if I had a soul, too, and what that soul was capable of.

I turn as Robin touches my arm. 'Do you think Abby is going to come clean about her conversation with Ashley?'

'She's going to have to,' I say, 'whether she likes it or not.'

'And if it's damning?' asks Mark.

'We meet it full on. There are already far too many unknowns in this case.'

After I say my goodbyes to Robin and Mark, I dial Alex. If she's found out anything on the Handcocks, I can't afford to wait any longer. Abby's belated relationship with them is still bothering me. Why take the girl in, only to ship her off to Boston and the Rotterdams so fast?

When Alex answers, I don't waste time with pleasantries. 'It's been a while, Alex,' I say. 'What have you got?'

If she's offended by me jumping straight in, she doesn't mention it. 'The Handcocks are into a lot of shady stuff, but I'm still digging.'

'Tell me what you have.'

'Rumours of financial irregularities, back-handers, that kind of thing. There's even talk of them hiring heavies to lean on people who don't play ball. And it seems Jim Handcock is prepared to grease palms to get what he wants, too, and stronger tactics, if he doesn't.'

'I guess none of that surprises me.'

'So far, nothing substantial has stuck, which means he's also good at protecting himself.'

'And Alice?'

'Chances are she knows things. You can't live with someone and not know something. I'm exploring another avenue too, but it might be nothing.'

'Tell me anyhow.'

'When I have something solid, you'll be the first to know.'

'Is it connected to the Handcocks, to Abby?'

'I'm not sure yet, but I'll be making a visit to your hometown very soon.'

'Corham?'

'One and the same.'

Before I have a chance to ask her any more, she kills the call. Maybe it's Alex mentioning Corham, or perhaps it was seeing Lucas again, but driving out of the city, instead of heading home, I make a detour to the place where it all began.

In less than an hour, I'm on the coast road, seeing the ocean with its small whitecaps hitting against the rocks. The tide is coming in. Seagulls swank and swoon above me. Within minutes, I'm on the narrow road to our old house. I think about all the years I've put between myself and this place, and how, ever since I went to the Handcocks' house to discuss Abby's case, I knew I would end up back here, in a place I have avoided for far too long, the place where my mother was killed.

As I get closer to the house, I see the extent of how much Mother Nature has taken over, but still, even within the overgrowth, and the sense of abandonment, it feels right to be here.

I park the car out front, then walk towards the old fir tree, remembering how my height was marked on it by my mother each birthday. The tiny slits stop at age ten, almost as if, even now, out there somewhere that young girl might still exist, ready to pick up another year of life. I see the torn rope of a child's swing, one of the few things my father ever built, and then, like all the previous times, a new memory comes back; it is both unexpected and without warning. I'm not sure what age I am, but I'm on the swing, and the sun is coming in and out of focus. As I go higher and higher, I hear my voice shrieking with excitement, imagining I could fly. In that moment, I feel anything is possible. Then, just as suddenly as the flash of memory arrived, it's over. I have an immediate sense of loss, before I realise what it is: the loss of the life that little girl once had.

Walking towards the front porch, I look down at my heels and kick them off, thinking about years before when I used to slip into a pair of my mother's shoes, the ones she wore if she and my father went somewhere special. I think about her precious mementoes, how she kept them in that red box, including the miniature elephant. Maybe it's thinking about the box, but now I'm remembering something else. How, after Mia died, my mother started writing in that journal of hers. She used to keep it in the red box with her mementoes. She told me she was given it for her sixteenth birthday and had never used it before, but now, when she got sad, especially after we lost Mia, it was her way of making sense of things. That was when she also told me it was okay to be fragile, but that I needed to be strong too – *Be fragile, be strong.*

Where is the journal now? Where are her mementoes? Are they destroyed? After the killing, Grandma Lorrie got rid of most things, as if wiping away our old life. But what if she'd kept the box, as a reminder of the daughter taken from her, the one, as parents, both she and my grandfather abandoned?

Out of nowhere, I hear the click-click of my mother's heels across the floor. It feels good, sensing her so close. Then I see her wearing a simple black dress, but something isn't right. She looks fearful, as if in need of protection. Who is she afraid of? My father? Someone else?

I step onto the porch, but I stop at the front door. Something is holding me back from going inside. Before her killing, the house was often filled with raised voices, angry outbursts, the sounds of a disappointed marriage. I see that red box again, and the pages of her journal, perhaps a reminder of a different life, the one she had before marrying my father. Was her life full of regret, thinking about her failed marriage, two people so mismatched they made each other miserable, and later still, her sadness compounded when she lost Mia?

Suddenly I don't want to go inside. I can't. Instead, I head back towards the trees, deciding to lie down on the pine needles, so that for the briefest of moments, I can allow myself to forget about everything, my past, the trial, even Lucas. The moisture from the ground tingles my feet, and soon, flat on my back, I'm staring up at the branches, which now look like stuck-out arms, some so thin they remind me of how my arms and legs were long ago, when I stopped eating for a while. How, in my teens, Grandma Lorrie sent me to the rehabilitation centre, as she called it. Severe anorexia. Delayed post-traumatic stress disorder. Memory loss. I had all three, yet somehow they pieced me back together. When I returned to this town, no one seemed any the wiser, except me, Grandma Lorrie and Daniel. I left this place one way and came back another, or so I thought, until much later when I found other, less obvious, ways of hiding my pain, such as not allowing others to get close.

I retrace my steps back to the house, and this time, on the porch, I grab the handle of the front door, turning it hard. It's locked. I search for the key in an old herb plot, overgrown with weeds. It's still there, like my old life, lying in wait. I enter the musty, abandoned house with fresh resolve. There are large damp patches on the walls. I look around, and it's almost as if someone else is walking into the kitchen to stand in the very spot where my mother was killed. I think about Gerry Gillespie's newspaper article, reliving it all over again. The refrigerator is gone from the kitchen, but I want to swing open the imaginary door, to be my mother, and to know what thoughts were inside her head, especially the day she died. That day, when she opened the door to get milk, did she know she would soon be killed?

The upstairs bedrooms are empty too. Whatever little furniture we had was sold off in a garage sale, as if Lorrie wanted to sweep away the past as something of no consequence. Perhaps she did the same with my mother's mementoes and journal too. The house, though, was kept, never sold, left to rot. I used to wonder why my father didn't get rid of it. Maybe even he couldn't bear to profit from her death.

Standing in the doorframe of my old bedroom, I imagine my bed there, instead of the mouldy floorboards. I see my younger self curled up reading a book, reaching out as far as the bedside locker to switch on and off the lamp with the sea nymph at the bottom, remembering how her pink body, covered with glitter, sparkled under the light. I turn towards the baby's room. Again, I stop in the doorway. This time, I know I can't go inside.

My heart thumps a little faster, and I'm about to walk away when I hear movements outside. I tell myself it's probably a fox on the prowl, or the trees creaking, but still I can't shift the sense of danger. Walking downstairs, I glance towards the kitchen, and as I do, I see my younger self pulling down my mother's skirt to cover her bruised legs. It's only then I see something I haven't remembered before. The memory is so clear, it's as if it's happening here and now. I watch my younger self walk back upstairs, a ten-year-old girl, who desperately needs to get something from the baby's bedroom. What?

I'm so consumed with my thoughts, I don't realise he's in the house until he's standing right beside me.

'Why did you come back?' I ask, staring ahead, instead of turning to face him.

'Eventually, Heather, we all have to face our demons.'

'You're not wanted here, Lucas, not by me or this town.'

'I've never been wanted here. It didn't stop me before, so why should it stop me now?'

'You shouldn't have come back.' I turn. 'You have no right.'

'Don't I?'

I steady my breathing.

'Heather, do you still think I killed her?'

'Does it matter what I think?'

'Yes, it does.' He is staring at me, eyes locked. 'I understand,' he says. 'Sometimes it's easier to hold on to old beliefs, even if they're not true.'

'Don't lecture me.' I take a step back, away from him.

'You look like her,' he says, so quietly I nearly miss it.

'What do you want, Lucas?'

'It's not about what I want. It's about what I need to do for your mother.'

'Don't talk about her,' I shoot at him. 'She was *my* mother.' I visualise her box of mementoes, and how he, too, gave her things, which she kept from my father.

'You know I loved her?'

'You're not the only man who gave her things,' I say, wanting to hurt him.

His jaw sets, rigid, as if a thought is forming in his mind, his forehead creasing, as he concentrates hard.

'I remember the book of poems you gave her,' I say. I see the inscription in his handwriting on the inside page: *Keep hoping, keep dreaming, and be free.* 'You shouldn't be here,' I repeat. 'I don't want you here.'

'I think about your mother all the time, you know.' His words are so earnest, it would be easy to believe him.

'You weren't the only man in her life,' I say, wanting to hurt him some more.

'I know.'

A silence settles between us.

Neither of us mentions Jim Handcock but, deep down, we both know who we're talking about.

'Your mother guarded her secrets well, Heather,' he finally says. 'I guess we all did.'

'Is that why you killed her? Because she might have loved someone else?'

'You were so young. Too young to understand. I never harmed your mother. I loved her.'

'It seems to me, Lucas,' a fresh sharpness in my voice, 'my mother's life was filled with men who supposedly loved her, but brought her far too much pain.'

'I know,' he says, his head bowed.

I remember the doll left at my place, and a new rage takes hold. 'Were you in my apartment, Lucas?'

'No.' He pulls back, surprised.

'Did you leave that doll on my bed? Were you trying to scare me? Is that it?'

'What doll?'

'Stop lying.'

'I'm not.'

'I won't let you frighten me. Leave me alone and leave this town. Being here isn't helping anyone.'

'I can't.'

'She isn't coming back, Lucas. She is gone.'

'I know that too.'

'Then why stay?'

'I have my reasons and, besides, I need to talk to your father. He'll be in Corham tomorrow to sign some legal papers, something to do with Lorrie's estate.'

My father didn't tell me he was going to be in Corham, but then again, why would he? I don't share my life with him. Why should he share his with me?

'There are things you didn't understand back then, Heather, truths you were too young to know.'

I don't want to listen to him any more. I don't want to hear about *his* truths.

'You are still grieving,' he says. 'I can see that now.'

I can't think straight. I need to get away from him, from this house. I don't even bother searching for my shoes. Instead, in my bare feet, I head straight for the car, but then I stop, seeing his black sedan parked out front. So, it was him. He followed me that first day after I left the Handcocks' house. Perhaps he followed me other times as well. Is he lying about the doll too?

I put the car swiftly into reverse. 'She is gone,' I scream, into the empty car, 'and she is never coming back.' I grab the steering wheel tight. No one understands, unless they've been through it, how it feels to lose a parent, a mother. How the compass that once guided you is suddenly gone, and sometimes the only means of finding your way back is to keep on pushing forward.

For so long I believed Lucas killed her, and even when I had my doubts, I shut them out. I never looked beyond him, not properly. I didn't want to. But there were other people in my mother's life, people capable of killing her, including my father, especially when he got angry, and Jim Handcock too. I may have been a child when she died, but still, like everyone else in Corham, I understood that Jim Handcock ruled everything. I also knew that being part of her life meant he most likely wanted to possess her, just as he managed to get everything he ever wanted, just as he owns this town, which is both small and powerful in equal measure.

After Mia died, when Lucas and my mother became close, Jim must have hated them, but did that make him a killer?

Lucas is right about one thing. I am still grieving. I will probably grieve her until the day I die, and no matter what people have said about my mother, or how, at times, I know she couldn't always be the mother to me she wanted to be, I also knew she loved me. After she died, I felt lost, like a deer caught in headlights, ready to look in whichever direction Sheriff Hodgson pointed, and that direction led me to Lucas García.

# 16
# VIVIENNE

Vivienne Rotterdam stands on the back terrace of their home in Garden Street, West Cambridge. The first day of the trial is over, but it has already taken its toll. She watches her husband drink a large glass of red wine in the living room. He often drinks too much now, saying the emotional pressure is weighing him down, one of many things she has learned to hate about him.

The sleeping tablets prescribed for her are neatly stacked in the medicine cabinet upstairs. Unlike Morgan, she isn't looking for a place to hide, not a drug-induced sleep or alcohol-fuelled oblivion.

She presses the small of her back against the trunk of a cypress tree in the centre of the three-tiered decking. This place used to bring her joy, but now the designer exterior, with its boxed plants and different levels, positioned beneath the large pink magnolia, seems different. The tiers are in shadow, and the elongated picnic table and chairs, where guests once sat with a good view of the Boston horizon, are empty. All of it feels like a lifetime ago. She doesn't want to talk to Morgan, but she doesn't want to leave him in peace either. Moving closer to the living room, she calls through the French windows, 'You plan on drinking the whole bottle?'

'What's it to you if I do?'

His words hurt but, then, everything hurts in this new reality, the one she cannot escape from – ever.

It doesn't take Morgan long to wander outside. She can hear the television blaring. It's set to CNN business news.

'Glad to see you're still keeping an eye on your investments,' she says sarcastically.

He still looks handsome, she thinks, imagining once more how easy it must have been for him to charm Abby.

'Do you object to me watching television now?'

'No,' she says. 'I just don't know how you can.'

'The same way you keep going to that gallery of yours, pretending you're needed.'

She hasn't gone for weeks, but she isn't going to tell him that.

'What I need,' Morgan says, raising his glass, finishing the wine, 'is to keep things on track because one of us has to.'

'Is that what you're doing?' Her question is mocking. She lets out a tiny laugh.

The small veins visible beneath his eyes throb. 'The house is so quiet without him, isn't it?' he says, staring at her.

She doesn't answer.

'Fine,' he adds, his tone business-like, the sort he uses with his clients, who want him to invest their money and make them a whole lot richer.

They are emotionally separate, she thinks. Yes, that is the correct term. In the past, they had secrets, especially Morgan, but now even the secrets are of little consequence.

'Finlay rang earlier,' he says.

'What does he want?'

'To ask us again why we had Abby working for us as a nanny.'

'We've already answered that question.'

'He obviously thinks there's more to it.'

'What did you say?'

'Nothing.'

'All he ever wants is answers.'

'He's on our side, Vivienne, and your attitude isn't helping.'

'Sorry, I forgot. Am I supposed to be obliging?'

'Sarcasm doesn't help either.' He walks back up the steps, keen, she decides, to refill his glass. She shouts after him, 'Why, Morgan?'

He turns. 'Why what?'

'Why did we have her here? As far as I recall, you were the one who pushed the point home.'

'You know why.'

'No, I don't. I know some stupid story you fed me, about how she'd be great with Jacob. Isn't that what you said? Wasn't that part of the lies?'

'Yes, I said that. Happy now?'

'I shouldn't have listened to you. I hate myself for that.' She stares at him, almost spitting out her words. 'You've lived a messy, complicated life, Morgan. Now, your mess has taken away our son.'

'You can't blame me.'

'You couldn't keep your dick in check, could you?'

'I've already told you. Nothing happened between us.'

'Don't lie to me. It only makes you more pathetic. Do you remember what you said to me, way back at the beginning?'

'About what?'

'About lovely innocent Abby. How you swallowed Jim Handcock's words that his niece was reserved, which some found odd, but she was a girl with a good heart, especially with children. You both made her sound like a fucking angel.'

'Are you feeling better now?'

'Nothing makes me better – not you, not Finlay, not alcohol or sleeping pills, and especially not myself.'

'Vivienne?'

'What?'

'I'm hurting too.'

His self-pity revolts her. He reaches out to touch her arm, but she pulls away. 'We're only living this charade, Morgan, because Finlay wants us to. If I had my way, you wouldn't be here.'

He takes a step closer, his face angry now. 'Go fuck yourself.'

'Would you like to know what I really want, Morgan?'

'What?'

'I want never to have met Jim Handcock or that wife of his. I'd do anything not even to know their names.'

He turns to walk away again.

'That's right, Morgan. Pour yourself another drink. Pretend our child isn't dead, that right now he isn't lying in the ground alone, all the life taken out of him.'

'Jesus, Vivienne, stop it.'

'Why? So you can sanitise things, turn them into the truth according to Morgan, wrap them up, like you've always done, pretending shit doesn't happen? At least, not to the wonderful man you think you are. To hell with you. You can't do that. Not this time. Your shit is hanging out to dry, and our son, our beautiful baby, is gone. And nothing anyone can say or do will change that.'

She closes her eyes, feeling the trunk of the tree at her back, steadying her.

'What will I tell Finlay?'

'Tell him your cock went into overdrive.'

'Be sensible.'

'I'm the essence of sensible. I'm not the one getting drunk.'

'I'm not drunk.'

'Not yet, but I have the utmost confidence in you. You've always been a high achiever. Isn't that what everyone says about you? You're a safe pair of hands in the risky world of finance. How safe will they feel now, putting their money with an alcoholic who fucked the hired help while his son was slowly dying?'

'I'm not listening to this shit.'

'Good for you,' she mocks. 'I stopped listening long before you stopped talking.'

'Have it your own way, Vivienne. You usually do.'

When she's alone, she breathes in the last of the evening smells, wishing more than anything she could simply close her eyes and make the horror go away. How hard would it be to take those sleeping pills? There are months of pills she could swallow. End it, finally. Why not?

She already knows the answer. It's the same reason she can't talk to Morgan, not properly, not any more. It feels almost biblical, an eye for an eye, a tooth for a tooth. And because of that she's going to keep on suffering, day by day, hour by hour, second by second, millisecond by damn millisecond. She can't undo the deeds of the past, but she can carry on feeling the pain. She doesn't deserve oblivion. What she deserves is hell on earth.

# 17
# ELIZABETH

*Strange things have been happening lately, things I don't fully understand. Jim carries so much hatred inside him too, his rage constantly bubbling over, becoming all-consuming, especially his anger towards Lucas, even though my affair with him is now over. Soon, I know, because of Jim, he will be leaving town. Lucas never felt accepted here, not in a place run by the Handcocks. Jim only looked for Lucas's help when Alice got really sick, out of a form of desperation, but being needy isn't one of his strong points either, which is another reason why he made things difficult for Lucas, slowly turning everyone in the town against him.*

*There are times I still feel like Jim's possession, although our affair ended shortly after Mia's death. It's as if his need to keep controlling me is getting stronger by the day instead of the opposite. He understands I'm married, in the same way I understand he has a wife, which is why Charlie will always be of less consequence than Lucas for his rage.*

*Lately, I think someone is watching the house too. Small things have gone missing. I am now keeping this journal with my mementoes in the red box. I try to keep it well out of sight. With Charlie away most of the* time, it's only me and Heather in the house. I worry about her, which is why I've started playing a game with her, a hiding game. I figure if we play it enough times, if something was to happen, if danger was to come to our door, she would know what to do. She would know how to protect herself.

Today I thought about the first time Lucas and I made love. Afterwards he told me I reminded him of a sea nymph, someone not of this earth. I thought about the sea nymph on Heather's bedside lamp, all pink and glittery. I started to laugh, but soon the laughter changed from something happy and ordinary to a crazy kind of laughter, and in that moment, I had wondered if I had finally gone mad.

After Mia's death, I had asked myself the same thing. Was I slowly losing my mind? Was her death a punishment for my adultery? It's partly why I began writing things down. Back then, I didn't understand post-natal depression, or how it can creep up on you unknowing, and how, when I lost Mia, all my thoughts became clouded, turning me into someone different, someone I hated.

All I knew was that when Lucas held me tight that day at the beach, and we made love, in that tiny microcosm of space, ever so briefly, as the waves hit the shore and the seagulls squawked, like an infant's unanswered cry, for a time I felt loved again.

# 18
# HEATHER

Before my pre-trial meeting with Abby this morning, in a small interview room close to the courtroom, I replay an audio recording of an earlier conversation between us. I hear myself ask her what kind of parents Morgan and Vivienne were.

'Edgy,' she replies.

'How?'

'They argued all the time, about the smallest things.'

I stop the recording, staring ahead of me, remembering how my parents used to argue too. I think of another afternoon when I crept downstairs, neither of them knowing I was listening in, and the memory is so vivid, it's as if I'm reliving it second by second. My father is screaming at my mother, accusing her of encouraging Lucas's attention. He hasn't been back home long, having spent months away working in Maine, wanting to put as much distance between him and his family as he could. He is also drunk. My mother stands at the kitchen sink, trying to ignore him. The window is open, and the curtain flaps in the breeze, billowing, like a pregnant woman. When the shouting gets too loud, I put my hands over my ears. I don't want to hear them. Instead I hear a hum, like an insect buzzing, relentless, but then it gets louder, and the words of the argument drag me in. I open my eyes in time to see him grab her, before shoving her against the wall. I think he's going to kill her, but somehow, she gets free, pushing him back, and he falls to the floor in a drunken stupor. I feel relieved, because he can no longer do her any harm.

I pull myself back to the here and now, as I hear someone pass the interview-room door. I press the audio recording again. I hear my voice asking, 'What did Vivienne and Morgan argue about?'

'Anything. Everything. How long Jacob slept for. If they should wake him. The toys he played with, even where he would eventually go to school. Jacob picked up a lot of infections too, with coughs and high temperatures. When he was sick, they would get even more stressed, especially Vivienne, constantly worrying about germs, afraid Jacob would get a bad infection before his immune system was fully developed. Sometimes it felt like the two of them were trying to get one up on the other, make out one of them was the better parent.'

'Was there a better parent?'

'Morgan idolised Jacob. Vivienne was harsher.' Abby's voice has an edge to it. 'Vivienne made the house rules.'

I pause the recording again. I already know from Jim and Alice that her relationship with Vivienne was strained.

I press the recording once more. I hear Abby's voice. 'If I was late back or she thought I was spending too long on the phone, she would have it out with me, turn stupid things into something big.' Then her tone changes, becoming kinder, as she says, 'He was nicer than she was.'

I shut off the recording, thinking about the shift in her voice, switching from the harsh edge when she was referring to Vivienne to something softer when it came to Morgan.

There is a knock on the door. Robin brings Abby in. I wait for her to sit down before I say, 'You haven't been honest with me.'

'What do you mean?' She looks startled. Good.

'Your conversation with Ashley, for a start.'

'I already told you, it's not important.'

'I'll be the judge of that.'

She looks away.

'Was it to do with Morgan? Did you talk to Ashley about him?' I wait, her silence telling me I've hit a nerve. 'Well, did you?' I push her.

'It's not what you're thinking.'

'Were you obsessed with him? Is that it?'

'I liked him, that's all. He was nice to me.'

I hear her voice from the recording: *He was nicer than she was.*

'Abby, did you have sex with Morgan Rotterdam?'

'What would it matter if I did? It's nothing to do with what happened to Jacob. Besides, it wouldn't have meant anything.'

'I think it means *something*.' My voice sounds incredulous.

'If you must know, we didn't do anything,' she blurts out. 'He flirted with me, that's all, and we messed around a bit, but it was nothing.'

'Did you discuss Morgan with Ashley?' I ask, a hard edge coming to my voice. 'Is that what the mystery conversation was about, the one you conveniently forgot?'

Robin gives me a look that warns me to take it easy, unless I want to risk Abby clamming up completely.

I soften my voice. 'Did you talk to Ashley about Morgan?'

'Yes.'

'Did Vivienne know about this thing between you and him, his flirting with you?'

'No, I don't think so.'

'You can tell me, you know. It would be protected under client-attorney privilege.'

'What does that mean?'

I study her, wondering what else she's capable of not telling me. If she's capable of lying about her conversation with Ashley, pretending not to remember it, and potentially covering up something between her and Morgan, what else is there?

'Robin,' I say, 'can you give me and Abby a couple of minutes.'

I wait until she leaves the room, then say, 'Client privilege means I cannot share any information you give me with the authorities, or anyone else …' I pause, knowing how loaded my next words will be '… even if it is in relation to a past crime.'

'I didn't kill Jacob.'

'And I want to keep believing you.'

'Believe what you like.' Her tone is suddenly hostile, knowing how much doubt has crept into my words.

She stares past me at the wall. 'If you don't believe me, Heather,' her voice so low, I almost miss it, 'then who will?'

'Look, Abby,' I say, wanting to reassure her, 'I'm still on your side.'

'But what if you're like everyone else?'

'What do you mean?'

'What if you're not really on my side? What if you let me down too?'

'I won't,' I say, earnest, 'not if you're telling me the truth about Jacob.'

'I didn't harm him.'

I don't reply straight away. Instead I stare at her, a girl who, like me, grew up without a mother, and who, I would wager, has spent a lifetime with people who have repeatedly let her down. I'm conscious of how difficult it must be for her to trust anyone, even me.

'Abby, if you're holding something back, now is the time to tell me.'

'There's nothing,' she insists, but the anger in her voice hasn't completely gone.

I hear a knock at the door. It's Robin. 'It's time, Heather,' she says. 'We're needed in court.'

I turn back to Abby. 'We'll talk about this again.'

'There's nothing, Heather, I swear.'

As I walk towards the courtroom, I know I need to get the next bit right. There can be no margin of error.

*

Like the previous day, during Finlay's opening statement, the courtroom is full to capacity. Only today all eyes are on me instead of him. The bailiff announces Judge Kendell, and then the jury is brought in.

Soon, filling the silence, I hear the words I have been rehearsing over and over.

'Ladies and gentlemen, we are charged in this trial with finding the truth.' I stand as close to the jury as I can, blocking their view of most of the room. 'The truth is something that can easily be broken down into something simple, so simple, in fact, that the simplicity may be lost in the sea of mixed messages the prosecution may want you to drown in.'

I wait for Finlay to object. He doesn't.

'Nor,' I say, my voice sombre, 'should the tragic loss of Jacob's life be further blighted by convicting an innocent person. Abby Jones may be older than Jacob, but she is still a young girl. More importantly, she has done nothing wrong. *Nothing*.'

I look at each of them, trying to read their faces.

'The only thing Abby Jones has done was find herself in the

wrong place at the wrong time. Put simply, she was there when Jacob Rotterdam became ill, when he first seemed a little poorly that morning, coughing and somewhat out of sorts. She was there when she settled him to sleep that day, and she was the only person there when, later, checking on him, he was unresponsive. She was the only person there when he became seriously ill. And this is where the truth should be simple, only it isn't, unless being in the wrong place at the wrong time is a crime.'

I pause, giving them time to take in the words. 'I don't believe it is a crime, and neither, I suspect, do you.' I take a couple of steps back. 'What if that person had been you, instead of Abby Jones?' Again, I allow them moments to take in my words.

'The state claims Abby Jones must have caused the injuries to Jacob Rotterdam, because the baby became critically ill while in her care, and that medical experts will testify to this. The latter ignores the fact that on the day Jacob wasn't the healthy baby the assistant district attorney purported in his probable-cause affidavit. The truth says something very different.

'For one thing, Jacob, as already mentioned, had small fractures to his arm, fractures that didn't happen on the day he died, fractures that, according to other medical experts, may have happened months before. Jacob wasn't the healthy baby the prosecution wants you to believe, and the big problem here is that they are hanging their case on a certain probability.'

Did I do the same thing when I convinced myself that Lucas was my mother's killer? Did I block out other options because, like Finlay, I was looking for a scapegoat, and in the absence of any alternative, I needed someone to blame?

I'm standing closer to the jury now.

'The prosecution also contend there wasn't a lucid interval between what they describe as internal injuries and when the baby displayed critical signs of failing.'

For a split second, I see myself at our old house, wondering what had happened during those missing hours, from the time I'd hidden in the blanket box to finding my mother on the kitchen floor.

'A lucid interval, ladies and gentlemen, is where you have an injury but you are lucid for a time. You are awake and functional. Externally, you look well and healthy, but some time afterwards, something changes and, in extreme cases, you die.'

A couple of the jurors write more notes.

'Basic medical evidence tells us that the prosecution's premise that a lucid interval didn't happen is false. As lay people, we have all seen numerous examples to contradict this. The player who gets an injury during a game, then appears lucid to the coach and the medical team, returning to the field of play only to become critically ill hours or days afterwards, and sometimes, as we know, this can be fatal.'

I pause again, allowing the information to sink in, word for word.

'The prosecution's forensic case is built on a perception that is simply incorrect, and they use this false premise even though, over a protracted period, many other people had access to Jacob. Yet the only person accused is Abby Jones. And again, I ask you, is being in the wrong place at the wrong time a crime?'

The oldest female juror looks at Abby. I hope she is seeing something other than a blank stare.

'We will argue that there are many other potential reasons for this tragic set of circumstances, including the possibility that Jacob suffered an undetected head injury some time before he became critically ill, which on that fatal day began to bleed, ultimately causing his death. Many of our witnesses are scientific experts, with decades of experience in the disciplines of neurosurgery, neurology, neuroradiology, emergency medicine, forensic pathology, paediatrics, child abuse and ophthalmology. They will explain in great detail many other possible causes for the tragic loss of Jacob's life, causes the prosecution is choosing to ignore.'

I catch Finlay's stare. I wonder what he is thinking. As usual, he is giving nothing away.

'Both of Jacob's parents are highly intelligent, mature, well-educated individuals. They will tell you they were unaware Jacob had any fractures. They will also tell you he showed no alarming signs of being seriously unwell, and not only that, but there were no outward marks on his body.' I pause again. Some of the jury are making more notes, others are watching me carefully. 'We will contend that of all the people who should have known something was wrong, they should. If they didn't, then how was Abby, an inexperienced young girl, capable of assessing the infant's wellbeing?

'The prosecution may have enjoyed their display of amateur theatrics yesterday, but that is all it was, theatrics.'

'Objection, Your Honour!' Finlay sounds incredulous.

'Sustained.'

I don't care about Finlay's objection because I already know what I'm going to say next.

'We will present medical evidence supporting our belief that, on the day Jacob died, he was a very ill child, so much so that even a slight jarring or trivial impact could have spontaneously caused a re-bleed of an older injury. And, sadly, in this case, it proved fatal.'

I walk back to the defence table. I drink some water from a glass already filled, hoping the emotional impact of my last statement will settle into their minds, remembering one of the first things I learned as a prosecutor. A court case isn't only about rational thought. Despite the many facts, it's an emotional thing, capable of being moulded.

'Unless all of us have been living under a rock for the last number of months,' I continue, 'we have been exposed to repeated incorrect accusations and scaremongering in the media, fuelled by the prosecution, about Abby Jones.'

'Your Honour, objection.' This time Finlay is standing. 'We cannot control the media. Neither would we want to.'

I glare at him. His arms are spread wide, and he looks as if he has been personally insulted. I detect a hidden smile.

'Sustained.' Judge Wilburn Kendell doesn't sound pleased. 'Lead counsel, please step forward.'

Both of us walk towards him.

'Ms Baxter, please refrain from putting the prosecution on trial, unless you want to take this conversation to my chambers.'

'No problem, Your Honour. I apologise.'

Walking back towards the jury, I pick up where I left off.

'Ladies and gentlemen, I spoke about simplicity earlier, and finding the truth, so I will keep my words equally simple and clear. To determine a fair and just verdict in this case, which I know and trust you will, it is imperative that you keep sight of all the facts, not the pre-trial hype, but the facts, the simple building blocks by which you examine the information coming before you. A child's life has been lost. This is a tragedy. A tragedy that none of us wants to comprehend. We all look for answers, but here, in this courtroom, we are also looking for fairness and truth. Abby Jones did not take this child's life, and when you consider at length, and in your wisdom, the thrust of the prosecution's case, you will not make her a scapegoat here, no matter how much we grieve the loss of a young life. And the reason why is simple. Ladies and gentlemen, the facts speak for themselves.'

I take another couple of steps towards them, a form of intimacy, before delivering my closing point.

'We also contend that there has been an overt bias towards our client, Abby Jones, which has been flaunted in some circles. If bias exists, you need to put it aside.

'This will be a long trial. You will hear and see a great many things over the course of it. Remember, we are here in search of the truth. And that truth, ladies and gentlemen, will give you no option other than to acquit Abby Jones.'

I sit down. I think some of my words have hit home, but I'm also thinking about the loaded terminology I have used – 'bias', 'incorrect accusations', 'scare-mongering', 'scapegoat'.

Was I guilty of that with Lucas? Did I rush to justice too?

It isn't long before Judge Kendell dismisses the jury for the second day, instructing the court to reconvene after the weekend when the first witness for the prosecution will be called. Abby is led away.

Out in the lobby, Robin picks up a discarded newspaper. She scans the front page before handing it to me. I stare at the headline: 'Killer Nanny Obsessed with Victim's Father'.

'Shit,' I say under my breath, reading the rest of the article.

'Finlay,' she says, 'is going to have a field day.'

I stare at the newspaper again.

'Do you think Ashley leaked the story? She may have been the only one in Abby's confidence.'

'Does it matter?' asks Mark. 'The point is, someone did.' His phone bleeps. 'Damn,' he says.

'What?' I ask.

Robin and I stare at him, waiting.

'It seems Finlay has called an impromptu media conference for an hour's time.'

'Bloody great,' I say, even though I mean the opposite.

# 19
# FINLAY

Finlay couldn't have been more pleased with the recent turn of events and the latest newspaper headlines implicating Abby Jones in some sordid obsession with Morgan. The girl is completely deranged, which is exactly what he's been telling any journalist prepared to listen for months.

Walking towards the media area, he senses the buzz of excitement, already tasting the pleasure he'll get when he closes the net even tighter on Abby. He recognises most of the faces. This trial is too high-profile for rookies to be covering it. He sees Tom Naylor, NBC News, with twenty years' experience, a sceptical old goat if ever there was one. CNN and Fox News Talk have more attractive contributors, with Jessie Leonard and Patti Goldbern. For Finlay, it doesn't matter how many reporters are in the room, or how experienced they are, because he has every intention of playing each one of them. You don't get to a position of power by being backward with the media. You need to know how to win the game, giving journalists exactly what they want, clear and effective soundbites, and plenty of fresh meat, all nicely wrapped up in the guise of news, the more controversial the better.

Jessie Leonard, with her slim frame and short dark hair, eyes him from behind her red designer glasses. Finlay purposely doesn't catch her eye: avoiding it will make her more eager. Tom Naylor looks relaxed after his month-long vacation. Finlay would lay money on him purposely working his time off around this trial. A seasoned press man like Naylor knows this is one of the biggest trials he will ever be involved with, and every dog and devil on the street knows it too.

Standing behind the podium, Finlay secretly hails America's First Amendment, protecting the freedom of speech, taking his time before speaking. He catches sight of one of Heather's snoops, Mark Hickman, ready to take notes. Heather, no doubt, will be watching the media conference from an adjoining room.

He decides to give the first question to Patti Goldbern, pointing in her direction.

'What comments do you have on the latest allegations about Abby Jones?'

He runs his fingers through his hair, a delaying tactic, and assumes a solemn air. 'Patti, I take it you're referring to the reports of Abby Jones harbouring an attraction for Morgan Rotterdam, the man who has lost his infant son?'

She nods.

'On that subject matter, Patti, I will keep my reply and comments clear.' He pauses to make eye contact with as many journalists as possible. 'Abby Jones is a young woman with a great many difficulties. She is not the innocent, law-abiding, shy teenager that the defence would like us to believe. I know that, and a great many other people know that, including, sadly, the late Jacob Rotterdam. As for the allegations you refer to, all I can say is this. The alleged behaviour wouldn't be out of character for her, behaviour that in many people's eyes is a depraved way of thinking, contrary to God's law and the law of any decent, moral human being.'

'Are you saying you believe the allegations?'

'Only Abby Jones knows what was on her mind, but in our opinion her fantastical nature wouldn't be wholly at odds with the allegation.'

Next, he points to Jessie Leonard. 'Yes, Jessie?'

She holds the microphone close to her mouth. He notices her full lips. He also notices the tiny cracks appearing in her lipstick as the words come out. He moistens his own in anticipation.

'According to these reports, the allegations came from a source close to the defendant.'

'I cannot comment on the source of the information.'

'I realise that, but you could hazard a guess as to who you think it might have been.'

'I am not in the business of guessing. I deal in hard facts, you know that.'

He is stringing her along, waiting for the right moment to land his punch.

'So, you are refusing to comment.'

'That is not what I said, Jessie. For the record, what I will say is that this trial, by its very nature, will mean a lot of unsavoury details about Abby Jones will become known. The prosecution over the coming weeks will share, in the interest of justice, many of these difficult details. A picture will gradually develop as to the kind of person Abby Jones really is, and it will not be a virtuous one.'

Tom Naylor doesn't wait for Finlay to look in his direction, blurting out his question: 'What has Morgan Rotterdam to say about this?'

He gives Naylor one of his stern looks, the kind that says he is asking something that is below the belt, bordering on offensive, but that he won't shrink from answering it.

'Tom, as you may appreciate, right now Morgan Rotterdam has a great many more important issues pressing on his mind, namely the loss of his child. It consumes his entire world, as it does that of Vivienne, his loving and devoted wife. Their life is filled with pain, and this sideshow in the sordidness of Abby Jones's desires, the killer of their son, is viewed with nothing but disdain. Vivienne and Morgan have handled, and will continue to handle, all of this with great dignity. I hope you respect them for that and will not drag them down to Ms Jones's level.'

Several hands rise. He sees a new face in the crowd, a young woman he hasn't noticed before. Her microphone tells him she is from the *Patriot Eagle*. She has a facial expression of purpose that he likes. It is a risk leaving the last question with her, but he likes risks, and temptation wins out.

'Ladies and gentlemen, we will have one more question, and I will give it to local news, the *Patriot Eagle*.' He points to the unknown female amid the sea of reporters.

'Thank you, Mr Clarke.' Her voice sounds strong, cheeky.

'Call me Finlay. We're all friends here.'

There is muted laughter from the crowd.

'Marcia Langan, of the *Patriot Eagle*.'

'Welcome to the madness, Marcia.' Finlay relaxes, giving her, and everyone else, one of his largest grins. The communal amusement continues to filter through. Even in big trials with high stakes, humour carries everyone some of the way.

'I have two questions, if that's okay.' Not waiting for him to answer, she continues: 'First, how sure are you, based on the media coverage to date, that the jury in this trial isn't biased towards a guilty verdict? And second, do you know if a psychological evaluation has been done on Abby Jones, as to whether she has the cognitive ability to adequately defend herself?'

Finlay has made a bad call, and he knows it, but he isn't going to duck it.

'Marcia, I will do my best to address your concerns,' he says, sounding sincere. 'In the first instance, I have the utmost faith in the twelve members of the jury, who are here to do what every good American is prepared to do, to uphold the right of an individual to a fair trial earnestly and wholeheartedly. Second, I can confirm that we have not carried out a psychological evaluation. Neither do we see the need for one. If Abby Jones's mental state is suspect, I will leave that to her defence team. What I do know is this. Her cognitive ability was adequate to kill Jacob Rotterdam.'

# 20
# BLANCO

Blanco isn't happy about getting the phone call from the park ranger early on a Saturday morning. If what Zach says is true, he needs to get to Setago Park, and fast.

Driving in through the gates, he spots the ranger waiting with his golden retriever.

'You call it in yet, Zach?' Blanco asks, rolling down his window.

'About to, now that you're here.'

Blanco listens as the ranger makes the call.

'Delta Seventeen to Base Control. Over.'

'Control answering, Delta Seventeen. Over.'

'Afraid we have a dead body here. Over.'

'In Setago? Over.'

'Affirmative. Over.'

'Which end of woods? Over.'

'Close to the bird sanctuary. Access via the south entrance a couple of kilometres in. Over.'

'Male or female? Over.'

'Male. Over.'

'Can you call ID on it? Over.'

'Yeah, I know him. Over.'

'Give us the positive. Over.'

'Lucas García. Over.'

'Are you sure? Over.'

'Not one hundred per cent, but close enough to make no difference. Over.'

'How long do you reckon he's been there? Over.'

'Not long. Parts of the lower body are missing. One leg severed. Most likely the animals had a feast overnight. Over.'

'Copy, Delta Seventeen. Are you alone? Over.'

'Affirmative. Just me and Max here. He picked up the scent. Over.'

'Give Max a pat from us. Over.'

'Will do. Over.'

'Copy, Zach. We'll notify the State Police now. Over.'

'Looks like there was an attempt at a burial too. Over.'

'Burial? Over.'

'The body is partly under the soil, although there wasn't much effort made to hide it. Over.'

'Anything else, Zach? Over.'

'Yeah. He took a couple of bullets to the back of the head. The victim is lying face down. As I said, he's not here long. Over.'

'Hold tight, Zach. Troopers will be with you shortly. Over.'

'Thanks. Over.'

'Set up a temporary perimeter? Over.'

'Will do. Over.'

'Roger that.'

'Okay. Delta Seventeen, signing out.'

'Control, over and out.'

Zach turns to Blanco. 'They won't be long.'

'Thanks for keeping my presence to yourself.'

'If anyone asks, I've just called you, okay?'

'Exactly. Now tell me what else you know.'

'As I said to the base, I don't reckon the body is here long. Hours at most. Max was probably drawn to the blood.' He kneels to pat the dog. 'There could be more injuries, but right now that's all I know.'

'The State Troopers will be all over this for sure.'

'I reckon you're right there.'

'And you're absolutely sure it's Lucas?'

'Yeah. He didn't last long in town this time, did he?'

'He was trouble, nothing surer.'

'He won't be causing any of it now.'

'I wouldn't be so sure.' Blanco lights a cigarette. He offers one to Zach. Both men blow bellows of smoke into the woods. 'You said he took the bullets to the head?'

'Yeah.'

'It might be a professional job, then.'

'You'd imagine they'd have done a better job hiding the body.'

'Maybe they were disturbed.'

'Or maybe,' Zach says, 'they wanted the body found.'

'You've been watching too much *CSI*. Why don't you leave the policing to me? Take the gold star for yourself and Max there, and stay out of things.'

'I have no interest in trouble.'

'Me neither.' Blanco looks beyond the park ranger into the woods. 'How far are you going to mark off?'

'Four yards all around, I'd say.'

'It'll be pushed out further than that, especially if they're following animal tracks. But let's leave that to the CPAC guys.'

'CPAC?'

'Massachusetts State Police, Crime Prevention and Control, or plain old State Troopers, if you prefer.'

'Will you be the lead?'

'Nah, I'll share it with some top-dog detective from MSP.'

'What's the protocol on this one, Blanco? I've never had a dead man in the park before.'

'Oh, they'll probably start with the body and work the perimeter outwards, scanning damn well everything with those metal detectors of theirs. Being part buried, it could be days, maybe longer.'

'Yeah?'

'They'll probably only extract a spoonful of soil at a time. Goddamn it,' he laughs, 'they might even take mugshots of the insects.'

'You serious?'

'Deadly. Those little guys and their larvae, wriggling around as we speak, will be able to tell them how long he's been down there.'

'What are you thinking, Blanco?'

'I'm wondering which assistant DA will be assigned to this.'

'Do you think it could be that guy Finlay Clarke?'

'Doubt it. He's tied up with the case of the murdered baby.'

'Awful stuff.'

'Awful,' Blanco repeats. 'Zach, why don't we have a look at that body before those State guys arrive?'

'It's your call.'

Both men approach the scene with caution, before Zach stands back, allowing Blanco to get far closer than he should. He leans in to examine the partial head, with part of it blasted away. Of what's left of the loose skin, he can make out Lucas's face, which has turned a mottled grey-blue. Beyond the corpse, he sees small pieces of brain. Eager vultures swoon above. For most, the sight of a rotting body is unsettling, the stuff of nightmares, but to Blanco what is uppermost in his mind are his own ideas on who killed Lucas García. One of them is more uncomfortable than he would like. If certain people wanted this body found, he decides, there sure must be a good reason for it.

# 21
# HEATHER

I hear the beep of my phone early on Saturday morning. The message is from Robin. More headlines have hit the weekend newspapers covering Abby's so-called obsession with Morgan.

Downstairs, I make myself a large pot of coffee, before getting stuck into my preparation for Boris Wesley's testimony on Monday.

When my cell phone buzzes again, I don't recognise the number. For a moment, I consider not answering it, wondering, after talking with Lucas, if it might be my father back in town. Instead I pick up. 'Hello,' I say.

'Hi, Heather.'

The female voice sounds familiar, only I can't place it.

'It's Marcia Langan,' she says. 'Sorry to be disturbing you on a Saturday, but I figured it would be good to hear your side of things.'

'About what?' I ask, irritated, already getting ready to hang up.

'Why, Lucas García, of course. Haven't you heard?'

'No.'

'Well, he's dead,' she says matter-of-factly. At first, my mind refuses to take it in. She keeps talking fast. I can't concentrate. He can't be dead. I hear her voice again, building up to tell me how he died, stringing it out, pretending to be caring. I feel my knees weaken.

'He was shot,' she says, her voice shrill.

Everything stops.

'Multiple bullet wounds.'

She takes my silence as a sign to keep talking.

'The body was partly eaten by animals.'

There are spots in front of my eyes. I look down at the low table in front of me, stacks of magazines coming in and out of focus.

'Do you have a comment?' she asks impatiently. 'You might as well give your side of things before someone makes it up for you.'

I go to hang up.

'You named him as your mother's killer, didn't you? Some people think it was a stitch up and that Sheriff Hodgson had it in for him.'

The phone is heavy in my hand.

'I went to see him in Salem a couple of days ago,' she says, 'Sheriff Hodgson, and he sure didn't like poor Lucas.'

Why is she calling him 'poor Lucas'? Because he's dead. Like my mother. They're both dead.

I hang up, dropping the phone at my feet.

'Lucas is dead,' I repeat aloud, trying to let it sink in, and when it finally does, I think about Jim Handcock and how much he hated him. And then I'm remembering again the day I walked with Lucas to the Handcocks' house. The afternoon was sunny. His Panama hat shaded his face. I had a rucksack on my back with a half-eaten sandwich and a bottle of water in it. He had a black cloth bag filled with small bottles of different-coloured liquids. There were bags of seeds too, and dried flowers with herbs wrapped in muslin. It felt like a long walk to the house, but I didn't mind. I was enjoying it.

I knew my mother trusted him, and she felt I was safe with him. I heard the waves hit the rocky cliffs, knowing that beyond the road, and the houses, there was a vast ocean. The thought of it made me happy.

I had never been to the Handcocks' house before, but when we arrived, we were ushered upstairs. I sensed something was wrong. I heard the adults talking frantically to one another – neighbours, who had called in to help – but no matter how hard I try to remember what they were saying, I can't.

Lucas seemed to be the centre of everything, like a ringmaster in the circus, turning around and around, smiling at the crowd. The voices subsided. Nobody noticed me, almost as if I was an extension of him, not a separate person at all. We went into Alice Handcock's bedroom. She was sick. She had a fever. Her mind was racing. One of the women from the town said she had the devil inside her, that he had taken hold of her thoughts. I heard Lucas call her name. 'Alice,' he said, over and over, as if it was a question hovering without an answer. The room was dark. It smelt of sickness, stale, heavy, sucking me in.

Lucas opened the bedroom curtains with a swish. The light from outside attacked the room. The sunshine didn't belong there. I watched as he sat at a table in the corner, mixing potions, still aware of the shape of Alice Handcock in the bed. The shape moaned, like an injured wild boar. The groans didn't sound human. I heard another voice. It belonged to Jim Handcock. 'Alice,' he said, 'it will be fine now.' Lucas pulled the sheets down. Alice was sweaty and blotchy, and her eyes were wild. I turned away, but she kept staring at me. Lucas lifted her forward, forcing her to sit upright. He poured a red potion down her throat. The liquid dribbled out at either side of her mouth, blood-like. She smiled as if she was enjoying the taste. I wanted to run away, but my feet were stuck to the floor, and all the

time the adults were growing larger, taller than me, towering over everything.

I ran to the door, but when I reached it, Jim Handcock blocked my way, standing over my small frame. I pushed past him, and that was when he grabbed me. I hated his hands on me. They reminded me of the afternoon after Grandpa's funeral, when Uncle Samuel asked if he could hold me. As a child, I'd thought it would be okay, but then he wouldn't let me go, and afterwards he gave me that ten-dollar bill and told me I was a good girl, and then I lied to my mother about it. And perhaps, for years, I've lied to myself too.

The cell phone rings. It's Marcia Langan again. I ignore it. Only it's relentless, like the sound of the insect buzzing in my ear on the day my father pushed my mother. I stare at the phone vibrating on the floor, suddenly not caring about Marcia, or the trial, or anything else.

I pack an overnight bag, needing to be somewhere no one can reach me. I drive aimlessly for about an hour, until I see a motel sign outside Quincy, shining luminous in the distance. The yellow neon 'vacancy' sign swings back and forth, making a metallic creaking sound, and it's as if my past and my present are doing the same thing, swinging back and forth, like a pendulum.

'Thirty dollars for the night,' says the woman at the reception desk. She takes my money, and hands me a key.

The bedroom is dreary, with dark, battered furniture and art-deco wallpaper. A single light bulb in the ceiling barely illuminates the room. There is a drip from the tap in the bathroom. Everything about the place looks as if it's been dragged from a seventies horror movie, where an unfortunate victim will soon be killed. I lie spread-eagled on the bed, listening to the water drip, sending myself into oblivion with the large bottle of bourbon I picked up along the way.

Hours later, I awake to a sore head and a throat that feels as if it's travelled the length and breadth of the Arizona desert. The empty bottle eyes me from the floor, inches away. It glints at me in the half-light. My stomach tells me I'm about to pay a price, and seconds later I'm in the bathroom, vomiting into the cracked basin. The filthy marks in it disgust me, but not nearly as much as I disgust myself. Deep down, I already know that this temporary attempt at escape is nothing more than a vain effort to run away from the truth, away from the knowledge of Lucas's death, in the same way I have run away for years from the knowledge that I left my mother to die.

I lie on the bed, part shivering, part sweating. I think about Marcia Langan's phone call again, still unable to fathom that Lucas is gone. But as I stare at the ceiling, and the tiny light bulb blurs my vision, seconds eventually turn into minutes, and minutes into hours, until finally the enormity of it all hits home. The man I accused of killing my mother is dead. Accusations don't confirm anything. They are speculative, unproven. Now there is a new fact. Someone has killed Lucas. That same someone may be capable of killing again. I think about the doll, the one wearing the fabric from my mother's blouse. I discarded it in the trash basket, but I know it's still there, waiting for me. If Lucas didn't leave it, I have to accept a fresh possibility: the person who left the doll may have killed him too.

# 22
# ELIZABETH

*Today, I went to Skating Pond in Setago Park with Heather. We walked past the bird sanctuary, a place I used to play in as a child, and the same place I secretly met Jim during our affair. The pond, surrounded by tall sycamores and willows, has been frozen for days. Heather brought her skates in case the ice was strong enough, but looking at it, I wasn't so sure.*

*The closer we got to the pond, the more it glistened, its surface a sheer sheet of ice. l could hear the birds flying between the trees, and I smelt the moss, too, still potent despite the chill. Heather begged me to let her skate. I scanned the ice again, and gave in. It felt good to see her happy. I knew the arguments with Charlie, and his constant disappearing acts, were unsettling her. She doesn't say anything, but I know she's becoming more and more withdrawn, almost as if she feels safer in a world of make-believe, blocking out the reality of her parents constantly fighting.*

*It is a few months since Lucas left town, and I guess all endings bring their complications. Increasingly, in both mind and spirit, I feel more and more isolated. It is only Heather and me now. We need to look out for each other, especially with so many strange things happening, and items going missing from the house. All of it tells me that danger is never far away.*

*Once on the ice, Heather's face lit up. She laughed when she slipped a couple of times. If I close my eyes now, I can still see her, swirling in her navy winter coat, then gliding forward, her hair flying free. I think about how her laughter echoed around us, and how, watching her, I smiled with a lightness I hadn't felt for so long.*

*It was when she was furthest from me that I heard that awful sound, the crack that stopped my heart. Suddenly, the birds seemed louder, the sun intensifying its reflection on the pond. My heart thumped as the pin-prickly touch of frost made my body rigid, petrified that I wouldn't get to her fast enough. Then I was running, only the closer I got to her, the more she kept disappearing under the ice. I could tell she was getting weaker. Within seconds, I couldn't see her. Sick with terror, I screamed at her to hold on, and jumped into the water. The freezing cold bit hard. Submerged, it was like everything was happening in slow motion, but somehow I managed to reach her small body, and soon we both emerged above the waterline. I feared the worst, but then she started coughing, and the water gulped out of her. Eventually, she opened her eyes. Instant relief flooded me. I'd lost Mia. I couldn't bear to lose her too.*

*In the car, I wrapped her shivering body in a blanket. Her face was so pale. I couldn't stop fretting about her. I was so absorbed in my own thoughts that I barely looked around as I put the car into reverse to drive home. It was only as I turned and stared back at the pond that I saw the person watching us. At first I thought it was my imagination, but even from a distance, with Heather shivering by my side, my eyes locked with theirs. The message was loud and clear. They will always be watching. They will never stop.*

# 23
# HEATHER

I climb into the shower of the motel room. The water is barely a trickle, but I stay under it for as long as I can. My mind feels stuck, thinking about Lucas, already knowing death has a habit of shutting things down, and all the stuff you thought vital stops being even vaguely important. A person dying changes things. There is no comeback after death. I understood that after I lost my mother. Each year that passed I would think of all the Mother's Day and birthday cards I would never buy her, staring at the cards filling the racks, knowing I have no need for them.

Years pass, but it doesn't change things much. People talk about grief, saying time is a healer, but that is only partly true. If you love someone, you will always grieve them, in the same way, that first day, I knew Abby would always feel slightly less whole, not having a parent, and my mother could never fully accept Mia's death. The horror has only just begun for Morgan and Vivienne. Soon, they will understand that they can never fully come to terms with Jacob's loss, because some deaths are like that: you can never entirely recover.

By the time I leave the motel room on Saturday night, a new resolve has formed in my mind. Dressed in fresh clothes, I consider my father again. He was supposed to meet Lucas, and now Lucas is dead. The issue of him wanting revenge after all this time, believing Lucas was responsible for my mother's killing, hangs in the air, like many other unanswered questions. When I was a child, there were times when my father pretended everything was a game. Before Mia died, he would make up stories, little mysteries full of puzzles. In his land of make-believe, he pretended we were a happy family, and I would pretend with him. After Mia died, he changed. The house became so quiet, and immediately afterwards, when my mother locked herself in Mia's bedroom, refusing to let anyone in, my father and I were like lost people, together but apart.

My stomach churns. I'm going to be sick again. Afterwards, I stare at my reflection in the mirror, catching a glimpse of my younger self, the girl deep inside me, remembering how, years before, alcohol could turn my father mellow, as well as angry. It was only when he was half-shot that he could show any kind of fatherly affection, his voice loving, sounding like someone you could love back.

After Mia died, I hated him for going away again. My mother had no one to care for her but me, and during those long months of depression, no matter how hard I tried, I couldn't fix her. When she started to feel well again, after she met Lucas, my father returned. Then she became increasingly anxious, on edge, and I thought about how much better our lives would be without him, and how much easier it would be if he was dead.

\*

In the car I switch on my cell phone, seeing several missed calls. One is from Alex. She's heard about Lucas. When I replay her message, I hear the concern in her voice, which is partly why I agree to drive over to her.

She answers the door in a long, flowing gold dress, wearing a pixie wig, her lips painted a deep maroon. She looks striking. I used to wonder why she wore wigs and changed her dress so much, until she told me it was like re-forming – it gave her a buzz, making her feel different from other people. I guess it aligns with her willingness to take risks. The threat of being ordinary, to Alex, being the scariest thing of all.

I step into the hallway. In the past, we have knowingly walked a tentative line, each aware of the sexual undercurrent existing between us. Up to now, I have always kept it at a safe distance, unwilling to get close enough to commit. Now everything feels slightly tilted, as if something unguarded could happen.

'You shouldn't have dressed up for me,' I say, lightening the mood.

'And you look terrible.'

'Thanks,' I say, sitting down. 'My father liked to reinvent himself too. Did I ever tell you that?'

She doesn't answer, sitting cross-legged on a set of cushions in the corner. I fire my overnight bag onto the couch opposite. She looks at it, but again, she doesn't comment.

'How did you hear about Lucas?' I ask.

'Does it matter?'

'I guess not.' I pause. 'I met him the other day. I told him to leave Corham, that he shouldn't have come back, and now he's dead.'

'Murdered,' she states for clarity. The word hovers.

I don't tell her about his planned meeting with my father.

'Do you have any theories as to who might have wanted him dead?' she asks.

'He was never liked in Corham.'

'Jim Handcock didn't like him much either, did he?'

'No,' I say, 'he didn't.'

She stares at me, then says, 'This might not be the best moment to bring this up, but I have more information on that new lead I mentioned to you.'

'Oh?'

'What do you know about Lexie Gilmore?'

'She used to work for the Handcocks, but then she left town.' I think about the newspaper article I read recently, and add, 'Lexie disappeared a few months before my mother was killed.'

'She was nineteen when she did her vanishing act,' Alex continues, 'and it seems, prior to that, she was happy and normal. She had only worked for the Handcocks for six months, but her disappearance created quite a stir.'

'Yeah,' I say. 'I know.'

'Eventually the police lost interest. It was put down as another young girl who simply got fed up with her job and headed out of town.'

'And you think different?'

'I do.'

'Why?'

'Because, so far, I haven't been able to trace her.'

'Maybe she changed identity.'

'That's a possibility. If she did, she wouldn't be the first person to get hold of a fake social security number and become someone else. But, then, the real question, Heather, is why?'

'What are you thinking?'

'Perhaps she was afraid of someone.'

'Who?'

'You tell me.'

'You're thinking about Jim Handcock, aren't you?'

She gets up from the cushions and sits beside me on the couch. 'Why the overnight bag?' she asks, ignoring my earlier question. Her voice is soft.

'I decided to check into a motel earlier, after I heard about Lucas, and drown my sorrows. I attempted oblivion – *badly* – with a large bottle of booze.'

'I can smell it,' she says, but her words aren't accusing.

'I guess, for a short time, I turned into my father, but mostly,' I say, angry at myself, 'my gut reaction was to run away, to hide from everything.'

Again, she keeps her silence.

'My father was fond of drinking, especially when he was miserable, and sometimes he wasn't so nice with it.'

Her hand touches my arm. An instant spark.

'I've been remembering more stuff,' I add.

'Oh?'

'It keeps happening when I least expect it, but now, it's happening more and more.'

'The brain can cause all kinds of weird stuff.'

'But there are still huge chunks of missing memory from the day my mother was killed.'

'Sometimes, Heather, the mind can only bear a certain amount of truth.'

'Is that what you learned in the Ding Wing, that psychiatric unit you used to work in?'

'That, and other stuff.'

She takes her hand away.

'But some of the new memory,' I say, 'is from before my mother was killed.'

'Perhaps you were already blocking out stuff. If you were, it would make sense that it happened that day too.'

I consider her words, wondering if it's possible.

She's still talking. 'It's called dissociation,' she says.

'Meaning?'

'It's a way of pulling yourself from reality, and it can be experienced in several ways, a mild detachment from a person's immediate surroundings to more severe detachment, especially if there are physical and emotional issues.'

'What do you mean?'

'You said yourself your father could get nasty with alcohol. Perhaps, as a child, your mind was already dissociating from certain experiences. Then, when your mother was attacked, it would make sense that you shut those things out too. The detachment explains the memory loss as well. You might not have been aware of the dissociation until the police investigation happened, and there were all those missing hours you couldn't account for. You probably thought it only happened once, but it could have happened before, and afterwards.'

'What are the main causes?'

'In children, typically trauma, sometimes prolonged, or …' she lowers her voice '… a history of abuse.'

'How can you tell if it happened to you, if you can't remember?'

'You can't, unless your brain allows you to.'

My mind flips back to the doll left at my apartment. If it wasn't from Lucas, then who?

'What's wrong?' she asks.

'Someone was in my apartment,' I say. 'I left the front door open, and they put a doll in my bedroom. It's like a voodoo thing. Lucas used to make them, but this one was ugly.' I'm talking too fast, in a rush to get the words out. 'He used to say a voodoo doll could be a good thing, a form of protection.'

'I don't understand.'

'The doll had fabric on it that had belonged to my mother. It's still at my apartment in Roxbury, in the trash basket in my bedroom.'

'Christ, who do you think put it there?'

'At first I thought it was Lucas, but now I'm not so sure.'

'It's obviously not someone random,' she insists, processing the information. 'They would have to understand the significance of the doll, and the fabric. Which means they know things about you, or at least enough to fuck with your head.'

'And they also have access to the fabric,' I add, 'to things that belonged to my mother.'

'Agreed,' she says, nodding, as if we're talking about an investigation. She must see the unease building on my face. 'Shit,' she says. 'I'm sorry.'

'It's fine,' I reply, although none of it is.

'Think,' she says. 'Who could have the fabric?'

'Lorrie cleared everything from the house after the murder. She could have held onto some things, things she kept secret from me.'

'Which means it could have been your uncle.'

'Or my father,' I add, finally willing to admit what I've been thinking ever since I heard about Lucas's death.

'Realistically, Heather, it could have been anyone who knew your mother.' She takes my hand. 'You don't really think it was your father, do you?'

'I don't want to believe it, but I have to consider the possibility.'

'You're going to need a firearm,' she says, so definite I stare back at her.

'No, I don't. I hate guns.'

'Someone is fucking around with you, Heather. You don't know what they're capable of, especially now, after what happened to Lucas.'

'Maybe it's not even connected.'

'Or maybe it is.'

I don't answer her.

Seconds pass. She lets it go. 'Abby,' she finally says, 'seems to be in deep shit too. Are the rumours in the media about her and Morgan true?'

'Possibly, but she says nothing of substance happened between them – flirting, no more.'

Again, she doesn't push it. Instead she reaches up to touch my face. She kisses my cheek gently, treading the line between friendship and something more.

'You are so beautiful,' she says.

I shake my head. 'At times, I feel like a broken thing.'

'Shush,' she says, kissing my cheek again. It feels good to be this close, but then I pull away. She takes it as a rebuttal, but it's not that. It's because, with everything that has happened – Lucas coming back to Corham, the Handcocks and the trial – suddenly, more than anything, I want to be a little girl again, to have a mother who will tell me everything is going to be okay, even if it isn't.

'Do you really think your father could have harmed Lucas?' she asks, sensing that whatever we had seconds earlier is already past.

'I don't know,' I say. 'I can't know anything for sure, especially when I can't trust my memory, or anyone connected to it.'

She stands up, putting more physical distance between us. 'Heather,' she says, turning around, 'human beings are capable of anything, including your father, and some of them carry an awful lot of hate.'

I walk towards her, wanting to undo any damage I have done.

'Why don't you stay the night?' she asks, with a hint of bravado. 'Hell, I have enough firearms in my personal arsenal to protect an army.'

'I don't know.'

'No strings attached, Heather, unless you call it different.'

# 24
# MORGAN

Morgan Rotterdam pours the end of the bottle of bourbon into his glass. Vivienne has been in bed for hours. He is biding his time, waiting. With a drink in one hand and his cell phone in the other, he walks to the back of his private den. The room is in darkness, apart from a solitary desk lamp.

He stares at the many photographs of Jacob in shadow on the wall, each one bringing the same reaction, a mix of love and grief. Taking a large swig from his glass, he slams it down on the small table. Right now he wants to kill someone, and if he had that bitch here, he would wrap his hands tightly around her neck and squeeze it until she choked. He can hardly bear to look at her in court, especially when he remembers toying with the idea of fucking her.

The images of Jacob look down on him. Some are from the day of his birth, others from the days that followed. He stares at the photograph of him wearing the T-shirt with *Dad's Number 1 Boy* on the front. He empties the glass. He has been thinking about making the next phone call all evening, but he hesitates before punching in the number.

Vivienne hates him. Perhaps she has always hated him. He knows something else too. He will never have another child. He doesn't want a replacement. He wants Jacob back.

He keys in the number. It rings only twice before he hears the voice at the end of the line.

He has had too many drinks to drive to the hotel to meet her so he orders a cab. A half-hour later, as he waits in the hotel room, he puts CNN on loudly in the background.

His cell phone bleeps with a text. She will be here soon. He opens a bottle of bubbly. Why the hell not? He's gone this far.

Ten minutes later, he hears a knock on the door. When he opens it, she's wearing a mid-length black coat, her long legs below it, twisted around each other, balancing on a pair of deliciously high heels. Her hair is tied up in curls, softening her face, with dark eyelids and red-stained lips.

'You're late,' he says, as he holds the door ajar, waiting for her to enter. His face is angry, lined, flushed with booze, as his eyes narrow. He is wearing a white hotel bathrobe and matching slippers. The robe is tied with an extravagantly large bow hanging beneath his waist. It is purposely loose. His companion unties it, the start of a ritual they have played many times in the past. He slaps her face. She doesn't wince. Good, he thinks, it's my turn to play rough.

The television is still on. A news reporter is talking about the murder of Lucas García, and how his body was found in Setago Park. They both stare momentarily at the screen, seeing images of the woods and the teams of forensics officers combing the site. Morgan switches it off.

'I have champagne chilling,' he says, pointing to a low table. She pours herself a glass. He watches as she swallows fast, bubbles, sharp, cold, with tiny droplets teasing her face. He pretends a lack of interest. She removes her coat. Underneath, she is wearing a pink bra and a pair of matching panties. His right hand pulls her hair, yanking it hard. He wants her to feel pain. He wants everyone to feel pain.

# 25
# HEATHER

I leave Alex's house early on Sunday morning, both of us having slept in separate rooms. Too many things are happening at the moment for anything more complicated. The chief medical examiner, Boris Wesley, will give his evidence in the morning, and irrespective of everything else that is going down, I need to be ready. Alex was right about Abby, too. This current media storm isn't helping. Another tough conversation with my client is well overdue, one in which Abby doesn't hedge in reply to my questions.

On the way home to West Roxbury, I phone Daniel. We agree to meet later today. Alex wasn't keen on the idea, but bottom line, he's one of the few people from my past I can trust, and after what happened to Lucas, not meeting him wasn't up for discussion.

After four hours of prepping for Boris Wesley's cross-examination, I leave the apartment, and with light traffic, I arrive early at Fox's cocktail bar. Walking in, I hear the piano playing, just as it did years before. The pianist is different, though, a younger man to replace the elderly Leo.

The bar has comfortable red couches, plump leather chairs and low tables, all with candlelit lanterns. The tiny flickers of light should be welcoming, only it doesn't feel that way.

For a moment I stall, as another night from my past forms in my mind, when the Christmas lights shone bright, and the tree was wrapped in silver and gold tinsel. I visualise the fake presents underneath, tied with silver bows, and how the lights looked heavy on the branches. Leo was wearing a new black shirt, and people were handing up pieces of paper requesting their favourite songs. The later it got in the evening, the more down I felt, and the need to get out of there grew. Soon, I found myself at Skating Pond, where I nearly drowned as a child and my mother had saved me, even though I couldn't save her.

Now, as I walk through the bar, I sense people staring. I know what they're thinking, that I don't want to be here, that I barely acknowledged my grandma's death, that I'm only back now because of Lucas, the man I accused of killing my mother.

I keep walking, pretending I don't care, and they don't matter.

I feel a tap on my shoulder. I turn. It's Daniel. His eyes are friendly, warm, but seeing him, I think about that Christmas night again, when I found myself at the pond and the water urged me towards the edge. After I'd stepped in, the tingling chill felt good against the pain. The low moon had guided me from the bar, out of the double doors, until I reached a point where I couldn't hear the music, and the Christmas tree lights stopped twinkling, and I knew, if I did this one thing, I wouldn't have to think any more about disappointing my mother. And when I was knee-deep in the water, then waist deep, the chill moved to bitter cold, and I was okay with letting go. Then the water changed, from cold to warm, and I thought, this is it, at last, it's over. I was ready to let go. And Daniel's arms reached in to pull me out, and a part of me thought my mother had sent him, that it was her way of telling me not to give up, to keep on fighting. *Be fragile, be strong.*

Daniel swore he would never tell anyone that I'd tried to kill myself. He'd said the same thing a few weeks back, when we spoke about Finlay, and both times I believed him.

He points to a table in the corner. 'You okay?' he asks, looking concerned.

'Yes. It's tough being back here, that's all.'

'Some of us stayed.' His words are clipped. I stare at the myriad faces in the bar. Many look away, others stare back.

I turn back to Daniel. He seems distant, tense.

'What do you really think of me?' he asks, as we take our seats.

'I don't understand.'

'Do you look down on me?'

'Of course not. Why would you think that?'

'Because I stayed, and you left.'

My eyes focus on the odd grey hair in his tight-cut beard, wondering about the boy I once loved, who is now a man, as I have changed from that girl to a woman.

'I don't think that,' I say, and I mean it.

He folds his jacket over the back of the chair. I open the top button of mine, the heat of the bar finally reaching me. Again, I think about how close we used to be, a million years ago.

'We were very young, weren't we?' I say.

'The enthusiasm of youth.' He laughs.

I laugh too.

'It has the power to make you believe things can be different,' he adds, sounding tense again. I think about him losing his parents late last year, annoyed at my selfishness in not mentioning it sooner.

'I'm sorry I wasn't here for the funerals,' I say. 'I should have been.'

'It doesn't matter.' He rearranges the items on the table, the beer mats, the stand with the menu of cocktails, the candlelit lantern, now flickering in the square silver tin with white paper napkins.

I consider his question again, about looking down on him for staying. 'I had my reasons for leaving, Daniel. You weren't like me. You didn't have to get away.'

'Do you want a drink?' he asks, as if he doesn't want to talk about it any more.

'A Coke is fine, thanks,' I say, thinking about the bottle of bourbon I'd consumed the day before.

I watch him at the bar, how he moves, how others stand back as he orders the drinks. Do I still have feelings for him?

'Here you go,' he says, arriving back, putting the glasses on the table.

'Okay,' I say. 'What's the collective gossip machine saying?'

'You mean the heartbeat of the community?' He glances around the bar.

I sip the Coke. 'Yeah.'

'They're thinking what happened to Lucas might tie into your mother's—'

I don't let him finish. 'I figured as much.'

'Some people have seen your father hanging around town too. They're wondering if it's connected, but I wouldn't pay too much heed to that. You know how they like conspiracy theories around here. It helps to make their lives more interesting.'

'So, my family is still a source of entertainment?'

'I didn't say that.'

'But it's what they're all thinking.'

'Heather, I'm not the enemy.'

'No, sorry, you're right. I didn't mean to—'

'It doesn't matter.'

Only I can see it does.

A few seconds pass. I ready myself to approach the main reason I'm here. 'Daniel, do you remember Lexie Gilmore?'

'Yeah. Why?'

'A friend mentioned her recently, and I read a news article about her a while back. It got me thinking about whether or not her disappearance could be connected to Jim Handcock.'

He looks at me as if he's considering the idea, as if, perhaps, the same thought has crossed his mind too. 'There was a woman who used to work with me,' he says. 'Her daughter got a summer job with the Handcocks, helping around the house. Only, at times, Alice could be erratic, shouting her mouth off. She made a remark once to the woman about keeping an eye on her daughter. Something about how her husband could devour young girls the same way a shark devours fish. She took the warning seriously and pulled her daughter out of there.'

'Then you agree. You think Jim Handcock could have been involved.'

He shrugs his shoulders. 'Who knows?'

'I've been remembering things,' I say, looking around the bar again, 'things from before my mother was killed, and other things from directly afterwards.'

I turn back to face him. He seems on edge. 'Did you ever see a miniature silver elephant at our house?' I ask, curious now as to how much he remembers.

He shakes his head.

'It belonged to my mother, and she had other stuff too, things I thought Lorrie must have gotten rid of.'

'What's so important about the elephant?'

'I don't know, but every time I remember it now, I see it buried in soil.'

The new pianist plays 'Mack the Knife'.

Daniel fiddles with his drink.

'What is it?' I ask.

'Nothing.'

'It can't be nothing. You remember it, don't you?'

'No.' He shakes his head again, perhaps a little too hard.

'Are you still taking your medication?' I ask, suddenly concerned about him.

'You don't have to worry about me.' His voice is defensive.

I back off, finishing my Coke in one gulp. I place the empty glass on the table, centring it perfectly on the beer mat, knowing he would prefer it that way.

'Photographs are a kind of death,' he says, staring at my glass. 'They're always about something that's already happened.'

'I guess,' I reply, wondering where this is going.

'That's why they're so important, because of their accuracy.'

I think about the autopsy photographs of young Jacob Rotterdam, how emotive they are.

'I have lots of photographs of you, Heather.'

'Daniel, I'm not that young girl anymore.'

'Maybe not, but a long time ago you *were* that girl.'

The pianist stops playing. The gap in the music feels like a vacuum. I study Daniel, noticing a slight movement in his facial muscles, his body posture telling me he's on edge. At law school, I learned how to recognise a witness under pressure, lines deepening on their foreheads, a slight rise of their shoulders, unnecessary hand movements, not making eye contact. Daniel is doing all of these things, repositioning his beer glass, now half-empty. His mind is churning something over. I remind myself that he's working for Finlay now. Irrespective of our past, I need to be careful.

'Finlay was asking questions about you,' he says, 'about your time at Harvard.'

'Why?'

'He's trying to connect the dots from your mother's death to the time you worked in the DA's office as a prosecutor.'

I look at him, confused. 'I don't get it.'

'He thinks your defence of Abby Jones is a sort of crusade, misplaced sympathy that, if he gets lucky, might reveal weakness.'

'There's nothing to find there,' I say, my mind flipping again, remembering arriving at Harvard and how, surrounded by books, like the ones in my grandfather's library, somehow I came back to life. How I loved arguing over case files with fellow students, fooling myself into thinking I was exactly like them, fresh, ambitious, keen to quantify the law with all its reasoning and foibles, debating implementation and interpretation, and how certain actions were at odds with the spirit of a law, how legal loopholes could uphold something askew with the original ideal. Now I wonder how much of it, deep down, was about being the daughter of a murder victim, with the crime never solved.

Daniel is still talking. 'When Finlay asked me to come on board, at first I was flattered, but it also meant I could get closer to you.'

'Daniel, don't. What we had is in the past, a childhood thing.'

He looks hurt again.

'It doesn't mean I don't care about you. I do. As a friend. A good friend. Even if I haven't shown that too much lately.'

'You never gave *us* a chance.'

'Didn't I?'

'After that night, when I pulled you out of the pond, everything changed.' He spins his glass in repetitive circular movements. 'You didn't want me in your life any more.'

'It wasn't that …'

'You couldn't bear anyone witnessing your weakness, not even me.'

'Did you tell Finlay?' I ask, suddenly uneasy. 'Did you?'

'Of course not!' he shoots back, but when we part company, I wonder if there's an element of *not yet* in his words.

# 26
# ELIZABETH

After leaving Skating Pond and arriving home, I couldn't shift the notion that something really bad was about to happen. I was frightened, mainly because I was unsure just how much harm the person watching us was capable of. They had kept their distance, but they must have followed us, which also means they've crossed a line. Later, when Heather fell asleep, I checked the house again, to see if anything else had gone missing.

At first I told myself I was overreacting, but then something caught my eye. I had left a pair of earrings on the dressing-table. They were a present from Charlie. One was gone. I looked everywhere in the room but I couldn't find it, becoming more convinced than before that someone had been in the house.

I thought long and hard about that day shortly after I came home from hospital with Mia. At the time, no one realised she was so ill. It was only after her death that they diagnosed septicaemia, a severe blood infection, capable of causing tissue damage, organ failure and death. She had looked such a healthy baby, full of life. Afterwards that was one of the hardest things to accept, that there had been no warning that anything was wrong.

It's impossible to understand the loss of a child unless you have lived through it, or to grasp how every day of your life, from that point on, you will keep imagining they are still alive, growing up as other children do. When you finally admit to yourself that none of these things is ever going to happen, that you will never hold them in your arms or be able to give them a mother's love, your heart fills with that horrible wretchedness again, the kind that never stays away for long.

That day, not long out of hospital, I was outside hanging laundry on the line. Now, I imagine Mia's clothes fluttering wildly in the breeze. I had the sense that something was wrong, and as the wind gained strength, it was as if even the rustling trees knew something bad was about to come a-calling.

A shiver runs down my spine as I think about it. The same way it did that day as, suddenly, I panicked about the baby. I started walking fast towards the house, carrying the empty laundry basket. When I reached the back door, and I saw their car, my walk turned into a run, imagining them alone with Mia, not knowing what they would do, or how far they would go to get what they wanted.

# 27
# HEATHER

Sunday evening, after leaving Daniel, driving back from Corham to my apartment, I notice the silver Honda Accord behind me. It tails me past the outskirts of town, out onto the highway. Lucas had followed me too, probably wondering when to make his next move, but now Lucas is dead. I put my foot on the accelerator, and soon the car turns off in another direction. I tell myself it's nothing, putting it out of my mind, but once I reach home, I decide to get rid of that damn doll.

The moment I open the front door, I sense something isn't right, and as I walk into the bedroom, to pull it out of the trash basket, in a way, I'm not surprised to find that it's already gone. Did the person who left it take it away again? I think about phoning Alex, then decide against it. I can't be ringing her every time I get spooked.

I stare at the basket again. Alex said that, under stress, the mind can do all sorts of things. Could I have already gotten rid of it, and forgotten?

I spend the night tossing and turning in the bed.

The following morning, I awake to even more headlines about Abby.

Inside the Mind of the Nanny

Nanny Obsessed

Disturbed and Rejected

Did She Kill for Love?

Later, when I arrive at Suffolk courthouse, Robin and Mark are already waiting for me.

'What are we going to do about the new headlines?' Mark asks.

'There isn't a lot we can do,' I say, irritated. 'Jurors go home. It won't matter a damn that this morning, and every other morning, they will be asked if they heard, read or saw anything pertaining to the trial, and if they did, if they formed any opinion as a result. An affirmative answer would get them tossed.'

'The rules are clear,' says Robin. 'They will be reminded at the end of the trial day, too, instructed not to read or watch the news, or discuss the trial with anyone, not even each other, and to keep deliberations strictly for the jury room. But with headlines like this morning's, if only one of them, even accidentally, reads something they shouldn't, who knows what damage it will do?'

'Which is why we need to remain focused on defending Abby. Let's agree to meet later today and examine everything we have on the Rotterdams, both Vivienne and Morgan. If Finlay's going to keep playing this out in the media, we need counterpunches.'

'I've been pushing the in-house investigators,' says Mark.

'Good, but let's push them some more.'

\*

This morning in the courtroom, there's an additional air of excitement because Boris Wesley, the chief medical examiner and the first witness, is about to be called. There is a sense that, after all this time, all the newspaper articles, all the build-up, the trial is finally going to begin.

I look around the room. Most of the faces are earnest. Others, especially members of the media, don't bother shielding their eagerness. Jim and Alice are both staring at me, as if to say, *You have a job to do, now do it.* I look across at Vivienne and Morgan too. No matter what dirt the in-house investigators dig up, they have still lost a child. They are victims here too. Abby is blank-faced, as if she isn't interested. Only she is. She's just doing a good job of hiding it.

All rise as Judge Kendell enters the room. Finlay calls his first witness. Dr Boris Wesley sits, ready to testify. Finlay stands in front of him with a solemn expression.

'Dr Wesley, can you explain to the jury what an autopsy is? Keep it simple and straightforward. We're not all medical experts here.'

'Certainly.' Wesley clears his throat. 'An autopsy is a detailed examination of a deceased body.'

Some of the jurors squirm, no doubt imagining young Jacob being examined.

I study Wesley, his dark hair and bushy eyebrows at odds with his small face and narrow nose. He reminds me of a satisfied rat, one with a very full belly.

'And what does the process consist of?'

'It begins as an external examination, where you examine the skin for the presence, or absence, of injuries, and any other significant findings.'

'After that?'

'The internal examination follows, with a full investigation of the organs. By that I mean from the brain downwards. The skeleton of the deceased is also examined.'

I don't look at the jury.

'And the purpose?' Finlay asks.

'Purpose?' Wesley looks at him, surprised, although I know they've rehearsed this point by point.

'Yes. What is the ultimate purpose of these examinations?'

Again, he clears his throat. 'Every aspect of the process, both the external and internal examination, serves to determine the cause of death.'

'What about trauma to the body? Would that be part of it?'

'Of course.' He sounds almost offended by the question. 'We look at all the medical factors involved, including the determination of trauma or lack of it. Disease is another important aspect. Finding and establishing indicators of this can be crucial to the overall results.'

'I see.' Finlay looks at the jury for the first time. 'And you would carry out these investigations using detailed forensic procedures?'

'Yes.'

'Consisting of several consecutive steps?'

'Yes.'

'Did you examine the brain of Jacob Rotterdam during these steps?'

Some of the jurors are obviously uncomfortable.

'It was examined, yes, but not my me.'

'No?' Finlay sounds surprised, although he isn't. It is more of his theatrics. 'Why not, Dr Wesley?'

'When I noticed the soft condition of the brain, I realised it had potential neuropathological relevance, so I made the decision to order a team of specialists to fix it in formalin.'

'Apologies, Dr Wesley, can you explain for lay people like me, and the jury, what you mean by formalin?'

'During an autopsy, formaldehyde solutions are used to fix human tissue and organs.'

'A preservative, if you like?'

'Yes.'

'Who was on the team?'

'Dr Douglas Feign, Dr Hilary Farrell and Dr Patricia Moore. Dr Feign was the lead neuropathologist.'

'And all three are attached to Boston Medical Center?'

'Yes, but they work in other areas of medicine too.'

'Which areas might they be?'

'It varies, but they have extensive medical experience.'

'Experts we can trust?'

'Certainly.'

'People at the forefront of medical analysis?'

'Yes.'

'I assume, Dr Wesley, that working at Boston Medical Center, they are also considered authoritative for the purposes of determining the medical truth in a case.'

'Certainly.'

'And as the chief medical examiner, you consider the results of the autopsy in this case to be beyond reproach?'

'Absolutely. Medicine isn't about uncertainty. It is about taking a group of hard facts and arriving at a solid conclusion.'

'And in the case of Jacob Rotterdam, what was the medical conclusion, based on the results of the autopsy?'

'The triad of symptoms presented, along with the various bone fractures, are all consistent with physical abuse, or in plain language, Shaken Baby Syndrome.'

'Thank you, Dr Wesley. That will be all for now.'

Finlay has kept it short. He will question his witness again, when I finish.

I approach the witness. He looks calm and relaxed, a seasoned professional who likes to answer direct questions with direct answers, which I aim to use in my favour.

'Dr Wesley, thank you for your concise introduction to the procedure of autopsy.'

He nods.

'I take it that, as chief medical examiner at Boston Medical Center you oversee all procedures, whether directly carried out by you or by others. By oversee, I mean you are responsible for them.'

'Yes.'

'You are therefore ultimately responsible for all the decisions surrounding the diagnosis?'

'Based on the medical evidence presented, yes.'

'You are the one in charge? Yes or no.'

'Yes. I am the one in charge.'

'Including of the team?'

'Yes.'

'And responsible for their decisions?'

'Yes.'

'How many medical cases of abuse have you been involved with?'

'Numerous.'

'Can you be more exact?'

'Since my time at Boston Medical Center, somewhere between seventy and eighty.'

'And before that? In your previous positions as a medical specialist elsewhere?'

'Over a similar period, I would say the numbers would be consistent. Sadly, abuse isn't confined to geographical areas.' He looks towards the jury.

'That is a high number of cases.'

'I work in busy hospitals.'

'But you've been involved with more than most?'

'I can't categorically say that but, yes, I have plenty of experience.'

'Are fractures a commonality within them?'

'They are one of any number of factors.'

'And your team found fractures in Jacob's upper arms?'

'Yes.'

'Which in your estimation were the result of abuse?'

'Yes.'

'In your description of an autopsy earlier, you described it as a method to ascertain the cause of death.'

'That is correct.'

'The cause is the same as the means?'

'Generally, yes.'

I pause for a couple of seconds, aware silence can be just as intimidating as a difficult question. I look at the jury, then ask, 'Is it logical to assume, based on your experience and authority, that while carrying out an autopsy you form an opinion on the cause of death?'

'Yes.'

'You work out the *how*?'

'As far as is medically possible, yes.'

'Is it ever your role to determine the *who*?'

'Sometimes there is evidence that opens a window towards identifying the *who*.'

'What kind of evidence?'

'DNA analysis, finger markings on the body, blood traces. Any or all of these can identify an individual assailant or abuser.'

'And was there any in this case?'

'Yes, there was.'

'Can you expand?'

'Certainly. There were various DNA samples found.'

'These were identified?'

'For the most part, yes. Several samples were linked to a variety of individuals.'

'Can you tell us who these people were?'

'Hair follicles and sweat marks found on the deceased matched the DNA components of Abby Jones.'

'Anyone else?'

'Yes.'

'Go on.'

He fiddles at his cuffs. 'Morgan and Vivienne Rotterdam.'

'Did you find any DNA that isn't identifiable at this time?'

'Yes, but there could be any number of reasons for that.'

'Thank you, Dr Wesley. The defence has no further questions.'

It doesn't take Finlay long to be back on his feet.

'Dr Wesley, just to clarify here. The DNA comparisons included those of Abby Jones?'

'Yes, they did.'

'And the injuries were consistent with abuse?'

'Yes. That is correct.'

'And the lethal damage done to Jacob Rotterdam prior to his death, in your opinion, required sustained shaking?'

'That is also correct.'

'The DNA matches found would be consistent with all three parties having spent time with the infant?'

'Correct.'

'In your medical opinion, Dr Wesley, based on the extensive data compiled, how relevant is the time line in this case?'

'Extremely.'

'Please expand.'

'The sustained shaking, the trigger for the haemorrhaging, took place within hours of the infant's failing condition.'

'And at that time he was in the care of Abby Jones?'

'Yes. I believe that is correct. I have no reason to doubt it.'

'And Abby Jones herself has confirmed this?'

'I think so, but my area is medical expertise, nothing more. I leave the policing to the police.'

'And rightly so, but to be absolutely sure, for the benefit of the jury, Abby Jones's DNA was found during the autopsy?'

'Yes.'

'The injuries to the infant happened within a timeframe, in your opinion, close in proximity to his admission to the hospital, and his ultimate death?'

'Objection, Your Honour.' I am on my feet. 'Counsel is deliberately putting words into the witness's mouth.'

'Overruled. Carry on, Mr Clarke.'

'Is it your medical opinion, Dr Wesley, as the lead medical examiner at Boston Medical Center, that the fatal injuries which caused the death of Jacob Rotterdam happened within the window of the preceding hours?'

'Yes.'

'And the only person with matching DNA who would fit within that timeframe was Abby Jones?'

'Yes, to the best of my knowledge.'

'Is there anything else you would like to add?' Finlay asks, raising his eyebrows.

He wants Boris Wesley to say something else, something, I assume, they have also practised.

'There is one other thing.'

'Go on.'

'The force necessary to sustain the damage to the brain was both prolonged and violent.'

There is an audible gasp from almost everyone in the room. I close my eyes, visualising what everyone else in the courtroom is imagining.

'That will be all,' Finlay concludes. He has a traumatised look on his face, as if he, too, is taken aback. It's all a game for him. One he's playing well.

Kendell looks in my direction. 'Would you like to cross-examine the witness a second time?'

'I would, thank you, Your Honour.'

I walk towards the witness. I hadn't planned to introduce the next line of questioning so soon, but I don't have any choice.

'Dr Wesley, isn't it a fact that medical opinion is divided on the triad of symptoms as proof of abuse?'

'The triad of symptoms is clear but, yes, some hold different opinions on them.'

'And there has been a series of medical papers since the seventies that clearly offer explanations other than abuse for these symptoms?'

'Objection, Your Honour.' Finlay is back on his feet, looking as if someone has taken away his favourite toy. 'Counsel is deviating from the grounds for SBS, the standards applied to it and its analysis within accepted medical practice. Surely we are not in the business of speculating here.'

'Overruled. I would like to hear what Dr Wesley has to say. Keep it brief, Ms Baxter. Dr Wesley, you may answer the question.'

'Yes, there has been a series of medical papers on the subject, in the same way there has been a series of papers on any number of issues, but the facts remain, these triads of symptoms present themselves in situations of abuse.'

'In your opinion.'

'Yes, in my opinion, and in the opinions of a series of medical experts the length and breadth of this country whom I respect and admire.'

'Again, in your opinion.'

'Yes.'

'Do you agree, Dr Wesley, that despite your own beliefs, a great many other respected medical experts disagree with you?'

'Yes, I do.'

'Thank you, Dr Wesley. I have no further questions.'

# 28
# HEATHER

As I drive to the office for the late meeting with Robin and Mark, I don't bother turning on the radio. I need the silence to realign my thoughts. My coming into this trial so late was always going to be a disadvantage but, right now, we need something solid, and fast. Let's hope Mark's latest information on the Rotterdams proves useful, but all of it feels like catch-up, rather than a controlled forward-thinking strategy. I remember Alice's words about Abby's previous defence attorney, him being an addict but still functioning at the top of his game. If the stakes weren't so high, it would almost be laughable.

I think about Finlay's words to Daniel, too, saying I was on some kind of crusade. It has touched a nerve, but then again, that's exactly what Finlay wants. But is he right? Am I on a crusade? How much of this has been about the similarities between me and Abby, both navigating the world without a mother, fired into awful situations too young and inexperienced to deal with them, and me wanting to save her because, all those years ago, I couldn't save the person I loved most in the world, my mother?

Waiting for Robin and Mark to arrive, I scan more newspaper reports from around the time of my mother's killing. Almost by accident I come across an article, which at first doesn't look important, but something about it pulls me in. It's another piece from the *Patriot Eagle*, covering the carnival I went to with my mother and Daniel all those years before. There are lots of pictures of people from town, but the main image is of Jim and Alice Handcock. They are smiling for the camera as part of the town's elite. I am about to move on when I see my mother's grainy face in the photograph. She stands in the crowd behind them, holding my hand. Daniel is there, too, with his new camera around his neck. It feels strange to see her, as if she is a ghost from another time. I wish myself back to that moment. Was she thinking about her past affair with Jim Handcock? Did she see herself as less worthy, as he smiled for the camera, the most important man in town?

I keep staring at the image and, all of a sudden, I can see myself in her. In the past, others have commented on our similarities, but as I study my mother from over two decades earlier, for the first time I realise how strong the resemblance is. She wouldn't have stood a chance in Corham, disowned by her parents, ostracised, and with very little money after marrying my father, especially in a town run by the Handcocks, where their power made her, and others, an easy target.

Alex said memory loss and dissociation are the means by which the mind protects you in time of trauma. If I'm remembering things now, is my brain telling me it's the right time to find out more?

I replay an earlier message from Alex, telling me the police will soon want to talk to my father. According to Alex, when he first arrived back in Corham he booked into a small lodging house, but soon checked out again. That he didn't contact me doesn't surprise me. He doesn't behave like other fathers. Perhaps, after the lodging house, he decided to sleep at our old house instead, or even to sleep rough. He's done both before.

A guy called Blake Lynam is heading up the investigation. I wonder if he knows my father was supposed to meet Lucas. Even if my father had nothing to do with the killing, I know I should tell them. As I'm thinking this, another idea jumps into my head. It feels odd that I didn't consider it before. What if, after all this time, Lucas wanted to tell my father *who* killed my mother? What if he knew?

Once the thought takes hold, it won't go away. Perhaps, at the start, Lucas didn't have the answer, but then, at some point, he discovered something. It might explain why he came back to Corham. Is that why he ended up dead? He had finally worked out who had done it so they had to kill him too?

# 29
# VIVIENNE

Vivienne is drinking heavily. She no longer cares about the argument she had with Morgan, or that he has gone out yet again. She doesn't care that she's being weak, behaving like her husband. She started with a chilled bottle of Chardonnay, emptying it in half an hour, and followed it with a heavy Rioja, one of Morgan's favourites, in celebration of her pointless life.

Laughing aloud, she bumps into a doorframe, and some of the wine spills onto the carpet, large drops, then smaller ones, like tiny tears. Negotiating the stairs is difficult, but eventually she makes it to the top, knowing exactly where she's going, down the hallway towards her home-office and her private space. Morgan doesn't have a key to this room. It is her sanctuary.

'Fuck him,' she roars into an empty house.

The lock is trickier than normal, so she places the half-empty glass on the floor. It tips over, creating a large bloodlike stain. She watches it spread, as if it's happening in slow motion. She doesn't care, not any more. She turns the key. The door swings open.

More than anywhere else in the house, this room is where she belongs. There are items from the art gallery, sample brochures, letters, books, and a couple of large canvases presented to her as gifts. There are photographs, too, some from art shows of the past, happier times, but it is the two identical boxes on the large shelves that she is most interested in, one with 'Jacob' on the front, the other labelled 'Annabel'.

It's good to have them side by side. Two babies: her son and her sister. Apart from her memories, the boxes are all that remain of them.

Today she can't bring herself to open Jacob's box. If she did, she would take those sleeping pills and end it all. The tears well up in her eyes again. She tries to block out thoughts of her beautiful son. Instead, she reaches for the box covered with a layer of dust.

She can't remember where she left her wine. She had it a few seconds ago. She thinks about going downstairs to get some more, then decides against it, lifting the lid off the box. It is filled to the brim. She sways a little, but soon steadies herself, moving her hands across the contents, feeling the softness of baby clothes. Some of the dresses have little bows. She imagines them smelling of baby powder. There are others with teddy bears and clowns, and one has a teddy with a bunch of red balloons. Another with a white stork. She lifts a powder-pink dress. Something about it doesn't look right. She spreads it out, fixing the white ribbon laced through the neckline. No matter how hard she tries, she can't get it to look right. Her head is fuzzy, but she keeps on trying. She wants to cry again. Her sister hardly had a chance to wear any of these clothes. She imagines Annabel, small and soft and gurgling. She imagines Jacob too, as she lies down on the floor, her sister's dress held tight to her heart, the dress of another dead child.

# 30
# HEATHER

When Mark and Robin arrive, we concentrate initially on Boris Wesley's earlier testimony, and whether or not our first strike, of casting medical doubt, made any headway with the jury.

'I think we have to accept,' says Robin, 'that establishing doubt on the medical evidence is going to be a prolonged and repetitive process, with most of the traction happening once we present the case for the defence and call one medical expert after another.'

'I agree,' I say, turning to Mark. 'Let's move forward. What new intel do you have, and how does it connect to what we already know?'

He flips open the large clipboard in the corner. 'Okay,' he says. 'Let's start with what we know.' He writes Vivienne and Morgan's names at the top of a blank sheet, adding terms we've used before, like married, professionals, well-educated, wealthy, and bereaved.

'Right,' he says. 'Shortly after the birth of Jacob, according to close friends, Vivienne became overwhelmed.' He adds the word 'overwhelmed' to the listing under Vivienne's name.

'The Handcocks alluded to something similar,' I say, 'during our first meeting.' I flip through my handwritten notes. 'Morgan believed Vivienne needed help with the baby.'

'But, ultimately, Abby and Vivienne's relationship became strained,' Robin adds.

'True,' says Mark, 'and we already know that Morgan and Vivienne, unlike Abby, had normal, and privileged, childhoods.'

I stare at the chart for a second, wondering if we might have missed something in their earlier joint history. 'Before we get into the new information, Robin, let's go over again how they met as undergraduate students and formed their relationship.'

Mark adds 'privileged childhood' and 'long-term relationship' under both their names.

'It wasn't until the spring of 1980,' says Robin, 'that they became romantically involved, to the surprise of many.'

'Because Morgan was more sociable,' Mark puts in, 'and well known for his lack of commitment, particularly towards women.'

'Not unusual in a young student,' I reply.

'But he continued to be unfaithful after they were married,' adds Mark, 'meaning this was a part of his lifestyle he wasn't prepared to let go.'

'Even after Jacob was born,' I reaffirm.

'And despite Vivienne's conservative upbringing,' Robin walks towards the wipe board, 'she appeared willing to ignore that side of his life.'

'As I said before, maybe she saw something in him others didn't,' I say. 'Anything else, before we get to the new stuff?'

Both shake their heads.

'Okay, Mark,' I say. 'Let's hear it.'

'It seems Morgan likes to play rough.'

'How rough?'

'We have anecdotal evidence of physical violence, consistent with sexual dominance.'

'Anything we can use?'

'According to our intel, none of the women want to go on the record.'

'What does this tell us about his relationship with Vivienne?' I quiz.

'That she's prepared to accept the sleazy side of her husband's life,' replies Robin, 'in exchange for getting what she wants in other areas. Socially, they're perfectly matched.'

'Is that enough?' I ask.

'It can be,' she replies.

I look again at the listings of Vivienne and Morgan on the board. I remember Lucas's words about my mother guarding her secrets well.

'I think there has to be something more,' I say, 'beneath the exterior Vivienne is presenting in court, something else lurking.'

'What makes you so sure?' Robin asks.

'Because Finlay is micromanaging the two of them.'

'He might already be aware of Morgan's reputation,' adds Mark, 'and wants to avoid either of their masks slipping.'

'What if there is another angle?'

They stare at me. I walk towards the board. 'I don't think that story about Abby and Morgan breaking in the media came from Finlay, even if he revelled in it.'

'Then who broke it?' Robin queries. 'Ashley?'

'If it was Ashley,' I say, 'chances are we would have had a personal exclusive by now, which means someone else is meddling.'

I write a question mark on the board under both Morgan and Vivienne's names. 'Mark, where are we on Vivienne's medical history?'

'Nothing much new.'

'We need to find something. As of now, the media love her, which is exactly where Finlay wants them to be.'

I am staring at the words 'privileged childhood' on the board. 'Something has always bugged me about the Handcocks and Rotterdams' relationship,' I say.

'What?' asks Robin.

'I'm not seeing an obvious connection.' I regurgitate Alex's words about Jim Handcock's shady dealings. 'What if there's another connection between them, other than friendship? Something shady or illegal? What if either Morgan or Vivienne was under financial strain, or something else, something that might cause them to crack?'

'How will that help us?' asks Robin.

'It may not, but so far, when the jury looks at Abby, taking into account her young age, her history in foster care and lack of experience, compared to Morgan and Vivienne, whether we like it or not, she is the one the jury is most likely to see as the potential abuser. If we can pull the Rotterdams down from the pedestal Finlay and everyone else has them on, other doubts may creep in.'

'If there is something shady going on, it could be hard to pin down,' adds Mark, 'but not impossible.'

'Let's look for anything that links the two families. Check out Morgan's business dealings, investments, private funds, offshore accounts, anything that might give us a reason to look deeper.'

\*

The following day, Finlay calls his second medical expert from Boston Medical Center. It is almost a repeat of the day before with Boris Wesley. The more Finlay repeats the same thing, the more he hopes the jury will believe his version of events. I need to ensure I do the very opposite.

After another long trial day, stuck in bumper-to-bumper traffic heading home, with several lines of cars in front of me, a car horn honks impatiently in the distance. The weather is cooling. Most of the leaves have fallen from the trees now. When I finally reach the Charles River, I roll down the window. The water smells salty and earthy. A fresh breeze wafts in an aroma of grilled meat and garlic from a restaurant close by. Ahead, I see yet another construction site, billowing out a cloud of dust. As I get closer to it, the noise of the machinery is louder. I close the window. College students on their bicycles are weaving in and out of the congestion. I think about Lexie Gilmore again, imagining her cycling down Main Street. I remember how young she looked, just like Abby. I see the wheels of her bike turning over and over, wondering for the umpteenth time what happened to her.

Once I get out of the centre of the city, things speed up, but with every second I get closer to home, exhaustion is hitting me. I haven't slept properly in days. Parking the car, I walk towards the front door of the apartment block on autopilot. I spot Abel, going in the opposite direction, ready to head out.

'You have a visitor,' he says.

'What? Who?' I stare at him, wondering what he's talking about.

'Security let your dad in. He said you were expecting him.'

Before I have a chance to say anything more, Abel is gone.

Seconds later, inside the apartment block, I see the light glowing from underneath my door. I feel instantly annoyed. He's only here because he's in trouble, because he wants something. Opening the door, I hear humming from the kitchen. I hate the way he thinks he can come into my life without any explanation.

I go into the kitchen. He's standing at the refrigerator peering inside. He doesn't even turn. 'Where do you keep your eggs?'

Anger stops me answering him. Instead I open a cupboard and fire a small tray of eggs onto the counter.

'Are you hungry?' he asks.

'Why are you here? And don't bullshit me.' I pull out a kitchen chair.

'Can't a father visit his daughter?' He sounds surprised.

'Normal fathers can.'

'I see,' he says, as if that covers everything.

'You heard about Lucas?' I ask.

'Yes.'

'Did you kill him?'

He looks at me aghast. 'Of course not.'

'Other people might disagree.'

'I don't care about other people.'

'No, I'm sure you don't. You never did.'

He cracks three eggs into a bowl, stirring them briskly with a fork, then adding salt. He is wearing a pair of black jeans and a black polo top. His shoes are narrow, pointed and shiny, as if they're brand new. I visualise him in all his reincarnations, the biker phase, the slick businessman, the outdoor orienteer, the angry husband, the drunk, the man who couldn't be a father, not a proper one.

'It is considered illegal to gain entry to someone's home without permission,' I say, my voice still enraged.

The whisked eggs hit the empty pan on the stove, covering the bottom, making a sizzling sound. He adds pepper to the mix.

'Why did you come back?' I ask.

'I needed to sign some legal papers. There was a messy clause in Lorrie's will that meant I might have some future claim on your inheritance. The lawyer thought, considering everything, I would be happy to relinquish any rights.'

'And did you?'

'Of course.' He puts the cooked eggs on a plate and sits down, fork in hand, as if all of this is perfectly normal.

'Where are you sleeping?'

'I stayed at our old place last night,' he says, adding more salt, 'but it was horrible.'

'Lucas said he was going to meet you.'

He gives me a blank stare but keeps his silence.

'Did you meet him?'

'No.'

'Why should I believe you?'

'Believe what you want.'

He fills a glass with water from the tap – familiar. I wait while he sits down again, watching him eat the same way he did when I was younger, when at times I was frightened of his temper, the seething anger caused by his disappointment in himself. Was *he* partly why I shut myself off from the world, why I dissociated, as Alex called it? Mostly, as I watch him clear his plate, I want to ask him the biggest question of all. Why he left my mother and me when we needed him most.

'You've done well for yourself, Heather.'

'I work hard.'

'I don't doubt it. You always did. And having Lorrie's money to pay for your education was a godsend.'

'I didn't want her money.'

'But you took it,' he adds, raising his fork.

'You left me, remember. I was ten years old. I didn't have much choice.'

'I know.'

Is that regret in his voice?

A silence hovers.

'Can I stay,' he finally asks, 'just for tonight?'

'I'm not like you.' I stand up, kicking the chair from the table. 'I don't turn my back on family.'

'You're right. You're not like me. You're exactly like her. You're strong, and so was she.'

Is he making excuses for himself? Trying to imply that he was the weak one, the one needing help?

'You weren't even with us the day she died.'

And suddenly I'm back there, at our old house in Corham, remembering how scared I was. I could hardly breathe in that blanket box, but finally I got out and walked downstairs. I saw my mother's bloodied and broken body on the kitchen floor. My ten-year-old self went into shock but I knew I needed to do something important. I left the kitchen. I went upstairs. The door to the baby's room was ajar. I pushed it, opening it some more. I walked towards the crib. I heard the imaginary lullaby playing from the mobile. I looked around the room, making sure no one was watching me. My mother had secrets. I lay on the floor, stretched my arms underneath the crib and, lowering my head, I crawled further in, knowing the thing I was looking for was hidden in the furthest corner.

# 31
# HEATHER

I make up a bed for my father in the guest room. He says he'll be gone first thing tomorrow. I don't want to stay in the same place as him. Neither can I tell him to leave. Instead I grab an overnight bag with a set of clothes for the morning, feeling more and more like a fugitive running from my own life.

When I arrive at Alex's house, she doesn't push me for answers. I tell her about my father's visit and ask if I can stay. I don't mention the latest piece of memory, the one where I climbed under the crib because I knew my mother had hidden something underneath it.

'Did you find out anything more about Lexie Gilmore?' I ask.

'I'm still digging, but there's something I wanted to tell you ...' She stalls.

'What?'

'I've managed to get more information on the García murder.'

I sense this isn't going to be something I want to hear.

'Blake Lynam and I have history.'

I don't like the tentative look on her face.

'Spit it out, Alex.'

'There isn't any good way of saying this. They're going to pull your father in.'

'But it's only days since—'

'Well, shit happens fast.'

'What do they have on him?'

'They made a DNA match from a pair of boots found near your old home. They were covered up, out back.'

'Why did they look there?'

'A tip-off.'

I think about my father's shiny new shoes.

'There were leaf particles found in the soles of the boots from a birch tree. It turns out birch trees have their own special DNA.' All of this is making her uncomfortable, but she is now in information mode. 'The particles were a perfect match for one of the trees near the burial site, and they know the boots belonged to your father.'

'How?'

'They're a particular type from out of state. They had markings, and he was seen wearing them.'

'It doesn't mean he did it. It may place him at the crime scene but—'

'It puts him in the wrong place at the wrong time.'

I think about my opening address at the start of Abby's trial, how being in the wrong place at the wrong time doesn't make you guilty.

'Anything else?'

'Motive.'

'Revenge?'

'It's the oldest reason in the book.'

'There's more, isn't there?'

'They've linked him to the murder weapon too.'

'Shit.' I close my eyes.

She keeps talking. 'All firearms have a serial number, and sometimes, if the cops get lucky, it will tell them where and when a calibre and design were registered. They are sequential. That way, when a firearm is sold, it can be traced back, and this time they've traced it back to your father.'

'They have the gun?'

'No, but they have the bullets fired from it, and they have been forensically identified.'

'Against what?'

'The same bullet type was used in a previous crime.'

Less than an hour earlier, my father was scrambling eggs, adding pepper to the mix. He couldn't have looked less like a killer.

'Turns out, Heather, after your mother was killed, your father went AWOL for a while.'

'What?'

'He had an argument with someone and fired a couple of shots in warning. That's how they matched the bullets.'

'Who?'

'Samuel Lawson.'

'My uncle?'

'The records stayed on the database.'

'When was the gun purchased?'

She stalls again.

'When, Alex? Tell me fucking when.'

'The year your momma was killed.'

'Before or after?' I wait for her reply.

'Before.'

'Shit,' I say again, trying to remember if I ever saw a gun in the house.

'They're out looking for him right now.'

'I need to warn him.' I reach for my cell phone. He answers on the first ring.

'The police want to talk to you,' I say, sounding like a little girl again, protecting him without fully knowing why.

'It's okay,' he says, his voice calm. 'They're already here. Just as well you didn't come home tonight. It might have implicated you. Neither of us would want that.'

Is he being sincere? Is this another of his acts? He hangs up before I can ask him anything more.

'They're already there,' I tell Alex, my mind jumping in different directions. 'He wouldn't be stupid enough to kill Lucas, would he?'

'That depends,' she says, 'on whether or not, despite not being the best of husbands, he still believes Lucas killed your mother.'

'To make amends for his own sins?'

'He wasn't there to protect her, Heather. Guilt has a habit of eating away at people.'

'Not being good enough can do that too.'

'What do you mean?'

'I don't think my father ever felt he was. It was partly why he kept running away,' I say. 'Because he felt such a failure.'

And right now, I'm wondering, by not protecting her, if I am guilty of that too.

# 32
# ELIZABETH

*Before they took Mia's body away, I laid her on the mattress of the crib. I locked the door to the baby's room. I didn't want anyone else coming in. Piece by piece, I removed her clothing, all the time talking to her, kissing her soft skin. I didn't want anything separating us, not clothes, not death. I wanted it to be the two of us, safe in our tiny cocoon.*

*She looked perfect, but unbearably still, and as I cradled her, she felt so light, I worried I would drop her. I stroked her forehead, as I had done with Heather in the past, when she was deep in sleep. I told myself Mia was sleeping too, resting in my arms. For a time I needed to believe she was still alive. I needed to hold onto the joy of her life, before the inevitable sorrow.*

*I re-imagined all the things she would never get to do, the hours, days, months and years taken from her. I thought about how her hair would never grow, how I wouldn't get the chance to braid it, or dry it after a bath, or see it go lighter with the summer sun.*

*Something changed inside me the night she died, and even though afterwards they told me about the septicaemia — caused by an infection*

*I didn't know I had in pregnancy, a strain of streptococcus – and how, once it took hold of Mia, she wasn't able to fight back, that first night I believed, if I tried hard enough, I could still be with her. The more I pushed away the thoughts of all the things she would never do, the more I created a surreal existence for us both that only Mia and I could understand. It was something I clung to, when everything else was lost.*

*There are times even now when I relive that existence in the darkest crevices of my mind, knowing a part of me will never let her go, because a mother can never let go of her child.*

*Lately I have been wondering if soon my fate will be the same as Mia's, suddenly and without warning. As each day rolls into the next I become increasingly aware of the growing danger. Perhaps, like her, when I am attacked, I won't be able to fight back.*

# 33
# HEATHER

The following morning, I shouldn't care about my father being brought in for questioning, but I do, which is partly why I'm back in the city before the court reconvenes, to go for a run. I have a spare set of running gear in my locker at the office and, changing into it, I tell myself I need to remain focused and win this trial.

I mark out a three-mile stretch along the river, meeting other joggers and dog-walkers along the way. The early-morning air is crisp, with the low hum of commuters and a city coming back to life. As my feet get into a more uplifting rhythm, I can't but think about that last new slice of memory, how I crawled under Mia's crib to find my mother's box of secrets. I hear my breathing becoming heavier.

I made a promise to myself a long time ago to face things head-on, but now I realise I've failed in that regard. I never pursued a proper resolution to my mother's killing. Initially I was too young, but later, instead of questioning, I was content to blame Lucas. I took the easy way out because I didn't, or couldn't, contemplate another.

Last night I made up my mind to somehow gain access to my mother's cold-case files. I remember Alex's words, about her and Blake Lynam crossing paths before, and right now I'm wondering how close they might have been, and if I can call in a favour.

An hour later, at the courthouse, my mind is still in overdrive when Finlay spots me before I see him.

'I heard about that nasty business with your father.'

'I didn't doubt you would.'

'Lucas and you go back a long way, no?'

'You could say that.'

'I hear you harassed him in the past.'

I go to walk past him. 'That's none of your business,' I say.

'It may have been a few years back but you were like a stalker.' He emphasises the last word.

Who told him? It couldn't have been Daniel: he wouldn't have known I followed Lucas when I was at Harvard, seeing myself as some form of amateur detective. I got an unofficial warning to back off, and I did. Nothing was put on the record, so the only way Finlay could know about it was if someone from my Harvard days had told him, the same way we've been digging into the Rotterdams. I should have known he would do the same to me, even if I'm not the one on trial.

'That was a long time ago,' I say, facing him.

'I only bring it up, Heather, because I'm curious.'

'About?' My voice is sharp.

'Whether you might be involved with his death.'

'Don't be ridiculous.'

'I hear your father was in your apartment last night when they brought him in.'

'I wasn't home,' I say, overly defensive.

'No?'

'How did you find out, Finlay, about me following Lucas?'

'Because, Heather, sooner or later I plan on finding out everything about you.'

I go to push past him again, and this time I don't look back. I wait until I've placed a decent distance between us before I dial Corham police station, knowing sooner or later I'm going to have to talk to my father.

'Sheriff Blanco,' I say, 'it's Heather Baxter. I believe you have my father in custody.'

'That's right.'

'Has he been charged?'

'No, but he won't be going anywhere anytime soon. A man has been murdered, and I don't need to explain the workings of the law to your good self.'

'Has he been assigned an attorney?'

'He says he doesn't need one. He thinks everyone is out to get him, trying to pin the killing on him.'

'Are they?'

'Now, now, Heather, we have a lot of hard evidence against your daddy, and sometimes a man needs to settle old scores.'

'He waited a long time to settle *old scores*, as you call them.'

'Things can be complicated. Ever since Lucas came back to town, he set about making folk uneasy, asking questions about things he had no business looking into, dredging up the past. By opening those old wounds, he was only asking for trouble and your daddy made him pay.'

'But he's only been in town for a few days.'

'Days can be awfully long when you have murder on your mind.'

'He needs an attorney.'

'Are you going to help him out?'

'I can't.'

'Oh, that's right. I forgot. You're up in the city defending the child-killer. I imagine it takes up a lot of your time.'

'I want to see him,' I say, keeping my tone level, professional.

'That's your prerogative.'

I close off the call once we've agreed a time for me to visit. A heavy rain shower hits the courthouse windows. It rained heavily the day my mother locked herself in the bedroom with my dead sister, and it doesn't matter how long ago it was, the memory still causes the same hurt and sadness. I am halfway to the courtroom before I realise I'm crying, but I wipe the tears away, long before anyone can see them.

# 34
# VIVIENNE

Vivienne makes a point of scanning the courtroom, taking in everything from the eager, inquisitive faces of the journalists to the empty chairs where the jury will soon sit. The clock on the wall ticks away the seconds. Everything about this trial feels alien, staged.

Nobody here understands her either, not Finlay and certainly not Morgan, who didn't come home again last night. Finlay won't be happy if he gets wind of something sordid going down, especially after those headlines about Abby being obsessed with Morgan. But that's Morgan's problem, not hers.

She watches Heather Baxter, before Abby is brought in. The likes of Heather are always busy, juggling so many things at once. What does she know about being a mother? Nothing.

Morgan touches her arm. It's his signal to tell her to be careful, not to look angry. He wants her to wear the face of the grieving mother, to do exactly as Finlay dictates. He's a fine one to be giving advice when he can't keep his dick to himself. The only reason she's playing along is because not to would shine a light on something no one must ever know.

She looks at Heather again. The driven career professional. Vivienne laughs inwardly, but then, as if Heather realises Vivienne is judging her, she returns her stare. She puts on the grieving-mother façade. Heather gives nothing away.

There was a time, she thinks, when she didn't have so much hate inside her, but that was a lifetime ago, before Jacob drew his last breath.

She stares at Abby's birthmark as the bailiff indicates the girl should sit down. The mark looks different today, pulsating like a throbbing vein. She swallows hard. If the truth became known, Abby would probably walk free. Doubts would be raised about who was responsible for her son's death. That can't be allowed to happen.

Jim and Alice Handcock are in the courtroom too, stiff-backed and dressed solemnly for the occasion. They don't want any of this shit coming back on them. They care too much for their reputation, their so-called status in society. Fresh money is so vulgar.

She looks at Morgan, taking in the tension of his expression. He is looking as far away from Alice and Jim Handcock as he can.

Judge Kendell enters the room. The ritual of it all, she thinks, affords solace of sorts, as everyone else carries on this stupid charade.

# 35
# HEATHER

In the courtroom, I am still reeling after Finlay's mini-interrogation. There is the usual buzz of noise, a mix of voices all talking at once, until everyone rises for Judge Kendell.

Mark leans down to whisper in my ear, getting my attention before Kendell opens proceedings. 'I've been thinking about the Rotterdam and Handcock connection.'

'What about it?' I ask, keeping my voice low.

'Maybe you're right, and Handcock had something shady on them, or Morgan, to be precise.'

'Like?'

'Investment properties are the easiest place to launder money. Morgan has property portfolios, doesn't he?'

'Yeah, and other stuff.'

'Perhaps Handcock was giving Morgan money to hide.'

'Possibly,' I say, still keeping my voice low.

'I think Handcock knew exactly what he was doing when he put his niece in there.'

'Are you talking entrapment?' I whisper. 'Do you think he used Abby as bait?'

Judge Kendell calls for the jury to be brought in.

'Precisely. Then, if Morgan misbehaved, Handcock had something else on him to keep him in check. That's how he seems to operate. First, Handcock gets the dirt on a person. Then he uses it to get what he wants.'

Mark's theory is more than a little presumptuous, but I wouldn't put it past Jim Handcock all the same. I sit in silence as Finlay calls his next witness. I think about our earlier conversation, knowing Finlay is capable of almost anything. He is wearing another of his sombre faces, as if troubled by the questioning he is about to instigate, warning the jury, visually, that this is yet another nasty insight into the life of my client, Abby Jones.

'Dr Perrotta, can you tell the court why Abby was referred to you in 2011?'

'Yes, indeed. She was eleven at the time. She had been placed in several foster homes by then, but had recently spent time with the French family, Stephen and Jillian.'

'Was there anything unusual about her time with them?'

'Yes. While she was in their care, question marks arose.'

Perrotta pushes his glasses further up the bridge of his nose. 'Child Protection Services had concerns about Stephen French, and alleged child abuse.'

'Were formal charges made by CPS?'

'Eventually, but at the time my consultations with Abby were purely exploratory.'

I hold my breath waiting for this bombshell to explode. I look across at Abby. She's nervous.

Finlay opens the front buttons of his jacket. 'Dr Perrotta, at the time of your first consultation with Abby, she was going to be assigned new foster parents. Is that correct?'

'Yes.'

'Because the rumours of sexual abuse needed to be investigated.'

'That is my understanding.'

'I see.' Finlay walks closer to the jury. 'And how would you describe Abby's state of mind?'

'Troubled, withdrawn, anxious.'

'Behavioural emotions to be expected, considering the circumstances?'

'Yes.'

'Were there any other worrying factors around Abby's behaviour?'

Perrotta hesitates. Everyone in the courtroom waits.

'Take your time, Dr Perrotta.'

The doctor clears his throat. 'I spent many hours with Abby. For a long time, our sessions didn't prove particularly helpful. I felt she was holding something back.' He looks at the jury, before turning to Finlay. 'Initially I put her aloofness down to self-preservation, which would be normal in cases of traumatic stress, the mind withdrawing as a survival instinct.'

I think about Alex's words again, and how I might have done the same thing.

Finlay turns to glance at the jury. 'Can you tell the court if your initial findings altered?'

'Yes, they did.'

'Why is that, Dr Perrotta?'

'I began examining other aspects of Abby's life for potential influences of trauma. It took a while before I realised what was happening, and it was partly why forming a concrete conclusion became problematic.'

'Go on, Dr Perrotta,' Finlay reassures him. 'We're only interested in getting at the truth.'

'I wasn't sure at first,' Perrotta continues, 'but over time, I realised that Abby, despite her young age, was displaying behaviour consistent with a process known as "transfer".'

'That is a psychological term?'

'Yes.'

'Can you explain to the jury what it means?'

'Transfer, or transference, is the redirection of strong feelings, desires and wants onto someone else, often found to have its core base within the gestation of childhood.'

'A misplacement of feelings?'

'Yes.'

'Can you expand?'

'Certainly. It occurs when a person feels heightened emotions, but then redirects them towards others.'

'Attention-seeking?'

'Not exactly. An individual may feel abandoned and have a desperate need to be loved. What is interesting about clients who display transference is that they direct these feelings in an inappropriate way, often towards strangers, and in doing so they become whatever the other person wants them to be.'

'You mean they pretend to be something they're not?'

'Yes, even though they're not always aware they're doing it.'

'Objection, Your Honour. Mr Clarke is putting the *child Abby* on trial here.'

'Overruled, Ms Baxter. I'd like to hear what Dr Perrotta has to say. You will get your opportunity to cross-examine.'

Finlay fights hard to hide the smug look on his face.

'Thank you, Your Honour,' he says, then turns back to Perrotta. 'This transference of feelings you speak about, could the other person be aware that someone is redirecting emotions on them, fabricating a false scenario about the kind of person they are?'

'Unlikely, unless they have training in psychology.'

'Which you have?'

'Yes, and it became clear to me that Abby had found someone to transfer her feelings upon.'

'Who?'

'I believed that person was me.'

'Your Honour, I have to object. My client was eleven years old at the time. How can this be relevant?'

'Overruled, Ms Baxter.' Judge Kendell looks towards Perrotta. 'You may continue.'

'I asked a colleague to read my case file on Abby, and then to view my recorded sessions with her.'

'Video recordings?'

'Yes.'

'And did your colleague agree with your concerns?'

'Yes, she did. We both believed that Abby had, consciously or otherwise, used transference during the sessions.'

'And how did this transference manifest itself?'

'Verbally, her responses were split. Either she told me things she believed I wanted to hear, or she withdrew communication altogether, seeking additional attention. Also physically. Through her facial expressions, she displayed severe anxiety and fragility, but importantly, this changed on several occasions, especially when I wasn't looking at her directly.'

'Did Abby know the sessions were being filmed?'

'No. The camera is there for the protection of both parties, and patient knowledge could complicate matters.'

Finlay is trying to push home the point that Abby is an expert liar.

'I see.' Finlay puts his hands on his hips, demonstrating he is thinking deeply. 'Did you believe Abby told you things she wanted you to hear?'

'Yes.'

'Dr Perrotta, at the time did you and your colleague form an opinion as to why?'

'Yes. We believed Abby desperately sought affection and attention.'

'Did you talk to Abby about this?'

'I did, or at least I tried to. I told her I could no longer be her therapist.'

'This is standard, where transference or attachment issues come into play?'

'Yes.'

'And how did Abby react?'

'With hostility.'

His words cause a low murmur around the room.

'Can you expand?'

'She had to be sedated.'

'And your assessment of her hostility?'

'She viewed my decision to assign another psychiatrist as rejection. However, it was the level of hostility and violence towards myself and my staff that indicated deeper psychological problems.'

'Did Abby, over time, progress through these deep psychological problems?'

'I can't say.'

Finlay looks surprised. 'Why not?'

'In subsequent therapy sessions, she changed – she was happy, responsive, almost as if she had put the entire period with the French family behind her.'

'You don't believe such a recovery is possible?'

'No, I don't.'

'Can you explain to the jury why?'

'The human mind doesn't suddenly snap into something different. The underlying issues arising from Abby's potential abuse and other elements of her life are unlikely to have gone away. Medically, the best one can hope for is acceptance, and establishing survival or coping mechanisms.'

'What can you tell us about her aggressive behaviour, Dr Perrotta, when you rejected her, as she saw it?'

'I believe she used it as a release valve.'

'And this, without proper help, is unlikely to have changed over time?'

'In my opinion, it is unlikely to have changed.'

'No further questions, Your Honour.'

Judge Kendell looks towards me. 'Ms Baxter, you may cross-examine.'

'Thank you.' I stand up, taking my time walking towards him.

'Good morning, Dr Perrotta.'

'Good morning.'

'You say my client was traumatised as an eleven-year-old?'

'Yes.'

'Because of abuse?'

'That is correct.'

'And you stopped treating her because of this phenomenon of transference?'

'Yes.'

'You describe it as the redirection of feelings, needs and wants that are consciously or unconsciously displayed, which potentially have their origin in childhood.'

'Yes.'

'Isn't it the case, Dr Perrotta, that we all do this? For example, your angry boss in the office may remind you of an aggressive father so you subdue or manifest your feelings accordingly. Or someone standing beside you at a bus stop looks like an old friend, so you may say something to them, something humorous, that you know your friend would enjoy?'

'Yes, but—'

'Transference happens everywhere, doesn't it?'

'Yes.'

'Even here today, we are all making judgements, reacting to others in a way that is not wholly based on the realities of the situation but, rather, based on the history of our minds, what we see and hear, and how we view and respond to things.'

'I agree, but—'

'Yes or no, Dr Perrotta.'

'Yes.'

'Would it be reasonable to assume that if transference happens everywhere it will also happen within a therapeutic session?'

'Yes, but the level is relevant. Abby's behaviour was clearly, and overtly, an attempt to influence my reaction. Specifically, I might add, by doing and saying certain things she believed I wanted to hear.'

'To impress you?'

'Yes.'

'But psychiatric therapy of any kind, Dr Perrotta, would surely intensify the level of transference, simply by placing it under a microscope.'

'It can do.'

'A simple yes or no, please.'

'Yes.'

'And you have had no such interaction with Abby since her childhood? Is that correct?'

'Yes.'

'Which means there is no proven professional substance to your earlier testimony as to whether Abby has recovered from a potential abuse situation or not. Or, indeed, if her angry outbursts as a child weren't simply because she was a young girl who had gone through a difficult experience.'

'No, Ms Baxter, I don't have the data to confirm or deny the latter part of my testimony, but I stand by my opinion.'

'No further questions.'

As I return to the defence table, the jurors look perplexed. Medical opinion, where doubt exists, can be pulled in different directions, but common logic will usually prevail. Bottom line: no matter how much doubt I cast on Perrotta's opinion, as a young girl Abby was psychologically damaged. Therefore her perceived judgement and future actions are potentially damaged too. Confirmation of her aggression, even if she was a child, no matter how understandable her behaviour might have been, will stay in the jury's minds too.

# 36
# HEATHER

Before I leave the courtroom, I get another text from Alex. My father has been officially charged with Lucas García's murder, and I am about to face my own media shitstorm.

I hear the reporters clambering outside. I have probably faced worse in the past, but usually the subject matter isn't personal. It's about a witness or a defendant. Now, it's about my father, and therefore about me.

Opening the doors, the flashing lights are immediately blinding. Cameras and microphones are pushed into my face as I try to make my exit.

'Any comment on your father's arrest?' asks a male voice from the back.

'No comment.'

'Will this interfere with your ability to defend your client?' asks another.

I keep walking. 'No comment.'

'Do you believe he's innocent?' This time it's a female voice.

'No comment.'

The pack follows me as I move forward.

'Will you continue to defend Abby Jones?' the same female voice asks again. I recognise it as Marcia Langan's.

'Yes.'

'Will you defend your father?' asks another voice.

'No comment.'

'What is your connection to Lucas García?'

I see the end of the corridor. 'No comment.'

'Do your clients still have faith in you?'

'NO COMMENT.'

I keep walking, pushing past a couple of reporters as they walk backwards in front of me. I already know the images of me leaving the courtroom, and my refusal to talk to the media, will create problems, but I can't do anything about that now. Out of nowhere, Robin appears. She puts her hand on my back, steering me down another corridor to an interview room where Mark is already waiting with the Handcocks.

'What in hell is happening?' Jim roars, as I close the door behind me. 'You're letting your damn personal life fuck things up.'

'No, I'm not,' I say, drawing in the breath I didn't realise I was holding.

'So, what's that shitstorm out there?'

'I can handle it.'

'You damn well better. You may not care about your reputation, but mine is on the line here, and I won't have my niece become a fall guy for you or your father's stupidity.'

'Don't let her upset you, darling,' Alice chides.

'You damn well better have a good game plan up your sleeve, Heather. Otherwise I don't know why I'm paying you all that money to bring trouble to my door.'

'Jim,' I say, my voice calm. 'I appreciate your concern, but perhaps at this point it's best if we talk alone.'

He grunts a reply but looks as if he's considering it. 'When and where?' he finally asks.

'The Paramount Café, in an hour.'

'This is ridiculous,' says Alice, clearly irked at being excluded.

Jim makes eye contact with her. 'It's okay, honey,' he says. 'I'll make sure it won't take long.'

*

When I arrive at the Paramount on Charles Street, it's already crowded with diners. I order a large still water and a guacamole and pepper jack omelette. I haven't eaten properly since yesterday. A waiter brings me to a table for two.

The door of the café is constantly opening and closing, with people coming and going. I hear a clatter of plates and cups behind me. A man to my right shouts into his phone, 'Are the police there yet?' Near the front window, a mother encourages her daughter to eat her pancakes. Seconds later, I see Jim Handcock opening the door. I raise my hand to get his attention. He nods back.

He sits opposite, his large, bulky frame making the small table and chairs seem even smaller. He holds a mug of black coffee. He looks relaxed, as if, in the intervening hour, his mood has improved.

'Not hungry?' I ask, gesturing at the coffee.

'I had something to eat with Alice. She's already on her way home.' His words sound like reassurance that Alice isn't going to get in the way.

Looking at him, I remind myself that I might be sitting opposite my mother's killer. The enormity of it isn't lost on me. 'Tell me, Jim,' I say, keeping my voice professional, 'are there any business irregularities between you and Morgan?'

'We have cut *all* financial ties.'

'Were there any irregularities in the past?'

He sips his coffee.

'Were you putting Morgan under pressure? Maybe you got some dirt on him and decided to twist it to your advantage, including using your niece as bait.'

He almost chokes. 'You think I'd sink that low?'

'I don't know how low you'd sink, if the right motivation existed.'

We stare at each other.

'I like the noise in here,' he says, 'don't you?'

I don't answer him.

'This media mess with Charlie isn't good.'

'Tell me again, whose idea was it for Abby to become the Rotterdams' live-in nanny?'

'You heard Dr Perrotta today. The girl spent far too long in foster care. She needed someone looking out for her, someone who could help her set up a new life.'

'And that's what you were doing? Looking out for her?'

'She is my niece, for God's sake.'

I think about Alice's words of warning, and his unhealthy obsession with Abby. 'You like to use people, don't you, Jim?'

I've hit a nerve.

'I don't have to take this from you,' he says, leaning back. 'You have no fucking idea what I'm capable of doing or not doing.'

'What motivates you, Jim? Power, success, money—'

'Look,' he says, cutting me off, 'let's be clear. I don't want any of that old stuff coming back into the public domain.'

'By "old stuff", you mean my mother's killing.'

*This is the reason we're here. We both know it. The rest is window-dressing.*

'A man has been killed, Jim. I can't control what comes to the surface.'

'No, but you can tell your father to keep quiet.'

'Why don't you tell him yourself?'

'I reckon it's best if Charlie and I keep our distance.'

'Because you can't be seen visiting a potential felon? Is that it?'

'Something like that. Deliver the message, Heather. Tell him Jim sends his regards. He will understand, and if he does what I ask, leave sleeping dogs lie, I'll do my best for him.'

'How?'

He pushes away his coffee cup as if it's spoiled goods. 'You don't need to know about that.'

'Is this about my mother?'

He shakes his head.

I don't believe him. Everything goes back to her.

'I have to think about Alice now,' he says.

'What about her?'

'She gets stressed about the smallest of things. I don't want old wounds upsetting her.'

He's talking about his affair with my mother.

'My wife may put a brave face on things, but certain issues go deep.'

'Alice doesn't strike me as the sensitive type.' I want to roar at him that my fucking mother is dead and his messed-up wife is still alive, but instead I say, 'Are you worried my father will say something to the police, something you don't want Alice to hear?'

'Just tell him to keep his mouth shut.'

'He isn't usually obliging when it comes to helping law enforcement.'

'Then it shouldn't be a problem for him. He'll listen to you.'

'I wouldn't be so sure.'

'Besides,' he says, 'you owe me.'

'You may be covering Abby's legal costs, Jim, but I don't owe you anything.'

He doesn't respond straight away, just stares at me, as if considering the next thing he's about to say.

'Your mother was one of the most beautiful creatures ever put on this earth.'

'Leave her out of this.'

'You think you know so much, Heather, don't you?'

He's laughing at me now, as if suddenly I'm the butt end of some joke.

'I know enough.'

'You don't realise, do you?'

'What?'

He leans forward. 'Your grandma Lorrie wasn't the only person to put a silver spoon in your mouth.'

'What do you mean? Did you give my mother money? Is that it?'

'You're an intelligent girl. I'm sure you'll figure it out, and it would do you a whole lot of good to do as I tell you.'

'Are you threatening me?'

He stands up. I feel as if I'm being dismissed, like a child, but as I watch him walk away, it is as if everyone in the restaurant is moving except me.

I hear Lucas's voice. We're walking to the Handcocks' house. Lucas has his bag of magic potions. I see the crazed Alice Handcock in bed. I want to get away, but Jim blocks the doorway. I push against him and, somehow, I escape, but then he follows me, out of the house and into the barn.

I think about his words: *Lorrie wasn't the only person to put a silver spoon in your mouth.* I wish I didn't understand but I do: that day, when he followed me out of the house, and I tried to hide, it didn't matter how long I held my breath or how quiet I tried to be, because the only thing that mattered was that soon, in the barn, he was beside me. This man. This powerful man, capable of crushing anyone who defied him. Back then, my child self didn't recognise the look of obsession in his eyes, but my adult self can see it now for what it was, how his attention towards me became elevated because I was a miniature version of my mother.

'You could be *my* daughter,' he whispered, when he found me hiding. I had pulled back, even more scared, not understanding what he meant, but now I'm remembering something else, a time when the creditors were looking for my father and he had high-tailed it out of town. Jim came to our house. I saw him in the kitchen with my mother. He gave her money. Isn't that what Mark said? Handcock gets the dirt on people, then twists things to make them pay. Did he help my mother, only later to demand she do his bidding? Was that my mother's price?

# 37
# FINLAY

Warren McKenna taps on Finlay's office door before entering. His frame is bulky, and he moves as his physicality demands, warning others to be careful.

'What's your take on the media focus on Heather Baxter?' he asks, sitting down, holding a file in his hand.

'I don't intend to look a gift horse in the mouth, that's for sure.'

'In that case, I'm about to give you more. I've pulled up something on Paula Shafer.'

'The defence's neuropathologist?'

'Yep.'

'Spit it out.'

'After her time at the medical examiner's office, she wrote a research paper on SBS.'

'And what did the good doctor have to say?'

'She applied certain criteria to the determination of inflicted injuries in the case of abuse.'

'I'm assuming it differs from her recent findings, considering she's a witness for the defence?'

Warren scans the pages of the file. 'First,' he says, 'she discusses the subdural haematoma, blood gathering between the dura mater and the brain, tears in the bridging veins crossing the subdural space, cerebral oedema, and an excess accumulation of fluid in the intracellular or extracellular spaces. She goes on to discuss retinal haemorrhages, which she describes as a disorder of the eye whereby bleeding occurs in the light-sensitive tissue at the back wall. But this is the important bit. She states quite clearly these triads of symptoms are the established signs a medical examiner needs to determine abuse. If these medical pointers exist, SBS is cited as the primary suspect. And it doesn't end there. She also states that in serious head injuries found in infants and children, it is an inescapable fact that outside of major accident trauma, brought on by a car crash or some other impact of severity, the acquired injuries are definitively a result of abuse.'

'That is all good news, Warren.'

'Yes, except she retracted her opinion ten years later, publishing another paper contradicting her previous findings.'

Warren flicks through the file, reading from the text. 'She says, in the past, it was the accepted diagnosis that if a child or a baby had the triad of symptoms as mentioned in the above segment, the child or baby was deemed to have been abused. Subsequent scientific studies have contradicted this dogma. It is now accepted that not every subdural haemorrhage is abusive, and not all swollen brains are the result of inflicted trauma. As a result, she continues, the latter justifies a reassessment of the earlier belief system on paediatric head injuries.'

'She can retract all she likes, Warren, but you and I both know that claiming one thing, then saying something else years later will weaken her in the jury's eyes. Put simply, how can they be sure she won't change her mind again?'

'She is not the only medical expert for the defence.'

'I know, which is why I want you to pull together the financial costs associated with all of them. Handcock's pockets are deep. It's about time we find out precisely what these medical experts are being paid. If the jury sees big money pay-outs, they'll question their credibility even more.'

'Will Kendell let it fly?'

'We'll argue the potential bias card. He's a right-winger. He'll allow it. He'll want to be seen to have examined everything beyond reproach. The first time he lets it pass, it becomes our modus operandi. If we convince the jury the defence experts are hired spokespeople, with an unhealthy allegiance to the defence, their so-called medical expertise will drop like a body into quicksand. Get me those figures, Warren. A financially fuelled defence is worthless once its integrity is questioned, and I have every intention of doing just that.'

# 38
# HEATHER

After I leave the Paramount, Jim Handcock's words repeat in my head. I put a call through to Alex. If my mind is telling me now is the right time to discover the truth about my mother's killing, even if it is in the middle of a murder trial, I'm not going to get answers from disjointed memory alone.

'Alex, it's Heather. I need to ask you a favour.'

'What kind?'

'You said you knew Blake Lynam from before.'

'Yep.'

'With Lucas's killing, do you know him enough to find out if he's going to pull my mother's cold-case file?'

'That depends.'

'On what?'

'On how he feels about it. Blake Lynam is usually a by-the-book kind of guy. He may feel I'm using him, in the same way you're most likely using me right now.'

'Alex, if there was another way, I wouldn't ask. If he's going to pull the file, a fresh pair of eyes might make all the difference.'

'Okay,' she says reluctantly, 'leave it with me, but I'm not promising anything.'

By the time I reach home, I have another two hours before I'm due to meet my father in Corham. In the apartment lobby, I empty my mailbox. Most of it is standard stuff, except for a small rectangular box wrapped in brown paper. It spikes my curiosity, with my name and address handwritten on the front. Even after all this time, I recognise his writing, the same as the inscription on my mother's old book of poetry. I'm holding a package from a dead man.

Inside, I rip open the paper to find an empty velvet box, which I assume, based on size and shape, once held a necklace. I turn it over a couple of times, examining it, seeing a worn gold sticker underneath. At first, I can't make out the words, but then I see it's place of origin – New Orleans. Did Lucas give my mother a necklace from this box? It has to be important, or why would he have sent it?

On its own, it means nothing, but Lucas obviously wanted me to have it. It has to be his way of telling me something. Perhaps he planned to talk to me after he met my father, but he never got a chance. Now, more than ever, when I see my father at Corham police station, he needs to give me answers.

*

Waiting in the station, I imagine my father being taken from his cell. I wonder what thoughts are going through his mind. When I see him pass the glass panels of the interview room, he looks as if he has shrunk. I watch him being marched towards me, like any other prisoner, only he isn't any other prisoner. He is my father. His shoulders are stooped, his eyes fixed on the floor. Do I see a broken man, or is this another of his performances?

I think about the box from Lucas, the cryptic message, and immediately steady my resolve. If I'm to get answers, I need to visualise my father on the witness stand, use my training to separate attorney from witness.

'They've matched you to the murder weapon,' I say, as he sits down.

'I didn't kill him.' He stares at me.

'The police don't believe you. They have a record of you registering the gun.' I wait for a reaction. Everything he does and says is important now.

'Back then, I needed it.'

'Why?'

'Protection.'

'Against whom?'

He doesn't answer.

'Who did you need protection from?' I push him.

'It wasn't to protect me. I needed it to protect you.'

'From what?' I ask, slightly taken aback.

'Can't you guess?'

'I'm not in the mood for guessing.'

He turns away, struggling with something.

'Look at me,' I say. 'Tell me the truth.'

'Okay,' he says at last, sounding defeated.

I need to be careful. He can twist things too easily.

'If you must know, I never trusted your uncle.'

'Why?'

'I hated the way he looked at you. I could tell what that bastard had on his mind, which was why I warned him off.'

I want to say, *Damn you*, but instead I say, 'You left me in the same house as him.'

'I didn't have a choice.'

'You always had a choice.'

'I did my best.'

'Well, it wasn't good enough, was it?'

He turns away again.

'Look at me,' I say, 'the daughter you left behind.'

He turns back. We lock eyes.

I keep my breathing steady. I need to be Heather Baxter the defence attorney, because she can get through this.

'Did you ever use the gun?'

'Yes.'

'When?'

'After your mother died. I couldn't stay in this shithole any longer. Nor could I take you with me. I threatened Samuel before I left. I told him I'd kill him if he ever touched you.'

'You could have taken me with you.' My voice is cracking. It sounds needy, the way it used to sound years before when I desperately wanted him to come back for us.

'No, Heather, I couldn't.'

'What happened to the gun?'

'I'm not sure. I drifted for a while, going from place to place. I thought I left it in our old house.'

'Where exactly?'

He looks as if he's thinking hard.

'Out back,' he says at last, 'in the shed, up on one of the shelves. Yeah, that's it,' he adds, sounding surer.

I visualise our old house as, in my mind's eye, I walk towards the shed. I see the tools, and other bits and pieces, and as I do, I see myself with something in my hand. It's night time. I look down at my hands. I'm carrying a garden shovel. I need to bury something.

I look at my father, pulling myself back to the here and now. 'You met Lucas, didn't you?'

'No, I didn't.' He shakes his head.

'Stop lying.'

'I'm not.'

'Lucas told me he wanted the truth to come out.'

He shakes his head again.

'So, you took the coward's way out, didn't you?'

He doesn't respond.

'Everything is always about you,' I say, 'isn't it? You and your pathetic survival, your hurt, your pain.'

Still, he doesn't respond.

'Do you want to know what I used to think?' I roar, years of pent-up rage spilling out.

'What?'

'That the reason you left me behind was because, like everyone else, you blamed me. You thought the same thing they did, that I could have saved her, but I didn't.'

'Heather, no, I swear I never thought that.'

'And now you may have killed Lucas, only you slipped up this time, didn't you?'

'My God, Heather, I didn't kill him. You have to believe me.'

'Stop lying. He told me he was going to see you.'

'Yes, that's true, but, as I told Blanco, he never turned up. I went to Raintree, but he wasn't there. I hung around for a while, and then I figured he'd changed his mind.'

'You're only spinning this story out now because you have to. Isn't that your style, to keep your secrets until you have to own up to them?'

'Lucas never turned up.'

'Why should I believe you?'

'Because it's the truth.' He puts his head into his hands.

The deputy sheriff taps on the glass. He points at his watch. I nod. This whole conversation is useless. I stand up to leave. My father lifts his head from his hands, and I'm about to go, when I remember my conversation with Jim Handcock. I glare at him.

'Jim Handcock's sent you a message.'

'About what?'

'Keeping your mouth shut. He said you'll know what he means.'

'That fucker's always looking to save his own ass.'

'I guess that gives you two something in common.' I don't attempt to hide my contempt. 'He said, if you stay quiet, he'll do his best for you.'

'Maybe he's my only hope.' His words mocking me now, angry.

'What's wrong with you?' I move a few steps closer. 'This isn't a game, or some made-up story, it's real life.'

The deputy sheriff taps on the glass again.

'Don't you realise you're also jeopardising my case?'

'Is that what's important to you, Heather? That trial? While your father sits in a prison cell?'

I tighten my fists, wanting to strike out for all the things he didn't do, or might have done, but most of all for not giving a damn about me or anyone else other than himself.

'Are you going to tell me what he wants you to keep quiet about?'

'That man likes to bury his secrets.'

'What do you mean?'

'Lexie Gilmore.'

I stare at him. 'The girl who disappeared?'

'Yeah.'

'What about her?'

'Maybe she ended up dead too. No one ever found her.'

'You're saying Jim Handcock—'

'I'm only saying what others thought. And I wish that man had never met your mother.'

'You're blaming him for that too?'

'He would have had his reasons.'

'Like you had for killing Lucas?'

'If you don't believe me, Heather, what is the goddamn point?' His rage the same as when I was a child, angry at himself and everyone else.

'Do you know what?' I say. 'I don't give a fuck about you any more. Whatever game you think you're playing is nothing to do with me.'

'Heather, please …'

'Save it for someone stupid enough to listen.'

I pull the interview room door open, sending it back on its hinges. The deputy sheriff is waiting, smirking. 'I'm done here,' I say.

'Good, because Sheriff Blanco wants to see you.'

'What for?' I ask, unable to hold in my anger any more.

'I don't rightly know, but he doesn't like to be kept waiting.'

*

I knock on Blanco's door. I hear the radio blaring from the other side, with a running commentary on the latest Red Sox game against Orioles. I knock again, harder, opening the door this time.

'You wanted to see me?' I say.

'I see you're not standing on ceremony.' He turns down the radio.

'I don't have a lot of time.'

'What's wrong with folks, these days? Nobody has any time.' He gestures for me to sit down. But I'm still emotionally charged after talking to my father.

'I don't have to remind you, Heather, it was out of the goodness of my heart that I approved your late visit this evening.'

'I appreciate that,' I say, my words clipped.

'His legal counsel will soon be assigned. There are some good public defenders out there, but others,' he shrugs, 'not so good.'

'I'm sure he'll be fine.'

'You know, Heather, I was only in the force a few days when your unfortunate mother got killed, and this mess with your father, it isn't good. Not good at all. A man's past can define him, don't you think?'

'I guess that depends on your life philosophy,' I say, 'but I would appreciate you getting to the point.'

'They never did find out who killed your mother, Heather, did they?'

'No, Sheriff, they didn't.' I look him straight in the eye. 'The police failed her in that regard.'

He doesn't rise to the bait.

'How is your uncle?' he asks.

'Fine, as far as I know.'

'He got himself into a bit of trouble recently.'

'I wouldn't know anything about that.'

'No?'

'The last time I saw Samuel was at Lorrie's funeral.' I remember my father's words about threatening him with the firearm years before. Could Samuel have come across the gun after my father left town?

'I guess, these days,' Blanco continues, 'finding someone with a finger of heroin isn't a big deal.'

'As I said, Sheriff, our paths haven't crossed lately.'

'He took your grandma's death shocking bad, and the way I see it, Heather, your family haven't had an easy life here in Corham. I felt I needed to cut him some slack, about the heroin and all.'

'I'm sure he appreciated that.'

'I'm on your side. We're the good guys, you and I.'

'Glad to know,' I say, keeping my face and voice deadpan.

'In the end, Heather, I made the whole thing go away. It was a first offence, so a warning was enough. You and Samuel,' he continues, 'are part of the heart of this town. Letting your uncle off like that, well, it was the least I could do.'

He's making me feel dirty.

'But your father,' he sighs, 'he is a whole different ball game, and you … well, you're practically a celebrity now.'

'I wouldn't put it like that.'

'You're on the news every day.'

'Sheriff Blanco, what do you want?'

'Just touching base, Heather, that's all. One fellow citizen caring about another.'

'I don't live here, not any more.'

'This town,' he smirks, 'sinks into a person's DNA. You know that more than anyone. I would hate for anything bad to happen to you.'

I think about my last conversation with Jim Handcock. Is he putting Blanco up to this?

'I'll be fine, Sheriff, unless there's something you're not telling me.'

'Unsolved crimes like your mother's murder are simply that, unsolved, and, hell, for all we know, her killer could still be out there.'

'If that's all, Sheriff, I think I've already taken up enough of your time.'

In the car, I catch a glimpse of my reflection in the rear-view mirror. Tonight wasn't the first time I've argued with my father, but it felt different somehow. Things were said that can never be unsaid.

I stare out into the night. Blanco was right. My mother's killer could still be out there, and right now no one, including myself, is any closer to finding them.

# 39
# MARCIA

Marcia is the only one left in the office. It is eerily quiet when her cell phone lights up. She stares at the screen. No caller ID.

'Marcia Langan,' she sings into the phone.

The voice at the other end is muffled, the caller trying to disguise their voice.

'Who is this?' she asks, mildly irritated.

'It doesn't matter. You'll want this story. I'm going to give you an address. Be there in half an hour.'

Marcia picks up a pen, irked by the caller's authoritarian tone. 'Go on,' she says, scrawling the details on a sheet of paper, but before she has a chance to ask anything else, the line goes dead. 'Damn it,' she says aloud.

She likes an adventure as much as the next person and, with an address in Central Boston, this could be connected to the Jones trial. God knows she's been working at the *Patriot Eagle* for long enough. What she needs is a decent break. It can't do any harm to check out the tip. She considers what she's wearing, a short black skirt and heels far too high for chasing anyone with her camera phone, but she doesn't have time to worry about that now. Before she leaves, she raids the petty-cash box. Beside it, in the drawer, is a small pocketknife. She puts it into her purse too, just in case.

Outside, she hails a cab, fixing her make-up in the back seat. Who knows, she considers, there might even be someone at the location worth impressing.

She arrives before the directed time and, outside the hotel, she briefly hesitates, wondering who or what she's supposed to be looking out for. She checks her phone. No more calls. She tells herself there has to be a reason the person called her, and if there is a story, she isn't going to miss it.

The lobby is crowded, but she doesn't recognise anyone. She nods to the smiling concierge. His ID badge says his name is Chad. He has dark skin, wiry hair and a beard that frames his smile. He might prove useful. She has the money from the petty-cash box in her purse. It will be enough, if she needs to buy information.

At the reception desk, a couple are arguing over their bill. Neither looks familiar. She spots a reading room to her left, and a bar off the lobby. She checks out the bar first. A man, a stranger, offers to buy her a drink.

'No thanks,' she says, and having found nothing of interest in the bar, she heads for the reading room instead. It, too, proves a waste of time. The whole thing is starting to feel like a bad idea, until out in the lobby she spots Morgan Rotterdam. She keeps her distance, watching him take the lift to the thirteenth floor. It's time, she decides, to have her chat with Chad.

A hundred dollars later, Chad has given her the instructions she needs, and before taking the lift, in the ladies' restroom she loosens the top button of her blouse, moving her skirt up a little. She applies the darkest shade of red lipstick she can find in her make-up bag, adding a touch of shimmer, and mascara to thicken her lashes. She runs her fingers through her hair. She looks like a woman with bad things on her mind, perfect for any *private party*. In the reflective glass of the lift, she examines herself again, before putting on the masquerade mask, given to her by Chad. His instructions were clear: on the thirteenth floor, go to the silver door at the end of the corridor, ring the bell five times in rapid succession. She hopes this isn't going to be a bad call, but it's now or never, she tells herself.

After ringing the bell, the door is opened by a man wearing a masquerade mask. Walking inside, she takes in the room. The window blinds are drawn, blocking out the streetlights. There are candles lit everywhere, on the low tables, the walls, in the chandeliers overhead. The room is opulent, decadent. The music sensual.

She realises everyone in the room is wearing a mask. There are young girls dressed provocatively. Waitresses wear scant black uniforms, serving glasses of champagne on silver trays. She drifts towards a shadowed area, searching for Morgan, wondering if she looks a little out of place.

A hand grips her buttocks.

'What's your name?' asks the male, who is obviously out of it.

'Marnie,' she lies.

'Nice,' he drools. His words are slow. He is either drunk or high on something, or both, so it should be easy to get away from him.

'Slow down, tiger,' she says.

'Are you playing – hard – to – get?' He pushes her against the wall, his tongue already lapping like a dog at her chest.

'Get off,' she tells him, attempting to push him back.

'You – want to – play – rough?' he asks, still thinking she's interested. Then, without warning, he hits her hard across the face.

Shit, that really hurt. Panic grips her. She's thinking about a time, when she was barely seventeen, at a party outside of town and a guy had started knocking her about. Eventually, she'd got away, but it was after that she'd learned to defend herself.

'You want to push that big boy of yours inside me?' she asks, taunting him.

'Oh, yeah.'

She drops her hand to his crotch, grabbing him hard, so hard, he falls backwards, bending over to numb the pain. By the time he looks up again, she is on the other side of the room.

She tries to calm her breathing as she hears a man from a group of three say, 'Equity leverage is key.'

'Why Boston?' asks another.

'The city attracted me.'

They mutter between themselves, before the first man says, 'I hear there's a cellar in Cambridge with millions of dollars' worth of wine. I'd like a large piece of that shit.'

'That's mainly for celebrities. Fantastic value item, though,' agrees another.

'And when their divorce comes,' laughs the first guy, 'they'll sell it to the Chinese. We did two point seven million last year.'

They all laugh.

Marcia moves on. More men talk loudly.

'American business is suffering,' says another, 'and our president needs to back up his words with action. America is on its knees.'

She eyes the room again, spotting a narrow corridor opposite the door she came in. Within seconds, she reaches it. Along it, there is a series of numbered rooms. Inside one, through the half-opened door, she sees a young Asian girl with pigtails doing some sort of dance on the bed. Two men ogle her. Marcia keeps on walking. In another, a man wearing a mask, but nothing else, is strapped to the bed. His fat belly is pig pink and revolting. The girl with him, dressed in bondage clothes, lashes him with a whip. Marcia passes a few more doors, tentatively opening them and peeping inside. It is at the last one that she sees Morgan. He is talking to another guy. Again, she pulls back. She feels as if she is watching a play unfold. There is a young girl too, wearing nothing more than a white hotel bath towel. Her short dark hair is wet, and she is barefoot. There are watermarks in the carpet from the girl's feet. She can't be any more than sixteen. Morgan pulls her to him, dropping the towel to the ground. The second man walks away, the girl's nakedness out on show.

Marcia has her phone ready to take a photograph, even if Morgan, like the others, is wearing a mask. She is so absorbed in what she's doing that she doesn't notice the man from earlier coming up behind her, until he pulls her around.

'So, you want to inflict pain, do you?' he snarls, twisting one of her arms behind her. 'I'll give you pain.' He opens the zip of his trousers to reveal the dick that, a few minutes earlier, she had grabbed within an inch of its life. Dropping her phone, she uses her free hand to pull out the pocketknife in her bra. He feels the cool chill of it, and says, 'What the fuck?' as he pulls back. She will cut off his dick if she has to, but he is already retreating.

Neither Morgan nor the girl seem to have taken any notice. She grabs her phone again, still clutching the knife as she lines up the shot. Her hands are shaking. The image might be out of focus, but it will have to do. She hears Morgan talking to the girl. He grabs her hair. The teenager smiles back at him, as if it's part of some sad, fucked-up game. Prick, she thinks, clicking more images. Because of the masks, she doesn't know the identity of the other men at the party, but she has heard Morgan Rotterdam's voice, and when this story breaks, he'll feel the heat, as the words 'reliable source' swirl around in her head.

# 40
# HEATHER

By the time I get home it's nearly midnight, and the argument with my father, Blanco's overt threat and my earlier meeting with Jim Handcock are still playing out in my mind. All of it feels as if Abby's trial and my past are on a collision path. Getting ready for bed, unlike the voices in my head, the apartment is eerily quiet, which is why the noise in the downstairs living room stops me in my tracks.

Just like on the night a few weeks earlier when I thought I saw someone outside, part of me wants to go downstairs, and another part wants to stay where I am. I pull a robe tight around me, as if the act of doing so offers protection. I listen again, partly wanting to hear something more, confirming my suspicions, while also wanting to dismiss it as nothing of consequence. I tentatively walk towards the bedroom door. My heart beats a little faster. Someone is moving things. Maybe they want me to go down. It could be a trap. It might even be the same person who left the doll breaking in again because they can.

I hear a door opening and closing, then footsteps outside the bedroom window. I rush towards it, seeing a shape moving from the apartment block, a thief in the night, their identity hidden.

Walking downstairs, I can't stop my heart racing. I take each step cautiously, wondering if there could have been more than one of them. I check all the rooms, but the apartment is empty, except for me.

Did they leave or take anything this time? There isn't anything obvious, until I reach the living room, and on the coffee table, I see the silver miniature elephant, his trunk pointing upwards towards the sky. He looks shiny and ominous. The table has been moved too, with dent marks in the carpet where the feet once stood. Someone is purposely trying to freak me out. The doll, the elephant are connected to my past, to my mother, and to me.

I check the doors and windows, eventually finding the downstairs window from which the intruder must have gained access. I think about the cross-examination of Abby's friend, Ashley, tomorrow morning, wondering if it's possible that this break-in is somehow connected to the trial, perhaps someone trying to knock me off course. It can't be my father. He is in Corham police station, and it's not Lucas. A dead man doesn't break into an apartment. The Handcocks hired me to defend Abby, so why would they try to unhinge me in the middle of the trial?

I pick up the elephant. It feels cold against my skin as I wonder again who leaked that story about Abby to the media, meddling, causing trouble. I hear a sound from the kitchen. My cell phone is ringing. I barely get there in time to answer Alex.

'Hello,' I say.

'You sound edgy.'

'Someone was in the apartment again.'

'I'm coming over.'

'No, they've already gone, but they left me a gift.'

'What?'

'Something that belonged to my mother.'

'Heather, I'm on my way.'

'No, don't. They're gone now.'

The phone goes silent for a millisecond too long.

'Why did you call?'

'I wanted to warn you.'

'What?'

'You and Blake Lynam will be getting acquainted shortly.'

'Why?'

'They found some things in Lucas's place, newspaper clippings about the trial, lots of them.'

'I don't understand.'

'Blake Lynam thinks he could have been obsessed with you. In one of the clippings, he circled your face in red, as if it was a target. They found a doll too.'

'Like the one left here?' I start to pace the room.

'This one had fabric matching a top you wore in one of the newspaper articles.'

'Which one?' I ask, but as I wait for her to answer, I'm already running upstairs.

'A green blouse with tiny butterflies.'

I search the bedroom, including the laundry basket. It isn't there.

'Blake Lynam will be at court tomorrow, when the proceedings finish, so be prepared.'

'Is he looking at my mother's cold-case file?'

'Yes, I think so.'

'Okay,' I say, calming my voice.

Hanging up, I pick up the miniature elephant, turning it in the same way I examined the empty necklace box Lucas sent, wondering why all of this is happening now, and why Lucas had those newspaper clippings.

# 41
# BLANCO

Blanco has made a dozen unanswered calls since sunrise. Parking outside Corham police station, he taps the steering wheel in frustration. Charles Baxter has been relocated to the city, which means things are moving away from his control. As he gets out of the car, he punches the same number into his cell phone, annoyed that, so far, none of his calls have been returned. It was bad enough having that state trooper Blake Lynam on his patch with the García killing, but now it seems the cold case of Elizabeth Baxter is being reopened.

'Fuck you,' he says, as the call once more goes to voicemail.

In his office, he takes a stick of gum from the top drawer of his desk. Chewing helps him to concentrate. He needs to work out how best to protect himself. Slamming the drawer shut, he punches the number into the cell phone again. This time there is nothing more than a crackle at the end of the line. He swears again. He did everything asked of him, he thought. What did he get for his loyalty? Damn all.

He thinks about calling at Billy Townsend's place and applying some pressure but, really, Billy is no more than the hired help. The only person worth talking to is the one pulling the strings, the one ignoring his calls.

The cell phone vibrates on the desk. 'Finally,' he says, grabbing it. He has every intention of giving the motherfucker a piece of his mind.

'You took your time,' he roars down the line.

'Relax, Blanco.'

'And what? Listen to you get me into a shitload more trouble? I want out, do you hear? I'm not going to fucking prison for you.' His voice lowers. He's aware that his deputy sheriff is close by.

'It won't come to that. I'm always one step ahead.'

'This thing could go curveball at any time, do you hear me? I can smell it. Now Blake Lynam is digging into the Elizabeth Baxter cold case. I don't like it. I don't like it one bit.'

'I told you, I have it under control.'

'What about Heather Baxter?'

'What about her?'

'That girl's big trouble, even if she's knee-deep in that trial of hers.'

'Not to mention her daddy's arrest.'

'You got anything to do with Lucas's speedy demise?'

'Do you really want to know?'

'I have a couple of theories.'

'Let's keep it that way. I don't want you troubling yourself about Blake Lynam either. There's nothing to be found. If there was, it would have turned up a long time ago.'

'What if folk didn't look in the right places?'

'It's history, Blanco.'

'I don't want another body appearing on my turf.'

'Are you scared?'

'Should I be?'

'Not if you keep playing ball.'

# 42
# HEATHER

Like everyone else in the courtroom, I await Ashley Connolly's testimony. If Finlay has his way, she will be another notch in his scorecard, yet another attack on Abby's reputation. I study her as she is sworn in. The girl looks unsure of herself. She seems reluctant to be here. I'll use that. She avoids Abby's glare.

Finlay doesn't waste time. 'Ms Connolly, or can I call you Ashley?'

'Ashley is fine.' Her voice is low.

'Can you speak up, Ms Connolly?' asks Judge Kendell.

'Okay.' She clears her throat. 'Ashley is fine.'

Finlay moves closer to her. The eyes and ears of the room follow him. 'Thank you, Ashley.' He smiles. 'I'll keep my questions simple.'

She nods.

'Do you know the defendant, Abby Jones?'

'Yes.'

'How long have you known each other?'

'Ten years.'

'That's a long time.' He looks to the jury, then back to Ashley.

'During this time have you ever had concerns about your friend's wellbeing?'

'I don't understand.'

'Have you ever been concerned about her, in general, as a friend?'

'Sure. A few times.'

'So, your answer is yes?'

She nods again.

'Can you answer the question for the record?'

'Sure. Yes.'

'Will you tell us when in the past you may have had concerns about Abby, including the time you were both in foster care, and how those concerns manifested themselves?'

'Abby used to get into a lot of trouble.'

'*A lot?*' Finlay emphasises.

'Well, often enough.'

'Really?' He lets his question hang, intimidating her to fill the void.

'Abby told me once, when things build up inside her, all she can see is black and she can't help herself exploding.'

'I see.' He looks to the jury again, and away from Ashley. 'Did she ever physically hit out, *explode*?'

'Objection, Your Honour.' I leap to my feet. 'The prosecution is leading the witness.'

'Overruled. Let's hear what Ms Connolly has to say. You may proceed, Mr Clarke.'

'I'll repeat the question, Ashley. Did Abby ever physically hit out?'

'Yes.'

A murmur goes around the room.

Finlay holds his composure. 'When?'

'She attacked someone in the foster agency.' Another low gasp circulates. Ashley immediately defends her friend. 'She didn't mean it. She isn't a bad person. The woman was always on her case, annoying her.'

I look at the jury. They have already forgotten about Abby's possible abuse in foster care. Now they're wondering how far she's prepared to go to release her anger.

'Were there any other incidences?'

'Yes.' Ashley's voice is low again.

'Speak up, Ashley, so everyone can hear.'

'Yes,' she says, louder this time.

'Were the outbursts frequent?'

'I guess.' She swallows hard. 'If she was out of it.'

'Out of it?'

'On stuff, you know.'

'You mean illegal drugs?'

'Booze, too.'

'This was when the two of you went out socially?'

'Yes.'

'And on these occasions, when Abby was *out of it*, how would she behave?'

'She could be moody.'

'One of these occasions happened late last year. Is that correct?'

'Yes.'

'When Abby was working for the Rotterdams?'

'Yes.'

'The two of you were drinking in a bar in Hingham?'

'Yes.'

'What about other illegal substances?'

'Some weed, nothing more.' She shrugs her shoulders.

'Tell the court what happened.'

'Abby was in an awful mood. She said she was fed up working for them.'

'The Rotterdams?'

'Yes.'

'Did she say why?'

'Vivienne kept picking on her.'

'She told you this in the bar, in Hingham?'

'Yes.'

'What happened next?'

'Some woman looked at her, because Abby was talking really loud.'

'Is that when Abby attacked the woman, this casual stranger?'

I'm on my feet again. 'Your Honour, what is happening here? Mr Clarke clearly wants to be giving testimony himself.'

'Sustained. Mr Clarke, tread carefully.'

Finlay nods, his face in deep thought. 'Ashley, after this woman looked at Abby, can you take us step by step through what happened next?'

'Abby walked over to her and pushed her.'

Every single juror, men and women, stares at Abby. I hear people shifting and murmuring behind me.

'And then?'

'She pushed her again.'

'What happened next?'

'I had to pull her away, to calm her down.'

'Do you know why Abby got so angry?'

'She thought the woman was laughing at her, like she was some kind of freak.'

'Was it to do with her birthmark?'

'I don't know, maybe.'

'After this incident, Ashley, she went back to work for the Rotterdams. Isn't that correct?'

'Yes.'

'I see.' Finlay stands closer to her. 'You said earlier Abby was angry about working for them.'

'Yes.'

'Did she ever discuss Jacob?'

'Sometimes.' Her voice is tentative.

'What would she say?'

'How it was hard to get him asleep.'

'He was a bad sleeper?'

'That's what she said.'

'Did she say anything else about his sleeping?'

'She said that at times the crying would go on all night, and that he was a difficult baby.' Ashley glances at Abby, her face flushed.

'Thank you, Ashley. No further questions.'

I approach the witness. 'Ashley, do you believe Abby harmed Jacob?'

'No. I mean, if I did, I would have said.'

'Did Abby ever say, or indicate, that she intended harming Jacob in any way?'

'No.'

'Did she ever discuss losing her temper with him, while he was in her care?'

'Never.'

'She trusted you, right?'

'I think so.'

'She told you things she didn't tell other people.'

'Yes.'

'And she never mentioned harming or intending to harm Jacob.'

'No.'

'Did you ever see her angry with him?'

'No.'

'Did you ever feel the need to warn anyone that Jacob might be in danger?'

'No. Abby was good with children. I think she preferred them to adults.'

'Thank you, Ashley. No further questions.'

I have dumbed down Finlay's questioning, but harm has been done. In the jury's eyes, Abby is capable of angry outbursts. Jacob wasn't a good sleeper, often awake at night. They will draw their own conclusions, irrespective of Ashley saying Abby preferred children to adults.

Kendell looks at his watch. 'Proceedings are adjourned until midday tomorrow.'

The late start tomorrow afternoon, mainly because Kendell has legal business elsewhere, should feel like a reprieve, but as everyone makes their exit from the courtroom, I brace myself for another media torrent, only this time, as I look towards the back of the courtroom I spot a man leaning against the wall. Mid-forties, tall, broad and bald, he is wearing grey slacks and a matching grey shirt. Square-jawed, he looks more like a thug than a police officer, but I already know he's Blake Lynam.

# 43
# HEATHER

'We can take my car,' Blake Lynam says. 'It'll be a quicker ride through the city.'

'Am I under arrest?' I ask. 'Because if I am, I haven't heard my Miranda rights.'

'Relax, Ms Baxter. Right now, you're a person of interest, nothing more.'

'In that case, I'll take your offer of a ride.'

Passing through the media skirmish, once again, I refuse to answer questions. If anyone recognises Blake Lynam as a detective, they don't mention it, but they will soon work it out.

At Cambridge police station, he buzzes his way past the front desk. I have been here many times before, but never as a person of interest. We walk past the room with the security cameras trained on the holding cells below and the public areas. Further down the corridor, we pass the Crime Analysis Unit. His office is behind it. I'm surprised we're not in an interview room. I'm also surprised we're alone. I take a seat, looking around the room for audio recording equipment or a camera. I can't see either. There is a wipe board on a wall, headed 'Hot Points', and underneath the heading, there is a series of city addresses.

'Are you expecting some sort of riot?' I ask.

He looks at the board. 'Something like that.'

'Is this an official interview?'

'Official enough, Heather. We're both here, aren't we?'

I nod in agreement. I wonder if he has my mother's case file in the room. It's a long shot but, still, I take a look around. There isn't anything obvious.

'Let's start small,' he says, meaning the opposite, 'and chat about you stalking Lucas García.'

'No charges were brought.'

'But it happened?'

'Yes, it did.'

'And now Lucas is dead.' He swirls his swivel chair from side to side, looking in no rush to move things on.

I sit upright.

'Your father has been moved from Corham,' he adds.

'Oh?'

'We thought it best.'

'Is he in Boston?'

'He's downstairs in a holding cell, as we speak.' We stare at one another. 'He will stay there until we find him more permanent accommodation.'

The idea of my father in a cell below me isn't a good one. 'Why move him from Corham?'

'We considered it best.'

'Again, why?'

'Let's just say I have a dislike of small towns, especially ones with history.'

'Because of my mother's cold case? Or was Blanco getting in your way? I hear he has his own unique methods of investigation.'

'You already know I'm not going to discuss detailed police business with you. That's not how it works, Ms Baxter.'

'Heather, please.'

'Heather.'

'Has a public defender been appointed?'

'Yep. Miriam Echols.'

'She's good.'

He stops swirling in his chair. 'Why did you follow Lucas?'

'I guess I couldn't move on from my mother's killing. Following him made me feel like less of a victim.'

This is where, if I was representing myself, I would advise against saying another word, but part of me wants to engage with him, mainly because this man is a means to my mother's case file. I'll string him along for now.

'I guess that's understandable.' He pauses. 'When was the last time you saw Lucas?'

'A couple of days before his body was found.'

'And after you heard about his death, what did you do?'

'I went to a liquor store and made a substantial purchase.'

'And after that?'

'I booked into a motel to be alone.'

'You were in shock?'

'You could say that.'

He isn't writing any of this down. I search the room again for a camera. He stands up to walk around, as if considering his next move.

'We found a number of things at García's place, and there were several items of interest connected to you.'

'Oh?' I say, unwilling to let him know that Alex has already filled me in.

'There were several newspaper clippings about the trial, and a strange-looking doll, like a voodoo doll.'

I look at him, perplexed.

'Do you know anything about it?'

'No,' I reply, still conscious of the need to tread carefully. He's telling me all of this in the hope that I'll give him information, but the truth is, I don't know why Lucas had the clippings or the doll.

'He had your name, and your home address was on his notice-board too. Why do you think he needed your address?'

*Because he wanted to send me that box with the New Orleans stamp of origin.*

'Perhaps he wanted to contact me.'

'Did you consider him a threat?'

'We weren't exactly friends.' It's an understatement, but I don't want to give Blake Lynam any more reason to see me as a person of interest.

'It seems,' he says, 'all the evidence in this case points to your father.'

'It would be great, Detective Lynam, if all police cases were as neat as the one stacked against him.'

He doesn't bite. 'Call me Blake.'

'My father may be a lot of things,' I say, 'but he isn't stupid.'

'No?'

'He wouldn't have used a firearm traceable to him, not unless he wanted to be implicated, and having spoken to him recently, I don't think that's the case.'

He opens a slim file with photocopies of newspaper clippings, turning it to face me.

'This image on the top,' he says, 'is from the *Boston Globe*, and the article is about you. The photograph was taken outside the courthouse.'

I study the image.

'Lucas had a copy of it pinned to his noticeboard, with your face circled in red. We found other clippings too, but this one appears to have been particularly important to him. Otherwise why circle your face in red?'

I shrug my shoulders.

'Do you think he was obsessed with you?'

'Perhaps he had an interest in the trial.' I look around the room again, seeing another wipe board covered with an American flag. I turn back to face him. 'Can I see the doll you found?'

'That isn't possible.'

'An image of it, then? It might jog something.'

He pauses, considering my request. I'm not feeling optimistic, but then he says, 'Okay, I'll see what I can do. Wait here.'

I'm surprised to be left alone in the room, although he takes the file of clippings with him. I stand up, checking again for a camera, before going over to the wipe board covered with the flag. Under it, there are more handwritten street locations, but at the bottom, scrawled beneath the block headed 'EB', is a list of names, including Lucas García's.

EB has to stand for Elizabeth Baxter. I quickly scan the names written in blue marker, memorising them before sitting down again.

Soon I hear the door open behind me. Blake is back. He hands me a photocopied image of the doll.

'As you can see, Heather, it's handmade. We think it's a miniature version of you. A bad one, I admit, but I'm sure you recognise the fabric.'

I nod.

'What do you know about voodoo dolls?'

'Not a lot.' I consider what Lucas told me about them, that they weren't as sinister as people make out, although some could have a dark side. 'Voodooists believe in a good God,' I tell him, but as I look at the image some more, I'm already doubting this is Lucas's handiwork. He would have been more careful with the stitching for a start.

'Well?' he asks, 'has the image jogged anything?'

'I don't think Lucas made the doll.'

'Why do you say that?'

'He could be a perfectionist,' I say, staring back at Blake, and in that moment, I decide to tell him about the doll left at my place. I need him to be looking beyond my father. I need him to be even more curious about my mother's cold-case file. 'I got one very similar a short time ago.'

'Oh?'

'Someone left it in my apartment.'

'Who?'

'I don't know.'

He considers my response. 'How did it get into your apartment?'

'I left the front door open, and whoever left it must have slipped inside.'

'They entered your home illegally?'

'Yes.'

'Did you report it?'

'No.'

'Why not?'

'I'm not sure,' I say, not prepared to admit that I was hoping it was a kind of message, and a fresh link to my mother.

'Do you still have it?'

'No. I fired it into the trash basket, but then it disappeared.'

I can tell by the look in his eyes that he's wondering what I'm holding back. I consider telling him about the miniature elephant, then decide against it. I've given him enough.

'Is there anything else I can help you with?' I ask, still thinking about the names from the wipe board.

'Not right now.' He stands up. 'I'll get a couple of our officers to drop you back.'

'I'd appreciate that.'

'I'll walk you to the public entrance.'

'That's okay,' I say. 'I know the way.'

Twenty minutes later, back at the courthouse, I punch the names I have memorised into my phone. I search for the original *Boston Globe* article too. I hesitate before scrolling down. My father's possible connection to Lucas's death hasn't gone away. After all, he was due to meet him, but what if Blake is right and Lucas had become obsessed with me? I study the date on the article. By then Lucas had already moved to Corham. He was there in early July, before I visited the Handcocks. According to Blake, Lucas had this newspaper clipping pinned to his noticeboard. So it meant something specific to him. There isn't a lot about what they found at Lucas's place that makes any real sense but, right now, what is uppermost in my mind is not the news clipping or the doll, but the names underneath the American flag in Blake's office – Kevin Howe, Henry Mills, Gerard Russo, John Brooks, Terry Clancy, Billy Townsend and Lucas García. They are all connected to Corham, and also known to me.

I pull out a legal pad to make some notes. Howe was into gadgets. He liked boats too. He lived with his wife and two small boys, both barely crawling at the time of my mother's killing. He did odd jobs for Jim Handcock, and as I note this, I wonder if this is the original list of suspects from my mother's case file.

I consider Henry Mills, originally from New York, and how he used to cause a stir when he visited Corham to meet Jim Handcock, always being flash with money. I know he was in Manhattan at the time of the killing. Gerard Russo, John Brooks and Terry Clancy are connected to Jim Handcock too, but then again, so is everyone in Corham. I concentrate on the name above Lucas's. I never liked Billy Townsend. He always made me uneasy, not to mention being related to Sheriff Hodgson. Grandma Lorrie said all the original suspects had alibis, apart from Lucas, but alibis can be fabricated, especially if you know someone in the Sheriff's Department. Billy Townsend was capable of being violent, too, and as far as I know, he still lives in the same place at Popfinn Beach. I keep staring at Billy's name, imagining him from years before, in the hardware store, wearing those grimy overalls of his, or during mass on Sunday, when he used to hang out at the back of the church. He and Samuel played poker together. I guess bad apples have a habit of attracting others.

When I reach my car, I decide, despite it being a half-crazy idea, to drive out to Popfinn Beach and find his house. The closer I get to my destination, the simple act of doing something feels good.

Driving along the shoreline, I lower the car window, wanting to hear the waves bash against the beach, the same way I used to listen to them as a child, when I would go down to the water's edge to be alone, wanting to be close to something bigger than me.

When I arrive at the beach, the bars are already in full swing. The lights and noise have a dangerous feel, and when I park outside the low wooden bungalow belonging to Billy Townsend, I tell myself to be careful. Billy isn't Lucas. Irrespective of whether or not he's connected to my mother's death, he can be hostile, and he won't take kindly to being watched.

I take in everything about the house, the porch running around it, the paint peeling off the woodwork, the lights in the various rooms. I can't tell if he's home, but through the windows I see his wife, and although I have no way of being sure, she looks like a kind person. The two children seem content too. They're laughing at some silly story, or so it seems. I look away, feeling hollow, with a longing for the family I never had. Maybe that's why I think Billy's wife looks kind, because I want her to be.

I wait outside in the car long enough to see her put the children to bed. He obviously isn't there, but still, I reason, if I hang around long enough, I might see him.

I imagine him again from years before, leaning on his truck, watching me as I walk into town. I try to imagine him dressed in the dark overalls of my mother's killer, his face covered. The pain in my chest grips tightly, as I think of how I allowed Sheriff Hodgson to put all those words into my mouth. 'Your description fits Lucas. You need to do the right thing, especially for your mother. She would want it that way. It doesn't matter if you didn't help her. What matters is that you do the right thing now.'

I visualise Billy driving from the beach road, heading home. From where I'm parked, I would see his car as soon as it turns the bend. I imagine his headlights ahead, and how I could switch mine on full blast, and if he was my mother's killer, I could drive straight at him. I'm so engrossed in my thoughts, I nearly miss the first hint of his headlights until they hit me full on, and I realise he's here.

I lock the car doors.

He walks towards his house but pauses before reaching the porch, turning and looking straight at me. I feel like a target, but still I stare at him, trying to second-guess his next move. Is he amused to see me here? Will he face me down? Will he walk over? Challenge me? I know only a crazy person would have driven out here tonight, but all those years before, when I hid in that blanket box and felt trapped, I learned something I've spent a lifetime trying to unlearn: fear. I know how it erodes your confidence, affecting your ability to take things on, or live like other people. I also know, at times, I've forced myself to do things because of that fear, and sometimes, like tonight, I push too far, unwilling to be trapped in that blanket box ever again.

As I'm thinking this, the biggest question of all still hovers, like a nightmare you can't wake up from. Is this the man who killed my mother?

I keep watching him as he takes a couple of steps away from the porch, as if he's considering walking towards me, but then he stops and turns away again. He goes inside. I switch on the engine. The lights of my car illuminate the silver Honda Accord. Is this the car I saw tailing me, after I left Daniel on Sunday?

Driving away, a part of me is glad that Billy saw me tonight, for the same reason I didn't go to the police when that doll was left in my apartment: if any of this is connected to my mother's death, if someone has information, I want them to know I'm here. I'm waiting.

*

Once back on the highway, I ring ahead to Alex, deciding I don't want to be alone tonight, and by the time I reach Dorchester, the rain is already thundering down.

I get soaked running from the car to the front door, and inside, I blurt out everything that has happened, including my meeting with Blake, and my crazy drive to Billy Townsend's house. She doesn't tell me I was foolish to go there, or that I should have told Blake about that stupid elephant and the empty box Lucas sent me. Instead she waits, as if she knows I need to get all of it out of me.

I can see she's turning the information over in her head, including the list of names from the wipe board in Blake's office. A silence hangs between us. I'm the one who breaks it because now I want to tell her about my mother, how unhappy she was with my father, and later, after Mia died, how she had no one to turn to, how she shut everyone out, as if the grief was hers alone, and that it hurt me more than the whole world when she shut me out too.

'Grief changes people,' she says.

'There were days,' I tell her, 'when I used to see glimpses of how she used to be, the mother who braided my hair, who made me better when I was sick.'

'Hang on to those memories, Heather.'

'Before she died, she started playing a new game with me, a hiding game, in which I would hide and she would search for me. I used to practise holding my breath, so she wouldn't hear my breathing. In the beginning, she would find me straight away, but then I got better at it.'

'Do you think she knew her life was in danger? And the game was her way of protecting you?'

'I don't know,' I say, seeing my ten-year-old self hiding in the blanket box for hours on end, keeping my breathing steady, trying to think about happier things, shutting out the sound of her screams, willing myself to forget about the man, telling myself it was only a game, until finally I had to climb out of the box to find her.

Alex pours us both a whiskey. It burns my throat. I don't realise I'm crying until the tears pour down my face. She wipes them away. It feels intimate.

I stare at her

'It's okay,' she says.

I nod, as if I'm a child, wanting someone else to decide on things.

'Right now,' she instructs, 'you need rest.'

It feels good allowing another person to care for me, only it's bittersweet too, because when someone does care, you realise how hard it is always to be alone.

# 44
# ELIZABETH

*Every day my fear of something terrible happening is growing larger, as if the evil is inching ever closer. I daren't say anything to Heather, I don't want to frighten her, but I also know I need to protect her.*

*We are still playing that game, the one where she hides and I try to find her. It's a small house and it doesn't usually take long to work out where she is, but today I explained to her that if I listened hard enough I could hear her breathing. I got her to practise keeping her breathing low, imagining she wasn't hiding, forcing her mind to go to a different place, thinking about happier things, becoming lost within her thoughts, the way you would lose yourself in a dream.*

*Today I found it harder to hear her breathing. She has worked out better hiding places too. None of it is any guarantee, but I keep reminding myself, I am the one despised, not her.*

*I guess it takes time to build up enough hate to kill someone. It takes planning too, especially if you want to get away with it. Part of me wonders still if I'm imagining all these things and if, like after Mia's death, I'm slowly going mad.*

*If I was to tell anyone about this, I know they wouldn't believe me. They would say I was insane. They would put it down to my depression, my strangeness, my inability to keep a grip on reality. They would talk about the day I went into the woods to find Mia after she died, calling for her, hoping to hear her crying, so I could find her.*

*None of them understand that even now I can still see her, a little older, skipping behind shadows, like a beautiful ghost, at times a toddler, then older still, imagining all the years she will never live, and all the love lost, the memories never given because they didn't exist, and I admit there are moments when I think I might be better off dead, but then I remember Heather and push all those dark thoughts away.*

*I remember how someone told me once that the earth's rotation is slowing down ever so slightly over time. A day is now a millisecond longer than it was a century ago, and I dare to hope that Mia might be within that millisecond, the one that never existed before.*

*There is a chill in the nights now and I have the sense that I am running out of time, which is why, more than ever, I need to write everything down, and revisit all the things that have happened since I began my affair with Jim Handcock.*

# 45
# HEATHER

Despite it being early, Alex is already in work mode when I join her in the living room, with a series of notebooks and pages spread out beside her half-eaten breakfast.

I sit opposite.

'The way I see it,' she says, putting her notes aside, 'is that someone is trying very hard to rattle you. All of it, the breaking into your place, putting that doll there, and then that elephant, it's a way of them saying they're in control, they know things about you, things you may not even know yourself, things you may not even remember.'

'Blanco and Jim Handcock have both made overt threats.'

'I want you to stay here with me,' she says, resolute, 'until we get a better grasp of what's going down.'

'No, Alex. I've no intention of running away or hiding.'

'You're not. Just think about it – even for a couple of nights.'

I stare down at her notes. 'Are you going to fill me in?'

'Everyone on Blake's list has a direct link to Handcock.'

'Agreed.'

'I've been thinking about Billy Townsend's alibi.'

'What about it?'

'He clocked into work at the lumber mill two hours before your mother's killing and clocked out six hours later.'

'How do you know that already?'

'I have some sources close to Blake.'

'Okay, go on.'

'Time clocks can be rigged. It wouldn't take a rocket scientist to pull a fast one.'

The television in the corner is on mute, but I do a double-take when I see myself on the screen. 'What the hell?' I say.

Alex turns up the volume. 'Christ,' she says. 'This looks like a right shitstorm.'

Vicky Johnson is in the middle of a *Breaking News* story. 'These images of Morgan Rotterdam,' she says, 'have come from a reliable source at the party.'

I see a man wearing a masquerade mask.

'Shit …' I say, but I can't take my eyes off the screen. Vicky, the news anchor, is looking perfectly presented, with her slick blonde hair, figure-hugging dress, and blue eyes that stare right at you. Only now I'm not looking at her any more. I'm looking at the image on the side screen beside her, the one with Morgan wearing a mask, a naked girl beside him. The girl's face and parts of her body are purposely blurred out.

'It is believed these photographs,' Vicky continues, 'depict Morgan Rotterdam with a teenage girl, possibly underage. Morgan Rotterdam is the father of the deceased infant Jacob Rotterdam, and a couple of weeks ago in *Breaking News* we brought you the fresh information about the nanny accused of the young boy's murder, and how she may have had an amorous interest in her male employer.'

A picture of Abby appears on the screen, followed by another of Morgan Rotterdam, this time holding Vivienne's hand outside the courthouse, looking bereft, but within seconds the image of Morgan with the mask is back on the screen. I take in as many details as I can, including the large four-poster bed behind them. The naked girl looks tiny, and Morgan, in comparison, a giant.

I hear Vicky Johnson's voice again. 'I am joined this morning by clinical psychologist Dr Oliver Meehan, and the journalist Marcia Langan, who broke this story.'

I stare at the serious faces of Oliver Meehan and Marcia Langan.

Vicky is still talking: 'Marcia, can you tell us a little more about this? It's certainly a shocker.'

'A shocker indeed, and as you mentioned earlier, Vicky, recently Abby Jones was accused of being obsessed with her employer, Morgan Rotterdam.'

'And this, Marcia,' Vicky butts in, 'sets a whole new context, doesn't it?'

'It turns the whole thing on its head.' Marcia points to the side screen. 'This image was taken at what was referred to as a *private party*, where everyone wore a mask, but there is no doubt, despite the blurriness of the image, that the man is Morgan Rotterdam.'

'And the girl,' Vicky pipes in, 'looks around fifteen or sixteen?'

'She does.'

'In Massachusetts, the age of sexual consent is sixteen years of age, isn't it?'

'Yes, but there is an older law still on the books which gives eighteen as the age of consent.'

'Meaning Morgan Rotterdam could be involved with the sexual exploitation of a minor?'

'It would seem so.'

The camera goes back to Vicky. She blinks into the television screen. '*Breaking News* has tried to contact Morgan Rotterdam this morning, but so far he has declined to comment.'

'Oliver,' Vicky asks, 'what do you make of this?'

'If it's true, it's likely to be a long-standing pattern of behaviour.'

'You mean Morgan Rotterdam would have been involved in this kind of activity before?'

'More than likely, yes.'

'For how long?'

'Impossible to say, but a pattern of behaviour is developed over time, and in sexual-predator terms, the level of depravity increases across a prolonged period.'

'If I could interject here, Vicky?' Marcia asks.

'Certainly.'

'This goes far beyond the sexual exploitation of minors, considering, according to the source at the party, Morgan Rotterdam's obvious aggression towards the young girl.'

'It doesn't paint a pretty picture.' Vicky looks towards Oliver Meehan. 'Does it, Oliver?'

'It doesn't.'

'I suppose the big question here, Oliver and Marcia, is what does this tell us about Morgan Rotterdam? What else is he capable of?'

I move closer to the television screen. I listen intently to Marcia's words.

'Until this point, Vicky, everyone has been pointing the finger at the young nanny in the Rotterdam household, Abby Jones, but the contents of this breaking story make it very clear that at least one other member of the Rotterdam household is capable of aggressive outbursts, and that person is not Abby Jones, the young girl on trial, but rather the dead child's father.'

'Oliver, is it possible that Morgan Rotterdam was aggressive with his son?'

'Well, Vicky, that is a difficult question, and it's hard for me to comment without knowing the full facts, but what I will say is this: aggressive, predatory behaviour is often aligned to control, and this can manifest itself in extremes, which, if left unguarded, can lead to dangerous outbursts of violence, particularly in males.'

The camera zooms in on Vicky again. 'We're staying with this story, and after the break, we'll talk more about these shocking images, in particular what they tell us about Vivienne Rotterdam, the mother in the middle of all this. How can a woman trying to cope with losing a child, and who is currently in the middle of a trial, deal with such sordid details about her husband? Did Morgan Rotterdam, as a predator, lure Abby Jones into their home? And how many victims are involved here? Jacob, Abby, Vivienne?'

Alex turns down the volume. 'What do you think?'

'I think shitstorm is a good description.'

'This will help you, right?'

'Kendell isn't going to allow it in, not in a million years, but more than likely one or more jury members will have seen it, even if they don't admit it.'

'Finlay will be livid.'

'I know.'

'Are you surprised – about Morgan, I mean?' Alex asks.

'We have some intel that isn't a million miles off, but so far no one wants to go on the record.'

My cell phone rings. I look at the caller ID. It's Jim Handcock.

'Once again,' he says, 'I've made your life a whole lot easier.'

I stare at the television screen. 'Are you behind this shitstorm?'

'I figured it was time to level the playing field.'

'It could backfire on Abby. It's her life on the line, not yours.'

'Take it from me, Heather, you needed this.'

'Bastard,' I say, as he hangs up.

Alex is still staring at the screen. 'Morgan isn't the first guy in the world to want extra honey,' she says, 'but it seems he really likes to rough his women up.'

'The man is supposed to be bloody grieving,' I say, disgusted.

'Losing his child might have pushed him over the edge.'

I tighten my fists. 'How dare he be so fucking selfish – especially now, when his wife needs him most? My father did the same thing to my mother, abandoning her when she was at her lowest point.'

'Steady, Heather. If you let this get personal, it'll cost you the trial.'

'It got damn personal a long time ago.'

# 46
# FINLAY

It takes only one phone call for Finlay to verify that the images on his television screen are authentic, and that Morgan Rotterdam, the idiot, has messed up big-time. This media scoop will get endless traction, with the father of the victim shown as some form of sexual predator, an aggressive one at that. The implications are obvious.

He needs to change game plan, and if one parent is fucking things up, the other will have to play ball. The public loves Vivienne, the grieving mother who has lost her child, and who now also happens to have a son-of-a-bitch for a husband.

He flicks around the channels. Every media outlet is focusing on the same thing: her loss, her husband's infidelity, her stoicism in the face of great adversity, confirming for Finlay, right now, that in the eyes of the public Vivienne can do no wrong.

Finlay knows he needs to keep the media pressure up on Abby too. Alone in his office, he decides to replay the video recording of an earlier police interview with Abby. He has already watched it three times, studying her physical movements and expressions. It is prior to her arraignment, and at that point the case was still fluid. Abby hadn't yet been assigned legal representation, but her request to have her uncle present was allowed.

Finlay sees Detective Masterson enter the interview room, aware that other officers are studying Abby's behaviour and responses behind the three-paned mirrored glass on one of the walls. The interview room is a windowless box with four white walls, similar to the holding cells below. There is a red panic button near the door, more for the police than the interviewee. Within the room, there is a tubular table with four matching chairs. Abby and her uncle sit on one side, the interviewing officers on the other.

Finlay hears Glenn Masterson announce his presence, stating the time and date for the benefit of the recording. Darren Watkins, his fellow detective, is silent beside him.

'How are you doing, Abby?' Masterson asks.

'Okay, I guess.' Her voice sounds shaky.

Finlay watches Abby and Jim Handcock, conscious that the normal physical interaction expected between close family members doesn't seem to exist here. Is that what's bothering him? Both look straight ahead, with their chairs a significant distance apart. Even in the opening moments of the interview, when it's apparent that the girl is upset, Jim Handcock makes no physical gesture to comfort her. Why the remoteness?

He rewinds the tape again, this time watching with the sound turned off. Again, he notes the physical distance between Abby and her uncle, how they both stare directly at the camera and the police officers. Five minutes into the interview, when Masterson stands up to get water from the dispenser, Finlay pauses the tape, then rewinds it again. Turning the sound back on, he notes the detectives are using the usual techniques of repeating questions and applying redirect.

Abby asks, 'Why would I harm Jacob?'

Masterson replies, 'I don't know, Abby. Why would you?' Turning the question back on her.

The girl gets flustered, and that's when Jim Handcock repeats the action he made moments before, when Masterson stood up to get water. He puts his hand on Abby's upper thigh – an intimate act, but so fast it's easily missed. The girl doesn't respond. That bothers Finlay, too.

Maybe, he thinks, instead of concentrating so much on Abby, he needs to find out more about her uncle. He makes his second phone call of the morning. This time it's to Daniel Petersen. 'I want to run something by you about Jim Handcock.'

'Okay.'

'Is it possible there was something unsavoury going on between him and his niece, something sexual?'

'Incest?'

'Precisely.'

'I wouldn't put anything past that man, but for the record, I'm not aware of——' He stalls.

'Spit it out, boy. I don't want any teenage crush between you and Heather Baxter interfering with my trial.'

'It isn't.'

'When you said you wouldn't put anything past Handcock, what did you mean?'

'It's not important – gossip.'

'Let me decide on that.'

'Handcock likes to shop around where female company is concerned. There was a girl a few years back who quit working for the Handcocks because of something Alice said, how the girl needed to be careful or she might find herself in dangerous territory, and that Jim could devour young girls the way a shark devours fish, only caring about filling its belly.'

'Is that right?' Finlay replies, but he senses something off about Petersen today, a hesitancy, a reluctance that he can't quite put his finger on. He decides to approach it full on. 'Are you holding something out on me, Daniel?'

Seconds pass. Finlay waits.

'There was another girl,' Daniel finally says, 'a Lexie Gilmore. She worked for the Handcocks too, only one day she disappeared without warning. No one knows what happened to her. That's all I know.'

'Then find out more, boy.'

'I'm not your *boy.*'

'I only meant—'

'I know what you meant.'

The line goes dead.

'Well, I'll be damned,' Finlay says, to an empty room.

He switches on the television again in time to see an image of Heather Baxter on the screen. She's looked rattled over the last few days. He'd put it down to her father being arrested, and the media onslaught, but what if there's more to it? What if Heather has some nasty secrets of her own? For all he knows she could have been involved with the García murder. If there was a link between her and the investigation, she would have to be removed from the case, and Kendell would pull the plug. With all this baggage going around about Morgan, the opportunity to regroup may not be such a bad idea.

# 47
# DANIEL

Daniel is seething after his conversation with Finlay. The arrogance of the man, calling him a *boy*. He paces the floor. The house is cold this morning, so he lights a fire, inspecting the area to make sure everything is as it should be, checking the cushions on the couch, which now aren't sitting right. He fixes them again, standing back to check. Ever since his parents' deaths, he has made sure the house is exactly as he likes it. The two large couches are placed opposite each other, with the fireplace in the middle, all in perfect balance. The fire looks comforting too, but the ash around the grate is irritating. He needs to clean it. He also needs to phone Heather, but instead, he measures the distance between the couches, making sure they are still an equal space apart.

Walking towards the bookshelves, he takes down the photograph albums from the top shelf. There are eight in total. Most of them are of family images, but soon he finds the picture he's looking for, a photograph taken in Raintree woods. Heather has a serious look on her face. He glances at the other images beside it, all taken shortly after her mother lost the baby. He skips through more family pictures, of him and his parents, then finds another set with Heather. They are from outside her old house. He still knows the exact distance between each of the windows, and the height of the front door. He knows the number of steps on the staircase too. Heather's home wasn't always tidy, and that used to bother him, but then he learned to concentrate on the things he could depend on, like the width and height of the doorframes, the number of spindles on Heather's sister's crib, or the rectangular shoebox underneath it.

The first time he saw the box, he wondered why it was hidden there. Heather said it belonged to her mother, and to leave it alone. Her answer had felt dismissive. He thinks about how Heather went away and never came back. He flicks through more pages of the album, finding an image with the old swing in Heather's backyard. They used to take turns on it, making up stories, but that was long before Heather moved to Lorrie's house.

He never told Heather, or anyone else, how he used to go back to her old house after her mother was killed, spending afternoons out in the backyard, thinking about him and Heather being together. The first time he went there on his own was the day after her mother's funeral. At the time, he wanted to pretend that everything was the same, only it wasn't because Heather wasn't there any more.

# 48
# ALEX

Alex waits in the car park opposite Cambridge police station. The place is already a hub of activity, with a couple of junkies having a domestic outside. It isn't long before the two are pulled in. She isn't wearing any disguises today, other than a pair of dark sunglasses. She knows Blake is due to start his shift soon.

She spots his car arriving and starts up the engine. Once he is parked, she pulls in right beside him, lowering her window. 'Morning, Blake.'

'Is that you, Alex?'

'None other.' She smiles, taking off her shades.

'To what do I owe this pleasure?'

'Your little chat with Heather yesterday.'

'What about it?'

'She tells me you left her alone in your office.'

'So?'

'A bit sloppy of you, wasn't it, leaving an attorney to nose around?'

'Is that what she did?'

'Don't mess with me, Blake.'

'Why? What did she see?'

'A list of names, including Billy Townsend's. Only I started thinking, why would Blake do that, leave vital information hanging around?'

'Did you come up with any theories?'

'None, other than that you wanted her to see those names.'

'Could be.'

'She paid a visit to Billy Boy last night. I think she spooked him, and I'm guessing Billy isn't the kind of guy who likes to be spooked.'

'I don't doubt it.'

'You gotta understand something, Blake.'

'What's that?'

'My friend is in a tough place right now, what with Lucas and all the other stuff going on, and you using her as bait, well, that's not what I call good police practice.'

He gets out of the car. 'You can hold the lecture, Alex, for someone who really cares.'

She isn't put off. 'Considering, Blake, you put Heather's life at risk, I figure you might as well tell me the latest on Lucas's killing.'

'That would be tricky,' he says, leaning into her window.

'Why?'

'Maybe this is a bit close to home for you.'

'Looking out for a friend, Blake, nothing more.'

'Well, you tell your *friend* I'm here if she wants me.'

'And the Elizabeth Baxter case?'

'What about it?'

'You've pulled the files.'

'I might have.'

'Don't bullshit me. You know we go back a long way.'

'As far as I recall, Alex, our past relationship was extremely brief.'

'But memorable.' She smiles.

'True.'

'So, what was the police work like?'

'No comment.'

'What if I were to give you a fresh lead?'

'What kind of lead?'

'Lexie Gilmore. You know the name, don't you?'

'I might.'

'I have some more digging to do, but I guarantee you'll want to hear what I have to say.'

'Okay,' he says, nodding in agreement. 'You let me know when you have something concrete.'

'So, what about that police work, Blake?'

'It was sloppy at best.'

'And at worst?'

'Let's just say I wouldn't have wanted it to be my mother.'

# 49
# HEATHER

The fresh media leaks about Morgan, despite my anger at his actions, is a positive for Abby, and if we can get someone to agree to go on the record, to become a witness for the defence, confirming his aggressive behaviour, even within a form of sexual deviancy, the circle of people responsible for potentially harming Jacob will at least have widened.

Taking advantage of the delayed trial start time, I walk the last few blocks to our offices to meet Robin and Mark, thinking about how else we can use this in our favour, and also how Finlay will respond to it.

I breathe in the city smells, the dry dusty heat now replaced by cooler, fresher air. There is a spicy aroma of sausage coming from a nearby grill, mingling with the fumes of steady traffic. Before leaving Alex's place, I got the call from Mark to say he has an update on Vivienne, specifically surrounding health issues. I'm hoping it's the breakthrough we need.

I know Alex is right about not allowing my personal life to

damage the trial. I've already resolved to put all thoughts of Billy Townsend temporarily out of my head, but as I continue walking past the various skyscrapers, the small artisan shops and cafés, I can't help but think about my mother again, wondering if she would want me to go easy on Vivienne Rotterdam, or defend Abby with all my might, no matter what it takes.

I look up at the sky. The clouds are thickening. I keep on walking, passing the kiosk with the fresh doughnuts, arriving at our offices early for my meeting with Robin and Mark.

I reread the list under Vivienne's name – privileged childhood, unfaithful husband, grief-stricken, overwhelmed. She and my mother are different people, but they are also two women who have lost a child.

My cell phone bleeps. It's a message from Paula Shafer. People are asking questions about how much she's being paid to attend the trial. She thought the enquiry was from a random journalist, but then the caller said they were part of the judicial team, a man called Warren McKenna. She wants to make sure she's done the right thing in giving him the information. I message back, telling her not to worry. A lot of things are riding on her testimony, and if finance is raising its ugly head, I already know Finlay is out to use it to his advantage.

While waiting for the others, I flip over a new sheet on the board, heading it 'Good Fact/Bad Fact'. Good Fact 1: there is no direct evidence linking Abby to Jacob's death. Good Fact 2: Morgan's aggression towards women may open up the possibility of him harming Jacob. Good Fact 3: medical opinion on SBS is deeply divided. Good Fact 4: multiple DNA matches were found on Jacob, including Vivienne, Morgan, Abby, and other unknown sources. Bad Fact 1: Abby was the last person with Jacob. Bad Fact 2: her history of erratic behaviour portrays her as unstable. Bad Fact 3: the time it took her to alert others may be problematic. Bad Fact 4: her opening statement to the police is still damning. Good and Bad Fact 1: her inexperience can be seen as either good or bad. Good and Bad Fact 2: assuming Abby is innocent, nobody, including the police, actually knows what happened.

Robin opens the door. She reads the list. 'Basically,' she says, 'there is no conclusive link to Abby.'

'Agreed.'

Mark follows soon after, with a file tucked under his arm. He reviews the listing.

'What's this new medical information on Vivienne?' I ask, wasting no time.

'It's not on her directly,' he says, opening the file, 'but, rather, her sister. She had a sibling who died in infancy.'

'Another infant death? Is there a direct connection?' As I ask this, I'm also thinking about Mia.

'There could be, but it's still too vague.'

'How so?'

'Vivienne was a teenager at the time. The infant was jaundiced after birth, along with other worrying aspects of the delivery. However, after the child went home, there were several footnotes in the family physician's case files, some recording the baby as having persistent bouts of coughing and changes in mental function.'

'Do we know what caused the changes in mental function?'

'Possibly a side-effect of the baby's persistent coughs and fevers.'

'What were they attributed to?'

'Repeated viruses, which happened in conjunction with a variety of symptoms.' Mark looks down at his notes again. 'The first reports are from a private hospital. The follow-up notes are from the family physician.'

'And the cause of death?'

'Respiratory failure.'

'It's broad, all right,' I say, looking from one to the other. I walk over to the listing. 'And not enough to establish an absolute genetic abnormality.'

Robin stands beside me. 'Kendell won't entertain it, unless we have something solid to go on. He isn't going to put the grieving mother on trial.'

'There is something else you need to know,' I say.

They both stare at me.

'That latest scoop on Morgan Rotterdam was instigated by Jim Handcock. Most likely, he gave the media the tip-off about the party, which means he's prepared to do anything to get Abby off the hook, including dirty tactics.'

'Great,' adds Robin, 'a rich rogue family member, playing his own game of criminal justice.'

'And speaking of playing dirty, it seems Finlay has been investigating the financial details behind one of our expert witnesses.'

'It shouldn't surprise us,' Mark says, closing the file, 'after his character assassination of Abby via Ashley and Dr Perrotta, and now Abby's ex-boyfriend later today. It all adds up to one thing, the state's willingness to prejudice the jury against her, which, factually, has nothing to do with any evidence of guilt.'

'Finlay would describe it as offering an insight into Abby's mindset at the time of Jacob's death, but I agree, their whole case is conjecture, possibility and prejudice, but if we can make any kind of a credible link to genetics regarding Vivienne's sister, or something equally damning, it could all blow up in Finlay's face. This could turn into the breakthrough we've been looking for.'

As we're leaving, I instruct Mark to email me the contents of the entire file on Vivienne's sister. Robin is right. Unless there is a definite link, Kendell won't entertain it, but there is no denying the tentative connection. If we can get it into court, if I can see the link, a jury will too.

*

At the courthouse steps, the cameras flash at speed, but I keep pushing forward with Robin and Mark.

Mark's phone bleeps.

'What is it?'

'Finlay's given another impromptu media conference.'

'Anything interesting?'

'A few vague references to Abby's lack of moral fibre, and how there will be more scandalous information about her and her family to follow.'

'Did he mention Jim Handcock?'

'Not yet.'

Another crowd of reporters are inside the courthouse.

'Heather, what is your reaction to allegations of Morgan Rotterdam as a sexual predator?' asks Jessie Leonard from CNN.

'All we're concerned with right now, Jessie, is our client getting a fair hearing.'

'But what about his anger-management issues?'

'No comment.'

Several other hands rise, and as I open the doors of the courtroom, Tom Naylor shouts after me, 'Do you still believe in your client's innocence?'

I turn to face him. 'Yes, Tom, I do.'

Robin and Mark follow me to the defence table. 'Robin, I need you to contact all our expert witnesses. Tell them if anyone asks about financial arrangements for court appearances to direct the enquiries to us.'

'Okay.'

'And one other thing. I want to talk to Abby again. Dr Perrotta's testimony has been playing on my mind. Arrange something for after things wrap up today.'

Looking around me, I immediately sense the aggression in the room. Practically every woman, including Alice Handcock and the female reporters taking their seats, is staring at Morgan Rotterdam as if he is now the devil incarnate. Vivienne's hands are folded on her lap. Both appear expressionless, but she must be going through hell.

*

The testimony of Abby's ex-boyfriend, as expected, is damning. More background on her erratic behaviour with far too much pleasure displayed in his descriptions of her outbursts after they split up.

Afterwards, walking towards the interview room to meet Abby, I think about my father, now moved to Cedar Junction, the maximum-security facility near Norfolk. Like Abby, he may soon be fighting for his life, and the thought doesn't sit easy on my shoulders, no matter how good his defence attorney may be. I check my phone. There is a new text from Alex. I scroll down her message, reading the fresh information about Lucas, how he was renting the shop and the rooms above it from Jim Handcock. As the Handcocks own practically everything in town, this piece of information isn't surprising, except it adds yet another link to Jim Handcock.

When Abby enters the interview room, Dr Perrotta's testimony is replaying in my mind. I hadn't pushed her too deeply on her time in foster care before, mainly because originally it hadn't seemed relevant, but what if her experience there is the key to the things she is still holding back?

'Abby, I'd like to talk again about Stephen French.'

'What about him?'

'Dr Perrotta spoke about potential abuse. I think it's something we should discuss a little more.'

'He said other shit things too, about what's wrong with me. That's the way *they* talk. What Abby did. What Abby didn't do.' Her voice is mocking, hostile.

'You're upset. I get that.'

'What do you want me to say? That he fucked me? Is that it?'

'Yes, if it's true.'

'What difference does it make?'

'Maybe none but, still, I need to hear it.'

She stares at me for what seems like a very long time, but finally she says, 'He took me to the park once. I thought it was a treat. We were supposed to feed the ducks. I even had stale bread in a brown-paper bag.'

'Go on.'

'When we got there, there was this broken-down carousel.' Her words seem softer now, her voice sounding younger, as if she's back there, remembering everything that happened.

Even before she says another word, I know this conversation is important, because it also means … I've gained her trust.

'The carousel had different animals on it. There was a horse, a zebra, a giraffe, an elephant and a unicorn,' she adds, as if proudly listing them off.

I imagine her as a little girl.

'I didn't notice anyone else around. The carousel was empty. Even though it wasn't moving, I pretended it was. I pretended I heard music too, but what I remember most, Heather, is their eyes, the animals on the carousel.' Her own eyes bulge out. 'It was like they were looking on, watching what he was doing to me. I tried to block out what was happening, telling myself it wasn't real, and that instead of what he was doing, I was on the carousel, happy, only I wasn't happy.'

I think about hiding in the blanket box, how I pretended too, pretended that what was happening to my mother wasn't real.

'More than anything,' Abby says, 'I wanted to be like them, the animals, all stiff and plastic, without feeling.'

I stare at her. Out of nowhere, another memory comes back to me. A door is opening and closing. I see the shape of a man's back. He is walking out of a room.

Is it Samuel? What age am I? Why am I so scared?

'He called me a whore,' Abby says, 'and he kept saying it was all my fault.'

Even though I'm still listening to Abby, I visualise the man walking out of the room. I'm at our old house. My mother is downstairs. I want the man to turn around, so I can see his face, because I need to know who he is, just as I need to know the truth about who killed my mother.

'I had a white ribbon in my hair,' Abby says. 'It came loose, as if it was breaking free. The wind caught it, swirling it on the grass, but then it went high up into the trees. Sometimes I imagine it's still there, in the park, swirling around, and that the little girl I used to be is still there too.'

I take Abby's hand, holding it without saying a word. I want to undo what happened to her, even though I can't. I wonder if I feel the same way, if I want to be my little-girl self again, the one I used to be before my mother was killed. Only, like Abby, I can't. She doesn't exist, not any more.

Abby looks away, pulling her hand from mine.

'What is it?'

She doesn't answer.

'If there is something else, something about Jacob, you can tell me.'

She shakes her head. 'I didn't harm him, Heather. I couldn't have, I swear. He was so innocent, the way I used to be, before I understood how bad people could be.'

She is visibly distressed. I probably shouldn't push her any more today, but I know I have to, especially on Jacob's medical history.

'Abby,' I say, my voice earnest, 'I want you to tell me, in as great a detail as you can, about every sneeze, high temperature, restless night and cough that Jacob Rotterdam ever had.'

'Why?' she asks.

'Because right now we need all the help we can get.'

# 50
# ELIZABETH

*Being honest with yourself can be difficult. I have lied to myself. I have pretended things were different from how they really were. It wasn't only lying to myself about Mia's death, it was all the other stuff too. How I pretended to fall in love with Charlie because I wanted to feel independent and free. How I denied his failures over and over, all his absences, and his inability to provide for us financially, his anger at his own regrets. When I began the affair with Jim I was in denial too. I didn't want to admit to myself or anyone else what attracted me most about Jim Handcock: that he was yet another means of escape, another means to pretend all over again.*

*I enjoyed his attention, but deep down, I knew I needed someone to pay bills, to keep a roof over our heads, especially with Charlie out of town. I prostituted myself in the name of love for money. I let Jim believe I loved him too. I let him think he was the most important person in the world to me. When you are desperate, you recognise it in others. I saw it in Jim. I gave him what he wanted, and I took from him what I needed, his money and his help. I had choices, but I chose the easiest path – or that was what I thought at the time. I couldn't have been more wrong because, ultimately, we all pay our price.*

*Billy Townsend called at the house today. He wanted to know if I needed him to do odd jobs. I told him I didn't have any money. I took his visit as another warning, telling me danger is as close as it needs to be.*

*Nothing is staying constant. First, there was the watching, staring at me from across the street in the grocer's or at the pharmacy. After that, I began sensing someone following me. I saw Billy Townsend too, walking too close to me, wanting to intimidate, playing the messenger again. I can't remember exactly when I first noticed things going missing from the house, but even before that, I sensed someone had been inside, like a hunter stalking its prey, waiting for the right time to pounce.*

*I know something else too. Inside I'm a different person. I'm stronger. All those months of being dead to the world, after Mia, then getting close to Lucas, changed me. When I finally emerged, the old Elizabeth Baxter was no more. I wasn't able to pretend anymore, and when more time passed, and Jim asked to rekindle our affair, and I refused, in the back of my mind, where the deepest of secrets are always kept, a part of me knew, soon, I would have to pay the highest price of all.*

# 51
# HEATHER

The next two days of the trial include individual testimony from the team responsible for fixing Jacob's brain in formalin. All three doctors reiterate the medical examiner's testimony, and again, I end my cross-examination on the same point, repeatedly drilling home that the DNA of others, including Jacob's parents, was found on the infant. The facts speak for themselves, but right now, I'm sensing we're losing this jury, and although in time we'll call our own witnesses, by then much of the damage might already have been done.

As yet, we still haven't been able to get anyone on the record citing Morgan's aggression, but at least, I tell myself, we have a potential link to Vivienne's sister to work on.

My phone bleeps with a reminder of my upcoming meeting with Dr Alicia Amel. After reading the medical data on Vivienne's sister, it's obvious that an awful lot could ride on this. I also know the risk of us getting the wrong verdict, and Abby going to prison for a very long time, is growing by the day. It was Paula Shafer who suggested meeting

Dr Amel, after I'd discussed the medical data on Vivienne's late sister with her. Alicia is a key player in the Innocence Project, the non-profit organisation aimed at helping people wrongly accused. We're due to meet in the courtyard garden at the Museum of Fine Arts.

As I enter the glass doors of the museum, throngs of tourists, parents with children, and art students are all eager to get inside. Part of me is envious of how carefree they seem.

I take a seat at the back of the garden, a good vantage point within the neoclassical architecture and lush greenery. I know from Paula that Alicia has been involved with several key criminal cases, but her expertise in genetics is the real reason I'm here. I order a coffee while I wait.

A few moments later, I see her, looking exotic with her dark skin and enormous eyes, like a beautiful lioness wrapped in her light fawn coat and fake-fur collar.

'Alicia,' I say, shaking her hand.

Once seated, she removes her tan gloves, then takes a sip from a glass of water already poured.

'I know from Paula you specialise in genetic disorders.'

'And you want to talk to me about a historical case?'

'Yes,' I say, moving my coffee aside, 'but I have limited information, although I'm still keen to hear your thoughts.'

She nods.

'You believe certain metabolic and genetic disorders, including bleeding and clotting disorders, can lead to symptoms mimicking SBS, isn't that correct?'

'In my opinion, it's beyond doubt, although not all medical professionals in the United States agree.'

'They're split right down the middle,' I say in acknowledgment.

'Heather, none of us want to put people in jail with bad science, but sometimes, sadly, we do.'

'Which is why you're involved with the Innocence Project, fighting injustice.'

'I don't see it as justice or injustice.' She shrugs. 'I'm not a legal professional. I'm a doctor of medical science, and to me, it's about getting the medical facts correct, and sometimes they aren't always clear.'

'How do you mean?'

'At times, it can be difficult to define them, especially in the case of an injured infant.' She sits back in the chair. 'Irrespective of whether an infant is alive or dead, realistically they can only act as witnesses via their individual medical story. In other words, what their body tells us. And this is often open to interpretation rather than absolutes.' She pauses.

I wait.

'You're defending Abby Jones,' she finally says. 'Isn't that correct?'

'Yes.'

'There were historical fractures found?'

'Yes.'

'And the triad of symptoms for SBS was present?'

I nod, agreeing.

'I'm sure you know, Heather, I've had some previous disagreements with the medical examiner in this case.'

'Do you have an opinion about his judgement regarding Jacob Rotterdam?'

'I'm not sufficiently familiar with the facts involved to give you that, but I can certainly tell you my opinion on some of Dr Boris Wesley's previous judgements.'

'Which is?'

'His judgements are at best overzealous and at worst suspect. He blatantly ignores all the data since the early seventies, confirming alternative reasons for the triad of symptoms, like viruses, genetic blood clotting, childhood illnesses. I believe, as do many of my colleagues, that in situations where we lack a definitive cause for the triad of symptoms, it doesn't mean a cause outside of SBS doesn't exist.'

'And the fractures to the body?'

'They can be genetic too. Nothing should be off the table.'

'Go on.'

'Unless someone has witnessed the abuse, in many cases no one can be completely sure how the abnormalities presented themselves. Unfortunately, with inconclusive data, other influences take priority.'

'Influences?'

'The socio-economic group you come from, the colour of your skin, your gender, previous history, like addiction issues or violent behaviour. All of these can influence people's perception of the data and, unfortunately, I know from working with the Innocence Project that this is particularly prevalent where infant mortality is concerned, and other medical professionals are sloppy.'

'Vivienne Rotterdam, Jacob's mother, lost a sibling to infant mortality. The cause of death was put down as respiratory failure.'

'And you think there is a connection to Jacob?'

'It's a possibility. The baby had a difficult birth, and later was sickly, and prone to infection. The infections were respiratory in nature, coughing, not unlike Jacob's own medical history. We are unaware if bone damage existed, but that is not to say it didn't. Also, there were multiple instances of high temperatures, fever, which the family physician put down to viruses.'

'Anything else?'

'The baby was jaundiced at birth, and some medical references noted altered mental functions aligned to the rise in temperature and fevers. I know the information is limited, but …'

'It could be HLH but, as you say, without more detailed medical data, it's impossible to be conclusive.'

'What's HLH?'

'Haemophagocytic lymphohistiocytosis, a syndrome of excessive immune activation. It mostly affects infants from birth to about eighteen months. Infection is a common trigger, both in those with a genetic predisposition and in sporadic cases, but it is challenging to diagnose because the symptoms can mimic those of common infections, such as persistent fevers, jaundice, respiratory issues, coughing and breathing distress, along with changes in mental functions.'

'But if an infant presented with these symptoms, would they not be tested for HLH?'

'Unlikely. Very often the greatest barrier to treatment of HLH is a delay in diagnosis.'

'Why?'

'Most paediatricians won't see a case of HLH during their careers. However, as far back as 2003, attention has been drawn to the potential confusion between HLH and child-abuse injuries.'

My body tenses, knowing everything Alicia Amel is about to say could be critical.

'As yet,' she continues, 'no one knows for sure how many cases there are worldwide, and the real tragedy is not just that parents are often wrongly accused, but that without prompt diagnosis and treatment, HLH can be fatal.'

'Let me be clear. You're saying that in a case of suspected child abuse, as with Jacob Rotterdam, the likelihood of testing for HLH is low.'

'Basically, Heather, the rareness of HLH and the commonness of child abuse can be a disastrous combination.'

'How does it manifest itself?'

'As I said, it can be genetic, or caused by infections such as glandular fever. Statistically, it is thought to affect only one in every fifty thousand infants. Many cases may slip through the net because of the lack of awareness among doctors, and the absence of a standard check for the disease, along with the fact that the link between brain symptoms and HLH in medical terms is relatively recent.'

'And the medical links are?'

'HLH occurs when disease-fighting cells called lymphocytes and macrophages fail to commit suicide when they're no longer needed. Instead they attack normal cells and inhibit essential processes such as the production of blood platelets. HLH has also been known to disrupt liver and bone-marrow function but, importantly, it can cause bleeding in the brain and eyes, which closely resembles the tearing and bleeding inflicted by sudden movement of the head and neck.'

'Shaken Baby Syndrome,' I say out loud. My body tenses even more. This could be it. The definitive link. The reason why Jacob lost his life. If we can prove HLH, or find a genetic link to Vivienne, the trial could collapse.

'Can it be cured?'

'Yes, if it's caught in time, although the prognosis for survival is still quite low. However, because affected people are now being diagnosed earlier, and treatment options are improving, the survival rate for people with HLH is likely to get even better over time.'

'Is there any way of proving an infant had HLH, or something similar, after death?'

'Yes, during an autopsy.'

'And if it wasn't looked for at that point?'

'If blood samples are available for analysis, they could be tested.'

'What should you look for?'

'Low white blood cells, traces of jaundice, anaemia, liver damage.

If these are found, then a further analysis of remaining bone marrow, organs, liver and spleen could be done.'

'And changes in the bone marrow would weaken the bones?'

'Conceivably, yes.'

'And lead to fractures?'

'Sure, it's possible. When infants and toddlers present with multiple unexplained fractures, alternative reasons can be overlooked as child abuse is often the diagnosis. Bone diseases associated with increased bone fragility can be subtle and difficult to diagnose too, especially if a clear medical history of a condition does not exist. It can leave both the carers and medics bewildered, but if you're looking for my advice, and you want to establish a genetic connection, you should consider testing the parents. Then, very quickly, you can confirm if either of them is a carrier of HLH.'

Despite how valuable this information is, I'm already thinking of how difficult it will be to get Kendell to agree to blood tests or any testing of the parents, especially without something concrete to base it on. Right now, all of this is theoretical.

'Alicia, in your experience, where parents are carriers and if, as in this case, the potential carrier had a sibling who died with similar symptoms, would they not be aware of the problem repeating itself? Wouldn't they be concerned?'

'Not if you're a parent in denial.'

'I don't understand.'

'Some parents don't want to believe the same thing is happening to their child.'

'So they put it down to normal health issues, deny the past?'

'It's often hard to accept, Heather, that something of life-threatening proportion is happening to you or a member of your family. Nor is it easy to accept that its manifestation may genetically be your fault.'

'You sound as if you've come across this before.'

'I have. And it is not, Heather, because the parents don't love their child. In fact, the very opposite, because when they do the weight of guilt can be even heavier.'

'What happens, Alicia, if a parent does nothing about it? If they ignore what's going on, deny it, as you put it? What then?'

'They may be too late. These things often accelerate.'

'And when a parent is no longer able to deny the truth, and the ultimate tragedy occurs, do they take responsibility for it or does the denial continue?'

'I'm not a psychologist, but sometimes accepting guilt can be too hard to bear.'

'Meaning a person may look for someone else to blame?'

She shrugs her shoulders. 'We're all human, Heather, and where trauma is concerned, anything is possible.'

Many questions are jumping into my head, but one keeps repeating itself. Did Vivienne's guilt cause her to look for someone else to blame? Was that someone Abby?

# 52
# HEATHER

Within two hours of parting ways with Alicia, I have set up a pre-trial meeting with Kendell and Finlay for early the following morning. By the time I get home, delayed exhaustion hits me again, but before I do anything else, I check that all the windows and doors are safely locked. Since the last break-in, I'm not taking any chances.

In the living room, I take in the mind maps on the wall. Lately, every opportunity I get, outside of preparing for the trial, I've been gathering information around the build-up to my mother's death, categorising various elements, using mind maps with my mother at the centre, with family, friends, lovers and even the possibility of a drifter put into the mix. The list of names from Blake's office is on the wall too, along with a second map with Lucas, outlining recent events, such as my father's arrest, and the makeshift doll left at my apartment. The miniature elephant, the empty necklace box, and the things found at Lucas's place are also included, along with the news clipping, my face circled in red, like a target.

I've always known the searching of the house was important.

It indicated a motive other than the sexual attack and killing. We didn't have anything worth stealing, so it makes sense that someone was looking for something specific. It might have been something my mother kept, a memento or her journal, which are now gone. I can't ask Grandma Lorrie about them, and even though I could ask Samuel, I'm also reluctant to seek him out.

Heading upstairs to bed, I realise, of late, it's like I'm two people, the attorney defending Abby by day, and the woman trying to make sense of her mother's killing by night.

Even though my mind wants to shut down, I think about Billy Townsend. If he was the killer, when I placed the blame on Lucas, he would have thought he'd got away with it. But then Lucas came back to town, and if the items found at his place mean anything, it is that Lucas was doing his own investigation.

I pick up a notebook from the side table. Over the last couple of days, I've started writing some of the memory fragments down too, in much the same way as my mother wrote in her journal. I flick through the pages, rereading earlier notes about finding my mother dead in the kitchen, and how, afterwards, I went back upstairs. I took something from the baby's room, but what did I do after that?

I visualise the swing in the garden. I flick to another page. It was snowing the day she died, and bitterly cold. I see the miniature elephant in the soil, only this time it is covered with snow. Did I bury it? Did I bury other things too, including her journal? Is that why I remember the shovel in my hand?

I concentrate on the swing. It feels important, drawing me in, in the same way that the voodoo doll did, the night it was left on my bed.

I imagine myself carrying something from the baby's room, then going outside. I have the shovel in my hand. I see my ten-year-old self walking towards the swing. I know I'm scared, but there's something else too. I'm looking around, sensing that someone is watching me – who?

Getting into bed, I shiver, as another thought hits me. At first, it feels ridiculous, but slowly it begins to make sense. What if the person watching me that night was Daniel?

I turn a fresh page in the notebook. I write – *Call Daniel tomorrow*.

As I attempt sleep, my mind keeps going back to the miniature elephant covered with snow, glinting at me, as if trapped like an animal in a snow globe. Soon I see other things too, other mementoes, and her journal. The journal seems to unlock more memories because then I realise I was burying more than the elephant that night. I was burying the contents of the red shoebox. I remember covering it with plastic to protect my mother's secrets.

My mother told me the red box was important, that I was to keep it safe, and not let anyone find it, which was why, that afternoon, when Daniel spotted it, I brushed him off. He was annoyed. He didn't like me shutting him out.

I get out of bed. I can't sleep. I walk to the bedroom window. As I do, I hear movement outside. I freeze. I wait for the next sound, sensing I won't have to wait long. I hear glass shatter. Panic grips me. I search for something to protect myself with. There is a letter opener in one of the drawers. I walk over to it, as quietly as I can, pulling on a robe. I hear footsteps downstairs. Whoever it is, they are walking around the apartment. I grip the letter opener tight in my hand. I should phone the police, or Alex, but what if the person downstairs hears me making the call? My fingers shake as I message Alex: *Someone is in the apartment again.*

I think about locking myself into the room, hiding, like I did all those years before, but instead I force myself to walk to the door, hearing more sounds coming from downstairs.

My breathing deepens with each step, and halfway down, I see the light underneath the living-room door. I think about retreating upstairs, waiting for Alex, but then I hear his voice, calling my name.

'Heather,' he says, from behind the door, 'I'm in here.'

The letter opener is still held tight in my hand. I reach for the door handle. When I open it, he stares at me from a chair in the corner.

'I thought I'd pay you a visit, Heather, return the favour, if you like.'

'People usually wait to be invited,' I say, glaring at him.

'Maybe you should have thought about that before you decided to spy on my family.'

'I wasn't spying.'

'No? I think you were. I saw *you*, remember.'

'Why are you here, Billy?'

He looks me up and down, as if inspecting me, before standing up and walking closer.

'Don't try anything tricky,' he says, pointing to the letter opener, 'or you could end up dead like your fucking mother.'

I can smell his breath, the whiff of alcohol.

'You look so pretty when you're scared,' he smirks, 'just like when you were a little girl.' His eyes crawl all over me. 'Some people think you knew more back then than you ever said.'

'I don't care what people think.'

'You see, Heather, I do.'

He is within touching distance. I think about the letter opener. I think about how Alex is too far away. I think about my mother, and whether or not Billy Townsend raped and killed her. The rage inside me is so strong, it's as if nothing else matters, only me and him, as in my mind's eye I relive the past, wanting to change it. This time I want to save her.

It feels as if time is standing still, but then he grabs my neck, and I let out a gasp, as he fires the letter opener to the floor, his other hand tight around my throat. He pushes me against the wall, the way my father pushed my mother that day.

'Was – it – you?' I plead. I can hardly breathe. 'Did – you – kill – her?'

'Your mother liked to tease,' he laughs, 'asking for it, she was, like the town's bitch, there for the taking.'

I try to pull away, but his grip is too tight.

'I don't plan on overstaying my welcome,' he says, 'but I need you to know something. If you mess with me, I'll kill you. No one will ever find you because, like Lexie Gilmore, you will disappear.'

I can't breathe. He could kill me here, right now, but instead, just as suddenly, he loosens his grip. I fall to the floor like a rag doll, gasping for air. His foot lifts my robe, exposing my bare legs. I think about my mother, how she lay on the floor too, and how her right to say no was of no consequence, as if her choice, and her life, didn't matter. Suddenly my fear is replaced with rage. I lunge at him, wanting to hurt him, but my fists are no match for him. He grabs my wrists.

'Jim Handcock wouldn't like to see you like this,' he spits, 'especially when his precious niece is desperately trying to save her skin.'

'Are you working for him? Is that it?' I scream, finding my voice again. 'Is that why you're here? To do his bidding?'

He looks amused, as if he's thinking about telling me something, but then changes his mind.

'Answer me,' I say, sounding braver than I feel.

'Why should I tell you anything? You work for Jim Handcock, too, like that freak of a friend of yours.'

I realise he's talking about Daniel. Why does he think Daniel is working for Jim Handcock?

He releases his grip, then walks away, as if suddenly bored. Seconds later, I hear him outside, then his car engine come to life. I stay in the same spot until I can't hear the car any more. What did he mean, people thought I knew more back then?

As I wait for Alex, I think about phoning the cops, but if Billy wanted to kill me, he would have done it tonight. Did he threaten me because I'm getting too close to something? I think about what he said about Lexie Gilmore, his hands on my neck, and all the horrible things he said about my mother. I think about Jim Handcock, too, and Daniel.

By the time Alex arrives, I don't need much convincing when she offers to stay until morning, but I also know that if Billy took the risk of coming here, someone is rattled.

# 53
# ELIZABETH

*The past is full of things you cannot see. I realise that now. How the casual look of another, held for a moment too long, may contain a secret, how others pretend to be something they are not. People are seldom exactly as you see them. To the rest of the world, I am still this crazy woman who went searching for her dead baby in the woods, the woman who neglected her little girl, caught up in her own darkness. I am the unfaithful wife, the disowned daughter, the silly girl who thought she could survive in this world alone, even though until she met Charlie Baxter she had been cocooned, protected. Back then, I didn't understand the world, and I trusted far too easily.*

*I have told Heather about the box underneath the baby's crib where I hide my mementoes and this journal. I refused to let Charlie take the crib away, no matter how much he wanted to. I need it close to me. No one, other than Heather and I, goes near it now. It's like a shrine to lost hope, reminding other people of death, of a life taken. Some people think the room is haunted. Heather told me that sometimes she imagines the lullaby is playing, even though it never does. I hope they're right, that Mia still haunts the room.*

*Even though Heather is still a child, she understands when I tell her something is important. She will not pry or look in the box. My daughter is older than her years in that way. She often frets about me, like a parent should worry about a child. I wish it was different. I wish a lot of things.*

*Lately, I have been yearning for everything to slow down, so I can capture all the things I might previously have missed, including loving and caring for Heather. I never wanted to abandon her and, like Mia, she is part of me, and I, too, will always exist within her. We form our individual pathways, but still we ripple through each other, a mother and her child, intertwined, despite whatever else is happening in the world.*

*My eyes are tired now, but I must write this down, because I know it's important. I should have realised that afternoon, when the washing line was filled with baby clothes, fluttering wildly in the breeze, and I saw that car in front of the house, that things would never be the same again.*

# 54
# HEATHER

By the time I wake the following morning, Alex is already gone. In the mirror, I see the early signs of bruising on my neck. I place a hand there, remembering Billy's threat – *If you mess with me, I'll kill you. No one will ever find you because, like Lexie Gilmore, you will disappear.*

I pick up my notebook, rereading my instruction from the previous night to phone Daniel. I make three attempts, then give up. I check emails. There is one from Robin about the pre-trial meeting with Finlay and Kendell. There is another from the *Boston Globe*. I had ordered a high-resolution copy of the image the police found at Lucas's place. I had almost forgotten about it. In the background, Finlay is talking to reporters. Morgan and Vivienne are there too, standing on the court steps behind him. Behind me are the Handcocks, and to my immediate right, Mark and Robin. It feels strange looking at it now, a clipping cut out by a dead man. My eyes fix on Jim Handcock. He is the common denominator in all this. He always has been. I can barely contemplate seeing him in court later today, but I have to. I know, too, it would be pointless tackling him over any of this. He would give me the same run-around he gave me in the Paramount.

I reopen Robin's email. She and Mark, like myself, are well aware that getting Kendell to agree to further testing is a long shot, but after my meeting with Alicia Amel yesterday, we have to try.

Before I leave, in the hallway, a waft of white light stretches across the floor. I think about my mother. Of late, despite everything, I feel her presence getting ever closer, as if by revisiting our shared past, with more memories slotting into place, she is coming back to me too.

\*

On the way to meet Kendell and Finlay, I try Daniel's number again but, like earlier, it goes to voicemail. I tell myself, Finlay and Kendell must be my focus now. Meeting Alicia yesterday had felt like a breakthrough, something that could turn this case completely around, but without Kendell's approval, the potential genetic connection might not get anywhere near the jury. The burden of proof is on us. We have to push for getting it into evidence, which also means, very shortly, it will be up to me.

When I arrive at Kendell's rooms, they're both waiting for me. Finlay is standing. Kendell is seated.

'You may begin,' Kendell instructs, even before I close the door.

For a second, I think about Billy Townsend's hands tight around my neck. I push the image aside.

'The state argues,' I say, 'that Abby deliberately harmed Jacob, which obviously tells us that all avenues must be explored.'

'Ms Baxter, I haven't dragged myself in early this morning to get a legal lesson from you. I'm willing to hear whatever concrete argument you have, but let's get on with it.'

I can see Finlay is amused by Kendell's annoyance.

'Of course.' I sit down opposite. Finlay stands behind me. 'We're far enough into this trial,' I continue, 'to know this whole case hinges on whether or not there are other reasons, outside of abuse, for the medical conditions presented by Jacob.'

'And you will have sufficient opportunity, Ms Baxter, to educate both myself and the jury as to how that is the case.'

'And as medical opinion is divided –'

'Again, Ms Baxter, tell me something I don't know.'

'– we believe the medical emphasis needs to shift from Abby Jones to the parents. We also believe further blood testing is necessary.'

'This is crazy.' Finlay lets out a mocking laugh. 'My colleague has lost her reason. The Rotterdams are not on trial here. Abby Jones is.'

'I'm sure, Ms Baxter,' Kendell says, 'you're going to back up this request with more than a whim.'

'I have taken an additional statement from my client, surrounding Jacob's ill health.'

'Your Honour, there is nothing new here,' Finlay protests.

'Let Ms Baxter finish.'

'And because of that I have re-examined my client's earlier statements, too, finding fresh elements of concern, with symptoms possibly indicative of an underlying genetic problem. Recently I spoke with a Dr Alicia Amel, a specialist in genetics, and it is her belief that—'

'This is preposterous,' Finlay interrupts again.

Kendell looks at him, unimpressed. 'Mr Clarke, please let Ms Baxter finish. We are here now. We might as well hear all of it.' He turns to me. 'I assume you do have more, Ms Baxter.'

'Yes, Your Honour, I do. We are all aware of Jacob's medical issues, and up to this point, they were not considered to be directly linked to his demise, but this is no longer the case.'

'Why not?' Kendell raises his eyebrows.

'We have found a potential genetic link.'

'Be more precise, Ms Baxter.'

'Vivienne Rotterdam.'

'What about her?'

'She had a sister who died in infancy.'

Kendell clears his throat. 'You have definitive proof there is a connection?'

'Not definitive, no, but—'

'Can I stop you there, Ms Baxter? Because if I don't, I assume Mr Clarke will. We are in the middle of a trial. We can't be halting proceedings or changing direction because of some vague theory on your part.'

'I understand, Your Honour, and I have no intention of requesting a postponement, but I do request the opportunity to rule out a genetic connection to the victim's death. A simple, straightforward testing of the parents is all we ask, and not to do so at this juncture could open the window to a retrial later on.'

'Again, Ms Baxter, I don't need a lesson in the law from you.' He turns to Finlay. 'Mr Clarke, what, if anything, do you know about Vivienne Rotterdam's late sister?'

'Sadly, infant mortality is an unfortunate aspect of life, but I also know that my colleague here is clutching at straws. Jacob Rotterdam presented with clear symptoms of abuse. The chief medical examiner of Boston Medical Center says so, and so do a great many other medical experts.'

'That may be, Mr Clarke, but I will give Ms Baxter the final word on this, before considering the request.' He turns to me.

'Your Honour, if we don't eradicate the possibility of a genetic connection behind Jacob's death, we will fail to pursue a potentially huge flaw in the state's evidence. It would be a travesty for everyone involved.'

'Ms Baxter, put together the proposed parameters of your *potential* testing. I'll expect them on my desk in the morning.'

'We may be looking at testing across a broad framework.'

'Indeed,' he says, his voice weary. Right now, I can't tell if this is a good or a bad sign.

*

That night, it is after nine o'clock by the time we finish putting the legal documents for Kendell together. We have done all we can so it's up to Kendell now, and very little is guaranteed.

In the car, I check my phone for any messages from Daniel – nothing. 'Damn him,' I say, 'why is he avoiding me?' It's not only that fresh piece of memory around the night my mother died, thinking Daniel might have been the one watching me, that irks me, it's also what Billy said, about him working for Jim Handcock. I decide, if he's not answering my calls, there has to be a reason for it, and I'm sick of waiting for answers.

As I near Corham, I see the silver Honda Accord again. After my escapade at Billy's house, I already know it's his car. I remind myself, if he wanted me dead, he had the opportunity last night, but it still makes me uneasy.

At the next crossroads, his car backs off, as if he's playing a game of cat and mouse, only I'm not sure if he's doing it for himself or someone else.

Closer to Daniel's house, I think about our conversation around him staying in Corham, and if I thought any less of him for it. He stayed in the same house, too, even after his parents died. He could have sold the place and started a new life, but he didn't – why not?

Ten minutes later, I pull up outside Daniel's place. I keep my headlights on. I look around for his car. It's not parked out front. I switch off the engine. At the front door, I press the bell. When I don't get an answer, I go out back. I spot his car there and call his name. If he's here, why the hell isn't he answering me?

My voice echoes back at me.

'Daniel!' I roar into the darkness.

I hear a rustle in the trees and, turning, I see something move in the undergrowth. I call his name again. In the distance, I hear the ocean swishing and swaying. When I least expect it, I hear my mother's voice too, warning me to be careful, as if the ghost of her memory is locked inside me, wanting to protect.

At first, as the figure emerges from the undergrowth, I wonder if it's Billy Townsend, but then I see him, the boy I once loved, the person who saved my life, the person, I thought once, who could be my soulmate.

'Why were you hiding, Daniel?' I ask, seeing the anxious look on his face, like someone at cracking point.

'I don't want you here.'

'You scared me half to death. Why didn't you answer when I called you? Why are you hiding in the dark?'

'I don't know.' He shakes his head. Everything about him feels unnerving.

He flicks on a torch and shines it in my face. 'I haven't been honest with you, Heather.' His words are chilled, hostile.

'About what?'

'Back then, when your mother died, I couldn't tell anyone the truth, especially not you.'

The torch is blinding me. I put up a hand to shield my eyes.

'People,' he says, 'might have thought I was strange. I don't want to be strange, Heather. You understand that, don't you?'

'What couldn't you tell anyone?'

'I did something I shouldn't.'

He drops the light from my face.

'Are you talking about my mother's murder?' I take a few steps forward. 'I swear, Daniel, if you've been lying to me, if you had anything to do with that, so help me—'

'I went back to your house.'

'When?'

'Afterwards.'

'After she was killed?'

'No.' He shakes his head, but the movement is too fast. I think about his panic attacks at school before he started taking his medication. I can't worry about that now. If he knows something about my mother, I need him to tell me.

'When did you go back to the house?'

'After your mother's funeral. I wanted things to be the same. I didn't want you in Lorrie's house. I wanted to be with you, like before, so I kept going back there, to your house, but that first day, after the funeral, things weren't right.'

'What wasn't right?'

'I should have told you—'

'Tell me now.'

'The soil out back, by the swing.'

'What about it?' I stare at him. 'You said you did something. That things weren't right.'

'Under the swing, the ground was mucky, but it was spread out wider than before. You know I always measure things, and I thought maybe someone had dug it up.'

'What did you do?'

'I dug it up too.'

'The soil?'

'I had to find out if something was buried there.'

It hits me then: what if Daniel has my mother's things?

'Jesus, Daniel, do you have them? Do you have my mother's mementoes, her journal?' My voice is high-pitched, strained. Has everything been with him all along?

'No, no.' He shakes his head again.

'Tell me the truth, Daniel, or I swear …'

'There was nothing there, Heather, except—'

'What?' I roar at him.

'An empty box.'

I visualise the red box from under the crib. I'm carrying it downstairs to bury it under the swing because my mother had told me it was important. She'd said she didn't want anyone else to find it.

'It can't have been empty,' I scream. 'I put it there. You're not talking sense. Did you give Jim Handcock the things from the box? Daniel, tell me—'

He stops me in mid-sentence. 'Heather, I haven't been taking my medication. Everything is mixed up. You don't understand. Jim Handcock, he wanted me to—'

'To what?'

'I owed him money.' He shakes his head a third time, looking away.

'My mother's things, does he have them?' I scream.

'No, no,' he insists. 'The box was empty.'

'I still don't understand.'

'I started gambling,' he says, putting his head in his hands, 'after my parents died. I got in deep. I mortgaged this place, and built up so much debt, Handcock was the only way out, but he wanted me to do things for him.'

'What things, Daniel?'

'I had to steal the money, don't you see?' he says, talking fast.

'What money?'

'I needed to pay him back. It was the only way out.'

'Daniel, slow down. You're not talking sense.'

'I stole from my clients, the people of this town.'

'How much money?'

He doesn't answer me.

'How much, Daniel?' I push him.

'Fifty thousand.'

'Jesus.'

'At first, Jim Handcock wouldn't take it. He said he liked me being in his debt. Then he started talking about Abby's trial, and how useful I would be for him, especially as I was working with Finlay. I didn't know what to do, but in the end, I wasn't any use to him. Finlay only wanted me to rattle you. So, finally, he took the money back.'

I can't believe what I'm hearing. 'You stole from your clients,' I say, trying to take it all in, 'to pay Jim Handcock back?'

'Yes, and now I don't know what to do. If I don't return the money, and someone finds out, everyone in this town will be against me. I could go to prison.'

I don't say anything for a minute, still trying to make sense of it all. I think about him saving my life, about how, when I had very few people to turn to, he was there for me, and how, if he isn't taking his medication, he isn't thinking straight.

'The money isn't important,' I say. 'I can get it for you. I know what it's like having this town against you.'

'I can't take it from you,' he says, turning away.

'Yes, you can. And you will. You need to put the money back. Besides,' I say, 'it's not my money. Most of it came from a trust fund Lorrie set up. I don't want it. I never wanted it. Lorrie only took me in because she felt she had to. It was never out of love.'

He wipes his eyes.

'Daniel, you have to stop working with Finlay, too. If this gets out and people hear you were in Handcock's pocket, while working for the opposing side, your career is over.'

'Isn't it already over?'

'Not if you put the money back, and keep as far away from the Handcocks as you can. Tell Finlay you're taking a leave of absence because you have personal issues to deal with.'

'I hung up on him the other day.'

'Good, then it won't come as any big surprise. And you need to go back on your medication. Promise me you will, or I won't give you a dime.'

'Okay,' he says, 'but I don't know how I can repay you.'

'Pay me back by getting well, by being the guy who looked out for me. Can you do that?'

I take a step closer to him. I put my arms around him. He seems calmer. 'Look,' I eventually say, pulling away, 'you can help me in other ways too.'

'How?'

'The police found a newspaper article about the trial at Lucas's place. I'm sure it means something, only I haven't been able to work it out yet.' I reach out to touch his arm again. 'Lucas circled my face in red, as if I was some kind of target.'

'Do you think he wanted to harm you?'

'I don't know. Can I send it to you? You're good with details other people miss.'

'Okay,' he says, sounding more like his old self.

'Daniel?'

'Yes?'

I breathe in deep. 'Do you still have the red box?'

'Yes, it's in my bedroom.'

'I want it back.'

I follow him inside. I wait, while he goes upstairs. I visualise the box filled with my mother's things, and my ten-year-old hands wrapped around it, trying to protect her secrets. When he returns, it looks smaller than I remember it. I take it from him. I touch each of the sides. I think about my mother, imagining her opening and closing it. I open the box, too, half wanting to believe I might still find her things inside, but, like her, they are gone. I breathe in the smell of it, hoping, even after all this time, to take a piece of her back.

Walking away, I think about all the things Daniel said to me. How the soil was disturbed after the funeral, as if someone had dug it up. At first, I'd thought he was talking about me when I buried her things, but maybe I was right. Perhaps someone did watch me that night. Then, later, they came back, taking the contents of the box and her journal. It wasn't good enough for them to kill her, they had to have her precious possessions too.

I carry the empty shoebox in the same way I must have carried it as a child, traumatised, in shock, aware, as I am now, how grief feels, with that awful heaviness inside, and how you have to build a wall around yourself, especially when something special is severed, a bond formed before you were born, in the womb of the woman who carried you to term, and the loss, and your love, is scooped out and ripped apart.

The box should be heavy, filled with her things, her journal, her words, but it isn't. The lightness echoes the hollowness I felt all those years before when she was taken from me, when I understood what heartache meant, and now that lightness feels as if her love has been pulled from me again.

Driving away from Daniel's house, I make myself a promise. I don't care how long it takes, or who gets hurt in the crossfire, including myself, but I am going to find my mother's killer. I owe her that. I have always owed her that.

# 55
# MARCIA

A pile of take-out coffee cups forms a mini-mountain on Marcia Langan's desk. She despises the coffee from the machine in the office and, right now, she despises the office, too. The buzz of evening commuters has slowed down to a trickle passing the window. There are only two of them left in the office, herself and Kevin.

It had been so thrilling being on *Breaking News*. She had felt immediately at home. She belongs there, in a big TV station, as far away from this dump as she can get.

'Do you have a cigarette, Kevin? I'm gagging here.'

He points to the no-smoking sign.

'Come on,' she says, 'Gerry isn't here.'

'Your funeral.' He takes aim and fires one at her desk.

She has a lighter in her purse. She lights up, sucks in hard, thinking about her next move.

The story with Morgan Rotterdam has already lost its original bite. She needs something fresh and, as of right now, there isn't a whole lot of information you could call fresh news.

'I'm done here,' she says, emptying her coffee cup and stacking it on top of the others.

'Going home?' Kevin asks.

'I'm thinking about heading back to the scene of the crime.'

He gives her a confused look.

She grabs her coat from the rack and kisses his forehead.

'Thanks for the cigarette,' she says.

'Thanks for the kiss.' He smiles. 'They call that sexual harassment, you know.'

She waves him goodbye, firing the office keys at him.

Out on the street, she knows it doesn't make a whole lot of sense to go back to the same hotel but, with the lack of any other bright ideas, that is exactly what she does. In the reception area, she studies the people coming and going. An hour later, she is tired of hanging around, but decides to have a quick drink before leaving. She orders a Cosmo. In front of her there is an array of bottles on mirrored shelves. From the vantage point of her bar stool, she can still see everyone coming and going. She spots a minor sporting celebrity, then a couple of well-known city investors drinking iced bourbon. None of it amounts to much, and a quarter of an hour later, she is out of there.

In the hotel parking lot, she flings her purse into the car, quickly followed by her body. She checks her phone for the umpteenth time – *no new messages*. She fancies another cigarette. Her resolve to give up is entering delusional territory. She knows the packet in her purse is empty, but she checks it just in case. 'Fuck it,' she says aloud, watching a black Mercedes, two rows up, reversing out.

'Well, I'll be ...' she says, almost whistling.

She recognises Morgan Rotterdam, the driver, straight away, before her eyes move to his female companion, who isn't his wife.

'It can't be,' she says aloud, as the car gets even closer. This is too fricking good to be true. She keeps her eyes fixed on them. Neither looks happy. Indeed, she would put money on the fact that they were arguing, but about what? And why are *they* together? Could she be his significant other? If she was, Vivienne wouldn't be the only female pissed off about his antics at that private party. It's one thing playing around on your wife, but a whole different ballgame messing with a lover.

She thinks about phoning Gerry, and running the fresh scoop by him, but why reveal this gem to him, or even reveal it now, especially as every journalistic bone in her body is telling her there's a whole lot more to this. If she went 'live' with it too soon, other hack journalists would jump on it, making it their own.

She starts the engine. She'll hold fire for now, or at least until she has every sordid aspect of this story. When all the shiny jewels are polished and ready to do their worst, she'll pounce. In the meantime, it might be productive to rattle a few cages, especially the one belonging to the high and mighty Finlay Clarke.

# 56
# VIVIENNE

Vivienne's head hurts. She drank too much wine last night. She didn't mean to, but she did. When she opens her eyes, Morgan isn't there. She doesn't remember him coming home, but she was probably too far gone. He must have slept in the spare room. The clock on the bedside locker comes into focus – six a.m. In a few hours they will need to be in court again.

Last night comes back to her in a blur. She was walking around the house, feeling sorry for herself. One glass of wine had led to another, and then to two bottles. She went to bed late. She wanted to talk to Morgan, but he hadn't come home. She had become so tired. Had she taken sleeping tablets too?

She opens the door of the spare bedroom, the one Morgan uses when he doesn't want to disturb her, or when he doesn't want her asking awkward questions. The bed is tossed. So, he was here last night. Maybe he's out running.

As she walks downstairs, she smells freshly made coffee. Is it a gesture to sweeten her up? She smells something else too, the aroma of another woman's scent. She's smelt it before, when Abby was living with them. But Abby isn't here so it can't belong to her.

She checks the garage. Morgan's car is there. More proof that he came home last night. The key fob is hanging on the wall too. She presses it. The inside of his car stinks with the same scent. Was he with someone last night? Did he take her into their house, into his bed?

Her husband doesn't give a damn about her. If he did, he wouldn't be out half the night with another woman. When Jacob was alive, they could pretend to be a unit, but not any more. Now the whole world knows about her husband's waywardness and, worse still, she has become a creature of pity.

After Jacob died, the psychiatrist explained the stages of grief to her – denial, anger, bargaining, depression, and not necessarily in that order, until finally there is acceptance. She has gone through the first four, the depression hitting last of all, which is why she's drinking so heavily now, the trial tipping things to breaking point.

All there is left is acceptance, and she isn't ready for that.

She hears the back door opening. It's Morgan.

She thinks about the scent again, still perplexed as to why it seems familiar, until it hits her. Surely not, she thinks. Not her. It can't be.

'I detest you,' she says, when he's within hearing distance.

He doesn't answer her. Instead, in his running gear, he sprints past her, as if she doesn't exist.

# 57
# ELIZABETH

*It's past midnight. The last few nights have been colder. There is talk of snow, even though I can already taste summer in the air. It's seeping out of the soil, as if, like me, it's fighting to get free. Charlie hasn't been home for months, but Heather and I are settling into a routine. I find myself savouring tiny things, like how peaceful she looks in sleep, or the way she seems so intent when she's doing even the smallest of tasks. Her body is changing too, although she's only ten. One day soon she will become a woman.*

*Items are still going missing from the house. I may be running out of time. Jim became so bitter after Mia's death, and harsher too. Charlie never said it, but I think he knew from the beginning that Mia was Jim's child. It was partly why he wanted to get rid of the crib, as if to cast it aside would also rid our lives of Jim. Even as an infant, Mia had the look of Jim about her.*

*I have learned of late to understand that a different kind of love is born out of necessity. Now in fear of my life, I know I shouldn't have feelings for Jim, but I do. Despite everything, despite Mia's loss, I recognise that, like me, he is damaged too. When he first entered my life, I hadn't expected love to creep up on me. I was so tired worrying about creditors calling at the door or trying to keep food on the table, I was there for the taking, at his bidding. But for a short time I grew to know a different man from the one other people knew, and very soon into our relationship, I discovered another truth. I saw in him the safety of my old life, the one I discarded to marry Charlie.*

*I was the one who let Jim Handcock into my life. I was the one who allowed him to take away my financial cares, who bore his child, and when her young life was cut short, when his anger became all-consuming, and his bitterness and hate came back with a vengeance, especially after he found out about me and Lucas, I saw the side of Jim that other people saw, only I saw it worst of all, because I knew how deep his sadness went, once he'd lost his child. Everything changes with the death of an infant, creating an emptiness that Jim filled with hate, knowing he couldn't bear the alternative.*

# 58
# ALICE

Alice Handcock stands in front of the full-length mirror dressed in a Ralph Lauren trouser suit of charcoal grey. She fixes one side of her honey-blonde hair behind her ear. It is now cut in a bobbed style, and she admires her new look as she picks up a pair of pale pink earrings to match her rose-quartz necklace. She hears Jim bellowing into the phone from the next room. She lingers a little longer, repositioning the necklace. The phone is slammed down. If Jim isn't careful, they will be late for court.

'Don't delay,' she calls, 'or we'll be stuck in that wretched traffic.'

She hears the shower running. 'Good,' she says to the mirror, before putting on a pair of Jimmy Choo heels. This whole mess with Abby is such a nightmare. Why did she ever agree to let that stupid girl into their house? Of course it's all water under the bridge now, she thinks, and best to keep a cool head, and ride out the nasty business.

She picks up a photograph of her and Jim from the bedside locker. It was taken a couple of years earlier, when they went skiing in Aspen.

He looks much more than twelve years her senior, but it takes hard work to look as she does. No one believes her age. They think she's at least ten years younger, perhaps even fifteen. On occasion, some have mistaken Jim for her father. It always makes her smile.

The shower stops. She braces herself for Jim's mood, which she already knows is bad. He has been like a man possessed all morning, and when he's like this, no amount of cajoling will make a damn bit of difference.

She waits. The bathroom door opens, and there he is in all his finery, a white bath towel wrapped around his roly-poly waist. His chest is flushed with red blotches behind the curled grey hairs, which are fluffed and damp.

'Not in a good mood this morning, Jim?'

'You could say that.'

'Who has upset you?' She drags out the words.

'The usual fuckers.'

'Don't let them get to you, darling.'

'I hate people who take me for a fool.'

'Who would *ever* do that to you?'

He discards the towel on the floor, marching towards the walk-in wardrobe.

'Anyone I know this time?' she asks, mildly curious.

'Daniel Petersen.'

'Who?'

'The Petersen boy. You know him. His folks died last year.'

'Oh, yes, I remember now. He used to have a squint, didn't he? He wore those horrible glasses.'

'Well, he isn't wearing them any more,' he says, walking back into the room. 'He isn't doing much any more.'

'He always struck me as a loser.'

'Loser or not, for a time I had him exactly where I wanted him.'

'I'm sure it'll all work out. You usually get your own way.'

'I had high plans for him, but now …'

'Now what?'

'Now nothing. I don't want to talk about it. What the hell does a man have to do to have peace in his own home?'

'You never did like loose ends, did you, Jim?'

'What do you mean?'

'Nothing,' she says, smiling. 'But you'd better calm down before we go to court. We cannot look as if we're unravelling.'

He walks towards her, fully dressed now, apart from his tie. He hands it to her and turns up the collar of his shirt. 'Fix this for me, will you?'

'Where would you be without me, darling?'

'Maybe,' he says, 'when this is all over, we should take a vacation, head off to Seal Harbor and visit your parents.'

'I don't know, Jim. Ever since they retired, I swear they're busier than ever. Sometimes I think Daddy loves that darn boat of his more than he loves me.'

'He made you that,' he says, pointing to the only reminder of Alice's old life in the room, a miniature New England-style doll's house, sitting in the corner and repainted every year to match the décor.

'I was a little girl then. I'm far from that now. There now,' she says, stepping back to inspect her work, 'you look perfect.'

'You look perfect too, Alice.' He places his hands around her narrow waist.

She laughs, fingering her rose-quartz necklace.

He stares at her. 'Do you think Heather Baxter was a mistake?'

'Only time will tell, darling, only time will tell.'

# 59
# FINLAY

Finlay punches the air in celebration. *Request for blood tests denied.* He hadn't expected to get the judgement back so fast, but he's practically humming when Warren McKenna knocks on the door.

'You're in a happy mood,' Warren comments.

'Kendell has ruled in our favour.'

'That's good, but it seems you have an early-morning visitor.'

Finlay checks his watch. 'Who?'

'Marcia Langan.'

'Tell her there isn't a press conference this morning, and even if there was, to get in line with everyone else.'

'She says you'll want to talk to her.'

Finlay lets out a sigh. 'Damn her.' He checks his watch again. It'll be another hour before things kick off for the day. 'Keep her waiting a few minutes, then send her in. But I swear not even a journalist is going to dampen my mood today.'

If Marcia is here this early, he considers, she either has something or is sniffing around for a story. His gut tells him, either way, he probably won't like it.

When Warren opens the door, Marcia follows close behind. Finlay greets her with one of his warmest smiles.

'Morning, Finlay,' she sings, taking a seat at his desk without being asked.

'Good morning, Marcia, why don't you sit down?'

She laughs. 'I do so love a man with a sense of humour.'

'I aim to please.'

She looks across at Warren and then back to Finlay. 'Due to the delicate nature of my visit, I think it best if we talk alone.'

Finlay nods to Warren, an instruction to leave.

'What can I do for you, Marcia, now that it's just the two of us?'

'More like what can I do for you, Finlay?'

The confident swagger in her voice annoys him.

'If you've got a story, Marcia, spit it out.'

'Would you like to guess what it's about?'

'No.'

'Oh, Finlay,' she says, 'you're no fun.'

'I don't think fun is going to be part of this conversation.'

'Oh, okay, then,' she says, her tone still annoying. 'I might as well come straight out and say it.'

'Appreciated.'

'I've been keeping an eye on one of your clients. Well, not your client exactly, with you working for the state and all, but for now, let's call him a client.'

'Which one might that be, Marcia?'

'Why, Morgan Rotterdam, of course.'

'There are laws against stalking.'

'I like to call it investigative journalism.'

'I like to call it harassment.'

'I'm not asking for your approval. I'm simply here to offer you information, and believe me, you'll want it.'

'I'm assuming you're not sharing this information out of journalistic kindness.'

'We've gotten to know each other so well, and over such a short time, haven't we?'

'What is it, Marcia?'

'Not so fast, Finlay. First, I need a commitment from you.'

'Commitment?'

'I want first pick of the cherry, not only during this trial but afterwards. You're a powerful man, Finlay, and when you go up even higher in the world, I want to be a part of that too. I don't plan to stay with the *Patriot Eagle* for ever. I like it here in Boston, and having a high-rolling gunslinger like you on my side sure would help me a lot in that regard. Heavens, I even hear you could be moving into the political arena, *especially* if you win this case. Wouldn't that be a fine thing?'

'And if I agree, what do I get in return?'

'I hold fire on my story, which, if you don't play ball, will make all that nasty stuff already in the media about Morgan look like a child's bedtime story.'

He stares at her for a moment. She thinks she's the one in control, but a journalist in control means nothing short of a whole heap of trouble. He'll agree to whatever she wants, but only for as long as it takes.

'Okay,' he says. 'It seems I don't have a choice so, in principle, I agree. Now, what is this story of yours?'

'Morgan went back to the scene of the crime, to the same hotel.'

Idiot, he thinks.

'I saw him there last night. You know the one, Finlay, where he was with that underage girl.'

'And?'

'I mean, I was surprised. You'd think a man like him would know better.'

'Perhaps he thought it would be the last place people would look.'

'You could be right, but what's especially important is *who* he was with.'

'Don't drag this out, Marcia, even if you're getting a whole lot of pleasure from it.'

'I would put down money,' she says, 'that the female he was with is the very last person in the world you would ever suspect.'

'You don't say, but as you still haven't given me her name, I cannot comment on that.' He clenches his fists below the desk.

'Alice … Handcock,' she says in slow motion, emphasising each syllable. 'I mean, heavens above, can you believe it?'

'Are you sure?'

'Of course I'm sure. I'm not going to make a mistake like that. And, from what I could see, it looked like she and Morgan had had a lover's tiff, because something sure wasn't happy in Eden.'

'There could be a perfectly reasonable explanation.'

'Oh, I doubt that, Finlay, and what with him having a reputation for kinky behaviour and all, heavens only knows what those two were up to. I sure wouldn't like to be Vivienne Rotterdam, would you? Hooked up with a husband playing around with any damn female on the planet he wants to. They used to be friends, right? The Handcocks and the Rotterdams?'

'So I heard.'

'Honestly, Finlay, it would give the House of Horrors a run for its money. Come to think of it, that's such a great headline, isn't it?' She laughs.

He clenches his fists again, as the fallout from her information accelerates in his mind. Alice and Morgan? For how long? Before or since the trial? There is Morgan's temper too, and the escalating frostiness between him and Vivienne. The man is obviously capable of being majorly stupid, but the bigger question is whether or not he could have lost his temper under pressure, and hit out at Jacob. And if he's thinking this, others will think it too. If this story gets out, the dynamics will shift considerably. Having a one-night stand at some private party, even with an underage girl, is one thing, but an affair alters everything.

'Marcia,' he says, 'I need to know I can trust you.'

'Why, of course you can.'

'Then here is what I want you to do.'

'I thought, Finlay, *you* were supposed to be helping *me*?'

'All in good time, Marcia, but for now I want you to get hold of any negative press you can on Abby Jones. I don't care if you have to repeat old stuff, or make it up, but keep it coming, and fast, do you hear me?'

'I hear you.'

'I promise you, Marcia, I will keep you in the loop.'

Trusting a journalist to keep quiet is about as sensible as sending a fox into a hen house. There will always be casualties. He needs to come up with another plan, and fast. All the negative news stories in the world on Abby Jones aren't going to cut it, not any more. Now something else is required. And if Morgan is a disaster zone, he has no option other than to use Vivienne. He hadn't wanted to call her as a witness, especially when it looked unnecessary, but damn the Lord, the public love her. The grieving mother, the long-suffering wife, showing strength and refinement despite untold adversity. The media have run that photograph of her from the first day of trial, the one with the single tear trickling down her face, so many times, it's practically a symbol of world grief. Meaning she could turn this whole darn thing around.

Still, he'll need to be careful. Even if Kendell has thrown out Heather's request for blood tests, if Vivienne is giving testimony she'll have to be rehearsed to within an inch of her life.

Looking out at the city landscape, he thinks about Marcia again. This story could blow up in his face at any time, no matter what she promised him, and it's the kind of story that always sticks. He'll need to scare Morgan into behaving, and ensure he keeps Vivienne on side too, by whatever means necessary. If she finds out about Alice, the whole thing will become one god-awful mess. Marcia was right about one thing: the Rotterdams are not his clients. He works for the state, which means they're no different from anyone else. They are there to be used in whatever way possible to achieve the right outcome.

He'll tell Vivienne today he's adding her to the witness list. He'll tell her in full public view too and see what comes from that. By putting the two of them under pressure, if he's lucky he can manage the damage control. There are only two absolutes here. He can't trust Marcia Langan to sit on this story for ever, and from here on, there is zero room for error. Starting now, the emphasis shifts squarely to Vivienne Rotterdam.

# 60
# HEATHER

I review Kendell's decision in depth, along with the conclusion that, unless concrete evidence exists to dictate further exploration, it is not the role of the court to investigate new areas. We knew it was a long shot but, still, it comes as a blow.

'You look dreadful,' Robin says, sitting down beside me at the defence table.

'I had a late night,' I say. All the emotion of the previous evening, thinking about my mother, carrying that empty red box, regurgitating everything that has happened since she was killed, including my estranged father still being in Cedar Junction, hasn't gone away, but this morning, somehow, I have to build a steel wall around myself, for my client's sake.

I turn to Abby. 'Are you okay?'

'I feel like a goldfish going around and around in a bowl with everyone staring.'

'Don't think about it too much,' I say. 'Sometimes when everything looks one way, it can turn. We'll get the chance to show our side of things soon.' Even to me, my words sound like rehearsed rhetoric. I watch Vivienne Rotterdam enter the courtroom with Morgan. She looks as if she's had a rough night too, only today she looks different, more defeated. I know that look. It tells the world to keep away. Finlay seems slightly rattled as well, which doesn't make sense. He should be happy with Kendell's decision.

'What's going down?' I whisper to Robin.

'I have no idea,' she replies.

I watch Finlay walk over to Vivienne. He whispers something in her ear.

'Christ,' says Robin. 'What has he said to her? Her face has gone completely white.'

Finlay must notice the change in her too, because he grabs Vivienne's arm to prevent her falling.

'What is he playing at?' I ask aloud, keeping my voice low. 'If Vivienne Rotterdam faints, we'll have another media frenzy on our hands.'

'Water,' shouts Finlay, as Vivienne's legs give way, and she collapses to her knees. The cameras immediately start clicking.

'At least Kendell and the jury aren't in yet,' Robin says.

'Will someone get some water?' Finlay repeats, looking all around him.

A female bailiff fetches Vivienne a chair, and a glass of water. Vivienne's hands shake bringing it to her lips.

'What should we do?' asks Robin.

'Find out what Finlay's up to.'

'You think he wanted her to faint?' whispers Robin.

'He wants to win,' I say, 'and he'll do whatever it takes.'

\*

It's late afternoon, after the day's proceedings have ended, when we discover the reason behind Vivienne's scene in court. I doubt she fabricated it, but equally I know Finlay intentionally told her the news about becoming a witness in full public view. He wanted to create a reaction, and he succeeded. The images of the grieving mother collapsing are all over the newspapers and television channels.

How Can A Mother Face Her Son's Killer Every Day?
Grieving Mother Collapses Under Pressure.
Mother On Her Knees As If In Prayer.
Nanny Looks On As Mother Cracks.
How Much More Can Vivienne Take?

'There has to be something we don't know,' says Robin. 'Finlay must have his reasons for changing tack and putting her on the witness list.'

'I agree, and if Finlay wants to escalate the grieving-mother card, something has shifted, something we don't know about.'

'It may be connected to Morgan,' Mark says, 'more dirt.'

'Possibly, but I wonder if Finlay's missing something too.'

Robin eyeballs me. 'What do you mean?'

'I don't know,' I say, 'but Vivienne is usually so composed. Even before Finlay spoke to her this morning, she looked different, almost crushed.'

'Marcia Langan has run another hatchet-job on Abby's so-called drug-taking,' Mark adds.

'Okay, let's think about this for a second,' says Robin. 'We may not be able to work out the *why* behind today's series of events, but at least we can attempt to determine the emotion fuelling it.'

'On Vivienne's part, anger,' says Mark, so matter-of-factly that we both stare at him. 'Well, she does have a lot to be angry about.'

'But she's been harbouring that anger all along,' Robin adds. 'It's nothing new.'

'Still, let's look at these things closer,' I say, walking over to the board. I write 'anger' on it.

'Loss of her son,' says Robin, 'grief.'

I write that down too.

'Her husband's infidelities,' adds Mark.

'Media spotlight,' I say, adding this as number four.

'Her potential guilt about Jacob's death,' pipes Robin.

I write 'guilt' and 'genetic connection' on the board.

'There is the loss of control,' I add.

'Legal trials can do that to people,' Robin agrees. 'All the decisions are made by others. It is disempowering.'

'Her emotional loss is disempowering, too,' I add, the memory of last night, carrying my mother's empty box from Daniel's house, still raw. 'By now, she could feel everything is slipping out of her grasp.'

'And Morgan's infidelities would feed into that lack of emotional control,' adds Mark, 'especially with his dirty laundry out there for everyone to see. She may feel she's the one being ridiculed in public.'

'Okay,' I say, 'this trial is obviously taking its toll on her, but even so, up until today she was managing reasonably well, considering.'

'Morgan's recent infidelities are nothing new either,' adds Robin.

'But what if there has been another form of betrayal?' Mark suggests. 'Perhaps this time his infidelity was too much for her to bear. It could even be with someone she trusted.'

'Or someone she hates,' I say. 'Let's look at this again. Finlay knows something we don't, or why change tactics? Agreed?'

'Agreed,' they say in unison.

'So, what if he didn't spot just how vulnerable Vivienne was today, before he started his circus? What if he's so tied up in trying to hide something that he missed her emotional shift?'

'I'm not getting you,' says Robin.

'Finlay may be keeping his cards close to his chest, but Vivienne has done this for a long time too. There is a chance that neither of them is telling the other everything.'

'You mean Vivienne's potential genetic connection to Jacob's death, and keeping that a secret?' asks Mark.

'Maybe, yes, but she also strikes me as a woman who can keep a lot of things to herself.' Nobody knew what my own mother was thinking, except herself. She didn't trust people to know things.

'If your point is correct, Mark,' I say, 'wouldn't it be the ultimate mockery if another woman, whom Vivienne knew, perhaps someone she trusted or someone she hates, is also having an affair with her husband? The ridicule goes up a notch, if someone close to her knows things she doesn't, laughing at her while playing around with her husband, especially when she's in the middle of suffering the worst loss of her life?'

I walk back to the board. 'The real question here is how we use it to our advantage, especially if we've spotted something Finlay hasn't.'

'In cross-examination, push her until she lets something vital slip,' Robin suggests.

'Tricky,' I say. 'With her getting the lion's share of the sympathy vote, we risk alienating the jury even more against Abby.'

'Finlay will prep her to an inch of her life,' adds Robin. 'He'll minimise any potential risks playing this card.'

'We have a couple of days before she testifies, so let's use them,' I say. 'We need to watch her like a hawk and study her reaction to everything and anything. If Finlay's missed something, we'll use that to our advantage, but we must be careful. If something or someone has backed him into a corner, rats like him always come out fighting.'

When they leave, I look back at the word 'anger' on the board. I think about my anger at my father, Billy Townsend, Jim Handcock and his schemes, including putting Daniel under pressure, and finally, Lucas's death, and how I blamed him for killing my mother. Mostly, though, as I walk towards the board, I think about how I've avoided Samuel, my uncle, for far too long. As a child, when I was lonely or scared, I would imagine I lived a different life, sometimes becoming a character in one of my books, separating myself from reality. That's partly why, at first, I doubted some of my old memories, not trusting them, but after talking to Daniel last night, I know some of them, at least, are true, not imagined, which is why, no matter how much Samuel makes my skin crawl, I plan on confronting him this evening.

# 61
# ALICE

Alice waits for Morgan, sitting in the front seat of her shiny new white Cadillac, with its alloy wheels and darkened windows. Trash blows across the motel parking lot of the Comfort Inn, which looks anything but comfortable. What a dump, she thinks, seething. All these months she's put him on a pedestal, not realising he was no better than her damn husband. She was there for him when he needed her. He cried on her shoulder over and over about that stupid baby of his. She listened patiently, even becoming a punchbag for his rage, believing all his empty promises.

Originally, they had agreed to avoid meeting during the trial, but he couldn't resist making contact again, and she went to that hotel room, after he begged to see her one more time, nearly crying down the phone. She did everything he wanted. What good has it done her?

Ever since the media scandal with the teenage girl at that private party, everyone is talking about poor Vivienne. No one gives a damn about how Alice feels, including Morgan. He said Finlay's on his

334

case and he has to curb things, as if he can switch her on and off like some water faucet.

'Damn it,' she says aloud, looking at her cell phone. 'There isn't even a proper signal here.' She's furious at him for even suggesting meeting at this dump. He didn't want them to be seen, with things being awkward. He'll pay for this.

It was so much fun in the beginning, sneaking around like young lovers, although she doubted young lovers got up to the things they had. It had taken her back to her younger self, and the adolescence she was forced to skip, marrying Jim. It was her time for enjoyment. She had the right to turn the tables. Sure, she'd had the odd fling before but, compared to Jim, she was practically a virgin.

She leans her head back, her thoughts drifting to Heather Baxter, thinking how that girl is a carbon copy of her mother.

Her cell phone bleeps with another text from Morgan. He's been delayed with Finlay.

She checks the phone for a signal to reply, but it's already gone out of coverage.

'I'm not waiting around here any longer,' she says to herself, looking in the rear-view mirror. She already knows what's going down, and she certainly isn't in the mood for giving Morgan anything more than she has given him already.

# 62
# HEATHER

The closer I get to my grandparents' house, with my uncle Samuel waiting for me, the more clusters of dark clouds form in the sky. A couple of miles outside Corham, revulsion at the prospect of meeting him rises like bile in my throat. Driving on the highway, I think about Lexie Gilmore. Billy said if he wanted me dead, I would simply disappear, like her, and no one would ever find me. My father talked about her, too, when he said Jim Handcock liked to bury his secrets. Now I imagine her cycling down Main Street, visualising the girl from the newspaper clippings, petite and slender. I see the imaginary wheels of her bike turning, as if she's caught in time, cycling forward without gaining any ground, like me, partly trapped in the past.

Outside my grandparents' house, the thought of meeting Samuel fills me with even more dread, but I take everything in, the barren trees in the garden, the untidy lawn, the old panelled front door, which, soon, I'll stand in front of. The place already looks rundown. Samuel doesn't care about appearances, he never did, and with each step I take closer to the house, it's as if I'm entering my past, one I'm still somewhat unsure of.

I steady my resolve, making my body more rigid, and capable of fighting back. When he opens the door, at first neither of us says anything. I hear the television in the distance, with church music blasting from it. I remember his new-found religious pathway but, like everything else about him, that isn't to be trusted.

Inside the hallway, as he shuts the door behind me, it feels as if the walls are closing in. I'm here now, I tell myself. I need to get answers.

'You didn't stay long after the funeral,' he says, as if I should be ashamed.

'I didn't want to.'

He mutes the television. 'Sit down,' he says. 'It's your home too.'

'It's never been my home.'

He smells of stale beer. He is unshaven, too. The big old house seems to stand in mockery against him. This can't be what Lorrie and Grey dreamed about when they had children all those years before. That their daughter would be murdered, and their son would turn out like this.

'I thought you found God,' I say, turning the tables on him, looking at the empty beer cans.

'What do you want, Heather? Because I know you want something or you wouldn't be here.' He waves his outstretched arms around in a dramatic gesture, taking in the house. I stare down the hallway to the door of my grandfather's library, where I first began thinking about the law. I stay standing, staring at him. I need him to tell me about my mother, and I need him to tell me the truth about *me* too. Abby's words, talking about her abuse, still linger in my mind. What if Samuel is the reason for my suppressed memory? What if, all those years ago, my father's warning to him not to touch me had come too late?

'You said you wanted to talk about Elizabeth,' he growls, angry.

'We've never spoken properly about her.'

'Sit down,' he repeats, and reluctantly, I do. 'What do you want to know?'

'Do you know who killed her?'

'You said Lucas did it,' he spits, his words accusing.

'I was a child. I was wrong.'

He laughs aloud.

'What's so funny?'

'You.'

The memory of the man walking out of the room replays in my mind. Is the same man in front of me now?

'Did you molest me as a child?' I ask, so suddenly I surprise myself, my voice separate, as if it's not part of me.

The musty smell in the room mingles with the stench of booze. I think again about the day after my grandfather's funeral, how Samuel gave me that ten-dollar bill. 'You gave me money once,' I say. 'Do you remember? After Grey's funeral. You put your hands on me. I didn't understand what was happening, but I knew something wasn't right.' The bile thickens in my throat again.

'I remember,' he says.

'You don't deny it?'

'What's the point? The Lord knows everything.'

'What else did you do?'

'Nothing.'

'I don't believe you.'

'Believe what you want. Lizzie warned me off you. Your father warned me off you, too, after she went and got herself killed.'

He keeps staring at me, as if he's wondering how to play this, as if he's the one holding an ace card. I hear my mother's voice, the same way I heard her that night when I was at Daniel's house. She's telling me to be strong, not to let him get to me, to stand up to him, because he's nothing more than a drunken fool.

'You sure felt sweet in my arms back then,' he says, smiling, 'but if it means anything to you, your father didn't need to warn me off.'

'No?'

'No. By the time Lizzie got herself killed, you'd already started changing. You were too old.'

'I don't understand.'

'A ten-year-old wasn't to my taste.'

'You're vile.'

'Think what you want, I don't care.'

'I have a memory of a man in my bedroom, when I was younger. Was it you?'

Behind him, the church choir on the television is still muted.

'Tell me,' I say, 'I need to know.'

'God has already forgiven me,' he mutters, 'for all my evil thoughts.'

'How convenient,' I fire back at him.

He leaps from the chair, tightening his fists, as if readying himself to hit me hard, but then he stops himself. 'You look just like her,' he says. 'It's like seeing her bloody ghost walking around taunting everyone.' His eyes are crazed. I see myself in my old bedroom again, after the man closes the door, but now someone else is in the room. They're standing over me. I let out a gasp, realising who it is. It's not Samuel. It's my mother.

'Yeah,' he finally says, 'I got close to you once, sneaked into your bedroom, but Lizzie warned me. She heard me upstairs and called out. She said she knew what I was up to, and if I ever tried anything, she'd kill me.'

'She threatened you?'

'Yeah.'

'Did you hurt her? Is that it? Was it you?'

'I don't need to answer to you.' He stares back at the television.

'You know something, don't you?' I scream.

'I know she lived in fear of her life, and that fucker of a father of yours didn't do anything to protect her.'

'How do you know she lived in fear of her life?'

'Because I read her stupid journal.'

'Do you have it?' I ask, barely able to believe it possible.

He looks at me, bewildered. 'No,' he smirks, 'I don't, but that afternoon you talked about, the one when I was in your bedroom, and Lizzie called out to me, while she was in the bedroom with you, comforting her little princess, I saw what she was writing in it.'

'Who was my mother afraid of?'

The lines on his forehead bulge, his eyes looking as if they're out on stilts, like a frightened animal ready to defend itself. 'The father of her bastard child, that's who.'

His words hang, and for a second I want to deny they exist, but then I say, 'Are you talking about Mia?'

'Of course I am,' he shoots back accusingly. 'You are every inch of Charlie – you were even back then, running away from any piece of shit you couldn't face up to.'

'I'm not running any more.' I breathe in deeply, my feet stuck to the floor, as immovable as my resolve. 'Who was Mia's father?'

'Who do you think?' He laughs. 'Your fucking boss.'

'Jim Handcock? Did he know about the journal?'

'That man knows everything.'

I relive that day in the barn, the one when Alice Handcock got sick, and Jim Handcock frightened me, and how, as an adult now, I realise his attention towards me was elevated because I looked like a miniature version of my mother. He said, 'You could be *my* daughter.' Was he lamenting Mia? Is Samuel right? Did he blame my mother for her death, making her live in fear of her life? And what about my father? Did he know Mia wasn't his child? Is that why he left, because he couldn't bear the truth?

'Why didn't you say any of this before?'

'The truth, no matter what God preaches, isn't all it's cracked up to be.'

'What makes you so sure Jim Handcock was Mia's father?'

He doesn't respond.

'Did you read it in her journal too?' I ask, pushing him.

'I didn't have to. I saw it in her face, with that mark on it, like the young girl you're defending, that baby killer.'

'Abby didn't harm the baby.'

He smirks again, turning up the volume of the television. 'I'm done talking,' he says.

He isn't going to tell me anything more. I slam the front door behind me, but as I leave, with each step I take towards the car, I consider everything he has said to me, about Mia, about her being Jim Handcock's child, about how my mother lived in fear of her life, and how I will be facing the same man in court tomorrow.

I can't go home, not yet. Instead, I drive towards the coast, and soon I'm standing at the water's edge, listening to the ebb and flow of the tide, in much the same way I used to do as a child, when I didn't want to hear my parents arguing, when I would look out at the world, pretending everything was okay when it wasn't.

# 63
# ALEX

Alex waits in her car for Daniel to leave his house. She has been watching him on and off for days. She doesn't trust him, even if Heather does, and she told Blake as much. Blake is still trying to find a link between the cold case of Elizabeth Baxter, Lexie Gilmore and Lucas García because, both Alex and Blake know, there is one.

While waiting for Daniel, in her mind she goes over the old police report on Lexie's disappearance. The day she vanished, she went into town. She paid a visit to the hardware store to pick up supplies. After that she tried on a couple of dresses at the only boutique in town. When she didn't turn up that evening, the alert went out. Her bicycle, which belonged to the Handcocks, was later found near the library. She was never seen after the last sighting at the boutique. Lexie didn't have any proper family either. Her father was dead. Her mother found being a widow difficult and became estranged from Lexie. She claims that at the time of Lexie's disappearance, she hadn't seen her in over two years. There were no siblings. So, the trail went cold with Lexie. Some people believed she hitched a ride to the highway and made her way someplace else, but Alex didn't swallow that. Lexie wasn't the kind of girl to up and leave. She didn't do wild stuff and, no matter which way Alex looked at things, Lexie's disappearance wasn't adding up. It smelt of something rotten, just as Elizabeth Baxter's case file stank to high heaven.

Now, more and more, she's wondering about Daniel Petersen, which is why she's sitting outside his house. It didn't take her long to work out he isn't the model citizen he presents. So far, the juicier bits of information have come from her cyber surveillance, unearthing his online gambling and half a dozen aliases. On most of the sites, he has prime membership, meaning he is in shit-deep. Gambling makes people do nasty things, including stealing from those close to them, and she sure doesn't plan on that being Heather. But when it comes to Daniel, Heather keeps most of the information about him close. Old loyalties carry weight. He was there when her mother was killed. They probably have their own secrets. Secrets bond people in unhealthy ways, often blinding them.

She watches him as he locks the house. He seems obsessional, checking the windows, the back and front doors, brushing his clothes down, examining the soles of his shoes. In the car, he readjusts his rear-view mirror, settling his tie, pulling across his seatbelt and rearranging the side mirrors. He's all cleaned up, unlike a couple of days ago, when he was hiding out in the woods. She keeps looking as he swabs the steering wheel with an anti-bacterial wipe. She watches him drive away, counting the exact minutes until she knows it's safe to get out of her car and casually walk across to his house.

She already knows where the alarm box is, the cables leading to it, and that it is not connected to a central station. When he returns, Daniel will see the severed cables. It will cause him anxiety. It will put him on edge. When people are on edge, they make mistakes, slip up.

As she enters the house, she concentrates on what it tells her about the man – orderly, minimalistic, obsessively clean. Jesus, she thinks, he must be up for hours before he even leaves this place. It makes sense with the gambling. Someone who is obsessed with things being orderly sometimes seeks out other outlets. He might have thought he could control the gambling, but even if you win big, you lose big too. Someone like him would be a perfect magnet for it.

Alex sets about photographing the house, including his home office. On the table, she sees Heather's face staring back at her. It's the image from the *Boston Globe*, the same one the cops found at Lucas's place, and immediately she wonders why it's there.

# 64
# HEATHER

After two more days of prosecution witnesses, and two more days since I faced down my uncle, I mentally prepare myself for the witness who could be the most important of all, Vivienne Rotterdam. Her testimony is critical. I know it, and Finlay knows it too. Trials have been won and lost on less.

I check my cell phone for messages from either Daniel or Alex: both have been oddly quiet over the last couple of days. It isn't unusual for Alex, but Daniel hasn't been in touch since he put the money back, even though he swore he was on his medication again.

Being so close to Jim Handcock, and knowing what I know now, has become increasingly difficult too, but none of this, I remind myself, is Abby's fault.

Vivienne's testimony will be broadcast to homes all over Massachusetts and beyond, no doubt watched by mothers who have dropped their children to school or by those who may be holding their babies in their arms.

Over the last couple of days, Vivienne's demeanour has given little away, but as I study her, she appears more composed than the woman who fainted a few days earlier. Finlay looks to have done his job well. His witness, on first impression, exudes strength with a certain vulnerability, as if her tears are being held back, but only just.

As she is being sworn in, Judge Kendell, in his robes, with the federal and government flags hanging behind him, waits. Everything about this moment feels solemn. The court clerk and the court reporter, both female, watch Vivienne too. She is the mother of the dead child. No one else, not even Morgan, comes anywhere close to her perceived level of emotional pain. Her losing Jacob so young defies our concept of nature, just as it did for my mother. If he was still alive, Vivienne could be holding him in her arms now, like all the new mothers tuning in to watch her.

Finlay will concentrate on all these things, because these are the things we understand, which society accepts as part of our attempt at an orderly existence. No one is going to rush Vivienne Rotterdam. Finlay will take advantage of that, too. I would do the same thing.

After she is sworn in, he approaches her tentatively. The silence feels like a heavy void, ready to suck all of us in. It is with near relief I hear his voice. I turn to Abby, who is fixated on Vivienne too.

'I know this must be difficult for you, Vivienne,' Finlay says.

'Someone has to speak for Jacob.' She looks at the jury, closing her eyes for a couple of seconds, and taking in a deep breath.

'A mother's loss is beyond words,' Finlay adds, acknowledging what everyone else is thinking.

'I have to be brave for my son.'

Finlay nods. 'Can I ask you, Vivienne, to go back to that fatal day?'

'I return to it all the time,' she says, 'over and over.'

I think about how I do the same thing, going back into my past, so many parts of it still unresolved. I look across at Jim Handcock, wondering, as I have done for days, if he killed my mother.

'Vivienne, when you were at work, did Abby Jones alert you at any point to anything being wrong?'

She takes a tissue from her purse. 'No, she did not.'

'And later, when you feared the worst, what were your first thoughts?'

'I thought about all the seconds, minutes, or even hours I had missed.' Her voice breaks. 'Sorry.'

'There is no need to apologise. Take your time.'

'Thank you.'

We're all imagining her pain. We wouldn't be human if we weren't.

'Mostly,' she says, 'I think about how precious little life Jacob had, and how vital that time was before he died, how it could have made a difference. How he might still be with me. If Abby had said anything to me that day, I would have been there in a heartbeat. I would have had those extra hours with him. I would have seen his beautiful eyes for longer. I would have held him, helped him. Every single second lost felt as if *she* took them from me too.'

I grasp Abby's hand under the defence table, squeezing it.

'Go on, if you can, Vivienne,' Finlay urges.

'It wasn't enough to harm him. She had to deprive me of those last moments.' She stares at Abby. I see the hate in her eyes.

Abby pulls her hand from mine. This is hurting her.

'It was *my* time with *my* baby,' Vivienne cries out, 'not hers.' She puts the tissue to her eyes again, breathing deeper. 'All it would have taken was a phone call, and I would have been there for him. She denied me even that.'

'Yet,' Finlay says, pausing, 'Abby had time to phone Ashley Connolly, her friend.'

'Yes.'

'And they talked for a very long time.'

'Yes.'

'While Jacob's condition was getting increasingly worse?'

'Yes, and—' Her voice breaks again.

'Do you need some water, Mrs Rotterdam?' asks Kendell.

'No. I'm fine.'

'Okay, if you're sure.'

'I keep thinking about Jacob in his crib,' she says, 'uncared for, suffering alone.' She stares at Finlay, desperation in her eyes.

I know that look because I have lived it, the memory of something too horrible to bear, my mother dying alone, frightened, knowing I can never turn back the clock and change any of it.

Another silence fills the room. Finlay lets it hover. The jury have eyes only for Vivienne Rotterdam.

'Every second he suffered, and I wasn't with him,' she says, 'adds to my pain. No matter how long I live, I will never know if things would have turned out differently if I had been with him, if he had been able to get help sooner. I will live with that torment for ever.' She looks at the jury. 'When everyone else finally leaves this courtroom, when all of this is over, I will be the one going home without my son.'

Finlay walks over to the prosecution table and pours a glass of water for her. He hands it to her as a small gesture of kindness. Part of me thinks this is rehearsed too, but after everything Vivienne has suffered, this small gesture reflects what we all feel: that we must do whatever we can to reduce the pain of her loss.

He allows more silent seconds to follow, and again, Vivienne's sorrow pulls us in, before Finlay picks up where he left off.

'Vivienne, you have been here since the beginning of this trial, arriving in court every day.'

'Yes.'

'You have heard a lot of the medical evidence.'

'Yes.'

'I can only imagine how hard that must be.'

'It has sent me to Hell and back.'

'Have you felt anger?'

'Yes.'

'Have you felt overwhelmed?'

'Yes.' Her hands grip the wooden support in front of her, in an effort to stop them shaking.

'Take your time, Vivienne,' Finlay says, so softly that even I believe his concern.

'I have felt all those things, and more,' she says, her voice temporarily defiant. 'I want justice for Jacob. I was deprived of the chance to help him when he was alive, which is why I need to be strong for him now, to ensure my son, even in death, is given a voice.'

*

Finlay's direct examination of Vivienne lasts the rest of the morning. During recess, aware of what I have to do next, I spend the time alone. I take a short walk to Boston Public Garden. The grey squirrels move fervently in the chill of the afternoon, coasting from tree to tree. I look up at the various skyscrapers from Arlington Street to Back Bay, the wind blowing in my face. I think about all the people in those buildings, going about their day, unconnected to this trial.

I pass skateboarders, lunchtime joggers, and others out walking their dogs, until I finally sit on a bench at the 9/11 memorial, the collar of my coat up around my neck. The smooth edges of the victims' names are scuffed, and the inscription, *September 11, 2001*, is only legible from a short distance. I contemplate how, so often, the past crumbles into the present. The image of the man falling from the tower solidifies in my mind. No one wanted him to be *their* son, husband, brother, father or friend. No one wanted to face that horror in their minds, to imagine how someone they loved went through such pain or think about how he felt before he made the decision to jump. But he existed, and his pain existed too.

The last thing I want to do this afternoon is pull Vivienne Rotterdam apart, but I can't allow Abby to be another victim. I did that with Lucas, and I was wrong.

I wonder even now if Vivienne truly believes Abby is guilty. Does she really think her son was killed or does she still harbour doubts? She must have questioned herself, and her genetic history. Is the need to blame someone else driving her now? Wasn't I guilty of that too? Perhaps Vivienne and I understand each other better than either of us realises.

I arrive back in the courtroom earlier than most, and as more people enter, I watch them as if I'm seeing a television documentary unfold. My eyes are the eyes of the camera, wondering where it will go next and who it will focus on. I can't bear to look at Jim Handcock so instead I stare at Alice. I think about how she couldn't have children of her own. I wonder if she resents this attention being given to others, to those who at least had the opportunity to become a parent, even for a short while. Since this trial began, she has always publicly kept her distance from the Rotterdams, which is why I'm surprised when I see her walk over to them now. What is she saying to Vivienne? Why is she whispering in her ear? Why does Morgan look so horrified? Is it because he blames the Handcocks too?

I look away from them, as Kendell arrives, and the jury is brought back in. Finlay's direct examination has left its mark on them. Each juror appears more sympathetic to Vivienne than before, looking at her or avoiding her gaze. Soon, they will look in my direction, and they may see me as the pariah. I have to prove them wrong.

Vivienne waits for my cross-examination, looking composed, somewhat nervous, and fragile. I have to tread carefully.

Judge Kendell looks over at me. 'Your witness, Ms Baxter.'

I approach. 'May I call you Vivienne?' I ask softly.

'Yes.'

'Thank you.'

The same hushed silence takes hold. I am as ready as I will ever be.

'Vivienne, can I ask you to go back to the beginning?'

'Which beginning is that?'

There is something about her tone that is a decibel too sharp. I wonder if she argued with Morgan in the interval or was it something Alice said to her?

'If you could go back to when Abby began to work for you.'

'What do you want to know?' Again, the soft voice of this morning has slipped. Instead, she sounds harsh and sharp. I catch a glimpse of Finlay. He is looking stern. Has she gone off-script?

'Were you happy with your husband's suggestion to employ Abby?'

'I had reservations.'

'But you still went along with it?'

'Morgan felt it was a good idea.'

'And you stand as a team. Is that it?'

She hesitates.

'Would you like me to repeat the question?'

'No, it's fine.' She recomposes herself, no doubt remembering her instructions from Finlay about how to look, how to sit, how to keep her voice soft, how to impress the jury. 'As far as Jacob was concerned, we both wanted the very best for him.' She pauses. 'And he seemed very taken with the girl.'

'With Abby?'

'Yes.'

'Did you vocalise your reservations to your husband?'

'Yes.'

'Can you tell us what they were?'

'I thought Abby was too young, too inexperienced.'

'Because she hadn't worked as a nanny before?'

'Yes.'

'And yet Abby was taken into your home to care for your son.'

'Yes.'

'Your only child?' I hear an uncomfortable murmur from the jury. Don't blow this. Don't push too hard.

She isn't ruffled. Finlay has groomed her well. If something unnerved her a few moments earlier, she's pulling things back on track. What did Alice whisper to her?

'As I said, Morgan felt it was the right thing at the time. The girl seemed to have a natural affinity with children.'

'Did you get along with Abby?'

'We didn't need to be friends.'

'But, still, it would have been good to have a positive rapport.'

'I gave her a chance.' She looks at Abby. 'I won't apologise for that.'

'I understand. Let's move on a little.' I'm standing closer to the jury now. 'Do you remember any instances when you and Abby argued?'

'Yes.'

'Was it more than once?'

'As far as I can remember, yes.'

'How many times?'

'I can't be sure.'

'What were the arguments about?'

'Her timekeeping mostly, staying out late, not doing her duties.'

'Do you mean in relation to Jacob?'

'Yes, that and her other chores.'

'Chores?'

'Nothing out of the ordinary, small household things, doing the laundry, changing the bed linen. That kind of thing.'

'I see.' I pause. 'So, Abby was a nanny and a part-time housekeeper?'

'Yes, if you want to put it that way.'

'Is that the only thing you argued about?'

'There may have been other things. I can't remember.'

I catch her looking at Morgan. She doesn't keep her attention on him for long, but it's long enough for me to wonder if something else has been added to her hostility towards him.

Finlay is on his feet. 'Your Honour, is there a purpose to this line of questioning? We are all familiar with the circumstances that led to Abby Jones living with the Rotterdams.'

'I tend to agree,' Kendell replies. 'Ms Baxter, can you move this on?'

I turn and look at Vivienne again. 'Jacob had a difficult birth, did he not?'

'He was breech, yes. The doctors thought he would turn in the final days, but he didn't.'

'And they made an external attempt to turn him?'

'Yes.'

'But it didn't work.'

'No, it didn't.' Her voice drops away, and her fingers go to her right eye, as if trying to stop tears.

'It was a complete breech, wasn't it, with the buttocks at the birth canal and the knees bent?'

Finlay jumps to his feet again. 'Objection, Your Honour. This form of cross-examination is both unnecessary and distressing.'

'Again, I tend to agree. Ms Baxter, is there a point to any of this?'

'Yes, Your Honour. It forms part of Jacob's medical history.'

'Fine, Ms Baxter, but do get there quickly.' Kendell looks towards Vivienne. 'You may answer the question.'

'Yes, it was a complete breech.' Her voice is low.

I need her to speak up. I'm relieved when Kendell makes the request for me.

'We were monitored throughout,' she says, louder. 'Despite everything, Jacob arrived safe and healthy.' She dabs her eyes again.

'Do you need a few moments?' I ask.

'No, I'm fine.' She draws in a huge breath. 'When Jacob was born … I fell in love immediately.'

'I understand.'

'Do you?' Her question sounds like a test, but she quickly picks up where she left off. 'I didn't think I could love anyone quite so much, but from the moment he was born, I loved him with a passion.'

She has the jury eating out of her hands. I keep my voice soft. 'And Jacob was also jaundiced soon after birth?'

'Yes.'

'Were the doctors concerned?'

'They said it wasn't unusual.'

'But you were worried?'

'Every new mother would be.' This time her voice has the earlier edge to it. She is being defensive again. She is harbouring something, I'm sure of it. Kendell disallowing the blood tests had been a blow, but at least with Vivienne on the stand I can attempt to bring in part of Jacob's medical history.

'Did you ever have experience with jaundice before?'

'Somewhat.'

'There is a history of it in your family, isn't there?'

'Objection, Your Honour.' Finlay is on his feet for a third time. 'Do we have to turn this whole thing into ridicule, with the defence aimlessly looking for mysterious needles in haystacks?'

Kendell considers. 'I'll let it go for now, Mr Clarke.' He turns to Vivienne. 'Mrs Rotterdam, you may answer the question.'

What do I see in her eyes? Hate? Anger? Guilt? All three?

'My sister,' she finally says, 'was jaundiced at birth.'

'Your sister was also breech, was she not?'

'Yes.'

'Did Jacob remind you of her?'

'A little.' She wipes away another imaginary tear. She's stalling. Either I've touched on something she hasn't covered with Finlay, which is unlikely, or something else has happened to knock her out of her stride. Perhaps Finlay senses it, too, because he is on his feet again.

'Your Honour, my client is obviously finding this very difficult. It has been a very testing day.'

'I agree, Mr Clarke. It has been difficult for everyone.' Kendell checks his watch. 'Considering everything, court will adjourn until tomorrow morning at ten o'clock.'

As he dismisses the jury, I can't help but feel I may have missed an important opportunity, and with the break in the proceedings, if I'm not careful, I could eradicate any gain I made.

# 65
# DANIEL

Daniel notices the severed cables as soon as he arrives home and, once inside the house, he examines everything, including his desk. Certain things have been moved, all of which he repositions to their proper place. He thought he saw that friend of Heather's on the highway the other day. The same girl who opened the door to Heather at that house in Dorchester. He shouldn't have followed Heather, but he wasn't thinking straight.

He stares at the desk again, studying the newspaper clipping Heather sent him. As yet, he hasn't said anything to her about it, mainly because he needs to be sure. He doesn't want to make any more mistakes.

When he phones the alarm company, they tell him they can't repair the cables until the next day. He hates the house being unprotected, but he needs to get some sleep. Now that he's back on his medication, the sleepless nights are catching up with him.

Walking upstairs, he checks the windows are all locked. He leaves his bedroom until last, and opening the door, he clicks on the bedside lamp, but he already knows someone is in the room.

'What do you want?' he asks.

'For you to stay facing the window.'

He does as he's told. The girl is sitting in his favourite chair. The one his mother nursed him in.

'I've been keeping an eye on you, Daniel.'

'Why?'

'Because I've seen you snooping around Heather.'

'I wasn't snooping.'

'Looking into other people's windows is a habit of yours, is it? I saw you at my house. Of course, I didn't know it was you at first, but then I started getting curious on account of your rekindled friendship with Heather. You can turn around now.'

The girl's hair is different today. It's raven-coloured, and long.

'You're on my property,' he says. 'I want you to leave.'

'I'd love to oblige, Daniel, only first I need a few answers, starting with why your bank account became suddenly flush with my friend's money.'

'That isn't any of your business.'

'I'm making it my business,' she says, standing up.

The cushions on the chair are flattened. He wants to fix them. At first, he doesn't notice the gun in her hand, until he feels the barrel pushed into his side. 'It was a loan,' he says.

'And your clients' money? Was that a loan too?'

'I put that money back.'

'Maybe you should ask Heather if that's legal. I'm pretty sure she would tell you it was theft.'

'I already told her.' He feels the barrel pull away a little. 'Didn't she tell you?'

The barrel is pushed in hard again. 'Why do you have that image on your desk downstairs?'

'Heather sent it to me.'

'Because?'

'In case I could work out why Lucas had it.'

'And have you worked it out?'

'No, not yet.'

'Not so clever then, Daniel, are you?'

He feels as if he's back at school, being teased.

'If you cause harm to Heather in any way,' she says, 'I warn you, I will come back here, and we will finish this conversation properly.'

He watches her back out of the room. He listens as she walks downstairs. He hears her open the front door and walk away. Somewhere in the distance, he hears a car come to life. He waits until he can't hear it any more before he walks downstairs. He studies the image from the *Boston Globe* again, especially Alice's necklace. When he has all the facts, he will tell Heather everything. He will show that friend of hers exactly what he's made of.

# 66
# HEATHER

In an interview room off the main lobby of Suffolk courthouse, with less than an hour before the trial is due to reconvene, I go over everything with Mark and Robin about Vivienne's testimony from the day before.

'We have to work out why she let her polished routine, perfected by Finlay, slip,' I say. 'If we don't, we could lose out on an important opportunity.' I can see the tension in Mark and Robin's faces.

'What's your best guess, Heather?' Robin asks.

'Honestly, at this point, I don't think it's to do with anything I said to her. Either something happened during the lunchtime recess yesterday, or it's connected to that conversation Alice had with her.' I pace the room. 'Why do you think Alice approached her yesterday? She hasn't done that before.'

'What are you thinking?' asks Mark.

'I'm not sure yet, but it's been bothering me.' I pace the room again. 'We can only assume that whatever Alice said to Vivienne, it hit her hard, especially if it caused her to go off-script.'

'Something connected to Morgan?' Mark suggests.

I replay the scene in my mind, seeing Alice walk towards Vivienne. Did Jim Handcock watch her, too? Samuel said Jim Handcock knew everything. Did he know about the journal, and Mia being his child? Was that enough to get my mother killed?

'Okay,' I say, 'let's break this down. We all saw Alice approach Vivienne.'

They both nod.

'Her walk was defiant,' I say, 'and she held her head high. She had her shoulders back too. Vivienne waited in silence as she approached. There was certainly a flicker of anger in her eyes, but it was as if she was stuck to the spot, rigid, her body stiffening. She remained that way even while Alice leaned in, unresponsive. Morgan looked even more horrified the closer Alice got to her, and although I couldn't see Alice's face, with her back to me, there was a marked change in Vivienne's expression.'

I let the scene replay in my mind, concentrating on Vivienne's reaction. 'For a second,' I say, 'it was as if Vivienne's mask slipped, and Morgan looked utterly terrified when Alice leaned in to whisper in her ear, almost as if he knew what was about to be said.'

'Do you have a theory?' Robin asks.

'We've discussed Morgan's infidelity at length,' I say, 'and how this time, if there was another scandal, it could be someone Vivienne knew, someone she hates, and how hard that would be to accept, especially with everything that has happened.'

'What are you implying?' asks Robin.

I glare at them, while simultaneously allowing the identity of the person to settle in my mind. 'What about Alice Handcock?'

Neither Mark nor Robin replies, but I can tell they think it's possible.

'Consider it,' I say. 'The two couples knew each other beforehand so, in theory, it's very likely.' I recall my first conversation with Jim and Alice Handcock, how Alice said they'd thought it would be good for Abby to work for the Rotterdams. 'What if it wasn't Jim's idea that Abby worked for the Rotterdams but, rather, Alice suggested it? It would give her the perfect excuse. She could be with Morgan on the ruse that she was visiting her niece.'

'Christ,' says Robin, the full enormity of it sinking in.

'I've always thought Abby was holding something back,' I say. 'What if she knew?'

'We could ask her,' Mark adds.

'If she does know,' I say, 'it would be reasonable to assume she didn't want to say anything about it, not while Alice and Jim were covering her costs. She wouldn't want to risk losing either of their support.'

'But why approach Vivienne now?' Mark asks.

'Does it matter?' Robin looks at him.

'Maybe not,' I say, 'but if this theory stands up, and Alice decided to tell Vivienne about something going on between her and Morgan, something must have prompted it.'

'A woman scorned?' Mark ponders. 'Perhaps Morgan dumped her.'

'Or,' I say, 'he was forced to. And, assuming we're on track, and it's a *big* assumption, more than ever now Vivienne is vulnerable and weak.'

'Which means,' Robin adds, 'this is Abby's best chance. You need to get her to crack.'

'Okay, let's play this out,' I say, a million thoughts crashing into my mind at the same time. 'The Rotterdams usually arrive early, probably because they want to avoid other people watching them take their seats. Then they become the spectators, not the other way around.'

'Mostly they keep their heads down, avoiding attention,' Robin says, 'but I have seen Vivienne look at people as they arrive. I thought it was a kind of black curiosity on her part, the way she studies them.'

'This morning, we need to gauge both Morgan and Vivienne's reactions to others as they enter the room, especially the Handcocks.'

Both nod in agreement.

'I know it's a bit unorthodox, Robin, but will you hold back from sitting at the defence table until the very last minute and watch them, especially Vivienne.'

'For what exactly?'

'Her reaction, or lack of it, to others, especially Alice Handcock. Study who she pays attention to. Go with your instincts. Try to work out what her face is telling you.'

Robin gives me a quizzical stare. She isn't happy becoming an emotional spy, but she'll do it. I check my watch. The Rotterdams should arrive in less than twenty minutes. 'Look,' I say, 'there's a real chance that Finlay has made a big mistake in allowing Vivienne to testify. If something was going on between Morgan and Alice, and Finlay found out about it, he would have changed tactics, using Vivienne as a pawn to keep the jury on side. He would also have made sure she was very much kept in the dark, and if we're right, perhaps Alice unintentionally spoiled his plans.'

*

The Rotterdams take their seats. Over the next fifteen minutes, the courtroom fills. The bailiff announces Kendell's arrival. The jury is called. Robin joins us.

'Anything?' I whisper.

'Vivienne eyeballed Alice Handcock from the moment she arrived. She didn't take her eyes off her, not once.'

'And Morgan?'

'He avoided looking at her at all.'

'What about Alice?'

'She seemed oblivious.'

'Anything else?'

'Yeah. After Finlay finished talking to the Rotterdams, he glanced at Alice Handcock. It was only for a split second, but it was pretty obvious.'

Vivienne has lots of reasons for hating Alice Handcock, including her and Jim financially defending the girl the Rotterdams contest killed their child, but if we're right about an affair between Alice and Morgan, how humiliated would that make Vivienne feel? How could she accept that the woman who had brought her child's perceived killer into her home is also having an affair with her husband?

I wonder again if, deep down, Vivienne still has doubts about Jacob's death. I think about Alicia Amel's words: that unless the abuse is witnessed, at times it can be impossible to know for sure what really happened. The overriding question is this: if Vivienne had doubts, and she shut them out, the truth being too painful to accept, has that changed? She has lost her son. Her marriage is over. Morgan has repeatedly humiliated her, but she kept on going. And now Alice Handcock is in the mix. Alice wouldn't be like any other woman in Morgan's life. Alice has always been a woman with a plan, and that plan would not include Vivienne Rotterdam.

Out of nowhere, I hear my mother refer to Alice Handcock as 'that woman', as if she is standing beside me.

I look from Vivienne to Alice. Vivienne's lips are pressed tightly together. She is sitting stiffly. Alice, on the other hand, looks smug, as if she's relishing the entertainment. When Vivienne's name is called, Alice is so focused on watching her move forward, she doesn't realise I'm studying her.

Once Vivienne is sworn in, I stand up from the defence table and walk towards her. Now that I'm closer, her eyes tell me even more. They are red and sore, and it isn't from crying. The tiny veins and glassiness immediately give away her hangover. Her coping mechanism, I think, may also be her weakness. Has Vivienne, like my mother, become increasingly isolated and, after suffering such a loss, shut the world out, except for those closest to her? Then, when the one person she should be leaning on, her husband, abandons her completely, what next?

The following seconds, as I stand to face this woman, feel like a lifetime. Am I going to push her further into Hell, be the one who finally causes her to crack? I hear Robin's words: this is Abby's best chance. Right now, I can't think about the pain other people have caused Vivienne, any more than on that dark day when my mother was killed, I could undo all the wrongs done to her too. Ultimately, like now, when a life is already lost, the only thing left to save is the truth.

'Vivienne,' I say, 'how are you this morning?'

'Fine.'

'It was a tough day for you yesterday.'

'All days are tough.'

'I understand.'

Her eyebrows raise. 'I doubt you do.'

Her body language is defensive again, her voice sharp, and I know Finlay is willing her to assume the grief-stricken persona with her anger well hidden.

'You're correct, Vivienne. I don't. Probably no one in this room does, but some of us have also lost people we love, even though your grief is yours alone.'

She stares me down.

'I lost my mother when I was a child, and a younger sibling too, so, like others, I'm doing my best to understand.'

I feel Robin and Mark's eyes burning into my back. I've gone off-script, and it's a high-risk strategy. 'I know, first-hand,' I say, 'how the loss of a child, an infant, can ripple through a family.'

She nods in reluctant agreement.

'And, of course, you lost a sister too, didn't you?'

Finlay is on his feet. 'Objection, Your Honour. I really don't see the basis for this trip down memory lane.'

I'm waiting for Kendell to shut this whole thing down, when I hear Vivienne say, 'I would like to answer that question.'

Seconds pass. Finlay isn't happy. Kendell is hesitant. I hold my breath. Will he deny a grieving mother the right to speak?

'Objection denied,' he says. 'Carry on, Ms Baxter, but I warn you, tread carefully.'

'Vivienne, do you remember my question?'

'Yes.'

I wait. Everyone in the courtroom waits.

'Yes, I lost a sister.'

'What age was she when she died?'

'Five months old.'

There are audible gasps in the room, acknowledging the similarity in age to the victim.

'The loss never leaves you,' I say.

'No, it doesn't.'

'What was your sister's name?'

'Annabel.'

'Mine was Mia.' I look across at Jim Handcock. He has a hardened look on his face. Is he thinking about his daughter?

'Did she look like Jacob?' I ask.

Tears build up in her bloodshot eyes. 'I didn't notice it at first,' she says, smiling through her tears, 'but then, later, I saw the resemblance. Perhaps I wanted Jacob to look like me …'

She puts her fingertips to her eyes like yesterday, this time holding back real tears.

'Sometimes,' she says, 'you miss things.'

'Like the similarities between Jacob and your sister?'

'Yes.'

'Did they have other things in common?'

She flinches. The anger is back. 'My sister died a long time ago.'

'But Jacob and Annabel died at a similar age.'

'Your Honour.' Finlay practically leaps from the prosecution table. 'This is absurd, not to mention mentally cruel.'

'I hear you, Mr Finley, but Mrs Rotterdam was happy to answer the original question, so I'm inclined to let this continue for now.' He gives me a stern look.

'Yes,' Vivienne says, 'they did.'

'Your sister had serious health issues, didn't she?'

'Objection,' Finlay bellows, furious.

'Can you both approach?' Kendell's words are an instruction, not a question.

'Ms Baxter,' he says, keeping his voice low, 'do you have something definitive to explore here?'

'Your Honour, I am simply establishing similarities in the medical history of Jacob Rotterdam and Mrs Rotterdam's late sister. As you said earlier, the witness accepted this line of questioning.'

'She didn't agree to be harassed,' Finlay retorts.

'Ms Baxter, I agree with Mr Finlay.'

'But—'

'Ms Baxter, I have made my decision.'

Walking away, I hear Kendell say, 'Objection sustained.'

I need to find another way around this. I look reassuringly at Vivienne, the same look I normally give to appease a client's fears.

'Jacob,' I pause, letting his name hang in the air, 'had some health issues, didn't he?'

'Nothing out of the ordinary.'

'He was prone to respiratory difficulties, coughing and high temperatures?'

'Yes, but as I said before, they were all normal.'

'When Jacob developed these various coughing bouts, and fevers, did he find it hard to sleep?'

'Sometimes.'

'That must have been difficult for you.'

'I was his mother. I loved him.'

'And Abby, did she assist?'

'At times, yes.'

'How did that make you feel?'

'I don't understand.'

'Did you object to Abby helping?'

'No.'

'Did she care for the baby during the night?'

'Yes, when I was tired.'

'Did you feel guilty about this?'

'A mother's guilt is not uncommon.'

'And after Jacob died, did you feel guilty then?'

I think about the dark places my mother went to, especially the afternoon she went missing in the woods, looking for a baby she would never find.

Vivienne stares at me.

I repeat the question. 'Did you experience guilt after Jacob died?'

'I felt a lot of things but, yes, there was certainly guilt.'

Other than swearing to tell the truth, she is under no obligation to do so. I take another step towards her, blocking the twelve members of the jury from her vision. I need her to feel we are simply two women having a difficult conversation but, mostly, I'm relying on her to do the right thing.

'Why did you feel guilty?'

'Like any mother, I wondered afterwards if there was anything I could have done differently.'

'And was there?'

The question hangs. I hold her stare. I can't be sure, but it's as if something else has shifted inside her. The earlier anger seems to be gone, but I'm not sure what has replaced it.

Is it acceptance?

Does Finlay see it?

I wait, sensing the next few seconds could be vital.

'I thought about Annabel, and how she suffered all those viruses before she died.'

There is another low gasp in the room. Internally, I hold my breath. This could be it. This could be the exact moment when everything comes tumbling down.

Finlay doesn't wait another millisecond. 'Your Honour, objection. You have ruled on this already.'

'That may be, Mr Clarke, but if the witness wants to talk about this, she is entitled to do so. Your objection is overruled.'

'Go ahead, Vivienne,' I say, my words soft, even though internally I'm screaming, willing her on. I daren't take my eyes off her. One wrong move and she could change her mind. All of this could slip from our hands.

'Annabel was a sickly child,' she finally says, breathing deeply. 'When Jacob came along, he felt like a miracle. I guess, somewhere in my head, I never thought I would be a mother.' The tears well in her eyes again.

'Take your time,' I say, still desperately willing her not to stop.

'When Jacob started to get sick …' she pauses, wiping tears from her cheek '… I thought about Annabel almost immediately. I kept checking with the doctors, asking if everything was okay. They assured me he was fine.' She wipes her eyes again. Her stare looks absolute, defiant. 'I didn't fully believe them. They said that about my sister too. None of it mattered in the end, when she died.'

'Like Jacob,' I say, part-finishing her words, determined to drill the message home.

Finlay is on his feet, but before he can say anything, Kendell signals for him to sit down.

'Do you want a break, Mrs Rotterdam?' Kendell asks.

She shakes her head.

'Carry on, Ms Baxter,' he instructs.

I soften my voice again. 'Was there an explanation, Vivienne, for your sister's death?'

'They did an autopsy, the same as they did on …' Her voice breaks.

'It's okay,' I say, 'take as much time as you need.'

Seconds pass. I wait. We all wait.

'They didn't find anything conclusive. In the end, they put it down to respiratory failure.'

'And this was how long ago?'

'Nearly a quarter of a century.'

'Medical science has changed a lot during that period.'

She nods in agreement.

I let the information settle into the jury's minds. It is a leap, but it may be enough, another infant death, partially unexplained, with similarities to Jacob's medical history. The possibility of a genetic connection will cast doubt. Doubt will make them reconsider the medical evidence, question the accusation of abuse and, hopefully, see other options. They already know medical opinion is divided on

SBS, and although they may have their reservations about Abby, they don't need a medical degree to understand the existence of doubt.

'Vivienne, are you okay?'

She looks distant.

I wait, before repeating the question. 'Vivienne, are you okay to continue?'

'Yes.'

'I know this is extremely upsetting for you.'

She nods again. She looks broken.

'Abby,' I say, looking at the jury, before turning back to Vivienne, 'stands accused of fatally injuring your son. If found guilty, her life will effectively be over. You understand that, Vivienne, don't you?'

She draws in a deep breath.

'None of us wants another travesty,' I say, 'especially if this trial ends in a false conviction.'

I hear Finlay behind me. 'Objection, Your Honour. Ms Baxter is taking some sort of cruel and convoluted, unearned high ground.'

'Mr Clarke, I have no problem with counsel reiterating what is at stake. Overruled.'

'A false conviction,' I say, picking up where I left off, 'would mean another person's life is over. No one wants that, and I don't think you want that either. I think everyone in this room understands the need to apportion blame, to have the consolation of an answer, a conviction, but it won't be a consolation if it isn't true.'

Vivienne stares blankly past my shoulder. She looks lost. I wait for Finlay to interject, but just as I think he's going to, her eyes snap back into focus, and she stares at me.

'My life is a complete sham,' she says. 'My marriage is a joke. You know it, everybody in this room knows it, and practically all of Massachusetts knows it too.'

Finlay doesn't object. Perhaps he knows it's too late to try.

'When Jacob got sick, part of me believed he would be taken from me.'

'Why, Vivienne?'

'Because I didn't deserve him. It's impossible to explain.'

'Is this connected to your sister?'

'I was jealous of her,' she says, so icily cold that everyone, including myself, is taken aback. 'Before Annabel came along, I was an only child. Suddenly she was the centre of attention. I used to wish she wasn't around any more, and then, when she died, I got my wish, and I blamed myself for it. I've spent my whole life taking the coward's way out. My marriage alone is testament to that. I didn't tell anyone about Annabel, and when I heard Jacob coughing at night, even though the doctors assured me he would be fine, I fretted. People thought I was being over-protective. Then, like my sister, he was gone.' She looks at Morgan. 'I even thought about killing myself, but I didn't deserve the easy way out.'

I need to ask her one more question, although a part of me fights hard against it, but my training, experience and knowledge of how justice works pushes the attorney in me forward.

'Vivienne?'

We look at each other, woman to woman.

'Did you blame Abby for your son's death out of guilt, because you couldn't accept it was connected to you, to your genetic history?'

Finlay leaps from his chair. 'Objection, Your Honour.'

I raise my hand to Judge Kendell. 'It's okay. I withdraw the question.'

The damage is already done, and walking back to the defence table, even though my knees are wobbling, internally, despite what I put Vivienne through, a part of me can't help but be elevated. I had to fight for Abby. I couldn't allow her to go to jail for a crime she didn't commit.

Everyone must know how huge this is. I know it, and when I look at Robin and Mark, I know they know it too. The courtroom buzzes with noise, people muttering loudly to each other. Kendell bangs his gavel down hard several times. As soon as a hush ensues, he looks towards Finlay, then the jury.

'Considering everything,' he says, 'this is an appropriate time to finish proceedings for today. The court will resume in the morning. Mr Clarke, you can re-examine the witness at that time.'

I watch Vivienne step down. She walks away from me, past her husband, past Alice and Jim Handcock, and past Finlay. I tell myself I did the right thing, even though I hate myself for it.

# 67
# MARCIA

Marcia studies Vivienne getting down from the witness stand. Things are shifting towards a victory for the defence. Multiple headlines arrive in rapid succession in her head: *Is the Wrong Woman On Trial?*; *The Sleazy Affair While a Baby Dies*; *The Wife, the Nanny, and the Other Woman.*

Journalists clamber after Finlay, but she isn't in any rush. She has an ace card, and it's simply a question of working out the pros and cons of breaking this sleazy sub-plot now or keeping her promise to Finlay. Every media outlet will cover the new revelations about Vivienne's sister, raising doubts, as the jury must be doing now, and drawing comparisons between the two infants, wondering how much of the medical evidence can be relied upon, especially when one set of experts says 'X', and another says 'Y'.

She can run with this story, too. There's certainly enough juice in it. But what about the current benefits of breaking the other scoop, the one Finlay wants her to keep secret?

It would put her ahead of everyone else, she being the only

journalist who knows about Morgan and Alice. Undoubtedly, there is always a risk with delaying, and obviously, there would be more television interviews too, raising her profile. She could even sell the story to the networks, now that things are lighting up in the trial, give exclusivity to the highest bidder.

Screw Finlay, she thinks, her mind progressing to another series of headlines. *Sex, Scandal, and the Rotterdams' Swinger Lifestyle!*; *What the Wife Knew!*; *The Deadly Love Triangle!*

The list is endless, and the TV channels will bite big on this, especially now that doubts about Abby's guilt are surfacing. She might even get a permanent slot in TV, on one of the top news channels. Heck, she could be on air every day for a month if she handles this correctly. Wasn't she the undercover journalist who first broke the hotel story?

It would be good to capture images of Alice Handcock and Morgan Rotterdam together, if she could get them. She considers tailing Morgan, but dismisses the idea in seconds. Other journalists will be on his tail. They will be camping outside the Rotterdams' 24/7. But, she thinks, no one is watching Alice Handcock. No one other than Marcia.

Another headline pops into her head: *What Did the Nanny Know?* It wouldn't be possible to gain access to Abby right now, but after the trial, if the girl is acquitted, she'll be free to speak to who the hell she likes.

# 68
# FINLAY

Waiting downstairs in the Rotterdams' home, Finlay's expression is a mixture of frustration and rage. He is still seething about Heather's cross-examination of Vivienne, and the media madness that followed. Predictably, the reporters were like scavengers eager for raw meat but, right now, he has other things on his mind, including the prospect of Kendell re-examining his decision on the blood tests. He didn't see Marcia Langan with the other journalists on the court steps either, which concerns him too but first he needs to focus on the conversation he is about to have with Morgan and Vivienne Rotterdam. As he waits for them to come downstairs, he is well aware that his reputation, his future career and his political prospects are all riding on this.

Morgan arrives first, pouring himself a large bourbon. Vivienne follows soon after, staring at Finlay as if he has no right to be in their home. Does she know about Alice Handcock? Is that what the dramatic confession was all about?

'Sadly,' Finlay says, 'things have not gone according to plan.'

He waits for a response.

Vivienne speaks first. 'What happens now?'

'The defence will probably put forward a new motion on the blood tests, and Kendell may well grant it this time. If he does, and there is something of substance, formal charges could be withdrawn, or the state will make the decision to proceed.'

'Withdrawn? You can't be serious,' barks Morgan.

'I couldn't be more so.'

'What about the fractures, the other evidence? You said it all pointed to abuse.'

'No one can say for sure that abuse didn't take place, but depending on the blood tests, with medical opinion divided, the emphasis will shift to alternative reasons for Jacob suffering those minute fractures.'

'They're minute now, are they?' Morgan says, his anger palpable.

'Lower your voice,' instructs Vivienne.

'What is important,' Finlay continues, 'is that if the cause of death is linked to a possible genetic connection we're on less solid ground.'

'Someone harmed my child,' Vivienne murmurs, tightening her hands into fists. 'I am not saying I didn't feel guilt, or that I didn't have my doubts, but I cannot accept that all of this has been for nothing.'

Morgan moves towards her, waving his glass. 'Your episode in court today didn't help.'

'Look,' says Finlay, 'we need to remain calm.' He stands between Morgan and Vivienne. She has to know about Alice, he thinks. It's there in the way she gazes at Morgan with such absolute hatred.

'If nothing conclusive comes from the blood tests, and the state decides to proceed,' Finlay continues, 'we can still be optimistic about the outcome.'

'I've heard enough,' Vivienne says, and both men watch her walk out of the room.

Morgan attempts to follow her, but Finlay grabs his arm. 'Leave it,' he says. 'We need to talk.'

Morgan pours another drink.

'Does Vivienne know?' Finlay asks.

'I think Alice told her, when she pulled that stunt in court yesterday.'

'Why?'

'She can be like that when things don't go her way.'

Finlay saw an overnight bag in the corner of the room earlier on. 'You plan on going somewhere tonight?' he asks, pointing to it.

'Vivienne wants me out of here, not that it's any of your business.'

'It's very much my business, if you're meeting Alice Handcock.'

'Being with Vivienne,' he says, 'was only bearable when Jacob was alive.' He puts his head in his hands.

Finlay waits.

'I loved him,' Morgan says, finally looking up, 'and it's such a special thing, having a son. You see yourself in them, you know. You feel almost immortal. I still can't believe he's gone. Even now, I expect someone to tell me all of this was one big mistake.'

'That isn't going to happen.'

'No,' he says, downcast.

'I've kept a story about you and Alice out of the media,' Finlay continues, 'but I'm not sure how long I can keep a lid on it.'

'I used to think I wanted revenge,' Morgan adds, ignoring Finlay's words about the story.

'And now?'

'Now everything is messed up.'

'When did this thing with you and Alice begin?'

'Over a year ago.'

'I thought you liked them young.' Finlay can't hide the annoyance in his voice.

'Alice was different. She liked the pain as much as I did, perhaps even more.'

'And after Jacob died?'

'I curbed things for a while.'

'Perhaps you should have kept it that way.'

'You don't understand. Vivienne kept shutting me out, blaming me. I thought I'd go mad. I tried to stop seeing Alice, but then it all got too much, and we agreed to meet. With her, I could forget all this crap. I could be myself again.'

Finlay watches him send a text message. 'Are you meeting her tonight?'

'I have to. I have to find out what she said to Vivienne.'

'I don't think that's wise.'

'I'm long past wise, Finlay. I'm long past a lot of things.'

# 69
# ALICE

Seeing Morgan approach the car, Alice rolls down the windows. He's carrying an overnight bag. His breath smells of bourbon. 'I'll organise the room,' he says, like she's nothing more than a cheap whore.

'Get in,' she tells him.

'But I thought—'

'I know what you thought.' Her voice is ice-cold. No man treats her like this, not Morgan, not Jim, not anyone.

He does as he's told, already looking like a little boy chastised. When he sits in, she slaps him hard across the face.

'What the hell?' He rubs his cheek, narrowing his eyebrows, staring back in surprise.

'Exactly.' She smiles. 'What the hell?'

'What did you tell Vivienne?' he asks, suddenly angry.

'I told your precious wife that I fucked you long and hard while your son was slowly dying. I told her I was still fucking you, and that every single day since, I take pleasure in seeing what a pathetic existence she leads.'

'Are you out of your mind?'

'You tell me. I don't care.'

'Finlay knows everything,' he says.

'Fuck Finlay, too.'

'He thinks the trial could collapse.'

'That's unfortunate,' she says. 'I wanted that horrible girl to be found guilty, to be rid of her for good.'

'Abby could walk free.'

She doesn't answer him. It was risky pulling that stunt with Vivienne, but she couldn't resist telling her a thing or two.

Morgan looks away, out into the night. 'I can't bear that bitch going unpunished for what she did to my son. He was my world, Alice, you know that.'

She wants to scream, *Fuck Abby, and fuck Jacob too*, but she holds back. Although, she muses, if he keeps up this grieving-father act, she can't be responsible for her actions. No one cares about her – *no one*. She has a knife in her purse. Lately, she has enjoyed carrying it around. The power of knowing it's there arouses her. He is still staring out the window, whimpering like a pathetic dog. She reaches out to touch his arm.

'I know this is difficult for you, darling, and, as you say, Jacob was your world. After all, he was the reason you couldn't leave Vivienne, wasn't he?'

He nods, breathing in deeply, his chest rapidly moving up and down.

'He was the most beautiful baby ever …' she sighs '… but difficult and all as this is for you, Morgan, nothing is going to bring him back.'

He lets out a loud gasp.

'In time, you will accept this, especially when we move on with our lives.' She already knows he's going to disappoint her, but she must test him all the same.

'Finlay says a journalist is about to break a story on us.'

'What do you want to do?' She keeps her voice neutral, but she is conscious of how important his answer will be. It will define everything from this point.

'Jesus, I don't fucking know. My life is falling apart, and you're asking me what I want to do, as if I'm deciding on a movie.'

The windows steam up. She considers taking out the knife, putting it to his throat, watching his blood drip, drop by miserable drop. How dare he. After all she's done for him, and all the long months of listening to his wretched self-pity, indulging his desires.

She starts to laugh, a loud, crazy laugh. The whole thing is so clichéd, it's ridiculous. A man has an affair. He tells the other woman he loves her. His wife doesn't understand him. He would leave, except for the child, or children. But there isn't a child any more. There are no more excuses.

'It's very simple, Morgan,' she says, controlling her laughter. 'You have to leave Vivienne.'

He looks at her as if she's mad and, in a way, she doesn't blame him. Her laughter does sound unhinged. 'She told me tonight she didn't want me back.'

'Then that should make things very simple for you, shouldn't it?' She smiles, but he keeps on talking.

'I'll stay here with you tonight,' he says, 'and after that, we can take it one step at a time.'

'I see,' she says, knowing he has no intention of spending his life with her.

'What about Jim?' he asks. 'Will he make trouble, you know, when the story breaks?'

'Jim is a dangerous man. He doesn't like other people taking things that belong to him.' She eyeballs him. 'He certainly won't like this, the two of us. Heaven knows what he might do. I'm married to him. I know him better than most, and I know he's capable of killing if the circumstances are right.'

'What do you mean?'

'Lucas García. Jim didn't take too well to him coming back to town, and then he ended up dead.'

'Are you saying—'

'I am not saying anything for sure, except when it comes to people and things that Jim holds dear, he can be ruthless.'

'Heather Baxter's father was arrested for that, wasn't he?'

'Jim doesn't like him too much either.'

She's pleased to see him panic, but she's angry too, the truth finally slapping her in the face. Everything that has happened – the death of Jacob, the trial, and all the time they have spent together – is reduced to one man caring about saving his own skin.

'You stay here tonight,' she instructs him, 'but I won't be staying with you.'

He looks at her, confused.

'There are things requiring my attention. Now get out.'

He goes to argue, but changes his mind, opening the door instead. She watches him walk to the motel reception area. He doesn't look back, not once.

She pulls down the car vanity mirror, applying more lipstick. A flash of light appears from inside the motel. It flashes another couple of times before she turns to look in its direction, the light flickering again, like a camera flash going on and off.

# 70
# HEATHER

There is a tentative combination of determination and deliberation in the office this evening as Robin, Mark and I work on the legal papers to re-file the motion for parental blood tests. We each know everything could turn on this, and there is absolutely no room for error. Collectively, we agree to hold off on the final amendments until Vivienne Rotterdam's full testimony is complete. The adrenalin from earlier today has now eased, with each of us still somewhat tainted by having to push a grieving mother quite so hard, even if, for Abby's sake, it was absolutely necessary.

When I get home, the gravity of the day hits me. I pour myself a glass of wine, and study the mind maps on the wall, at first allowing my mind to drift. It doesn't take long before I'm drawn to the map covering the trial, and a possible overlap between it, my mother, and Lucas's killing.

The two people linking my past to the trial are Jim and Alice Handcock, although Daniel has a tentative link too. I stare at Abby's name in the centre, with the word 'birthmark' attached to it. After my visit with Samuel, the possibility of Mia being Jim Handcock's child cannot be ignored. I draw a circle close to Jim's name, with the words – *Did he know?*

I switch to the map with Lucas at the centre, rereading the key points: his return to Corham, the empty necklace box, the makeshift doll, his scheduled meeting with my father, the newspaper clipping, his intimacy with my mother, the gifts he gave her. I step back, wondering about the possibility of my father being framed for Lucas's death. If he was, whoever did it most likely knew about the scheduled meeting between them, and they would have been in possession of the gun, too, which also means they could have everything else.

I walk closer to the map with my mother's name in the centre, revisiting the list of words around it: post-natal depression, Mia, fear, secrets, mementoes, journal, loss, affairs, rape and murder. I take the red shoebox down from upstairs. It feels like an anchor, and the physicality of holding something my mother held also seems important.

The shrill of my cell phone pulls me from my thoughts. It's the first time Alex has made contact in days.

'Hello,' I say.

'Heather, I may as well come straight out with it.'

'What?'

'I have a confession.'

'About?'

'I paid your friend Daniel a visit.'

'Why?'

'I got suspicious about him. I caught him spying a while back, and I wanted to check him out.'

'When? I don't understand.'

'It doesn't matter,' she says. 'What matters is, I didn't trust him, so I broke into his place, and I guess he didn't react too well.'

'Christ, Alex.'

'I found out about the money you gave him.'

'That was my choice. It was between me and him.'

'Maybe, but—'

'No buts. You don't know him the way I do. He hasn't been well.'

'And you don't know him either. People change, Heather, but that's not the only reason I'm ringing you.'

'What?'

'Blake is pulling Billy Townsend in.'

'On what grounds?'

'Suspected rape, perhaps even murder.'

'Of?'

'Lexie Gilmore. Look, I shouldn't be telling you any of this.'

'You shouldn't do a lot of things, but it hasn't stopped you before.'

'True.' She hesitates. 'I got talking to some people and it seems Billy made his sexual attraction to Lexie well known, only the girl wasn't keen. And if Billy liked you, and you didn't like him back, it made things awkward.'

'Are you working with Blake?' I ask, still unsure where this is going.

'In a way. When I heard about the Billy and Lexie connection, I figured Billy would show up somewhere else causing trouble.'

'And did he?'

'Yeah. When it comes to recording certain crimes across the States, crime-scene computers can tell you only so much. Sometimes you have to reach out to investigators and find the *right* detective to talk to. The police don't always share information state-to-state, and it can be a case of going down several avenues.'

'Alex, I need to understand everything – *everything*.'

'I may have matched Billy to two separate rape cases outside of the state. Hodgson would have had *The Rape Investigation Handbook*, and no doubt he shared some of the information in there with his nephew. Billy would have known that the best means of getting away with this kind of crime was to commit it in a different jurisdiction.'

'I'm listening.'

'There was a similar case in Washington a few years back, where a guy raped two women in two different suburbs, three months apart, and although there were striking parallels between the two cases, the police never pooled resources to investigate them. It took another victim to be attacked, and a female police officer sending emails all over the place, for all the files to match up.'

'Christ.'

'With two unsolved rapes, possibly linked to Billy, it's enough for Blake to pull him in.'

'And what about my mother's cold case? Does Blake think it's connected too?'

'Right now he's working on Lexie's disappearance, but it's anyone's guess where that might lead.'

'What links Billy to the unsolved rapes?'

'Like Lexie, neither of the girls had family support. They were similar in age and appearance, vulnerable and, most importantly, Billy was in all three places when the attacks took place, including when Lexie disappeared. If they match his DNA to either of those rapes, they've got him.'

'I want to be kept in the loop, Alex, do you hear me?'

'You will be. Look, Heather, I'm sorry about Daniel. I crossed the line. I should have run it by you first.'

'Yes, you should have.'

She doesn't respond.

'Look,' I say.

'Yeah?'

'Maybe we should cool things on the personal front for a while.'

'That's your call,' she says, but her voice tells me she's hurt.

'Thanks for telling me about Billy,' I say, attempting a consolatory tone.

Hanging up, I immediately phone Daniel. When he doesn't answer, it makes me nervous. I revisit all the things Alex said to me, and then, like previous times, when a fresh slice of memory comes back, there's no warning. Suddenly I'm in Raintree woods. I hear a woman screaming. I can hear something else too, footsteps moving fast, as if people are running. I'm not sure what age I am, but I know I'm scared. I can't work out where the screams are coming from either, or who they belong to, but then I see a man running fast, breathing heavily, as if in pursuit. I think about Billy's words, how in the past people thought I knew more than I was saying. Is it Billy running in the woods? Are the screams Lexie Gilmore's?

My cell phone bleeps with a message from Daniel – *I need to see you alone*. Immediately, I message back, telling him I'm on my way.

# 71
# JIM

Jim sits in the conservatory drinking a large beer. It isn't his first of the day, and it won't be his last. He's waiting for Alice to come home. She said she had something to tell him. He knows she's going to explain about Morgan, but he's known about that for some time. Alice has made a fool of him, and she'll pay, as will Morgan Rotterdam.

He hears the front door opening, and listens for her footsteps, the determined steps of a woman who could take you to Hell and back and still look for more.

He waits patiently, listening to her tell him the version of events that she wants him to hear, slanting things in her favour. When she's finished, he picks up his drink and fires it against the wall. She looked shocked as the glass shatters.

'I could destroy you,' he says.

'I could destroy you too,' she retorts, defiant. 'We're well matched.'

'Why do you stay, Alice, with me?'

'There was a time I might have called it love,' she sniggers sarcastically, 'but that was before Lizzie, and your obsession with that whore.'

'Don't call her that.' He wants to kill her, to crush her, to make her feel pain, slowly shattering every bone in her body, crack by tiny crack.

'But right now, Jim, I'll settle for money and power. They're far less complicated. I followed the two of you many times,' she mocks, 'back in the day, before Lizzie got pregnant with Charlie's baby. You couldn't stand that, could you?'

He walks closer to her. 'I could kill you.'

'But you're not going to, are you? And don't worry, darling, I've already taken precautions in case you decide to do anything rash.'

'Lucas was right about you. He said you were a witch.'

'I wonder sometimes,' she teases, 'if you and Lucas were in it together. After all, you both screwed her. Maybe that was why my womb became barren.'

'I don't need to listen to this crap.'

'Don't you remember, Jim, how he left that damn doll here all those years ago?'

'He said it would help, that the dolls could heal.'

'Either way, your baby never grew inside of me, did it?'

He doesn't answer her.

'For all your bravado, Jim, you are a pathetic man. Don't think I haven't been watching you with Heather too, and seen how she's rekindled that old obsession of yours. I've seen the desperate way you look at her.'

'Shut up, Alice.'

'She hates you, darling, and sometimes I can't help but wonder just how far she's prepared to go to make you pay.'

# 72
# HEATHER

The windscreen wipers whisk back and forth on the way to Daniel's. The rain, which has been threatening all day, is now a deluge, but all I care about is whether or not Daniel has worked out anything on that newspaper clipping.

At his house, I have to knock several times before he answers. I wait, eventually hearing him release a set of double locks.

'Sorry,' he says. 'I had to make sure you were alone.'

A fire is roaring in the grate.

'Billy Townsend has been brought in for questioning,' I say, taking off my coat. 'They think he could be connected to Lexie's disappearance.'

'Oh?'

'And I'm sorry about my friend, Alex. I know she paid you a visit.'

'She sat in my mother's chair.'

'She shouldn't have done that, but she was only trying to help me.'

'I want to help you too,' he says, standing close enough to touch me.

It feels too intimate. I step back. 'Daniel, did you spy on me, on Alex?'

'I wasn't on my medication …' He trails off, ashamed.

'Look, it doesn't matter now,' I say, because it doesn't. 'Why did you send the text?'

'I need to show you something.'

I follow him towards a set of bookshelves. Up close, I can see all the books are in alphabetical order. I see photograph albums too, remembering his keenness for photography.

'I went through everything,' he says, his words spilling into one another, as he takes down one of the albums, flicking through the pages. 'I wanted to be sure.'

'Of what?' There are loose photographs in the album, along with the printout of the newspaper clipping.

'At first,' he says, still talking fast, 'I couldn't find it, but then I remembered the old negatives of photographs that didn't go into the albums.'

'I still don't understand.'

'I got some of them printed. It delayed things, but I couldn't risk telling you until I was absolutely sure.' He hands me a photograph.

I stare at the image of myself. I look around eight years old, my hair tucked behind my ears, wearing a pink sweater and a fake pearl necklace. I look like a child expectant of a good life. Again, I see the uncanny resemblance to my mother.

He hands me another photograph. This time it is one of me and my mother. 'I had everything with a necklace developed,' he says.

For a moment, I don't want to leave the first little girl behind. My hands linger over her face. 'I look so young,' I say.

'When they found the clipping at Lucas's place,' Daniel continues at speed, 'the police obviously made the connection to you, and it must have added another layer to your father being involved, the idea of a family out for revenge.'

'Slow down, Daniel. Where is this going?'

'I started wondering if Lucas knew something other people didn't want him to know.'

'I have wondered that too.'

'Look at the clipping, Heather.' He pushes it into my hands. 'What do you see?'

'I see myself, Jim and Alice Handcock, the legal team, Finlay, the Rotterdams, some journalists.'

'Look at everything,' he insists, as if he is the teacher and I am his pupil.

I study myself again, my proximity to Mark and Robin. I stare at Jim Handcock, seeing the smug look on his face. I note Finlay in the distance, and the journalists, until finally my eyes settle on Alice.

'Look at her neck,' he says.

'She's wearing a necklace.'

'It's rose quartz,' he says, pointing to it.

'So?'

'It's supposed to mean love and protection.'

'Okay, but ...'

'I knew I'd seen it before.' His voice is more energised now.

I look from him to the clipping. 'You mean the necklace, right?'

He nods, placing the photograph of me and my mother beside the clipping. 'Look carefully,' he says, pointing to both images.

The photograph is taken at the carnival, the one we went to the summer he got his first camera. I think about the earlier news clippings I found while searching for articles about my mother and Lexie Gilmore, and how there was an image of Jim and Alice, with my mother behind them in the crowd. My fingertips rest on the rose-quartz necklace on my mother's neck in the photograph, before my eyes dart back to the *Boston Globe* image, seeing Alice wearing a similar necklace. I put my hand to my neck, thinking about the day my mother asked me to close the clasp of her necklace, and how she told me I had delicate hands. They start to shake as I see my younger self close the rose-quartz necklace around her neck.

'It could be a different one,' I say, unsure.

'Look at the link chain,' Daniel insists, 'they're identical.'

I let out a low gasp, staring at him, before pacing the room. 'Lucas sent me an empty necklace box. He was trying to tell me something. He wanted me to make the connection.'

Daniel is talking again. 'I researched everything I could on it. It took a while, but eventually I worked out it was made in—'

'New Orleans,' I say, finishing his sentence.

My mind flicks back to the last time I saw Lucas at our old house. We spoke about the book of poetry he'd given her, and how it wasn't his only present to her. He must have given her the necklace too. 'If Alice is wearing it,' I say, thinking aloud, 'then she got it from Jim, and when Lucas came back and saw the image in the newspaper, he knew she wouldn't have given it away.'

My mind is in overdrive, thinking and talking at the same time. 'Jim Handcock hadn't seen Lucas for years. He probably thought he would never return. Then when Lucas took an interest in the trial, and started working certain things out, he ended up dead. Perhaps he confronted Jim before meeting my father, and if Jim had the necklace, he also had the gun to frame him, but …'

'What?' Daniel asks, as I stall.

'Why didn't Lucas tell me this the last time we met?'

'You said yourself you were angry. Perhaps he thought you weren't ready to listen?'

'Maybe,' I say, considering his words.

'And if Jim Handcock took all your mother's things,' he adds, 'if he watched you that night, after she was killed, he probably wanted to remove any possible connection to him.'

'He wanted to do more than that,' I say, fresh anger gaining ground. 'Jim isn't the kind of man who's willing to share anything important in his life. That's why he hated Lucas, why he hated my father, and why he wanted to take revenge on them both.' I pick up my cell phone, still staring at the photograph of me and my mother. 'I don't remember burying the necklace,' I say.

'Maybe you didn't. Maybe Jim took it before your mother was killed.'

I dial Blake's number.

'Who are you calling?' Daniel asks.

'The guy who's pulled in Billy.'

'What are you going to tell him?'

'I'm going to tell him the Handcocks have a necklace belonging to my mother. I'm going to tell him everything I can because, even though none of this proves Jim killed her, the necklace is a connection. It's another piece of the jigsaw.'

# 73
# ELIZABETH

*No one really knows what's going on inside another person's mind. Billy Townsend has his own secrets, which is why he and Samuel hang out together. They recognise the deceit in one another. I have misjudged Alice Handcock too, I guess, in the same way people have misjudged me. In the past, I pigeon-holed her as a naïve young bride. I listened to the rumours in town about how her father lost his money in a big business deal, and even though afterwards he recovered from financial ruin, when Alice married Jim she was unable, or unprepared, to accept a different kind of life.*

*The first time I should have realised I was wrong about her was when, as a couple, they surprised everyone in how well they worked together. Despite the age difference, they mirrored one another in the pursuit of money and power. There was always two of them in it, which is partly why Jim's interest in me, at first, came as a surprise.*

*In the early days of their marriage, Alice liked to emphasise her new surname, as if she was reimagining herself, trying her new life on for size. The façade they presented to the world should have been a warning:*

*the more people stand firm behind something false, the more likely it is they have something even bigger to hide.*

*Samuel knows about this journal now. He discovered it the other day when I caught him in Heather's room. I was so panicked about protecting her that I left it out for him to see. I can't trust that he isn't going to tell others about it, especially when he shoots his mouth off with Billy.*

*Will the person I fear most in the world want to take the journal too, in the same way they have taken other things from the house, including the necklace Lucas gave me? For months, I've been followed, and watched, with Billy doing their bidding, because they have become more and more fixated. But mostly I worry just how far they are prepared to go. Am I, even now, risking too much by my silence? But who would I tell? Who would believe a woman who went searching for her dead baby, the woman with depression, who made a mockery of her marriage, being with other men, the woman who drove her husband away? I doubt anyone would believe that woman. I doubt anyone would care.*

*Tonight Heather had a bad dream. She said she heard screams in the woods, that a man was chasing someone, a woman. I wondered if she was scared about something happening to me. I lay down beside her on the bed, and before she fell asleep, I told her it was okay to be fragile, to be afraid, but that I knew, deep inside, she was also strong. Be fragile, be strong, I told her.*

*I remember her now as a newborn baby, her large eyes looking up at me, blinking at the wonder of the world. Back then nothing mattered, only Heather and me. I felt the same with Mia, even as I willed her back to life, touching her soft skin, her tiny fingers and toes, wanting her heart to beat once more, when everything had gone so still.*

# 74
# HEATHER

The phone call last night with Blake had been brief. He was interested in the information, but he also kept his cards close to his chest. If I want to find out anything more, Alex is my only option. After our parting words, though, I'm not sure that's such a good idea. Blake asked me not to mention the necklace to the Handcocks although, as yet, he doesn't seem convinced that it's connected. According to him, there could be several explanations for it being in the Handcocks' possession, but even so, in case it proves important, for now I'm to keep my mouth shut.

As everyone shuffles into the courtroom, I keep an eye out for Jim and Alice. When they arrive, all the anger I feel towards them resurfaces. Walking towards their seats, I stare at Alice's neck. Did she know the necklace belonged to my mother? Is there a chance they both knew? Perhaps they each took pleasure from mocking my mother. I despise them, their power, their warped motivation, their desire to protect themselves no matter what, but mostly, as I look at Jim Handcock, I see a man capable of killing. Abby and this trial may have become the linchpin between my past and my present, but within it, I have changed. No matter which way this verdict goes, I cannot ignore the past any more.

Finlay's re-examination of Vivienne takes up most of the morning, but it is lacklustre, as if even he has partly thrown in the towel, especially now that we've reintroduced our motion on the blood tests. He doesn't give in easily, but he is pragmatic. He will have worked out the best pathway forward – for himself.

Kendell postpones proceedings pending legal deliberation on the blood tests, warning the jury to avoid media contact, and not to read or listen to anything about the trial, keeping their deliberations for the jury room whenever he discharges them.

'There are rumours,' Mark says, 'of another story breaking, one that has gone to auction between the media channels.'

'Any idea of content?'

'No, but according to hype, it's explosive.'

We walk towards the interview room set aside to talk to Abby. Again, an armed police officer stands outside the door. I tell myself every piece of information is important, and if she knows something about Alice and Morgan, I have to get it out of her.

As I enter the interview room, she is fiddling with her hair, fixing it repeatedly behind her ears. The wait has made her nervous. I sit in front of her.

'Abby, a story is about to break, one connected to the trial.'

'So?'

'I'd like you to tell me more about Alice.'

'What about her?'

'You lived with her and Jim, you must know things.'

'Alice only tells you what she wants you to know.'

'Was there something going on between her and Morgan?'

She hesitates, then says, 'Maybe.'

'Either there was or there wasn't.'

'If I tell you, what will happen?'

'Like I explained before, client privilege covers most things.' I look across at Mark and Robin. They take the hint to leave.

'Abby, you are my client, irrespective of who is paying the bills. Anything you tell me, with one exception, is covered. I would only be free to reveal information if a client intends to physically harm someone, which isn't the case here. Nor, for the record, am I allowed to reveal information about a historical crime.'

'Something that happened before?'

'Yes,' I reply, holding my breath. What if she tells me she harmed Jacob? Oh, God, please don't let it be that.

'I knew from the beginning something wasn't right.'

'What?'

'When I started working for the Rotterdams, Alice kept calling to check up on me. Only every time she did, Morgan would be working from home, and Vivienne would be at the gallery. It kept happening, and I knew Alice didn't like me, in the same way I knew she wanted me out of her house.'

'Did you see something, Abby, something you shouldn't have?'

'When you're not important, people don't notice you much and, like I said, Alice kept calling at the house. A few times Morgan wasn't there. He'd get delayed at the office, and it used to piss her off. I'd make stupid conversation, but I soon gave up on that. After the first couple of times, I'd leave her alone and get on with my chores. She didn't care. I think she was happy not to have to make the effort, but sometimes she would walk around the house, as if it was her place, you know, touching the furniture, picking things up. One day I caught her lying on Vivienne and Morgan's bed.'

'Go on.'

'She liked to go through Vivienne's things, fingering her clothes, her underwear.'

I lock eyes with her. 'Anything else?'

'No.'

There's something she still isn't telling me. 'Abby, are you trying to protect someone? Is that it?'

She shakes her head.

'Is this about your uncle?'

'You can't make me say anything.' She shakes her head again, tensing.

'Did he threaten you?'

She looks away, but she's far too nervous for this to be nothing.

'Are you scared of him?'

She won't look at me. Whatever she's holding back, I already know she isn't going to share it now.

*What is going on? What am I missing?*

I study her, sensing her fear: she is a pawn in someone else's dangerous game. I visualise the mind maps in my living room, and how, in one form or another, everything leads back to Jim Handcock.

# 75
# HEATHER

Robin gets the telephone call informing us of Kendell's decision as we are about to pack up for the evening.

'At last,' she says, 'we have good news. He has agreed to everything we've asked for.'

'Assuming the blood results prove damning,' I say, 'and Vivienne is a carrier of HLH, or something similar, we'll unpick Finlay's case, bit by bit.'

'What about further testing on Jacob's stored samples?' Mark asks.

'After the parental blood tests,' I say, 'if the results go in our favour, we can push Kendell for more, so let's be prepared. We'll be looking for signs of low white blood cells, traces of jaundice, anaemia or liver damage, because if any of those factors proves positive, we can then press for further analysis of the bone marrow and other organs, including the liver and the spleen. If there are alterations to the bone marrow, and we have a weakening of the bones, it gives probable cause for the fractures.'

My phone buzzes on the desk. Finlay's name comes up on the caller ID. I show it to the others before answering.

'Heather, I'm sure you've heard by now, Kendell has agreed to the blood testing of both Vivienne and Morgan.'

'I have.'

'He has also decided to postpone proceedings until tomorrow afternoon, allowing time for the blood testing to be completed. The hospital has agreed to expedite the testing, considering the significance of the situation. With any luck, we should have the results before proceedings resume.'

'Are you planning on amending the charges? We both know if things don't go your way, it will be hard to pin this on anyone, least of all Abby.'

'Let's agree to talk after the results come in tomorrow.'

'Okay,' I say, hanging up.

I turn to the others. 'Things may move faster than we expect so, as agreed, let's be ready.'

When they leave, the office feels eerily quiet. I put a call through to Cedar Junction prison. I wait for my father to come on the line. It feels like for ever but, finally, I hear his voice. I'm still unsure if he knows about Mia, if he's always known that I am his only daughter.

'Heather, is that you?' he asks, his voice croaky.

I should say something about the two of us, about the last argument we had. I should say a lot of things, but instead I say, 'Boston State Police have pulled in Billy Townsend about Lexie Gilmore's disappearance.'

He doesn't say anything for a few seconds, but then he asks, 'Why are you telling me?'

'Because there's a chance it could be connected to my mother's killing.'

'I'm tired, Heather,' he says wearily. 'I'm locked up for a murder I didn't commit, and I stopped chasing rainbows long ago.'

'Don't you want to know? Sometimes all you need is one missing link, and once the truth is out, everything fits.'

'Like who framed me.'

'Exactly,' I say, as a fresh and horrible feeling grows inside of me.

What if, when I buried everything that night, I buried the very things that would have led to my mother's killer?

# 76
# HEATHER

The following afternoon an apprehensive hush fills the courtroom, as everyone waits for things to start up again. We got the results of the blood tests less than half an hour ago, but they are clear-cut. Vivienne Rotterdam is a carrier of HLH, and the completed paperwork for the testing of Jacob's stored blood samples is already in preparation. It may be a protracted pathway from this point to analysis of the bone marrow, but the way forward is clear.

I have also sent several messages to Alex, asking her to get in touch, but so far, nothing. I don't blame her. I was the one who said we should cool things for a while.

The absence of Finlay and his team isn't going unnoticed in the courtroom either. I look across at the Handcocks, tempted even now to ignore Blake's instruction, walk up to them and demand they tell me the truth. They look on edge. Maybe, like everyone else, they're wondering why the Rotterdams haven't arrived either. The obvious inference is that they are still in conference with Finlay.

Robin nudges me, spotting Finlay entering the courtroom. He

looks unperturbed by everyone staring at him as he walks towards me.

'Heather,' he says, low enough for only me and the legal team to hear, 'we need to have that talk. Kendell has pushed proceedings back another couple of hours. The bailiff will announce it shortly.'

I turn to Robin and Mark. 'You two stay with Abby.'

Once we reach his office, he doesn't waste any time.

'Heather, you know as well as I do this trial was always going to be a tough call – no eyewitnesses, circumstantial evidence, and now the blood results. For the record,' he adds, walking to his desk, 'I still believe Abby is capable of harming Jacob, but now proving it is a lot trickier.' He sits down behind his desk. 'Sit,' he instructs, and I do, knowing so much hinges on what he is about to say.

'The way I see this, Heather, when you and your defence team have the opportunity to put forward your side of the argument, things can only get worse. The doubt is already there and, sadly, I can't put it back in the box. Added to that, another story is about to break in the media about Morgan Rotterdam, and these unnecessary sideshows are not helping anyone, least of all anyone looking for justice.'

'What's the context of the story?'

'I guess you'll find out soon enough,' he says, 'but if you must know, it's about Morgan and Alice Handcock being romantically involved.'

'I see.'

'You don't look surprised.'

'I'm not.'

'Anyhow, here we are. With the blood results in, Kendell already has his doubts, and they're big ones. We both know he'll spend a lifetime charging the jury with the words "beyond reasonable doubt". He'll say it so many times they'll be reciting it in their prayers. All of which will tell the jury to find the girl not guilty.'

'Is the state dropping the charges?' My heart beats a little faster. I feel the adrenalin rush through me, the prospect of winning, of gaining Abby's freedom, rising by the second.

He stares me down, hanging on for as long as he can.

'That depends,' he says.

'On what?'

'You're preparing an additional motion for further analysis of Jacob's stored blood samples?'

'Yes.'

'I expect you'll get an official decision on that shortly.'

'If the decision goes in our favour, the results of the blood samples shouldn't take too long to come through, even if the others, including potential bone-marrow testing, will take a lot longer.'

'I agree, and you might as well know, Kendell has already unofficially given the go-ahead for the blood tests. If they confirm certain anomalies, it will be indicative of what we can expect to follow.'

I tighten my hands into fists, trying to keep my voice calm. 'And if we get a positive result later today, what then?'

'If the results are what we expect, we might as well get this circus over with as quickly as possible.'

'The state will drop the charges?'

'We won't have a choice.'

'The truth wins out,' I say quietly.

'Sometimes it does,' he replies, 'and sometimes it doesn't.'

\*

When the court reconvenes a couple of hours later, with the expediency of the testing through Boston Medical Center, we already have the blood results in our hands. Robin, Mark and I scan them for a second time.

'What is it?' quizzes Abby, oblivious to fresh developments, with none of us wanting to build up her hopes, just in case.

'Jacob's blood results show anomalies,' I whisper, 'consistent with HLH, and the earlier testing of Vivienne. They're damning, only we haven't heard from the prosecution as yet.'

'But ... it's good news?'

'Yes, it's good news.' I can't stop the smile coming to my face, the relief I've felt since reading the blood results gaining momentum all the time. 'Hopefully,' I say, 'this is nearly over.' I reach out to touch her arm. She's trembling. 'It's okay, Abby,' I say. I look at her birthmark, the same as Mia's, in the shape of a half-moon, recalling how, on the first day I met Abby, the easiest thing to do was walk away. I couldn't, because even though I wasn't able to save Mia, I could save this girl from suffering for a crime she hadn't committed.

I look at the Handcocks again. If things go our way, they'll be overjoyed too, and although I'm happy for Abby's sake, part of me is sick that I'll have to continue this façade with them. I doubt the breaking story about Morgan and Alice will bother them either, as I'm sure Alice has already told Jim about Morgan. They will put on a united front. Their kind never shows weakness. They will brazen out this slight on their reputation, and if the DA's office pulls the charges, as Finlay suggested, the Handcocks will milk it for everything it's worth.

The buzz in the courtroom tells me Finlay and his team have arrived. All eyes are on him as he hands a note to the bailiff.

The bailiff announces Judge Kendell. I take Abby's hand, as the jury is brought in. Everyone waits until they take their seats. The bailiff hands Kendell the note. Kendell looks across to Finlay.

Finlay nods. He steps forward, passing more documentation to Kendell.

Warren McKenna approaches the defence table. He hands Robin a piece of paper. She opens it. We all read it simultaneously, before staring at each other, not quite believing it.

Judge Kendell formally opens proceedings by requesting Finlay, as the chief prosecutor, to step forward.

Finlay clears his throat. 'Given the fresh evidence in this case, Your Honour,' he says, 'sadly, the state has no alternative but to withdraw all charges.'

A buzz of nervous excitement sweeps around the courtroom.

I tighten my hands into fists, staring forward, stuck to the spot.

Kendell bangs the gavel several times, calling for order.

'Mr Clarke,' he says, 'please continue.'

Finlay looks as if he is reading his own death warrant. This is hurting him.

'We know this is a painful decision for many concerned, especially the parents of Jacob Rotterdam, but this decision is guided by the law and the evidence presented to us. The evidence leaves the state of Massachusetts with no alternative other than to withdraw all criminal charges against the defendant, Abby Jones.'

The room explodes, and the gavel cannot be heard above the noise.

'It's over,' I tell Abby, grabbing her in my arms, still not quite believing things have turned around so fast. I keep holding her tight, and despite all the remaining questions about my mother, I can no longer keep the happiness from my face. 'It's over, Abby,' I repeat. 'You're free.'

A swarm of reporters snap their cameras. Kendell calls the room to order again, until, at last, a silence ensues. More time passes. The tension mounts. Everyone knows where this is going, and when at last the jury is discharged and thanked for their services, I feel a stillness inside similar to how I felt after my mother was killed, as if somehow I'm standing back from everything, becoming a spectator, separate.

Jim and Alice Handcock walk towards me. I'm relieved when a journalist blocks their way. The silence inside my head is deafening. Other journalists surround Finlay, shouting questions at him.

I turn to shield Abby.

'What happens now?' she asks.

'You'll walk free.'

For a moment I think the crowd is going to swallow her whole. I grip her hand and, losing her usual aloofness, she hugs me hard, crying, whispering, 'Thank you,' over and over.

I hope it is a new beginning for her, and that, for once, she believes other people haven't let her down.

Mark, Robin and one of the bailiffs push the stream of photographers and journalists back. Neither Vivienne nor Morgan is in the courtroom. No doubt Finlay advised them to stay away. More people hover around us and, out of nowhere, I see Alice glaring at me. Others in the room are sending messages on their phones as, right now, the decision is being announced on every news channel and radio station state-wide. Alice holds my gaze, but all I can see is the image from the newspaper clipping, and the rose-quartz necklace at her throat.

A hand grabs my shoulder from behind. 'Heather,' Jim Handcock bellows, beaming like a Cheshire cat, 'your grandpa would be so proud.'

I stare at him, the same man who followed me out to the barn that day after Lucas gave Alice Handcock the potion, the same man who wanted to use Daniel in yet another scheme of his, who probably loved and hated my mother in equal measure, who fathered her dead child, and took everything that had belonged to her so that he could save himself. Daniel was right: the likes of Jim Handcock never really suffer, but they leave plenty of casualties in their wake.

'I did my job,' I say, my voice ice-cold.

'It's like a dream,' Abby murmurs.

Alice is standing beside her, linking her arm, as if she actually cares about the girl. 'Keep hoping, keep dreaming, Abby darling,' she almost sings, 'and be free.'

Our eyes lock, unflinching. My skin prickles. In my head, I repeat the inscription from the book of poetry Lucas gave my mother – *Keep hoping, keep dreaming, and be free.*

I grab the edge of the defence table. I need to keep upright. For a moment, it's as if everything stops. I step back, telling everyone I need a few moments.

'Are you okay, Heather?' Mark asks.

I watch the Handcocks leave, waiting until they are gone from view before I say, 'I'm fine. A little overwhelmed, that's all.'

'They need you for a news conference. Do you want me or Robin to take it?'

'No, it's okay,' I insist. 'Has Abby gone with the Handcocks?'

'Yeah, and Jim Handcock made a big deal about us sending on our bill.'

'Screw him,' I mutter, fresh anger taking over.

At the podium, I lean towards the microphone. 'Hello everyone. I'll take your questions now.' I see the inscription inside the book of poetry, the words of a dead man, *Keep hoping, keep dreaming, and be free*, as Alice's words to Abby repeat in my head.

'Was justice done?' asks one of the journalists.

'Why isn't Abby here?' asks another.

'Please,' I say, 'one at a time.' I look towards the first journalist. 'Justice was served today. All charges have been dropped. The evidence for a conviction did not exist. Abby is innocent, and she is with her family now. She has been through a great deal, and I ask everyone at this time to respect her privacy.'

A sea of hands rises.

'What about the Rotterdams?' asks a voice from the back of the room.

'Our sympathies, as always, are with them for their loss.'

'Will Abby be issuing a statement?'

'That is her choice.'

'What will Abby do next?'

'I'm sure she needs time to reflect.' I see more hands rise.

'Did your father's arrest impact on you during this trial?'

'No comment,' I say, wanting to wrap things up. 'Thank you for coming here today. An official statement will be issued shortly.' I step back from the podium.

'Get me out of here,' I say to Mark, but once we're outside, there are more journalists clamouring on the steps. They are pushing together so tightly that some find it hard to hold their place, slipping down, like a rock fall. There are members of the public too, unwilling or unable to let go of a trial after weeks of obsession. The hashtags #casedismissed, #nannywalksfree, and #thejonestrial are already the three top trends on Twitter. Several TV programmes have rescheduled programming to bring live coverage from the courthouse.

'Come on,' says Mark. 'Let's go back in and find another exit.'

Inside, we pass the courtroom where the trial took place, now filled with a ghostly silence, as if the residue of something disquieting still remains.

I hear someone shout my name. I turn, expecting another

journalist, but instead I see Alex. 'I heard it on the radio,' she says. 'I figured you'd need some back-up.' It feels good to have her here.

Seconds later, we reach another exit.

'Leave your car,' she instructs. 'You're coming home with me.'

I don't argue. I tell Mark I'll speak to him and Robin later. He looks jubilant as he walks away, as I should be. But other than feeling relief at Abby's freedom, and the trial being over, I cannot shift Alice's words from my head.

# 77
# HEATHER

The landscape of Boston whizzes by in a blur, my mind temporarily shutting down. Alex doesn't bother with small talk. I don't ask her about Billy Townsend or the police investigation. Everything can wait, for now.

At her house, I reach down to pet Layla, her pitbull, on the head, as she settles at my feet. Alex pulls the blinds, shutting out the daylight, then reaches for a bottle of bourbon, and fills two shot glasses.

'Knock that back,' she orders.

We swallow together. I grimace. She pours another for each of us. The next goes down easier. She refills my glass for a third time, watching as I knock it back.

She takes my hand. 'You need sleep.'

I nod obediently.

'Everything will feel a whole lot better after some shut-eye. I'll stay downstairs, so you won't get disturbed.'

'You don't have to do that,' I say, but as we reach the bedroom, and she blocks out the light upstairs, I finally give in. I can't get Alice's words out of my head, the inscription in the book of poetry, knowing, deep in my gut, if Jim gave Alice that book, it was another way of discarding my mother's memory, as if she was of no consequence. I think about what Alex said to me months before, how human beings are capable of anything, as another thought slips in, that Jim and Alice were in this together.

As Alex reaches the doorway, I say, 'My mother saved my life once, when I was a little girl, skating on the pond. The ice cracked, and I nearly drowned. She protected me against my uncle Samuel too. She did everything she could, even during her months of darkness, after Mia, to love and keep me safe. She also taught me how to hide, to ensure, if anything happened, I would be okay. Nobody remembers her for any of that. Nobody cares about all the good bits.'

'You care,' she says, 'and that's what matters.'

I close my eyes, so close to tears I can barely breathe.

Alex shuts the door. In my mind's eye, I revisit the day my mother locked herself into Mia's bedroom, trying to cling to a life already gone. I want to reach back through time and tell her how much I love her. How I have always loved her. How Alex is right. Even if others don't care, I do. I don't expect sleep, not after everything that has happened, but somehow it's as if my mother is willing me to rest, telling me I need my strength, that eventually I'll remember everything, and if I let her guide me, I'll find the answers I'm looking for. *Be fragile, be strong.*

*

I have no idea how many hours have gone by, but when I wake up, I have the sour taste of bourbon in my mouth. Alex isn't in the room. I reach dry-mouthed for my phone to check the time. Eight o'clock. I've slept for four solid hours.

I hear Alex talking downstairs.

Getting out of bed, I go to the door, easing it open. I hear her voice again. I walk towards the staircase. She's talking to someone on her cell phone, unaware that I can hear her. There is something unsettling in her voice. It sounds agitated. Then, I hear her say, 'It's okay. I'm with her now.'

The person at the other end of the line must be talking, because a few seconds pass without her saying anything. *Why is she giving someone information about me?*

'Everything is under control,' she says, hanging up.

I lean against the banister. It creaks. She looks up, slipping her phone into her back pocket.

'Who was that?' I ask.

'No one important. Did you sleep okay? You were out for hours.'

I start wondering how much I really know about her. 'Look, Alex, maybe I should go.'

'But the weather has turned into a son-of-a-bitch out there.'

'I don't care.'

'Stay,' she says, but I'm already walking downstairs. She's so close to me now that her breath is on my neck.

I pick up my coat from one of the side-chairs, only then remembering I don't have a car.

'I'll drive,' she says, reading my thoughts.

I look at the half-empty bottle of bourbon.

'Maybe that's not such a great idea.' I point to the bottle. 'I'll grab a cab.'

She argues, but some of her earlier enthusiasm is already gone. It isn't like Alex to drink so much. Something has her under pressure. Perhaps she senses I'm uncomfortable because, thankfully, she doesn't push the point again.

The cab arrives soon after.

I step out into the horrible night, wet and windy, a new loneliness hitting home fast. I count the steps to the cab, part of me unsure until I'm safely inside it that she will let me go.

# 78
# HEATHER

Less than an hour later I pick up my car from Central Boston. Before doing anything else, I call my father again. I wait for him to come to the phone, hearing the sounds of a maximum-security prison down the line – the clanking of keys, footsteps of the prison guards, opening and closing of metal doors, ramblings from the inmates, and the crackle as the receiver is taken into someone's hand. Then I hear his voice.

'Heather, is that you?'

'I know you didn't kill Lucas,' I say, as if this must be our starting point – a fact that tells him I no longer believe he lied. 'I also plan on getting you out of there.'

'You owe me nothing.'

'You're still my father.'

There is silence at the end of the line, as if he's churning this over. 'Do you know why Lucas was killed?'

'I think so.'

'He worked out the killer, didn't he?'

'Yes.'

'Who?'

'There has only ever been one person.'

'Jim Handcock?'

'Yes.'

'You can't take him on, Heather. He'll crush you.'

'I have to face him. I have to know the truth.'

'I know I haven't been much of a father ...'

'It's okay,' I say, pressing my cheek against the car window, feeling the cold against the warmth of my face. 'It wasn't all your fault.'

'Heather, you need to be careful.'

As I hang up, I imagine him walking away, back to the prison cell, where someone will turn the key and lock him in, before everything goes black at lights out. I feel sadness for all the lost time we could have had, the lost life, the little girl I used to be. I thought I could put it all behind me, do the very thing my father has done his whole life, never fully facing up to things, but I can't. I know that now. My mother was seen as weak, only she wasn't. She was strong, and I am too.

Nearing Corham, the rain gets even heavier. I take the coast road to the Handcocks' house, just as I did all those months before. I'm driving so fast now that, at times, the tyres skid on the wet surface. I have no idea who Alex was talking to on the phone, or if my need to get away was either crazy or sane. All I know is that I need to push forward. I don't give a damn what Blake said about not approaching the Handcocks and keeping quiet. I've been quiet for far too long, a habit learned in childhood, the ability to be silent, to disappear. In the beginning, you believe it offers you protection, but it doesn't: it locks you in.

I take a bend too sharply, and for a few seconds I lose control of the car. In the moments that follow, when I pull it back from the edge, I think of how I panicked the day my mother died. I see myself fixing her dress, covering her bare legs, before walking back upstairs to get that red box. Soon after, I go outside, and with the shovel in my hand, in the snow, I dig a hole large enough to bury her secrets, her life.

Afterwards, I stood there, watching the snow create a brand-new layer, pure and white, as the flakes kept falling, as in my mind I pushed the horror to a place I couldn't reach it, burying my memories because I was unwilling or unable to face them. Even now, I have no idea how long I hid in that blanket box. Nor can I know for sure if my mother thought I did everything I could to help her, everything a frightened child could do, or if, lying on that kitchen floor, she wanted me to do more. 'I'm sorry,' I roar into the empty car. 'I'm sorry, I'm so sorry, so, so sorry.'

I wipe tears away, taking the next bend too sharply as well, then slowing down, my breathing heavy, feeling the rush of it, like a wild animal, startled, jerking, with everything suddenly becoming clear, a simple truth. All this time, I realise, I've been seeking more than answers. I've been seeking redemption, having failed the person I loved most in the world. Surviving defines you. I am who I am, not despite my past but because of it, and as I take the next turn towards the Handcocks' house, getting ever closer, the physicality of being back here feels as if I have come full circle. I hear a loud clap of thunder, before another deluge of rain hits the windscreen, and my mind splits into fragments.

I see Alice wearing the rose-quartz necklace, after Jim gives it to her as a present, mocking my mother. How could he do that, if he loved my mother, if he was the father of her dead child? How could he imagine he could superimpose my mother's life and everything precious to her on another woman? I think about Mia, wondering how much of everything that has happened was because of her, the baby who died too young. Did Jim see Mia in Abby too, a final chance to gain the daughter he'd lost, and the reason Alice believed he was obsessed with her? And all those years before, did Mia's death fill him with so much hate that he had to destroy my mother also?

I see Corham in the distance, the church steeple, the rows of shops, the library and other, smaller, buildings, all linked together, as if I'm Gulliver looking down upon Lilliput. A mass of grey cloud hangs low over the town. I remember thinking during the trial, how bad things can happen to good people, and how the death of a baby will bring out the best and the worst in people. But what about the death of a mother?

My hands tighten on the steering wheel. For a few seconds it's as if I can't breathe, as if I'm hiding in that blanket box again, a child, terrified and alone. I slow down as the road narrows. I think about Jim and Alice, jubilant earlier today. I think about Abby, and the nagging doubt that, even now, she may be holding something back. But more than anything, I think about how I've waited far too long for this moment, and nothing on earth is going to stop me facing my mother's killer.

# 79
# BLAKE

The interview room at Cambridge police station has a circular metal table bolted to the floor, surrounded by four metal stools, also locked down. The walls are painted white, and Blake is standing behind the three-paned mirrored glass on one of the walls. In front of him are two computers with keyboards, along with a direct phone line. Also on the table are boxes of files and notes from the García murder, the unsolved rapes in Washington, Lexie Gilmore, and Elizabeth Baxter's murder. Through the mirrored glass, he sees Billy Townsend looking like he doesn't give a damn about anyone or anything. Why is he so smug? Is it because he thinks someone is going to come to his aid and, if so, who?

Blake pulls up an image of Elizabeth Baxter on one of the computer screens, seeing the honey-blonde hair, the attractive shoulders. He looks in more detail at her face, and her almost mystical gaze, and how her eyes are like that of someone who has lived through many things, someone who wasn't ready to die. He has no intention of letting a lowlife like Billy Townsend get the better of him. He changes the image on the screen to one of the crime-scene photographs, seeing Lucas García's dead body partly covered in soil. He has a half-crazed look in his eyes, as if before he died he was surprised at who pulled the trigger.

It had all pointed to Charlie Baxter, but in his gut Blake knows the scumbag on the other side of the glass is linked somehow to all these cases, the rapes, Lexie Gilmore's disappearance, Elizabeth Baxter, and perhaps even Lucas García. Maybe Billy is the weakest link.

He re-enters the interview room, having left Billy on his own for over an hour.

'What's a guy got to do around here to get some water?' Billy asks.

Blake, square-jawed, with his tall and broad frame, ignores him. He kicks Billy's folded legs apart. Billy looks at the camera in the corner. Blake loosens his tie and the top button of his shirt. The door opens. Blanco walks in with Officer Hanratty. Billy looks instantly more at ease. Blake hadn't seen the harm in having Blanco involved, not until now. Could Blanco be another puppet for whoever is pulling the strings?

'Blanco, I think we can handle this from here,' Blake says. 'We'll keep you informed.'

Blanco isn't happy, but he doesn't argue. When he's gone, Blake sits down and switches on the recorder. He notes the time and date, and who is present in the room: himself, Officer Hanratty and Billy Townsend. He has a file in his hand. 'Do you know what I have here, Billy?'

'No.'

'The DNA profile of the guy who raped those two girls.'

'So?'

'We're running your sample through the system as we speak.'

Billy shrugs his shoulders.

'What do you think is going to happen if we find a match?'

'Dunno.'

'I'm going to tell you.'

Billy looks at the camera again, and away from the detectives.

'There are two possible scenarios, Billy. Scenario one, your sorry ass rots in jail for a very long time. Scenario two, if you help us sort out a few outstanding issues, you may have the option to plea-bargain, but obviously that depends on the information you give us.'

'About what?'

'About whether you did more than rape those two girls.'

'I'm saying nothing.'

'I'm going to ask you again, what do you know about the García murder?'

'Only what the whole damn town does, that Charlie Baxter was out for revenge.'

'Is that a fact?'

'I'm only saying what folks are thinking.'

'You ever watch any of those true crime documentaries on TV, Billy?'

'Sometimes.'

Blake looks at Hanratty, then turns back to Billy. 'I bet you're a bit of a pro when it comes to solving things.'

He doesn't answer him.

'The thing I've often noticed about those documentaries is that when the cops go investigating stuff at the beginning, it's rarely simple. Things are messy. I mean, they look at one thing, and then another, and soon they find themselves in one helluva complicated heap of shit. You get my drift?'

Billy nods.

'That's when it usually goes to an ad break.' Blake laughs. 'It pisses the hell out of me, because I love mess. The more shit there is to wade through, the more I like it. Do you hear what I'm saying?'

'I guess.'

'This killing of Lucas García, the one you have nothing to do with, is so full of shit it could send a man blind, and complicated too, very complicated.' He straightens his back. 'It's like opening up a cesspit, and before you know it, a load of stuff is crawling everywhere.'

Billy shrugs again.

'Do you want to know what I mean by that?'

'Nope.'

'Well, I'm going to tell you. Elizabeth Baxter's murder, for one.'

'I don't have—'

Blake holds up his hand. 'I know, you don't have anything to do with that either.' He puts his elbows on the interview table. 'So, Billy, when a man turns up dead, shot, and you start looking around for motive, you have to consider all kinds of things. It could be a revenge killing, sure. Or it could be something else.'

'I don't follow.'

'I'll take it nice and slow for you,' he says, looking towards the mirrored glass, remembering Elizabeth Baxter's face. 'If it was revenge, it's tied into the Baxter murder, right?'

'I guess.'

'Which happened a long time ago.'

'Yeah.'

'Now, let's just say between the three of us here, yourself, Hanratty and me, that some of the police work on that case was sloppy.'

'Not my problem.'

'Maybe not right now, but it could be.'

'How's that?'

'When police work gets sloppy, it turns up a whole host of

questions. Did someone want to protect someone? Did they want to lose evidence?'

Billy stares at him.

'I'm going to be straight with you, Billy. It disappoints the hell out of me when I start thinking about cops not being model citizens, but you see, Billy, no matter how many good apples there are in the barrel, or how big that barrel is, a few rotten ones always manage to get in. You know what I mean?'

'Do I need a lawyer?'

'No, not yet. Let's shoot the breeze for another while, on account you will want to hear some of the things I have to say.'

'I'm listening.'

'Corham is a mighty quiet place, isn't it? At times all you can hear are the birds a-singing.'

'I suppose.'

'Hardly a robbery, or the like, ever happens there, not to mention murder. Do you know, Billy, how many murders have happened in Corham in the last one hundred years?'

'No.'

'Two, Billy, that's all. Statistics don't lie. Remarkable, isn't it?'

Billy stares at him.

'And we both know which two murders we're talking about, don't we?'

He nods.

'Elizabeth Baxter and Lucas García.'

Billy shuffles his knees under the table, folding his arms tight.

'And, Billy, making my way through the statistics, do you know what the only other big incident was?'

'No.'

'No?' Blake looks baffled. 'Billy, you've let me down. Maybe you haven't watched enough TV after all.'

'Maybe not.'

'I bet, Billy, if either of us went into a local bar right now and asked anyone the same question, do you know what folks would say?'

Billy shakes his head.

'They would say it was that missing girl, Lexie Gilmore. Do you remember her?'

'Sort of.'

'I hear you two were mighty friendly.'

'I wouldn't say that. I bought her a drink a couple of times, that's all.'

'Did you now?'

'It didn't mean nothing.'

Blake smirks, keeping his eyes on Billy. 'For a while, when I was out there, rolling in the shit of those two unsolved murders, the disappearance of that young girl got me curious about you.'

'Oh, yeah?'

'Absolutely. You are a very interesting person, Billy. You have a temper, everyone knows that. You beat the crap out of your wife. Everyone knows that, too. And do you know what else people know?'

'No.'

'You like to travel.'

'No law against it.'

'I've been long enough at this game, Billy, to know people don't change all that much over time. And when we started digging into your past, we found you did some other travelling too, up around Maine, then further south. And I got to thinking, what else has Billy been up to?'

'Fucking police harassment, that's what this is.'

'I'll cut to the chase, Billy, shall I? Here is what I think. You liked that Lexie girl. You liked her a lot. Maybe you thought she liked you, too, but perhaps things weren't moving along fast enough for you.

She started to play hard to get. You didn't like that. Then one day things sort of got out of hand. You lost it. You flipped. Figured the best way out of this was to shut the girl up good and proper.'

'I want a lawyer.'

Blake softens his voice. 'Look, Billy, I know you're tied to that girl's disappearance, and do you know what else I know?'

Billy stares him down.

'When I started working my way through those old case files, I found something else mighty interesting.' He leans in. 'At the time of her disappearance, there was DNA evidence taken from the Handcocks' house. It seems Lexie Gilmore wasn't the only person in her bedroom the day she went missing. Now, I don't know for sure if this Person X got into that room uninvited, or if the circumstances were different, but what I do know is this. Sheriff Hodgson, your uncle, missed something important.'

'What was that?'

'The identity of the person in the room.'

'Yeah?'

'You see, earlier on, we checked your DNA sample against the one from her bedroom, and we got a match.'

'So what? Even if I was in the room, it doesn't prove nothing.'

'Doesn't it? It puts you in the girl's bedroom without the permission of the homeowners, which brings me nicely to the two unsolved rapes. I'm confident you'll go down for those, and because of Hodgson's sloppiness, we have enough to get a search warrant for your place. Right now, we're turning it upside down.'

'You won't find nothing.'

'But, Billy, here's the thing. This investigation is spreading out faster than a stone causes ripples in the ocean. And whereas I don't have a crystal ball, once you're done for the rapes, we plan on tying you to one of those two murder statistics too.'

'I didn't kill either of them.'

'You know, in a way I'm inclined to believe you. I've developed a good instinct about these things over the years but, you see, we may find something a helluva lot more awkward for you than your DNA in Lexie Gilmore's bedroom.'

'What?'

'We hope to match you to Elizabeth Baxter too.' Blake stands up. He walks around Billy. 'Now, I'll admit there was a fair amount of contamination of the samples. I mean, Sheriff Hodgson could have appeared at the O.J. trial back in 'ninety-five, the evidence collection was that bad, but the thing is, the State Police held onto some items from the original crime scene, including Elizabeth Baxter's clothing.'

'So?'

'Did you know, Billy, that technological advances in DNA are so good these days, that they can even make a composite sketch of a suspect from DNA? They did it right here in Massachusetts, with a twenty-four-year-old murder case. Hell, they can even extract DNA from the Neanderthals, who went extinct thirty thousand years ago, if they want to.'

Blake leans in over Billy. 'You couldn't resist having Elizabeth Baxter, too, could you? The same way you couldn't resist Lexie Gilmore, those other two girls and God knows who else.'

'I didn't kill Elizabeth Baxter.'

'No?'

'And I'm not the only one in this fucking mess of yours.'

'Is that right?'

'I want a lawyer.'

'I'm guessing you know who to call.'

Blake hands Billy the phone. He watches him dial the number of the Handcocks' house.

'I'm in Cambridge cop shop,' he roars down the line, 'and I need a lawyer, now.'

Blake waits until he hangs up before saying, 'Billy, I'm a reasonable man. I want to hear your side of things. When it comes to prison sentences, it's usually best if you're seen to co-operate with the police, especially when your balls are caught in a snare.'

'I have nothing to say.'

'Before your lawyer gets here and you two get all friendly, I'll tell you this. If you play along with us, tell us the stuff that will help our *complicated* investigation, then this whole situation doesn't have to turn out as bad for you as it could.'

Billy stares at him again.

'I won't lie to you, Billy,' Blake continues, 'this isn't a good situation. You will most likely go down for several counts of rape, and possibly murder one. I'm not shitting you, it's serious stuff. But multiple homicides, well, God, Billy, that's entering serial-killer territory and there isn't much worse than that.'

Blake looks at Hanratty, then says, 'Billy, I think someone helped you cover your tracks, someone other than your uncle, and heck, I wouldn't be surprised if it's the same person who was behind Elizabeth Baxter's killing and Lucas García's.'

'No shit?' says Billy, defiant.

'And if you want to opt for any kind of a plea-bargain, then after you get chatting with your legal representative, I'd advise you to get talking mighty fast.'

# 80
# HEATHER

When I turn into Hobart Lane, my cell phone rings. It's Alex. I pull off the road, still angry at her for talking about me behind my back. I don't want any more secrets in my life. 'Who were you talking to, Alex? No bullshit, not if you care about me.'

She hesitates. I wait.

'I was talking to Blake.'

'Why?'

'Something big is going down, and he didn't want you getting in the way.'

'What?'

'I can't say.'

'Yes, you can.'

'He doesn't want to risk people sending out alarm bells to those involved.'

'It's too late for that, Alex.'

'Heather, you don't want to mess things up now, not when the police are closing in.'

This time it's my turn to hesitate.

'Where are you?' she asks.

'Corham,' I reply, and kill the call.

I pull the car back out onto the lane. The cell phone vibrates. I ignore it.

Five minutes later I'm parking in the Handcocks' driveway, and seconds after that, I'm running across the gravelled drive. By the time I ring the doorbell, I'm already soaked, the rain pelting down my back.

The bell rings several times before Alice answers. She has a strange look in her eyes and, for a second, I'm not sure if she's going to shut the door on me.

'Are you looking for Jim?'

'Yes.'

'Then you'd better come inside.'

'Is Abby here?'

'She's sleeping, and Jim is in the study.'

I follow her, my wet clothes stuck to me.

She taps on the study door. 'Jim, you have a visitor.' She doesn't wait for him to answer, turning the handle to allow us both walk into the room.

He is sitting behind a large desk, and for the briefest of moments, I think about my grandpa doing the same thing. For the first time I see Jim Handcock as an old man, with a lifetime behind him.

'You're soaked,' he says, standing up. 'Alice, get Heather a towel.'

'Of course,' she says. I note a slight rise at the sides of her lips, as if she's hiding a smile, taking pleasure in seeing me wet through. I wait until she leaves to say, 'We need to talk.'

'It seems like no time at all, Heather, since you first came to visit us, to take on Abby's case.'

'And now you have everything you wanted.' My words are terse. 'Abby's freedom.'

He nods in acknowledgement.

'But then again, Jim, you always get what you want, don't you?'

He studies me. 'Alice thinks you hate me, Heather. Is she right?'

'I know about you and my mother.'

'What do you know?'

I remember my father's words, how Jim Handcock has the ability to crush me. 'I know you had an affair.'

He smiles. 'I used to call her Lizzie,' he says, as if we're taking a walk down memory lane, 'it was our little secret, and, sometimes, she used to call me James.'

'Why couldn't you leave her alone?'

'Because I couldn't resist her. And I think for a time she loved me too.'

'Until Mia?'

'She wasn't well after the baby died. She went to a very bad place, especially when the post-natal depression kicked in.' He sounds sincere, but I've no intention of letting him fool me.

'You have to understand, Heather, your mother went inside herself. She started to do crazy things. Going into the woods, looking for the baby.'

'She was called Mia,' I say, reaffirming her name.

He nods.

'You gave my mother that miniature elephant, didn't you?'

'Yes,' he says. 'How did you know?'

'Because I buried it with her journal and all the other things you took from her. You left it in my house. You wanted to scare me, the same way you scared my mother, the same way you took that gun and killed Lucas.'

He glares at me as if I'm crazy. 'I – I don't understand,' he stammers. 'Where did you bury them?'

'You know exactly where I buried them. Don't deny it. Out back, near our old swing. You watched me that night, didn't you? You, or someone you sent to do your dirty work. The same way you killed her, or maybe you hired some thug, because you couldn't bear the truth that she didn't want you any more.'

'That's not true.'

'You took her from me. You had to be in control of everything and everyone, but sometimes that means destroying people. That's what you're doing to my father right now, isn't it? And when Lucas came back, and saw Alice with that necklace, the one he gave my mother, he knew she would never have willingly given it away, and when he confronted you, you killed him too.'

His face contorts.

I wait.

'If you're correct about all this, Heather,' he says, his voice cold, 'if what you say is true, I could do the same thing to you right now, couldn't I?'

I hear a phone ringing in another room, then Alice's voice. She opens the door. 'Blanco has been in touch,' she says, firing a towel in my direction.

'About what?' Jim glares at her.

'Billy Townsend. It seems he's in trouble. He called earlier, looking for a lawyer.'

'Why didn't you tell me?' he snaps.

'Because you didn't want to be disturbed, but I knew you'd make an exception for Heather.'

They're talking as if I'm not in the room. I use the towel to wipe the rain from my face.

'It seems the police are investigating that missing girl from years back,' Alice continues. 'You remember her, Jim, don't you? Lexie Gilmore?'

I study the two of them. Jim looks as if he's trying to work something out. He must realise, if Billy is being questioned, the finger of blame will soon point to him.

'They're looking into the case,' Alice says.

'They've reopened my mother's, too,' I say, 'because of Lucas's murder.' They both stare at me, as if only now remembering I'm still in the room.

'Your loser of a father killed Lucas García,' Jim shouts, 'because Lucas killed Lizzie. He was looking for forgiveness, by doing something half decent, even after all this time, and I'm happy he's going down for it. And, God damn it, isn't that what you want too, Heather, forgiveness for leaving your mother to die?'

His words hit hard.

'Charlie has never been any good. He wasn't there for Lizzie when she lost the baby, or when she couldn't pay the bills. He ran away, like the coward he is.'

Why is he still blaming my father?

He turns to Alice. 'Heather thinks I killed her mother.'

Alice raises her eyebrows. 'Does she?'

'She told me other things, too, about how someone left a small elephant I gave to Lizzie in her house, wanting to scare her.'

He takes a step closer to his wife. I can't read his face.

'Heather also believes I gave a necklace to you, but perhaps you know better, Alice. Did you steal it from her?'

'My huuusband,' she says, elongating the word, 'adored your mother, but to me, she was nothing more than an annoying whore.'

'Don't call Lizzie that,' he spits.

Alice laughs, a mad, crazy laugh.

'Heather also thinks,' he says, his tone accusatory, 'that I watched her bury her mother's things, along with her journal, after she was killed.'

'Or someone did it for you,' I scream, looking from one to the other. 'I may have only been a child, but I was there. I can't be sure I buried the necklace, but even if I didn't, whoever killed her took that too, wanting trophies, mementoes, things that belonged to another person's life. Someone capable of stealing, of killing. Someone evil.'

Alice puts her hand to her neck.

Jim moves closer to her. 'Do you have Lizzie's necklace?'

There is something different in his eyes, a look I recognise, the same as when a jury member becomes certain of someone's guilt or innocence.

She doesn't answer him.

'Heather believes I killed Lucas. I thought Charlie did it, but maybe we're both wrong.'

'He was a horrible man,' she fires back at him. 'He made me barren with those concoctions of his and that crazy voodoo doll.'

My mind jerks back to the day Lucas brought me to this house, when Alice was screaming like a mad woman in the bed. I look at Jim. 'Lucas came to see you, didn't he?'

'I didn't kill him,' he says again, and his words are so emphatic, I almost believe him.

Alice smirks.

'You wore the necklace to the trial,' I yell at her. 'Was it because neither of you could resist laughing at my mother, even in death, wearing something that had belonged to a dead woman?' They stare at me and, once again, I wonder if they could be in this together, if this whole thing is some sort of warped charade. 'And when Lucas came here,' I scream at them, 'one or both of you needed him out of the way, because he knew whoever took the necklace probably killed her too.'

Jim is standing side by side with Alice. He whispers something in her ear, the same way she whispered to Vivienne days before. His voice is low, and even though I'm only a few feet away, I can't make out what he's saying. I study her face, seeing a hint of fear. What did he say to her?

I visualise her on the steps of the courthouse, wearing the necklace, and in much the same way as the orange glow of dawn illuminates a darkened sky, I ask myself if, after all this time, I've been looking in the wrong direction, blaming the wrong Handcock.

Was Alice the one who wanted control of my mother's life, who wanted to take everything that had belonged to her, including her life?

As I'm thinking this, the door to the study opens, and I see Abby.

# 81
# ELIZABETH

Heather was at school the day Alice Handcock came to the house. Mia was asleep upstairs, her eyelids having fought hard against it. Beforehand her eyes had a glint in them, bewitching, almost not of this world, until at long last she gave in to sleep, and I went outside.

I didn't hear Alice's car pull up. The washing line was filled with Mia's clothes, fluttering in the breeze. Walking back towards the house, I saw it, the car, red and shiny, and opening the door, I smelt her scent. I already knew she hated me, which meant she hated Mia too, Jim's only child.

I called her name, but she didn't answer me. I called it again, louder the second time, as a horrible thought took hold. Somehow I knew Mia was no longer in her crib. I also knew Alice Handcock had her. She was waiting for me to find them.

When I saw her in the rocking chair, with Mia in her arms, part of me died inside. I saw the pink pacifier too, the new one Alice had put in her mouth. My first instinct was to grab Mia from her, but then Alice said, 'Don't you worry, Lizzie, I won't harm the child. She's such a beautiful little girl. Isn't it such a shame she has that horrible stain on her face?'

'What do you want?' I asked, readying myself to grab Mia.

'Oh, Lizzie,' she laughed, 'we could talk about that all day.'

I despised the way she said my name, dragging out both syllables. I despised her calling me Lizzie too. I knew it was her way of telling me she had found out about me and Jim.

When she stood up and handed Mia back to me, it felt almost unexpected, but inside, a fear was growing, as if I already knew this wouldn't be the end of her. She took the pacifier out of Mia's mouth, and Mia cried, unsure of what had happened. I was filled with such relief, cradling her in my arms, that I didn't pay too much attention to Alice's parting words.

'I don't think either of us should say anything about this to Jim, do you? It can be our secret, and you know all about secrets, don't you, Lizzie?'

Afterwards I could have told Jim, but then Mia died. I became lost within myself, directionless.

Later, when he asked to come back into my life, I shut him out, knowing how dangerous his wife could be. I knew as soon as things began going missing from the house, including the rose-quartz necklace Lucas had given me, that Alice had taken them. That was why I needed to hide everything precious to me, including this journal, and why I told Heather they were important, and to keep them safe.

That day at Skating Pond, when Heather nearly drowned, and I saw Alice Handcock watching us, I also knew she would visit us again. She would never go away, because she couldn't take the risk that I might one day give Jim the very thing he wanted most in life, the one thing she could never give him: a child.

# 82
# ALEX

After she parks her car, Alex barely looks around her, sprinting across to Cambridge police station and entering the lobby seconds later.

'I need to see Blake Lynam now,' she shouts at the officer behind the glass. The police officer is female, African American, and doesn't seem keen on Alex's attitude. Alex softens her tone. 'Look, he will want to see me.'

'Name?'

'Alex Drummond.'

'Wait over there.' The officer points to the visitors' area at the side.

Alex has tried Heather's cell phone so many times that making contact with her at this point is no longer an option.

In the visitors' area, there are a couple of homeless guys, and a teenage girl trying to look older than her years. Up high, in the corner, is a portable television. Fox News is on. After a sport segment on the Red Sox, it turns to the trial. Alex sees Marcia Langan on the panel, but the chief anchor is doing most of the talking.

'Abby Jones,' she says, 'the nanny sensationally cleared of the murder of infant Jacob Rotterdam today, is seen here hugging her defence counsel, Heather Baxter.' An image of Heather and Abby from the court earlier appears on the screen. 'We are joined this evening by Marcia Langan, a reporter close to this unfolding story. Let me start by asking you, Marcia, is this the end of the road?'

'The end for Abby Jones, perhaps, but this verdict doesn't bring closure.'

'What about the parents? They weren't in court today, is that right?'

'They were noticeably absent, and it is fair to speculate that the decision to drop charges was probably too much for them to bear.'

'And Morgan Rotterdam? You've been keeping a close eye on him for some time, haven't you?'

'It isn't long,' Marcia says, 'since I broke the story about Morgan and the unnamed young girl in a downtown hotel.'

'His behaviour,' the anchor says, 'left many of us reeling.'

The old image of Morgan at the hotel with the girl reappears.

'I agree and, like the aftermath of the trial, this story isn't going away anytime soon.'

'Marcia, I understand you'll be staying with us as more of it unfolds.'

Marcia nods.

The news anchor turns to the camera. 'We'll be back in a few moments with an in-depth analysis of Heather Baxter, the lead defence attorney in this case. She sure must be happy this evening.'

Alex paces the waiting room. She's only going to give Blake one more minute before she barges down the internal corridor to find him herself.

She steps out into the lobby. The female officer behind the glass looks at her. 'He's on his way,' she says, in a tone that tells Alex to stay put.

She paces the floor again, eyeing the security cameras, knowing there are officers in the room to her left, watching everything.

'Alex,' says Blake, opening the double doors, 'what the hell are you doing here?'

'I couldn't get you on your cell, and I think Heather is heading into a shitload of trouble.'

'Did you tell her what's going down?'

'Some.'

'Jesus, Alex.' He stands back, indicating she should walk through.

'I think she's gone to the Handcocks' house.'

'Fuck.'

'I couldn't stop her. She was going no matter what I said to her.'

He opens the door to a small office and switches on the light.

'What has Billy Boy told you?' Alex asks.

'Not enough for us to make our move.'

'Did you turn up anything at his place?'

'No.'

'I warn you, Blake, if anything happens to Heather, there'll be hell to pay, and right now you're not filling me with a whole lot of confidence.'

'We need more time.'

'Then you'd better hope it moves fast because I'm going to the Handcocks.'

'You can't go until we have enough for a warrant.'

'We'll have to see about that,' she says, storming off.

Blake calls after her, but she ignores him.

Out in the public area, the news is still on. They are about to start an exclusive with Marcia Langan about *What the nanny knew*, but

Alex has no time for that. If she's lucky, she has a couple of minutes before Blake sends a car after her and, most likely, the trickiest part will be getting out of Central Boston. Once she's on the interstate, she has a chance of getting ahead of them.

Moments later, she hears the faint sound of a police siren in the distance, as she zooms between lanes, honking her horn to get every other goddamn vehicle on the road out of her way.

# 83
# BLAKE

Blake opens the door to the surveillance room watching Billy Townsend. He knows he needs to get him talking about Elizabeth Baxter's murder, and fast, but with his lawyer in situ, it's going to be difficult. He picks up the phone to call Hanratty. 'How long until the lab has the results back on Billy's DNA and the Baxter case?'

'Another quarter of an hour at most, but the results are in on the other rapes.'

'And?'

'They're positive.'

'Good, because we have a developing situation.'

'What?'

'Heather Baxter may be at the Handcocks' place, and a private investigator is heading that way too.'

'Who?'

'Alex Drummond, the PI who initially linked the rapes to Billy.'

'What do you suggest? We don't have enough yet to get a warrant for the Handcocks' place.'

'We convince Billy we've already made the connection to Elizabeth Baxter or, at least, keep him under pressure until we have what we need.'

'His lawyer will claim coercion. It's risky.'

'I'll be careful.'

'What makes you think the Handcocks are behind all this?'

'Elizabeth Baxter's rape fits the same MO as the other two, with rope marks on the wrists, bruising on the legs, and the attacker leaving the lower part of the body exposed, but if Billy tossed the place, there are only two reasons for it. Either he wanted to steal from the Baxters, who didn't have much, or he was looking for something specific. My guess is he was looking for something for someone else, and there aren't too many people with the power in Corham to keep this kind of thing under wraps. It takes someone good at covering their tracks, too, and it also takes money. I think García discovered something that got him killed, and if it wasn't Charlie Baxter, then it was someone else, and, yes, my money is still on the Handcocks. Chances are, by now Blanco has filled them in too.'

'I never wanted him here,' replies Hanratty.

'He brought Billy in and, anyway, he's out of the picture now.'

'Hold on a second,' says Hanratty, 'there's more coming in from the lab.'

Blake counts back from five.

'Hell,' says Hanratty.

'What?'

'They've matched the DNA from the Baxter case to Billy.'

'Right, have everyone on standby. We need to move fast once we get Billy talking. Start the process for the warrant on the Handcocks' place too. I don't want any legal loopholes coming back to bite us.'

# 84
# HEATHER

All three of us stare at Abby as she opens the study door. She rubs her eyes, walking in. 'I heard shouting. What's going on?'

'Go back to your room,' Jim tells her.

'Why is Heather here?'

'It's nothing to do with you, Abby,' he insists. 'Go back to bed.'

'I don't want to. I'm sick of being locked up, even if this isn't a prison. You were arguing. Tell me why.'

'It's okay, Abby,' I say. 'Your uncle is right. This isn't about you.'

'Is it about her?' she asks, pointing the finger at Alice.

I stare at Alice, the rain pelting hard against the large window behind her, with white gusts, like ghosts, flying in from the sea. Abby has been through enough, I think. I don't want her mixed up in this.

'Can I talk to Alice alone?' I ask, directing my question to Jim.

He puts his arms around Abby, protective, fatherly. Is this an act, or does he really care for her? Perhaps Alice hates her too. I don't expect him to agree, but then the door clicks shut behind them. I turn to face Alice. 'You knew about the affair, didn't you, between my mother and Jim?'

'Yes.'

'And you hired Billy to kill her, didn't you?'

She laughs. 'I enjoyed wearing her necklace, if you must know.'

'And what about the other things?'

'Worthless trash.'

'Not to my mother.'

She shrugs.

'Do you have her journal?'

'Perhaps I do.'

'Does Jim know?'

'After your little rant this evening, I think he's probably put some things together, but I doubt he'll do anything other than threaten me. I could ruin him if I wanted to.'

'You don't care about anyone, do you, other than yourself?'

Her eyes narrow. 'Shall I share something else with you, Heather, woman to woman?'

'What?' I tighten my fists.

'Billy didn't kill your mother.'

'I don't believe you. You paid him to kill her. I saw him – he was the intruder.'

'Such a pity you hid in that blanket box. You missed all the fun.'

'And before he killed her, he raped her too.'

'The rape part is true,' she smirks, 'an added bonus, but it may also be his undoing.'

'And yours, if he tells the police you put him up to it.'

'He won't tell the police.'

'Why not?'

'Because if he does, I'll tell them where he hid Lexie Gilmore's body.'

I take in all of Alice's words. I visualise myself again, the day of the murder, hiding in the blanket box, how time skipped by, and when I finally went downstairs, it was already dark, hours had passed. Sheriff Hodgson always thought there was more than one person involved. What if someone else was in the house that day, after Billy left? And what if, right now, I'm staring at that person – Alice Handcock?

'Billy searched the house,' I roar at her, 'looking for my mother's mementoes and her journal. He was looking for them for *you*, only he couldn't find them, could he?'

'I wasn't the one hiding upstairs.' She opens her eyes wide, as if willing me to fill in the blanks.

'Then after Billy left, when he came back empty-handed, you must have been furious.' I think about Billy breaking into my apartment. 'Did you pay Billy to threaten me?'

'Wrong again, Heather. He wanted to protect himself. He thought you saw something that might implicate him with Lexie, and when you started snooping around again, after Lucas's death, he wanted to ensure you kept your mouth shut.'

'I don't remember …'

'There are lots of things you don't remember, aren't there?'

I don't answer her, because it's as if every cell in my body is twisting and knotting inside.

'Sheriff Hodgson,' she scoffs, 'told me once that some people never recover from the kind of trauma you suffered. They find it hard to work out which pieces of memory are true and which are false.'

'You seem to know a lot about me.'

'I make it my business to know.'

'You came back to the house, didn't you, after Billy? It was you who watched me that night.'

'Yes, I did. I guess, in a way, I've never stopped watching you.'

I think about the day I first came here, to discuss Abby's trial, how I had felt someone was looking down at me from upstairs, imagining it was Jim but realising now it was Alice all along.

'Why couldn't you let her live?' I ask.

'I thought you'd have worked that out by now, especially after you met Abby.'

'You mean the port-wine birthmark, the one Abby has, like Mia?'

'Abby looks so like Jim, doesn't she? As did your sister. Birthmarks may not be hereditary but, fortunately or unfortunately, a person's DNA is.'

'What do you mean?'

'I went to see your mother shortly after Mia was born. You were at school, and she was out back, hanging laundry. I took your sister from the crib and I gave her a brand-new pink pacifier. When your mother found us, she wanted to grab that child off me so fast, it was almost cruel. If I hadn't hated her before, I hated her then. What kind of woman denies another a few seconds with her child?'

'The kind who wants to protect them.'

'I took the pacifier out of your sister's mouth. The child wailed, but the DNA results took no time at all. They told me what I already knew. Parental testing, even back then, was possible. Did you know it was one of the first uses for DNA? But then, conveniently for everyone, the baby died, and your mother went off the rails. Everyone thought she was crazy, not believing a word that came out of her horrible mouth.'

'You're evil.'

'But after Mia, I couldn't take any more chances, especially when Jim started sniffing around your mother again. I had no choice. I couldn't let her live.'

I move closer to her. The wind howls against the window. 'My mother was still alive, wasn't she, after Billy left?'

'Yes,' she smirks, 'she was.'

'Did you kill her?' I swallow hard.

'Yes, Heather. As her cowardly daughter hid upstairs, that is exactly what I did.'

And there they are, the words I've spent almost a lifetime running from. On that dark day in May when, for hours, I stayed hidden in that blanket box, for a time my mother was still alive and I could have saved her.

# 85
# BLAKE

Blake re-enters the interrogation room. Billy sits with his arms folded, legs crossed. His lawyer, Harry Ipson, sits beside him.

'Things have moved on, gentlemen,' Blake says, his tone upbeat.

'What do you have, Detective?' Ipson asks, sounding less than impressed.

'Triple rape and potential murder. How does that sound?'

'On what evidence?'

'We've matched Billy's DNA to both unsolved rapes, and to the rape and killing of Elizabeth Baxter. Your client's DNA is all over her clothing.'

'I told you,' Billy shouts, 'I didn't kill her.'

Ipson touches his arm, instructing him to be calm.

'So, explain to me, Billy,' Blake asks, 'if you didn't kill her, how come we matched your DNA to Elizabeth Baxter's soiled clothing – her undergarments, to be precise?'

'This interview is over,' Ipson tells Blake.

'Who was pulling the strings, Billy?' Blake leans forward. 'I know you want to tell me. I can see it in your face.'

'I didn't kill her.'

'But you raped her, didn't you?'

Billy doesn't answer him. Instead, he looks at Ipson.

'Hanratty,' instructs Blake, 'read this fucker his rights.'

'Billy Townsend, you are charged with multiple rapes, and the murder of Elizabeth Baxter. Anything you say may be used against you in a court of law. You have the right to consult an attorney before speaking to the police, and to have an attorney present during questioning now or in the future.'

'For the record,' Ipson says, 'I am instructing my client not to say another word.'

The telephone in the interview room rings. Blake picks it up.

The police officer at the other end tells him Jim Handcock is on the line.

'Put him through,' Blake says.

# 86
# HEATHER

Alice is laughing. I can't take my eyes off her, the woman who killed my mother. Nothing compares to this, the power of it, the hate I feel for her, my own shame, trapped inside for far too long, as all those missing hours replay in my mind.

Billy Townsend breaking into the house before he attacks my mother, leaving her so weak on the kitchen floor she cannot cry out for help. His failed attempt to find what Alice wanted, which meant she had to come back to find the things herself. Perhaps she and my mother looked at one another. Alice would have taken pleasure in seeing her suffer, knowing she was raped, soiled, near destroyed. Only that wasn't enough for her. It was Alice, not Jim or Billy or anyone else, who stabbed my mother, the woman she hated, and then she waited, watching, until the blood pooled around her body, and when she was done, she waited for me too, because she knew I would lead her to the things she needed to possess.

'You had to take everything from her, didn't you, her life, everything?'

'And what did you do, precious Heather?'

'Alice, you've lived the life of a dead woman all these years, and you will rot in Hell for what you've done.'

'Hell happens after you die, Heather, and I have no intention of that happening anytime soon, or anyone linking me to that crime. If someone is going to take the fall for it, it will be Billy, not me.'

'I can back him up.'

'You falsely blamed Lucas. For a time, you most likely wanted to pin the killing on Jim, too, and now you're desperately trying to say it was me, when everything points to Billy.'

'Don't twist things.'

'Do you want to know something else, Heather?'

'What?'

'Should I tell you why, after all this time, I wanted to scare you too?'

'Do I have a choice?'

'Because that day, when you came to this house, when Jim asked you to defend Abby, I saw the way he looked at you, as if he was seeing the ghost of his beautiful Lizzie, and I wanted you to feel the same way she did before she died, and then I could take pleasure in it all over again.'

'There's more, Alice, isn't there?'

'I wanted you to lose the trial too, if you must know, so I could get that girl out of my life. It was pathetic the way Jim behaved with her. He thought he could bring Mia back. He thought that mark on her face was a sign that all wasn't lost.'

'You leaked the story to the media, didn't you, about Abby's so-called obsession with Morgan?'

'Yes, I did.'

I stare at her, remembering her screaming in the bed years before.

'Is that what this is all about, Alice? The fact that you could never have a child?'

She doesn't answer me.

'Or was it because Jim never loved you, not the way he loved my mother? Hate surrounds you, hate for others, hate for me, and if you really look hard in the mirror, you will see the hate you have for yourself.'

'Only I'm the one still alive and, for what it's worth, you're right about Lucas. He came back here causing trouble, stupidly thinking, like you, that Jim gave me the necklace. He didn't live long after that, and your father will rot in prison for it, but what gives me the most pleasure, Heather, is seeing you now, even with all the many questions answered, how you still have those nagging doubts. Could you have saved her? Did you leave her to die? Did you abandon her? And now we both know the answer to those questions, and you know for sure that every second of guilt you've felt since that day is utterly deserved.'

I look past her, seeing myself as that ten-year-old girl, terrified, running upstairs, hearing the screams of my mother as Billy attacked her. I think about the hours that followed, as I stayed hidden in the blanket box. I see myself now, bending down, telling my mother that I will guard her secrets, that I will bury them, where no one will ever find them. But, right now, surrounded by Alice's hate, what I remember most is how much I loved my mother, and even though her death meant I would never see her again, or touch her face, or take her hand walking home from school, despite the anguish of the last few months, something huge has shifted inside me, because now I know that, somehow, my mother has been with me all along, loving me, and Alice's hate, no matter how strong it is, cannot take that away. A mother never leaves a child, no more than Vivienne can let go of Jacob, no more than my mother could accept Mia's death, going inside herself to try to find her but finally coming back to me. Over these last few months, despite everything, the passage of time, the regrets, the shame, she has been with me, getting closer all the time, telling me it's okay to be fragile, and that I am strong, and that no matter what has happened, or will happen, she loved me and always will.

Car lights flicker past the window. They cast a gleaming shadow on the wall. Alice looks away, but I see a slight hint of fear in her eyes.

'Were you going to leave Jim for Morgan?' I ask, realising, more than ever, just how pathetic she is.

'Yes, but it turns out Morgan didn't give a shit about me either.'

'History repeating itself,' I say, turning the cruelty back on her.

I hear loud voices in the hallway.

'All Jim ever cared about was your stupid mother and his dead child, and Morgan, the weak lowlife, wasn't any better, with that sickly child of his, who happened to end up dead, like your poor pathetic sister.'

'Did you harm him?' I ask, my words ice-cold. 'Did you harm Jacob?'

'You're the one who believed he died of natural causes.'

'I believed Abby was innocent,' I say, standing firm.

I hear Alex arguing with Jim Handcock. He's telling her things are under control.

I think about Vivienne and her beautiful son. My mother and Mia. I leap across the space between myself and Alice, pure adrenalin pumping through my veins. All the years of loss tumble into one another, my anger turning into a rage so dark it feels almost primal, surging me forward. I know I'm capable of killing her, of making her suffer, of taking revenge. But as I look at her, I see that is what she wants: she wants me to hurt her. A fresh smile spreads across her face until, finally, I loosen my grip.

'Do you still have the knife,' I ask, 'the one you used on my mother?'

'What do you think?' She laughs, recomposing herself.

I hear police sirens in the distance. They're heading towards the house.

I want to be my mother, to give my mother the strength to fight back, to undo all the wrongs done to her. If I had that knife now, I would scrape it along Alice Handcock's neck, along the line of my mother's necklace. I would want to see her blood on my hands, for everything she has done.

Alex is still arguing with Jim. I hear a crash in the hallway, a bang so loud it must be one of the large sculptures smashing onto the marbled floor.

Alice's eyes are wild. 'You're a coward, Heather Baxter,' she yells, 'just like your damn father.'

The police lights are ablaze across the windows.

The door to the study is flung open with such force it comes back on itself. Alex barges in, followed by Jim Handcock.

Within seconds, she is beside me, pulling me further from Alice. Through the open door, I see Abby halfway down the staircase, looking scared, the same way I did all those years before.

Blake and the other police officers fill the hallway. It seems strange to see them here, like miniature people, tiny, below the large white sculptures.

# 87
# HEATHER

In the moments directly after the police arrive, it seems as if everything is happening in slow motion, my mind examining each millisecond to ensure that the truth as it unfolds is clear and real. Alice has been bundled out of the house, on her way to Cambridge police station. The house is being searched. Alex is with Abby in another room, the girl traumatised by everything that has happened. I already know it was Jim who contacted the police, and I need to know why.

I'm sitting waiting for him in the expansive living room, a blanket wrapped around me to balance out the shock.

'Alice said she could ruin you.'

'She's already done that,' he says. 'She did it a long time ago, only I was too stupid to see it.'

'Financially, your business, she could destroy everything.'

'I don't care about that now.'

'You told the police where to look for my mother's things, didn't you?'

'Yes, but I can't be sure I'm right.'

'Why did you call them?'

'I turned a blind eye for too long. Maybe I didn't want to know.' The lines on his forehead deepen. He looks even older now. 'When you came here tonight, Heather, saying what you did, I knew then it was Alice.'

'But at the Paramount that day, you asked me to tell my father to keep his mouth shut because you were worried about her. You didn't want talk of the past coming back to upset her.'

'At first I thought it was the trial, or perhaps it was seeing you again. I had always suspected she knew about your mother and me, how deeply I felt about her. I didn't want Alice becoming even more unhinged.'

'Unhinged?'

'She started acting strange before the trial began. I found her with a knife one morning, twirling it in her hand. She didn't know I was watching her, so I waited. I saw her put the knife back in her purse. After that I had someone follow her. That was how I found out about the affair with Morgan.'

'You didn't challenge her?'

'I'm a lot of things, Heather, but I'm not stupid. I knew I had to bide my time. I started putting certain things in motion.'

'Things that would protect you if you split ranks?'

'Yes. I didn't realise, though, that it wasn't the trial that unhinged her but Lucas coming back.'

'And then she killed him.'

'Perhaps she had Billy in her sights too. According to your friend Alex, since my phone call to the police Billy has become very helpful.'

Blake walks into the room. He stops for a second, staring at us, as if we're the most unexpected allies he has ever seen.

'What is it?' I ask.

'We've found everything.'

'In the dollhouse?' Jim asks.

'Yeah.'

I stand up, dropping the blanket. 'What have you found?' I think about all the things I buried that night under the swing.

'The gun that killed Lucas, the one registered to your father. We found a knife as well. It's early days, but it could tie her to your mother's death.'

I brace myself, because I know there's more.

'We also found the rose-quartz necklace, earrings, and a lock of hair with your name on it, Heather, in a tiny envelope.'

I immediately want to run upstairs, into the room where everything belonging to my mother has been found. Blake fills the doorway. I try to get past him, but he won't let me through.

'We need to keep them, Heather,' he says, holding onto my arms, 'as evidence.'

'But they're mine,' I shout. 'They belonged to my mother. You don't understand. They're all I have left of her.'

His body is rigid, blocking my way.

'What about her journal?'

'We have that too.'

I start crying. I can't stop myself. I don't care about Alice, or anyone else. The only person I care about is my mother, and turning back time, making sure her things are safe.

'You'll get them back, Heather,' Blake says. 'I promise you.'

# 88
# ALEX

Alex didn't want to leave Heather downstairs, but in the chaos that ensued, someone had to take care of Abby.

'The police will want to talk to you again,' Alex says, as the officers go from room to room.

'What if I don't want to talk to them?'

'This time you're not the one accused, Abby.'

'No?'

'No.'

She studies the girl lying on the bed, with its pink quilt and lace canopy, taking in the old-fashioned floral wallpaper, the soft teddies, the glittery lampshades. 'Is this your room?' she asks.

'Yeah, but it was always like this, from years ago.'

'How come?'

'Uncle Jim said he knew I'd return some day. It was only a matter of time.'

'How did he know?'

She shrugs her shoulders. 'He told me he always wanted a little girl of his own. I guess when I came back here he wanted that little girl to be me.'

Alex doesn't respond. Instead she thinks about Heather's sister, Mia, and the affair between Elizabeth Baxter and Jim Handcock. It doesn't take her long to fill in the gaps, imagining how Jim must have created this room for Mia, the little girl who would never spend a moment in it. It would have irked Alice, all these years, its continued existence, but a room for a ghost was probably better than a room for a child he fathered with someone else. When Abby came back and Jim gave her this bedroom, Alice must have hated her for it too.

Abby sits up on the bed, biting her fingernails, looking nervous. Under the circumstances, her anxiety is understandable, but Heather always thought the girl was holding something back.

'Abby, why don't you tell me what's on your mind?'

The girl puts her face into her hands.

'I know there's something else, Abby, and Heather knows it too. Now's the time to come clean.'

Alex waits.

Abby lowers her hands and stares at the floor.

'Is this to do with Jacob?' Alex asks, pushing her.

'I didn't harm him.'

'I know, but you have to tell me whatever it is you've been hiding, or it will keep eating away at you.'

The girl's expression changes, a look of dread and relief interwoven.

'When Jacob was asleep,' she says, hesitant at first, 'there were times when Alice would go into his room. I knew she couldn't have children of her own, so at first I was cool with it. Jacob often woke up when she was there. I would hear him on the baby monitor.'

'Did she ever pick him up?'

'A few times.'

'There is more, isn't there?'

'I couldn't say anything, during the trial, because Jim and Alice were helping me.'

'Say what?'

'I noticed marks on Jacob's body a couple of times, red blotches on his arms and legs, as if someone had squeezed them hard. I thought perhaps they happened because he was lying on his side, but then I thought something else.'

'What?'

'I started thinking that the marks were only ever there after Alice had been with him.'

'Did you say anything to her?'

'Yeah, but she brushed me off. It was around then I realised something was going on between her and Morgan. When he was around, she was as sweet as pie, both to me and the baby, but when he wasn't there she was different.'

'How?'

'Her eyes would go all cold when she looked at Jacob in the crib, especially when she thought no one was watching.'

'Have you told any of this to Heather?'

'No.'

'You would have been covered under client privilege.'

'I couldn't. As I said, Alice and Uncle Jim were helping me. I couldn't let go of my only chance.' She puts her hands to her face again.

'Abby, you need to tell the cops.'

'But what if they don't believe me? I can't go through that again.'

'You can, and you will. I'm going to tell you something, Abby, something you need to remember for the rest of your life. Secrets are like open wounds. They fester, and grow, and turn you into someone you don't want to be. They change you, make you feel less worthy. You don't want that, Abby, do you?'

'No.'

'Then tell the cops.'

# 89
# HEATHER

This time when I walk through the doors of Cambridge police station to meet Blake, I already know Billy Townsend and Alice Handcock have been the ruination of each other, each in their desperate attempt to save their skins.

Alice tried to pin it all on Billy, saying she'd never meant him to kill Elizabeth Baxter and, after all, he was the one who'd killed Lexie Gilmore. She said Billy was blackmailing her, not the other way around. Billy had his own slant on things. Alice had put pressure on him after what had happened to Lexie, which was an accident. He'd had no choice but to do her bidding. He didn't kill Elizabeth Baxter: she did.

It would possibly have gone Alice's way, except for the gun, which tied her to Lucas's murder, and the knife used to kill my mother, both found at her home. Alice couldn't bear to let any of the possessions go. Like a magpie, she kept everything.

I wait in the public area for Blake. A television drones in the corner. Marcia Langan is still featuring high on all the news channels. Her face is everywhere because of the scoop she managed to get on Morgan Rotterdam and Alice Handcock, especially now that the investigation into the death of Jacob Rotterdam has been reopened. Abby did the right thing in the end. She told the police her suspicions about Alice. It was enough for Alice to be charged. Either way, with all the evidence stacked against her, my mother's killer is facing a lifetime behind bars.

There is a newspaper in the waiting area. In today's copy of the *Boston Globe*, Marcia Langan has written the lead column. 'Without a doubt,' she states, 'the trial and everything associated with it has taken its toll on Vivienne Rotterdam. She has lost her son, her marriage has collapsed, and the woman she allowed into her home, as a friend, is now being investigated for her son's death and the killing of two others, Lucas García and Elizabeth Baxter. Morgan Rotterdam is currently undergoing rehab, blaming himself for putting others before his son. Sources close to Vivienne say she has become something of a recluse. It is hoped that, after time, she can make a fresh start, but when it comes to the loss of her child, the horror for Vivienne will continue for years.'

I think about my own mother's suffering, after Mia, and I wish I could reach back to her to take away that pain. I wish I could do it for Vivienne too.

'Heather,' Blake says, opening the door, 'I'm ready for you now.'

I follow him in silence to his office, the place where, weeks before, I sat alone, looking at a list of names on a wipe board, trying to work out who killed my mother. I know the answer to that question now, and many others, but what I know most of all, sitting opposite Blake, is that soon I will get back everything belonging to my mother, the items which, as a child, I tried to protect.

'We found the skeletal remains of Lexie Gilmore,' Blake says. 'In the end, both Alice and Billy, in an attempt to mitigate charges, told us the location.'

'Who will bury her?'

'There is a relative, an aunt on her mother's side, but I don't know too much about that just yet.'

'I want to make sure she gets a Christian burial. It's partly because of her that we found out the truth about my mother. If necessary, I'll cover all the costs.'

'Okay,' he says, 'if you're sure. I'll let her aunt know.'

Once more, I see the fleeting image of Lexie cycling down Main Street, a smiling young girl with her life ahead of her.

'Anything more on Blanco?' I ask.

'He's under official investigation with Internal Affairs. Of course he's denying helping Alice Handcock, but in the meantime, he's suspended.'

'And Hodgson?'

'As you know, he retired to Salem. We're co-operating with the police there. If we get something to stick, he'll be charged too.'

'Did Alice tell you any more about the things you found in Lucas's place, the newspaper clipping and the doll?'

'She left the makeshift doll there, the same way she left the one in your apartment. She circled your face on the clipping too, in an attempt to put more pressure on you and keep the attention away from her.'

'When can I have my mother's things?'

'Not until after Alice Handcock's trial, and with three murder charges hanging over her, it could take some time.'

'I've waited nearly a quarter of a century so I guess I can wait a little longer, but I want a copy of my mother's journal.'

'I can do that,' he says, 'but leave it with me for a couple of hours. When I have it for you, I'll get in touch.'

# 90
# ELIZABETH

On a gravestone, there is a beginning and an end date, two moments in time, as if everything begins and ends in between. Life isn't like that. Some parts of it will carry on after you die, especially in the minds and memories of those who loved you most. That is why Mia will always be with me, and why, no matter what happens in the future, I will always be with Heather too.

Lots of things drive us as human beings – greed, power, fear, all kinds of human emotions – but there are few as strong as love and hate. I want to believe love is more powerful, but hate is part of us too. If anything happens to me, I need Heather to protect herself. I want her to hide. That is why we have played the hiding game so many times, until it has become instinctual.

I have told her over and over, if she is ever frightened, and if, for whatever reason, I can't be with her, she needs to protect herself first, to stay hidden, keeping her breathing low and steady, imagining happy thoughts, no matter how long it takes. If I can, I will find her, but she must always be safe.

*I have been thinking a lot about the past lately, how it cannot be changed, no matter how much you want to change it. How it influences your present and your future, how it is part of who you are, and who you will become.*

*If Heather ever reads this journal, I want her to know, despite my many faults, I loved her with all my heart. That, like Mia, she will always be a part of me, and me a part of her.*

*I see her now, skating on the pond that day, looking so happy before danger struck. It came without warning. I guess none of us can know what our future holds. All we can ever do is be true to ourselves, and to those we love most.*

*No matter what happens next, I will always be with Heather. I will stay with her, in her memory, held in the tiny fragments of our life together.*

*Sometimes all of us can fall out of life for a while. That happened to me after Mia, when I couldn't bear the truth. Now I understand that being fragile is part of being human, and in time, when each of us is ready, we can be strong again, even within a tragic loss.*

# 91
# HEATHER

An hour after I leave Cambridge police station, I meet Alex near Skating Pond, the place where Daniel and my mother saved my life. As I walk towards her, she asks me if I'm okay.

'Yep,' I say. 'Blake has promised me a copy of the journal.'

'How do you feel, after all this time, about reading your mother's words?'

'I'm not sure, but they exist, and because of them, I'll get another chance to be close to her.'

She nods in acknowledgement.

'I visited Jacob's grave yesterday,' I tell her, as we walk towards the pond. 'It felt right being there. I shed tears for him, for Vivienne, my sister, for Lucas and my mother too. The trial brought me back here to Corham, and during it, I changed. I'm a different person now. It's not only because I know who killed my mother, but because on that dark day, all those years ago, when I eventually climbed out of the blanket box, a part of me remained locked inside it. That's why I suppressed all those memories, and why I stayed away from here all that time. Now I know it wasn't my mother I needed the forgiveness from, it was from me.'

'Have you forgiven yourself?'

'Yes, a little more each day.'

When the pond comes into view, I explain to Alex how I reached a kind of truce with my father. 'I met him a few days ago at our old house,' I say. 'I asked him if he remembered making the swing for me. He said he did, and that it was for my sixth birthday. I realise now, as a child, lots of things happen that can scare you, and in his own way, he cared about me too.'

The closer we get to the pond, the more the trees thin out.

'Something else has been happening lately,' I say.

'What?'

'Other memories, happy ones, are coming back too, as if only now my mind is allowing me to see them because, perhaps, before this I didn't think I deserved to remember.'

She links my arm. 'Any word on your friend Daniel?' she asks.

'He's getting back to his old self but it'll take time.'

Sitting by the pond, I stare at the algae in the water, blurring my eyes, the way the ice did years before, covering the dangers below. 'Over the last few months, despite everything that has happened,' I say, 'I've felt closer to my mother. That night, when I drove to the Handcocks' house, wanting to face Jim down, I took the coast road too fast and she was there, pulling me back from the edge.'

'She's part of you, Heather. That will never change.' Alex fires a pebble into the pond. I watch the ripples spread out.

'I've been thinking a lot about Lucas lately, too, and how when something bad happens we all look for someone to blame. There is always a name put forward, the person everyone suspects. For my mother, it was Lucas. For Jacob, it was Abby. In the end, they were both innocent.'

Alex fires another pebble into the pond. I watch the ripples once more, and then my mind jerks back to a memory. It's totally unexpected. I stare at the pine trees. At first, I think I see my mother and Jim Handcock, but then the people become clearer, and I realise it's Lexie Gilmore, just before I heard her scream, and the man running after her is Billy Townsend.

'What is it?' Alex asks. 'You've gone completely pale.'

'I saw it, or at least part of it.'

'What?'

'I saw Billy and Lexie.'

'I don't understand.'

'That was what Billy was afraid of, that I would remember. I saw him with her before she was killed. That was why he threatened me.'

'It's okay,' she says, her voice soft. 'Now you know.'

'Do I?' I stare at her. 'What if there are more dark parts of my past, other things that, from fear, I've blocked out?'

'In time, they'll all come back. You're strong, Heather, you always have been.'

*

When I reach home, a police car is parked outside. A uniformed officer hands me a large brown envelope, in which, as Blake promised, I will find the copied pages of my mother's journal. I hold them tight, before going inside.

By the time I finish reading them, it's already dark as, once again, hours have slipped by. I know what I need to do. I turn to the blank pages at the back, and I begin to write the final entry.

# 92
# HEATHER

*Dear Mom,*

*A few weeks ago, I drew two stick people on a damp windowpane. One of them was me and the smaller version was Mia. When she died, I was probably too young to grieve her properly, but during those long days after her death, when you were lost to me, there were times I, too, believed she still existed. Like you, I felt her close by, and some days I would walk into her room alone and lean in over the top of the crib, staring at the emptiness. If I tried hard enough, the elephants on her quilt would come alive and dance, and I would be able to hear the lullaby from the mobile playing. I imagined her sweet baby smell filling my nostrils, as I reached down to touch her soft hair or kiss her warm cheek.*

*When I read your words about Mia, the times you, too, believed that, if you tried hard enough, you could still imagine her with you, or hear her cry when all was silent other than the sleeping night, now I can understand your loss a little more. That day when you went into the woods, half crazed searching for her, you believed she was calling you, and that somewhere, within the trees and the undergrowth, she might* still live on. The truth is, she does, in your love. She exists within me, too, the little sister I never got a chance to know.

After you died, everything became tilted, as if I couldn't fit into this world the same way any more without you. It was as if there was nowhere for my love to go, as if I was both full and empty at the same time. All that unspent love I wanted to give to you kept growing inside me, until it, too, became trapped, and the only way for me to deal with it was, at first, not to try. It has taken me a long time to realise that now I have to stop playing the hiding game. I have to face the hurt of everything that has happened, no matter how frightened I may be.

When those first glimpses of memory came back, I thought it was about finding the truth about your death, and other dark aspects of my life, the many things I had blocked out because my mind couldn't face them, but it was about much more than that. It wasn't only a question of putting all the missing pieces together, it was about understanding that, as a ten-year-old child, I did the best I could. If I could go back now and talk to my little-girl self, I would tell her it was okay to be afraid, and that she, too, was brave. I would take her hand, and we would both lie down beside you on the kitchen floor. I would tell her how great her love for you was, and always will be, and as the snowflakes covered the ground that night, she did what she thought you wanted her to do and buried everything. It didn't matter what everyone else thought, because everything she did, she did out of love. I used to think that little girl was weak, but she wasn't. She was fragile, but she was also strong.

I have learned to love her again, to forgive her, even though she never needed forgiveness, not for a single second, but in doing so, somehow, I feel more whole. Because of your words, I understand now that you wanted me to protect myself and, hopefully, over the last few months, you have been proud of me too.

You are right about love and hate. For a time, Alice Handcock got to relive her hate through me, but now that, too, is over.

*Of late, I've started remembering happy times, moments locked away in my mind, hidden for far too long, like that day we went to the beach, and I brought a flower in my pocket, a flattened orange marigold, to put on top of my sandcastle, and you laughed, saying you'd never seen such a beautiful castle. Or the night I wanted to stay up until after midnight, only I fell asleep in your arms, and when I woke, you said, 'Heather darling, say hello to tomorrow.'*

*Some people may not understand how important your words are to me, perhaps because, if they're lucky, they have yet to experience the loss of someone close to them, or understand what it was like to wait nearly a quarter of a century to read your words, re-imagine your voice, talking to me. They may not understand the joy I feel right now, writing to you not as the child, Heather, but as the grown woman you always wanted me to be.*

*So many years have passed since the day you were killed, but over the last few months, I've felt you nearer to me, as if before, by shutting out the hard stuff, I was pushing you away too, but you were always there, waiting for me to find you.*

*My heart still breaks a little, thinking about all the pages you'll never write, and how your life was cut far too short. This journal is your final gift to me and reading it has helped me to understand so much more. During the trial, I thought a lot about both Mia and Jacob, and the deep bond between a mother and her child, the same bond that still exists between you and me. The death of an infant changes everything, but the death of a mother, the break in the mother–child bond, changes everything too.*

*I will always cherish your words, even those written in the darkest of times, because they are the words of a mother, my mother, who loved me with her whole self, who cared for me as best she could, who was brave, and fragile, and strong.*

*Love always,*
*Heather*

# ACKNOWLEDGEMENTS

The spark for this story began in 1997 when as a young mother I watched the televised trial from Boston, Massachusetts, of Louise Woodward, a nineteen-year-old nanny accused of harming the infant in her care. The story never quite left me.

Several years later my mother died. It was the first time in my life I understood true heartbreak. Over time I began to reflect on my mother's life, especially the loss of my infant sister to a cot death, and later, my brother who was stillborn. Both tragedies deeply affected our family. For years my mother kept the unworn baby clothes of my sister and brother in a large cardboard box on the top of a wardrobe, unable to let them go.

Although this novel is not autobiographical, or based on my mother's life, I hope within these fictional pages a certain commonality of human experience is explored, sometimes within the context of loss, trauma, secrets and lies, and on other occasions, injustice, and murder.

The emotional anchor for this story is a simple one. The death of an infant changes everything, and the death of a mother, the break in the mother–child bond, changes everything too.

During the process of writing this novel many people have helped to make its publication possible. Firstly, I would like to thank my wonderful agent Gráinne Fox, of Fletcher & Co., New York, for being so passionate about this story, and giving her support to me every step of the way. Also, thanks to Ciara Doorley, Editorial Director, Elaine Egan, Publicity Director, and the rest of the team at Hachette Ireland, for their work and enthusiasm on publication of *The Hiding Game*. Special thanks also to Rachel Pierce for her assistance with each of the early drafts.

In the area of research, I am again thankful to a great many people, all of whom helped to make this story more authentic. If an error exists, it is mine alone, and not connected to the wonderful experts who gave of their precious time and knowledge. My sincere thanks to Detective Kevin Bradley of the Boston Police Special Investigations Unit, who was amazingly generous with his knowledge on many aspects of police and legal procedure. I would also like to thank the Senior Crimes Unit in Cambridge, and all the police officers within it, including those operating undercover, who each gave of their time and knowledge. My sincere thanks also to Peter Cummings, MSc, MD, of the Boston University School of Medicine, who opened my eyes to the many aspects of this subject matter. Also, Bob McKenna of the Attorney General's Office, Rhode Island, Bryan Leavy, Attorney, Andrea Carter, writer and ex-barrister, and finally, special thanks to Detective Tom Doyle (now retired) for his introduction to fellow colleagues in the United States.

Huge thanks also goes to the Irish Writers Centre, for facilitating my residency in Cill Rialaig Artist Retreat during the early stages of writing this novel, and the Tyrone Guthrie Centre in Annaghmakerrig, for numerous editorial visits. Also, enormous thanks to the Arts Council of Ireland, for granting me an Arts Bursary for Literature in support of writing this story.

I will never be able to repay the wonderful writers who read this novel in advance of publication, namely Patricia Gibney, Liz Nugent, Catherine Ryan Howard, Andrea Carter, Arlene Hunt, Sinéad Crowley, Cormac O'Keeffe, and Karen Perry (Gillece), all of whom I admire greatly. Thanks also to the amazing Irish Writing Community, a tremendous network of support for all writers, and special thanks to Vanessa O'Loughlin of Writing.ie and Irish Pen, for her ongoing support and knowledge. Thanks also to my readers, who have read, enjoyed and supported my earlier novels, and whom I hope will enjoy this one too.

Finally, I would like to sincerely thank my family, who have encouraged me from the early days of my writing journey, particularly my husband, Robert, and our children, Jennifer, Lorraine and Graham. Also, a very special thanks to my parents, especially my mother, who made me believe that anything is possible. A heartfelt thanks also to my sister, Monica, who died on the 5th of September 1964, aged 4 days, 21 hours and ten minutes. This novel is dedicated to her, and it is fitting that it is published on the fifty-fifth anniversary of her death. Over the years, I have reflected many times on the life my sister never got a chance to live, and if this novel acts as any kind of small acknowledgement towards her loss, then writing it has been very worthwhile indeed.

Louise Phillips